"Sharp, yet lusciously written . . . full of shocks, beautiful images, and new ways of seeing things." —*The Guardian/Observer* (London)

"Here is that rare and welcome book about love that's less concerned with how we find love than what we do with it, a book that deals not in moments of passion, but in moments of grace, a book about the frustrating, hilarious, embarrassing, transcendental business of living with love. Heidi Jon Schmidt's stories are filled with delightful wit, spellbinding feeling, and an emotional intelligence that rises to the level of essential wisdom." —Peter Ho Davies

"This collection has so many shining moments of humor, of heartbreak, of grace that readers might find themselves asking: Why aren't more stories this good?" —*Publishers Weekly*

"Schmidt creates a mood not unlike the tenor of modern life, lurching from giddy enthusiasm to embarrassment to frustration. Schmidt's take on contemporary phenomena is bracing." —*Booklist*

The Rose Thieves
• • •

"A graceful journey into the individual life of a young woman and the collective life of a family—and a fine debut." —*The New York Times*

"Laugh-out-loud comic, and really tragic at the same time. Beautifully, evocatively written." —*The Boston Globe*

"The stories are standouts." —*Chicago Tribune*

"Captures the rueful humor in family ambiguities." —*Publishers Weekly*

"Delightful . . . precise and elegant." —*Library Journal*

The Harbormaster's Daughter

HEIDI JON SCHMIDT

NAL Accent
Published by New American Library,
a division of Penguin Group (USA) Inc.,
375 Hudson Street, New York, New York 10014, USA
Penguin Group (Canada), 90 Eglinton Avenue East, Suite 700, Toronto,
Ontario M4P 2Y3, Canada (a division of Pearson Penguin Canada Inc.)
Penguin Books Ltd., 80 Strand, London WC2R 0RL, England
Penguin Ireland, 25 St. Stephen's Green, Dublin 2,
Ireland (a division of Penguin Books Ltd.)
Penguin Group (Australia), 250 Camberwell Road, Camberwell,
Victoria 3124, Australia (a division of Pearson Australia Group Pty. Ltd.)
Penguin Books India Pvt. Ltd., 11 Community Centre,
Panchsheel Park, New Delhi - 110 017, India
Penguin Group (NZ), 67 Apollo Drive, Rosedale, Auckland 0632,
New Zealand (a division of Pearson New Zealand Ltd.)
Penguin Books (South Africa) (Pty.) Ltd., 24 Sturdee Avenue,
Rosebank, Johannesburg 2196, South Africa

Penguin Books Ltd., Registered Offices:
80 Strand, London WC2R 0RL, England

First published by NAL Accent, an imprint of New American Library,
a division of Penguin Group (USA) Inc.

First Printing, August 2012
1 3 5 7 9 10 8 6 4 2

 REGISTERED TRADEMARK—MARCA REGISTRADA

LIBRARY OF CONGRESS CATALOGING-IN-PUBLICATION DATA:

Schmidt, Heidi Jon.
The harbormaster's daughter/Heidi Jon Schmidt.
p. cm.
ISBN 978-0-451-23787-3
1. Children of murder victims—Fiction. 2. Racially mixed people—Fiction.
3. Cape Cod (Mass.)—Fiction. I. Title.
PS3569.C51554H37 2012
813'.54—dc23   2012013108

Set in Albertina
Designed by Elke Sigal

Printed in the United States of America

PUBLISHER'S NOTE

This is a work of fiction. Names, characters, places, and incidents either are the product of the
author's imagination or are used fictitiously, and any resemblance to actual persons, living or dead,
business establishments, events, or locales is entirely coincidental.

The publisher does not have any control over and does not assume any responsibility for author or
third-party Web sites or their content.

For Marisa

"What see'st thou else, in the dark backward and abysm of time?"

—WILLIAM SHAKESPEARE, *The Tempest*

The Harbormaster's Daughter

PART ONE

1

Pleasure Boats

No matter how many years passed, Franco would find himself standing there with the bar rag, thinking back, trying to search out the flaw, the rusted bolt that held tight till it snapped, the knot that slipped, the exact place where the whole leaky contraption that was his life listed, took on water, and began to go down. If you rearranged the story by just one detail, Sabine could have lived, and worked herself into the fabric of the town one way or another, and now she'd own a little art gallery, or be the brisk, smiling hostess in the new bistro, married to a man who would of course have adopted Vita. The past would be past, and nearly forgotten.

When he came to himself, he would give up and go back to wiping the bar. He should have been harbormaster. That was the natural order of things and everything would have been different if it had been followed. At Manny Soares's retirement dinner, the men had clapped Franco on the back. It was his turn to oversee the harbor and they had faith in him. Franco had operated his dragger, the *Rainha do Mar*, from the same berth his father had used, and his grandfather before him. He knew every fisherman, every oysterman, in town, their families, their histories, their ways. It hadn't occurred to him that anyone else would apply for the job, much less that the new town manager would advertise it, and not only in the *Oyster Creek Oracle* but in the *Cape Cod Times*, the *Boston Globe*, and on Monster.com.

"Brian," he'd said, looking across the desk to the earnest, sandy-haired young man with his degree in city management and his devotion to fairness, excellence, and the public good. And his seer-sucker suit, his bow tie. How did you talk to such a man? Franco squinted, and considered. "You need someone who's comfortable on the pier."

Who else had such a full understanding of the delicate web of relations among the fishermen? It was in Franco's blood, to know how to pay appropriate respect to men whose brothers had been lost at sea or how to keep an arrogant SOB like Bobby Matos satis-fied so he didn't start throwing his weight around. He had grown up among these guys, fished with them, fought the town's fires be-side them. When Vince Machado had seen an odd pattern in the chop and realized a tuna had ventured too close to shore, he'd called up and Franco had run down Sea Street with the rusted old harpoon his father had found while digging a foundation out on Try Point. Vince went out in his dory—it was the nearest boat to hand—and speared the fish right behind its eye. The majestic crea-ture stopped still, its blood billowing into the water, and Franco swam toward it. That the tuna might thrash him to death . . . the last thing he thought of. He admired it; he wanted to know it, to feel it move while it was still alive. Bearing it in toward shore, he could hear his father's voice telling him never to speak with disdain of his catch. The fish—especially tuna—were a valiant adversary. Stand-ing beside it hoisted on the pier, he had understood this so well—he and this fish were a proud pair. And he and Vince Machado had had each other's backs from that time on, until Vince went down on the *Suzie Belle*.

Brian Sorel's mouth had twitched, as if he found it amusing to think he might need anyone, never mind a guy like Franco, who had dropped out of high school, and not just any high school, but Oyster Creek High School, where students interested in going on to college had been considered traitors to the town that had raised them, that needed them to man the draggers and the restaurants and the cannery. Of course the cannery was a condo complex now, but ... Franco had rubbed his eyes—he was allergic to every kind of pollen. When he was young he would start sneezing as they came into port, before they could even see land. They stood in Sorel's oak-paneled office, beside the high window that looked out on a bay full of little sails—pleasure boats. Pleasure boats—what an idea!

"It's difficult to enforce fairly when you've been part of the community," Sorel had explained, with an infuriating diplomacy. "I don't want to put that burden on you. We need a fresh eye on the harbor, someone who's not beholden to anyone."

So he'd hired Hank Capshaw, a guy from Newburyport who looked like a yachtsman, ruddy and weathered, and prone to clapping men heartily on the back. Franco would be assistant harbormaster. The washashores would trust Hank, so they'd make better use of the pier, bringing in more pleasure boats, more of the money that pleasure boaters had to spend. There were exactly nine draggers fishing out of Oyster Creek on a regular basis now, nine guys who would rather deal with Franco. Franco could name them, and their parents, and their wives, and their boats, and their stories.

Franco had a picture of himself on board the *Rainha*, when his father was captain and he was ten or eleven years old. The hold was so full that the fish had spilled over onto the deck and to get anywhere you had to climb through them, slipping and sliding, feeling one leg go out from under you suddenly, then floundering up again and finding a dogfish down the leg of your waders. And there they all were, his father and his uncle Eddie and Joe Matos, culling fish, sorting fish, filleting fish, climbing over hills and slipping into valleys of fish. Franco stood in the middle of it all, a skinny kid holding a fat silver cod out in his arms, while behind him Joe hosed down the bit of deck that was showing amid all the fish heaped everywhere. It had not occurred to him, not to any of them, that they wouldn't pull their nets in full and heavy like that every day for the rest of their lives.

When there was only water, everywhere you looked in every direction, and maybe another boat or maybe two, and that was all—you could no more imagine the seas being empty of fish than the ocean going dry. Like his father, and his grandfather, and the generations back to Portugal before they all followed the fish across the sea and landed here on Cape Cod, Franco was a fisherman. He knew there were other lives—both of his sons lived on the Pacific Coast now, working in offices, in cities, and though he'd visited, he still barely understood. You went up in the elevator, and then what? He was Franco Neves, captain of the *Rainha do Mar*. Or he had been, until the fish dwindled. Then the regulations began, the catch was limited, the number of fishing days was cut, the boat would just sit at the dock for a month until the engine clogged and mice built nests in the bilge pump. One winter he tied her to a mooring near the breakwater, meaning to give her a full overhaul in the spring . . . except that by spring it didn't seem worth it. He tried to get out to check the engine every few months, but it weighed him down just to think of it. Two hundred fifty a year for the mooring, more for the registration, checks that hurt him to write, but to have her junked, sold for salvage . . . It would be like spitting on his father's grave.

Sometimes he'd admit he ought to sell the thing, but Danielle, his wife, would always shake her head, no matter how much they needed the money. "It's you, Franco. It's what you do. You'll go back to fishing—I know you will. Look at the way the stripers have come back. Cod will, too." The relief Franco felt when she said something like this!

"You could be a professor at Wife College," he answered, and she smiled at the idea.

"A Neves has to go out to fish whether there's fish or not," she said, her voice deepening as it did when she was laughing at the poignant futility of everything, which was often. They both guessed he'd never go back to sea in the *Rainha*, but she recognized it as tragic, which gave him the comfort of seeing it as only a financial problem. He might have crumbled into dust if he'd really thought about all that old rust bucket meant to him, but bless her, Danielle did that for him.

He had to admit that he could understand the town manager's thinking. Arguments on the wharf tended to be settled by fisticuffs; in fact, Franco's father had a pair of well-used brass knuckles from his time as harbormaster. And Franco was not a fighter. His heart was easily swayed and his mind padded obediently along behind, explaining the other point of view and finding the best reasons to give in to it. This was a wonderful quality in a bartender, less so in a harbormaster. The old fishermen had been here before the laws, and they were alive because they had outwitted nature. Dunk Carlos used to say, "Lookit the pretty rainbow" when he poured his motor oil over the side of the boat. Franco listened to Dunk and others like him, night after night at his second job, tending bar at the Walrus and Carpenter. They were sure that the only thing standing between them and success was the law. Let Hank Capshaw keep these guys in line.

That was how Franco met Sabine. Bobby Matos had been selling scrubbed lobsters at the fish market, and though he swore he had bought them without realizing it, Hank boarded his boat and found a wire brush still full of the eggs Bobby had scrubbed off. It was the spring run, when half of the female lobsters caught would be bearing eggs, meaning you had to throw them back. But the eggs were just there on the outside of the shell—you could rub them off with your thumb, and you'd have a lobster you could sell. Bobby was guilty of possession: possession of egg-bearing lobsters, possession of egg-bearing lobsters from which the eggs had been removed, failing to display fish in demand—there would be heavy fines at the very least.

The Matoses did not like being called to account—years ago when the school principal said Bobby's son would have to repeat second grade, the man's car had burst into flames in his driveway in the middle of the night. Someone had tapped a nail into the gas tank and dropped a match. Bobby was coming in to the harbormaster's shack at ten to have a talk with Hank. Franco had set off on his Rollerblades at a quarter till. It had been one of the first warm days of spring and Franco had headed out along Breakwater Road and lost track of time. His nickname was Wheelie, from the times in high school when he'd ride thirty miles on his bike just to work off some of his excess energy. When his sons were old enough to skateboard, he had learned along with them, and then came Rollerblades. He loved his kayak, too—anything that let him skim over the world's surfaces. As soon as he was out of the shack—a small, tilting structure at the base of the pier, its cedar shingles curled with age—he felt young again, free as a butterfly.

That day as he passed the Beach Rose Cottages, he saw Sabine standing in her doorway, in jeans and a thick sweater, watching him with admiration.

"Hi, skater boy," she said, as though she'd stepped right out of a movie. Franco loved the movies.

2

CAFFE CORRETTO

Sabine was tiny, barely five feet tall, with thin, pale hair and dark circles under her eyes; he knew the type—the educated, poetry-reading type. They drifted into town clinging to some idea that never would have crossed a Portagee's mind—the light here was so intense that it was necessary to their painting, or they never felt alive except when they faced the salt wind. Truly, they were here because life had damaged them and they needed a beautiful vision to hold to against some inner darkness, a well of despair that no self-respecting local had time for. Oyster Creek, with its narrow streets angling down toward the harbor, the breakers rolling against the eastern shore while the bay on the west side rippled like a bolt of silk, was their place of consolation. They might have "washed ashore" here like flotsam, but they clung like barnacles, taking any work, it seemed, or any man, whatever could help them stay and make their lives here.

The local women—Danielle, for instance—belonged to an entirely different species. Romance was beyond their means, even in imagination. Their fathers were fishermen; their brothers and husbands had been raised on trawlers, hauling up load after load of cod, mastering a trade even as they were making it obsolete. They had learned to be tough, to survive. Danielle did love the smell of salt air, mostly because it meant warm water, safer for the men. She'd never liked the taste of fish; seeing a tourist eat steamed mussels, she remembered a story of someone who'd had to subsist on tree caterpillars during the war. A little beach cottage with rambler roses trained over the lintel and a window that looked out to the sea? She'd cleaned too much mildew, too many spiders out of places like that. She liked things brand-new, solid, clean. When the boys were young they'd lived in a raised ranch out in Cranberry Corners, a new development behind the highway with brickfront houses and pools in the backyards. And when the fish were gone, and the bank foreclosed on the house, she said, "Well, I'm glad I've vacuumed that place for the last time. It's too big for us now anyway." She stitched up curtains for the apartment over the bar, took a job behind the counter at the pharmacy, and never spoke a regretful word.

Life without Danielle—he couldn't imagine it. But the washashore women were like sunlight, wafting along the street in their flowery dresses, digging clams on a dim morning on the flats, their hair pulled back loosely so a few strands escaped, their laughter floating up through the fog along the beach, across the water. The unfulfilled dreams they sighed about seemed ridiculous to Danielle and her friends, but those yearnings gave women like Sabine a certain air; every move was full of art, of seduction.

"You need some real strength to use those skates that way," Sabine said. Her smoky voice had surprised him, coming from a woman so small. "Thighs."

He'd found himself shy. "My boys got me started skating. Builds the muscle . . ." Then he was sorry he'd mentioned the boys, making himself sound old, and irrevocably married. His wedding ring by itself had never seemed to daunt a woman; in fact, they seemed to take it as a challenge. But he'd sworn off women. He had.

"I just made some coffee. . . ."

"Oh, no, thanks. I gotta get back to work."

She smiled, blinking. "What is it you do?"

"I'm . . . I work in the harbormaster's office." He was forty-seven years old; he was not going to speak of himself as someone's assistant.

"I see," she said, looking down at the skates again, and up at him, with mischief. "Just take a little coffee break. Your skates won't rust. Grappa?"

"What?"

"A shot of grappa in your coffee. *Caffe corretto,* the Italians call it. Corrected coffee."

"Grappa . . . like aguardiente?" he asked. "The liquor from the grape skins?" Flirtation was a little like Rollerblading. You might be unsteady for a minute at first, but once you hit your stride you were lighter than air.

"Aguardiente?" she tried, syllable by slow syllable, so he'd watch her mouth. "Rolling the r?"

"That's the Portuguese word. Aguardiente."

She would love it; they all did. When he was young, families would put a particularly dark-skinned baby up for adoption, for the good of future generations—they were trying to bleach the Porta-gee out of themselves. Who would have guessed there would come a day when you could seduce a woman by telling her how to salt cod for bacalao? A woman like Sabine was looking for something real, something you could close your hand on and hold tight to—something like an ethnic heritage.

"But, thanks, not while I'm . . . at work." She wanted him; it felt wrong, unmanly, to refuse.

"Some other time, then."

"Yeah . . . some other time."

He skated away, feeling he'd dodged a bullet. Georgie Bottles went by on his bicycle with a clam basket hanging from the handlebars and a rake over his shoulder.

"Hey, Wheelie," he called to Franco. Georgie would always use a nickname—it proved he belonged here, that he was part of the family. He was the town drunk, or one of them, and he'd have counted that a proud title if he'd been aware of it. His big jack-o'-lantern's face was eternally arguing some enraging question and he would wag his finger if he had a free hand, though he rarely did, with the bicycle, the beer, and the clam rake. He pedaled along with his knees angled out, his long legs doubled, and the bike wobbling back and forth across the road.

"Hey, George. You goin' down to the flats?" The answer was obvious, but if Franco hadn't asked the question, Georgie might have felt ignored, or taken lightly. And you couldn't do that, not if you'd known him long enough. You could be miles out at sea on a dragger and Georgie would come along rowing a dory, fishing with a pole. He belonged here in a way even Franco didn't anymore.

Bobby Matos came out of the shack, hawking and spitting as if to rid himself of Hank Capshaw and any other authority, and swung himself up into his truck for the three-block ride back to the fish market. Bobby was a bastard, everyone agreed on that, but to some it counted as praise. Bobby owned his house, his boat, the fish market, the best oyster grant on the flats, and in the eighties he'd bought a couple of "unbuildable" lots for twenty thousand, built duplex condos on each and sold them for six hundred thousand apiece ten years later. Try to stop him. Franco avoided him, and now he intended to avoid Sabine Gray, too. He put the skates under his desk and swore to keep his mind on his work: annual report to the Division of Marine Fisheries, annual report to the Department of Environmental Protection, compilation of statistics for the Office of Coastal Zone Management. . . . His head ached. If he were harbormaster, he, too, would have given these jobs to his assistant.

But it was the month of May and inevitably the day arrived when the air was so fresh with salt that a surge of life came up in him. As soon as Hank took the boat out to check the recreational shellfishing areas, he laced up the skates and went straight down Breakwater Road. What were the chances he'd see Sabine, after all?

"I thought you'd given up skating," she said, in the voice of someone who knew exactly what a man was trying to give up. She was wearing soft old jeans and a man's shirt, sitting in the doorway of her cottage—Sea Spray, it was called. Just the fact that she was there seemed to be a sign.

The cottage was ten steps from the road, but she led him down the grass alley to a tiny patio surrounded by a privet hedge, shaggily overgrown. There were two plastic chairs and a rusted metal table barely big enough for the pot of impatiens she'd set there.

He swallowed. Danielle always planted impatiens; that was all that would grow on their little deck. She had two window boxes shaped like dories—or, really, they *were* dories. He'd built them with the boys, one for each, a way to spend some time together and get them comfortable with tools; helped them understand the water, too—all those mysteries that had to be passed along through physical experience. Danielle scraped and repainted them every year, a bright red enamel. She would not have peeling paint, or the slightest blister of rust, as if decay might overtake her life entirely if she didn't attend to it right away.

But this had nothing to do with Danielle. It was about stepping into a dream for a minute, into another life entirely. These wash-ashores, with their watercolor brushes soaking by the sink, their cellos resting in the corner, the frayed Persian rug some great-grandparent had left, the beach glass on the windowsill. LaRee and Drew Farnham had built their house entirely from salvage—beams, doors, windows—everything was a relic of something else, ill-fitting, unmatched. Everyone said it was charming, but to him it just looked unstable. People like the Farnhams and Sabine grew up in those big white houses on one or another Main Street and moved to Oyster Creek so they could live like shipwreck victims. It made no sense to him.

Not that it wasn't somehow magnetic.

"So, may I correct your coffee?" Sabine asked, and he smiled.

"It's so harsh, it's like medicine," she said, pouring the grappa. "But I love it. It makes me feel like I'm back in Florence."

Franco tried to respond, but his tongue was slow. He was in her power, falling toward her; it was the best feeling he knew. He sipped.

"Florence, Italy?" he managed to ask, realizing instantly that only a dumb Portagee who'd never been to college, who rarely went across the bridge to the mainland, never mind across the sea, would have asked such a question.

"I lived there for years," she said. "I was studying, and then . . . Anyway, I miss it sometimes. I'd have guessed you were Italian, in fact."

"No, Portuguese," he said apologetically.

"The great adventurers," she said. "Navigators, conquistadores . . . I should have known."

Something pricked in the back of his mind, a memory of his

father's pride—his father who had not gone beyond high school but who read and studied Portuguese culture and history as if those books were making him strong. "A thalassocracy, that was Portugal—an empire of the sea!" he would say. He had a map, a copy of a map from the year 1500, that showed the continents, or their coastlines, emerging from a vast unknown. "Vasco da Gama, Cabral, Corte-Real . . . all sailing under the Portuguese flag, into . . . *pfft!* Who could even imagine what they would find?"

The memory of his father's expansive spirit, more than the grappa, more even than Sabine's expert seduction, dizzied him.

"I like you," she said, a cool appraisal, paired with a glance so frank that something in him reared back—who was she, and who did she think she was? Then she laughed lightly. "Sorry," she said. "That's the kind of thing men say to women, you know. As if we were a bunch of goats lined up at a county fair. I don't like it any better than you just did. But I'd always wanted to see what it felt like on the other side."

With that, the mask of sophistication dropped and she became sad and looked away.

"I like you, too," he said, filled with tenderness suddenly. Not so much for her, but for every lonely soul on earth, everyone who was yearning for some connection, reaching toward it, in whatever way.

She looked up, quizzical. "No," she said, pinching a spent bloom off the plant, "you don't know me, that's all." Now her eyes were bottomless, and as he looked she leaned in and kissed his mouth, as sweetly as a child. Everything tender in him was awakened, but she had changed at the instant their lips touched— become hungry and harsh. So he took the part she gave him and played it in earnest, hands cupped to her ass, grinding against her. . . .

"I'm so wet," she said. Oh, she was not a local! He lifted her and carried her in to the bed. Soon she'd be saying, "Wait. We can't," in the same suffering tone, ending this little part of the drama. And he would give in to her scruple, swearing fidelity to his wife and making himself all the more irresistible. He thrust his hand up under her shirt.

"You . . . you . . ." she said. But not "wait."

"You," he said, unbuttoning the shirt, laying her breasts bare. Their eyes met. Where was "wait"? She lay there exposed and challenged him to resist her.

"I . . . I don't have any . . . protection," he said, feeling utterly unmanly.

"We don't need it," she said. "I don't, I can't . . . I'm barren, as the Bible would put it. . . . I mean, I probably don't know you well enough to tell you that, but . . ."

She laughed, sweetly, a tigress melted. Her skin was so pale beside his! The few lilies of the valley in the vase beside the bed gave off the sweetest fragrance. . . . She still seemed like she was in a movie, but now he had stepped in with her. And if this was more art than reality—well, he rose to the occasion; he knew every move. And then there they were, the dream had passed over them and a ray of sunlight was illuminating the flowers outside the window.

"Is it noon already?" she asked, sitting up. "I have a hair appointment in half an hour."

He knew the arc of the situation. Having given in to impulse, he could expect a flood of guilt. What was he thinking of? He loved Danielle.

"I can't come back," he said, just before he left, leaning against her as if he was deeply in her sway. Anything else would have been unspeakably rude.

"I'm not that way," she said lightly. "I don't want promises."

"My wife . . ."

"There's nothing to fear." She buttoned his shirt up, kissing his chest before she did the top few buttons. "See? Nothing's changed." She laughed lightly. "I've been in Europe so long, I've started looking at it the way they do. They have their dalliances; it doesn't interfere."

By "Europe," she certainly did not mean Gelfa, the town his grandfather had come from, where they had taken the boys to visit their cousins on their one trip across the Atlantic. Red-tiled roofs, a harbor crammed with boats, dogs sleeping in the alleys where they could shelter from a merciless sun. Men gathered in the square, their pants belted above their bellies, talking about the catch. Women in black from head to toe, gossiping in a tone he recognized easily though the words were foreign. The people from the next town could not be trusted; that was what they were saying, and they were speaking with pride. Of course, theirs was the best town, in the best country, in the world. On June 10, Portugal Day, they would celebrate the nation's heroic explorers and the conquests they'd made. They were not more sophisticated than the Americans he knew.

Though Americans did take a strange pride in their own shame, excoriating themselves for a history that had happened before most of their families had even arrived. Washashores were always eager to count off the ways that Europeans were better, kinder, braver, more honest, more sophisticated than Americans. Maybe they had only studied American history.

"It's like . . . swimming," she said. "You slip into another element for an hour."

Franco blinked, squinted at her. In the course of his life as a rascal, he'd never heard a woman say such a thing. They always wanted love, or at least possession. That little tug, and his pull against it, would define the relationship. Without it, what was the point exactly? The sweetness of wanting, of errant submission to an overwhelming force—that was the pleasure! Guilt was an essential part of Franco's life, even of his marriage. He had adored Danielle since he was fifteen—her body had been such a sweet revelation then, such a miracle. The years had strengthened the love, and coarsened it, until it was gnarled and twisted and maybe eternal, but his tender amazement was gone. The remorse that sprang up when he was with another woman could be counted on to rouse his feeling for his wife, sting him with love and longing for her again.

So a guilt-free liaison was not as appealing to him as Sabine might have expected. Her idea of an affair as a sort of spa treatment was strange. And . . . he didn't trust it. She was trying to keep him there with her, just the way they all did. Her trick was to flaunt her Continental attitude, to promise she didn't care. Jealousy, she insisted, was unknown to her. Sex was a kind of talent, didn't he think? Like dance, or music, it was inborn, wrong to deny. When she heard his skates on the road, she'd get ready for him, and afterward she'd blow him a kiss good-bye, still lying among the sheets, with a sleepy smile. "It's how I want you to think of me," she said.

3

HOOKED

Usually it was possible to make a graceful escape from such a liaison: One explained that one's guilt had become too great; that though one loved the woman, whoever she was, one's wife must come first. It was wrong, wrong to continue. There would be tears and protestations, all the more because a man who valued his wife as highly as Franco did became wonderfully attractive. The ache that followed would be sweet, and a little ribbon of tenderness would always connect the two hearts thus separated. And Franco could go home to a nice roast chicken and salad with Danielle's special dressing, have a beer, watch the game, whatever game, in peace.

Sabine's rules effectively barred this exit. "It's wonderful to tell you things, and know you're not going to use them against me. Men always do, you know. You admit your saddest little weakness and then they tell you that's why they're leaving." She held her hand up so the light struck through her opal ring. "My father brought this back for me, from Australia, when I was little. Look how it's green and blue and purple, just like the bay."

"It's beautiful," Franco said, taking her hand to kiss it. It was this he couldn't resist—the idea that his touch could heal. He did love her, but someday that healing effect would wear off, and the love would go with it.

"He was in the precious-stone business. Do you know what that is? No, I didn't either. Nor my mother. He'd come home and it was like a big celebration every time. But by the time I was in high school she was starting to figure it out—there was another family somewhere, in some country where women didn't ask so many questions. I could never understand why he didn't miss me the way I missed him...."

"But you deserve better," Franco said. "You deserve more."

She looked at him as if she'd heard a proposal and he started kissing her neck, diving back into the physical to escape, but she twisted away.

"Hank's gonna be back from Barrel Point," he said. "I gotta get going."

"See you Tuesday."

"I'm not sure I can come Tuesday...."

Her smile faded; she looked into the opal again. A stink wafted in through the window; Vinny Machado, his old pal Vince's son, was pumping out the septic tank next door.

"Maybe Thursday. I think Hank's going out of town."

"You know you're always welcome," she said, but the stench ruined the effect.

Franco avoided Vinny when he could. Vinny made Franco uneasy, guilty for staying alive when Vinny's father had gone down with the *Suzie Belle*. They went out on a cold morning and couldn't afford to come in when the seas got rough—they'd have lost one of the few fishing days the regulations allowed. The load, frozen with sea spray, shifted in the hold and before Vince could correct their course the boat capsized. Vince's nickname had been Gonna—for all the things he was "gonna" do one day, when he retired. His leg washed up six months later—all that was left of him. Vinny had always been small and slow, and the loss crushed him. He tagged behind Franco's sons at school, trying to act like he was one of them, but everyone called him Runt and left him behind. The town did what it could for him, which was not very much. Dunk Carlos gave him the septic pumping job and you'd find him on one corner or another, smiling in his goofy, red-handed way, with an edge of malice that grew over the years, as his fate was borne in on him.

"Hey, Wheelie," Vinny said. He seemed to be smirking, as if he knew all about Franco and Sabine and was going to use it against Franco somehow.

"Hey, Vin," Franco responded warmly. He must be going crazy if he imagined Vinny was any kind of danger. But that itself was a warning. It was time to break this affair off, before . . . whatever happened next. He could not imagine anything good happening next. He decided to take Danielle out to Tacoma to see Frank Junior. It would be worth maxing out the credit cards to make a clean break. When he got back he would just avoid Sabine, maybe say Hank was upset with his missing so much work. Or . . .

He was considering how to frame it when she told him she was pregnant.

"I swear, I never thought it could happen!" she said. "But I guess with you, anything can." She rubbed her hand along his chin. Five o'clock shadow was a noontime thing for him.

"But it's not what you wanted," he said.

"Oh, no! It's what I've wanted more than anything. But I thought it couldn't happen—the doctor said . . ."

What had the doctor said? Anything? She'd have learned to lie from her father; of course. People like that didn't know how to tell the truth.

She kissed his chin, drawing her mouth against his beard, speaking huskily as if they were about to make love. His stomach dropped.

"When I think about it, I think, when I saw you I knew, I just knew you were the one who could..." Where was her sophisticated distance, her ennui? She spoke in a breathless rhapsody, like a teenager.

"But I—" he said. His heart was slamming. Of course, hadn't he known it was an act? These people were acting all the time, pretending to poverty in their little cottages while they waited to inherit their parents' houses back in Westchester, pretending to art to excuse their idleness. They didn't know how to tell the truth. He took a deep breath. "I... well, so would you go back to Italy, then? You'd like to raise a child there?"

She looked as if he'd slapped her.

"I haven't thought it all out yet, but..."

"I'm a married man!"

"Oh. You remembered." This was the sound of a mousetrap springing, as if she had secretly despised him all along. And her face turned vengeful, vicious, like Bobby Matos when he was caught in one of his schemes.

"They never winterized this place," he said stupidly.

"No. I'm only here until September. Then I'm house-sitting for the Straubs, up on Sea Street. I cleaned their Jeff Koons last year. They're happy to have someone there over the winter. I only have to pay the utilities."

He could guess that "their Jeff Koons" would be a painting, and from the twist in her voice he knew that it was also a credential, one of the things that separated the sophisticated from the ordinary people. The Straubs had bought their cottage, a tilting old shingled cape, from Sal Bemba after his parents died. Sal bought Sea View Auto Repair and the Straubs gutted the place, put in skylights and maple floors and an alarm system so complicated that no one could really get it to work, so they needed to have someone in the house with the paintings. It was two blocks from the Walrus and Carpenter; Sabine would know when his car was there, when the lights were on, everything.

"But you said . . ."

"*You* said you loved me." Her voice was as hard as her eyes.

That was the beginning. It seemed there would never be an end. A few weeks later, Danielle had come home from the pharmacy with a bit of gossip.

"You know that girl who stayed over in the Beach Rose Cottages last summer? The little pixie one? She's pregnant—she came in for prenatal vitamins!"

Confidentiality didn't come easily to Danielle. Franco knew who was depressed, who was on Antabuse, whose prescription for Percocet seemed to come from a different doctor every time.

"I'm not sure I remember her," he said.

"Oh, you do," she said. Danielle had a deep voice and a seen-it-all laugh. She'd borne two sons and a stillborn daughter, years of poverty as the nets came up empty, a stint of terrifying wealth when Franco started using the *Rainha* to ferry cocaine to New Bedford. Her brother was known as Lefty: Three of his fingers had been torn off in a scallop chain when he was sixteen. The fact that her husband kept track of every pretty woman in town might have been upsetting to her when she was younger, but by now she was more concerned with the price of heating oil and the mice in the kitchen wall. "LaRee Farnham's friend from college, I think? Rode her bike like she was goin' into battle?"

"Oh, yeah, maybe. How is LaRee?" After LaRee Farnham's husband left her, she'd started taking Valium for anxiety and then Ativan for "acute anxiety," although her life looked to Danielle to be entirely untroubled. The husband had deeded their house over to her, she was a nurse, the steadiest job on earth, no kids—what could the problem be? She was so fragile, she seemed to be allergic to herself! Danielle laughed about it because it made her feel better about the way she made it through life, never letting the knot in her stomach win out.

She was not going to be distracted. "Pay attention—this is a good story!" she said.

"Yeah, I can picture her," he said, praying he sounded bored. "Pregnant, huh? She got a father for it?" His heart seemed to have stopped entirely.

"She said it's an old boyfriend. He bolted when he heard. Men—they're never there to deal with the consequences."

"You've only heard one side," he couldn't help saying.

She just laughed. "Oh, yeah, she's probably a rapist. Really, she seems like a nice girl. Don't know why I call her a girl; she's pushing forty. But it's her first. She's nauseous all day. She asked me what to do."

Sabine was proving to be a most subtle torturer.

"It's nice that somebody's interested in my opinion," Danielle said. "She's in the pharmacy every other day wanting to know something. She worries about every pound she puts on. I told her flat out—I never took off all the weight, either time. It's just part of being a woman."

The ultrasound, the amnio, the birthing classes . . . he heard about them all from Danielle. And then, the first place Sabine turned up with the baby was the pharmacy.

"About the cutest baby I've ever seen," Danielle said. "Black hair, if you could believe it with the mother so pale, and the brightest little eyes! Vita, she named her—it means 'life.' She said the father was a tourist, just passing through, but if you ask me, that baby looks a lot like a Portagee."

The first fish Franco ever caught with a hook and line had been a striper, a really big one, maybe twenty-five pounds. He remembered the tug, and the mastery he felt as he jerked the line back and the fish began to fight. "Let 'im go a ways," his father had said, "then you start reeling him in. Be patient—remember, every move he makes just sets the hook deeper in his mouth."

Sabine pushed the carriage past the harbormaster's shack daily. Franco tried to stay out on the water every minute he could. Then she began calling him, at the shack in the mornings, the Walrus at night. *Your own daughter, Franco, and you haven't even bothered to visit. A child needs a father. She looks more like you every day.* Then: *You don't have the balls, do you, to own up to what you've done?*

"No guilt!" he said. "You said it would be like swimming, an hour in a different element!"

"Not when there's a child involved."

"You said you couldn't . . ."

"I admired you," she said bitterly. "I thought you were different from the others."

Next she pushed the carriage right in through the shack's front door. "Can I talk to you?"

"Sure," Franco said. Hank, gauging the situation, said he was going out to check a mooring on Sequasset Neck.

"I need you to put Vita on your health insurance," Sabine said.

"What?" Franco was slow to anger, but Sabine seemed determined. If she couldn't inspire love, she'd settle for rage.

"You have a job with insurance. I don't," she said.

"Because you're living on a *trust fund*." He was whispering, though they were alone in the shack. Out the little window he saw the harbormaster's boat heading wakeless across the brilliant bay.

"No one can afford health insurance," she said.

He took her arm. "My wife sees all of that; she'd have to know."

Sabine shrugged, pulling away. "She's your daughter. I guess your wife ought to know about her."

His blood raced, he could feel his face blazing. "Well, I guess that's why you've been down at the pharmacy giving her the blow by blow for a year and a half now. What are you trying to do? Who the fuck do you think you are?"

"The mother of your child."

Danielle was used to bearing things. She bore this, too. Her misery was so sharp it broke his heart open and resuscitated every tender feeling that had ever lived between them. They made love as if it were a matter of life and death. This child cemented their marriage in the same way the birth of their own first child had. He had Danielle's name tattooed in a heart on his bicep—a rope heart tied at the point in a bowline knot, "which neither slips nor binds."

"Well, I always wanted a daughter," she said finally. "I guess a stepdaughter will have to do." And the next thing the town knew, she was showing Vita's picture to everyone. "Look at this, a new little Neves! Finally a girl and she looks just like her dad. I hope she's got more sense than the old tomcat." It was a forgiving complaint, the same she made when he forgot to take off his boots and tracked low-tide muck in at the kitchen door.

"She's acting like Vita belongs to her," Sabine complained. How was it that she, whose great-grandmother's portrait had been painted by J. M. W. Turner, was being outmaneuvered by a pharmacy clerk? "She doesn't seem to get it."

"I think she gets it," Franco said, proud of his wife, entirely relieved. "She's glad Vita's a part of her life."

"Good," Sabine said, "because I'm suing you for child support."

4

3:17

LaRee had been so deep asleep that the knocking was absorbed into her dream at first. She was with Drew again. They were picking apples in a vast orchard when the light went strange and a storm came out of nowhere. Everything blew sideways and she heard the apples going *splat, splat, splat* against the barn—the swaybacked barn behind the house she grew up in. Then they were inside the barn, crouching in the back corner while the storm sucked at the door. Together again, and safe, the way things were supposed to be. Then, suddenly, she saw that Drew was gone.

And woke up, enough to realize someone really was knocking, banging a fist on her front door. The clock read 3:17 a.m.; after this, she never saw the number 317 without thinking, *That's when my life turned.* Who could it possibly be at that hour? It was the bleak middle of January, and the pond road was so icy that she'd had a frightening skid coming home from the clinic, then tromped up the unshoveled driveway, shutting the door behind her so she could sink down on the couch to cry.

She'd had to have Rex put down the day before; he was so old his joints were gone, and lately he'd been whimpering even while he was asleep beside the stove. It would have been cruel to keep him alive, but his death seemed beyond bearing. Sabine had said to come over for wine and tears, but LaRee's grief seemed too awful to let show. Rex had been their puppy when she and Drew built the house, and losing him was like losing the marriage all over again. Two years and she was still undone by it; it was too sad and stupid to inflict on Sabine, and three-year-old Vita would be frightened to see an adult in such a state. So LaRee had counted it as "extreme anxiety," and knocked herself out with Ativan. When she woke up this morning she'd felt even worse, as if the weight of misery was dragging at her flesh until she barely had a human shape. It had snowed three more inches overnight, and she swiped the windshield with her arm and fishtailed off to work in the truck, managed the day of taking weights and blood pressures, came home to eat cold cereal for dinner and crawl back under the covers. She couldn't get herself to shovel. The snow would melt and freeze, the driveway would be hopeless all winter, but what did it matter? She didn't have to worry about Rex slipping and hurting his shoulders anymore.

So here she was, stark raving alone with someone pounding on the door. She used to be frightened out here all by herself. The other houses on Grace Pond Road were summer places, pipes drained and windows boarded before there was chance of a freeze. Rex would bark cholerically (wagging his tail all the time) whenever a car even turned around in the driveway, but in fact there had never been an intruder, all these years. If she was woken by some presence in the night, it would be a pair of raccoons fighting at the garbage pail or a deer tearing shoots off the burning bush plant outside the bedroom window. In Oyster Creek only the summer people locked their doors.

"Who is it? What's the matter?" She found her bathrobe and pulled it around her. "I'm coming—hold on!"

"Police!"

LaRee opened the door to see Hannah Stone in her uniform, carrying something in a pink Hello Kitty blanket.

"Hannah, what on earth?"

She had known Hannah Stone since Hannah was a little girl, standing for her measles vaccination with a set, stolid face, walking away proud. She still had that same look when she held up a hand to stop traffic so the schoolkids could cross to the bus. She'd found her place in town; she had the uniform and she was allowed to shout, "Police!" instead of the meek "It's Hannah."

Two wild eyes looked up out of the blanket at LaRee.

"Vita! What . . . ? Hannah! Where's Sabine?"

Hannah pressed her lips tight and gave a quick shake of her head.

"Mommy won't wake up," Vita said. "She's asleep on the floor."

A shot echoed in the woods and both women jumped.

"It's the ice . . ." Hannah said. She'd grown up in the hollow on the other side of the pond; her father had an auto repair business in the woods over there, not exactly licensed but trustworthy. Hannah wasn't someone who usually looked people in the eye, but now she let LaRee see right in, trying to get something across to her above Vita's head.

"I mean, the ice is cracking. There's no gun," she said quickly, a red blotch spreading up her neck from her uniform collar.

"No gun, but . . ." LaRee gathered Vita into her arms.

"Right," Hannah said. "But . . . something else."

"Hannah, stay a minute. I'll make some cocoa. It'll be like a little party," she said to Vita in that high, false voice people use to speak to children and animals when they don't know what else to do. Vita gazed up at her in silence, a rebuke. She had her father's dark eyes and his hair, all tangled now and matted ... with blood. LaRee could smell it; she felt through the child's hair to check for a head wound.

"She's okay," Hannah said. "It's not her, it's ... I gotta go back. We thought if she could stay here, at least for tonight. She knows you."

"Of course. Of course. But what about ...? Is ... is there anything else I ought to do ...? Anyone ... else who needs me?"

She turned, so Vita was facing away, and Hannah shook her head, grim. LaRee held Vita tighter, and the little girl snuggled in against her chest, sucking her thumb.

"Her clothes were ... We had to take them off," Hannah said, and for a second there was the sound of bitter judgment in her voice, as if whatever had happened was the consequence of Sabine's negligence, of the general license of the washashore community. Hannah glanced over at LaRee's sink, filled with the dishes of the past two heartsick days, and nodded, having confirmed her sense of things.

"I have to go back," she said. "She's got her teddy bear but ... she needs a bath and I expect she's hungry. The chief will call you. I have to go back. I ... You probably ought to lock the door."

LaRee heard Hannah's boots crunching through the snow as she made her way back down the driveway. The house had settled and the bolt didn't fit into its hole anymore, or maybe it never had. She tried to lift the door by the knob, then to shove it with her hip, but nothing would force the alignment, and she could feel Vita becoming frightened just from watching her face.

"How about some cocoa for you?" she asked. Vita shook her head. "French toast?" No. There was frost on the inside of the windows; she touched the top of the woodstove. Cold. "Here, I'm going to get a fire going, warm us up."

But as she bent to settle the child on the couch, a bare arm emerged from the blanket to clutch her neck. The other was still holding tight to her teddy bear.

"No, no, don't put me down!"

"Okay . . . okay. I'll just make myself some cocoa, okay?"

This she could manage with Vita settled on her hip, and Vita might want some once she smelled it. One little ordinary motion after another: take the pot down, turn on the gas burner, pour the milk. The cocoa powder spilled onto the counter as she opened the box; she stirred with the wooden spoon. Then she tried to lift the pan off the stove, saw that her hand was trembling too violently, and everything started to spin. Sabine was dead, or terribly wounded, by some . . . accident? Vita's hair was soaked with blood; she said her mother was asleep. Not a car crash. No gun. It was midweek, mid-January—the roads had been empty, everything was closed for the winter, still and silent. What had happened? What? She'd called Sabine the day before, as soon as she got back from the vet. "It's done," she'd said.

"And it . . . went okay?"

"I had him on my lap. So he was happy." She'd started to cry, of course.

"I only wish I could go that way," Sabine had said. "I'll probably fall off some scaffolding and go splat on the Sistine Chapel floor."

LaRee hadn't answered. Sabine was always giving herself little airs like this. She had studied art conservation in Florence, but she spent most of her time now restoring the wide, dull abstract impressionist canvases painted by the generation who owned retirement homes in town. Her parents' generation, Harvard alums who'd married Smith alums, who'd been analyzed by men who'd been analyzed by Freud, and dropped acid with men who'd dropped acid with Timothy Leary. Her own father had a degree from Oxford, or so he'd said. Sabine didn't even know whether he was still alive. Her mother—Bennington—had sold the J. M. W. Turner portrait and bought an apartment on Washington Square. So Sabine could afford to study art at NYU, while LaRee, her prosaic roommate, worked toward a nursing degree.

Sabine had loved that nursing degree. "You're so lucky to be *normal*," she would say—meaning that she, like Sylvia Plath, or one of the other great artists whose biographies she had memorized, was cursed with genius and madness, set apart from—*above*— the normal.

"Here, let's use the cups your mom brought me," LaRee said to Vita. They were simple and perfect, hand-painted in some town in Italy specially known for its pottery. LaRee usually used the big mugs she and Drew had picked out at the thrift shop, when they were young and poor and so in love they'd stayed awake all night just to feel themselves skin to skin.

"She cut herself, that's why she's so tired," Vita said, shaking her head very seriously. LaRee carried the cups to the coffee table one by one so she could keep her promise not to put Vita down. Then she pulled the quilt off the bed and wrapped it around the two of them, propping Vita's little teddy bear on her lap. As soon as Vita sipped, she relaxed, sat up suddenly, and became the bright little creature LaRee knew.

"She didn't even wake up when the police came."

"What made the police come?" LaRee asked.

"They had to wake her up! But she was sleeping too hard! Right by the front door and she didn't wake up in the morning!" Vita drained her cup.

"Do you want mine, too?" LaRee asked. Had the police called Franco? Of course, Vita didn't know he was her father, so what would have been the point? Vita took the cup LaRee handed her, but noticed something amiss.

"Where are the marshmellows?"

"Oh, sweetie, I don't have any marshmallows."

"We have 'mellows," Vita said suddenly, severely, as if she had just discovered LaRee was a criminal. "We always have 'mellows in cocoa!"

"Well, you know what? Tomorrow morning, as soon as the store opens, we will go straight there and get marshmallows. What do you think of that idea?"

Vita looked up at her, troubled and accusing, through the snarl of dark hair that had fallen over her face.

"I won't be here tomorrow. Tomorrow I'm going home."

As Vita spoke, LaRee saw her realize what she had no words to explain. She didn't know what death was, though she'd been alone with it for hours. When LaRee said "tomorrow" so easily, as if she expected Vita to stay, Vita understood that her mother was not going to wake up. She flung her arm out suddenly, dashing the cup away so the cocoa sprayed across the room, butting her head into LaRee's shoulder.

"I want marshmellows now!" she wailed, as if her heart was being torn from her chest. "Tomorrow I'm going home!" She threw the teddy bear down and when he hit the floor she began to scream as if she had killed him.

"Here, look, Little's fine," LaRee said. She picked him up, kissed him, tucked him into the blanket with Vita. "He didn't get hurt, see?"

But Vita had been sucked into a black vortex and flailed at

LaRee with her little fists, kicking until the quilt slipped off and left her in nothing but her nightshirt. She was tiny, filthy, terrified, and LaRee pulled her up onto her lap, holding her tight, taking one of her little bare feet in each hand. They were like lumps of ice—had she been without socks all this time in the cold?

"I'm right here with you, right here . . ." she said, and she felt the tense little body give in slowly to her warmth. The kicking stopped; she bent to kiss the toes. Was this what it was like to be a mother— you had to stand by, powerless, while life struck its blows? Who could bear it? No wonder Drew had been so set against having a child.

Then Vita was asleep, nestled against LaRee's shoulder, breathing steadily, sucking her thumb.

What had happened? What would happen next? In the morning . . . But it was the morning. Six a.m. and still so dark the windows mirrored her life back to her—the paperwhites she'd gotten to bloom on the countertop, the lamp over the couch, her book still facedown on the arm, and Rex's torn old bed beside the woodstove. She'd been bleary with misery a few hours ago; now her head was so clear it hurt. She covered Vita with a folded quilt and got the fire going, sat down beside her. Her curls were crusted with blood— LaRee rubbed them between her fingers to flake some of it away. The teddy bear was stiff with blood, too, so LaRee opened Vita's little fist with her thumb, stuffing a corner of the blanket into her hand to replace the bear, then ran the sink full of cold water and put him in to soak. She rubbed dish soap into the plush, rinsed him again and again. The stain wouldn't show too badly—he was, of course, a brown bear. Sabine had shopped obsessively for him, going through every toy store on Cape Cod to find this particular bear, whose black bead eyes and sharp snout made him look so poignant and alert.

It came over her, scalding—Sabine was gone. Sabine who had been so uncertain that her every word was a pose, so hurt that she had been willing to smash Franco's life to bits when he didn't fall in love with her ... so anxious for Vita to have the perfect soft toy. The bear looked up at her from the sink, with his bright, expectant eyes.

LaRee wrapped Little in a towel to squeeze him dry, then set him on a stool beside the stove. "Here's a nice warm spot for you," she whispered. It was good to offer comfort, if only to a stuffed animal with a sympathetic expression. If only she could have been so kind to Sabine. Surely there are worse sins than imagining yourself restoring the Sistine Chapel ceiling. She leaned against the sink with stiff arms, lifting herself off the ground for a second. She'd been a gymnast in high school, seventh in the state, and she still looked to the strength in her arms for reassurance. After all these years. The window over the sink looked east, up the hill to the back shore, and she saw through the trees the faint red glow of the new day.

5

TOMORROW

L aRee had never put a door on the bedroom, but a velvet drape hung across the opening. She had carried Vita in and settled her in bed there, while she waited for . . . whatever would come next. The television, muted, showed a banner across the bottom of the screen, which changed from "Body Found in Cape Town" to "Nightmare in a Dream Cottage" over a loop of the Straub place with its wide porch wrapped in yellow tape, police cars parked haphazardly, and the chief looking flustered and self-important as he conferred with the state cops. Last week's police report had listed two instances of Operating Under the Influence and one of Assault and Battery with a Dangerous Weapon (clam rake). There hadn't been a murder in Oyster Creek since 1974. They showed a picture from Sabine's Facebook page— LaRee had taken it, of Sabine and Vita making a pie at Thanksgiving, holding out their floury white hands.

The phone rang every five minutes: first, Hannah. "How's Vita?"

"Still asleep. Hannah, what on earth . . . ?"

"She . . . It happened a long time before we found her. Probably the night before last, but there was the snow yesterday and . . . I was driving by and the lights were on and the storm door was banging in the wind, so I went up and looked in. And . . . oh my God, it was an awful mess and Vita was just curled up in the crook of Sabine's arm. I called the rescue squad and they came over with the defibrillator and everything but . . . oh, my God, dinner on the table and blood and . . . I tried to straighten up some, but it was hard with the baby."

"Yes, she tidied up the murder scene," Charlotte Tradescome said a few minutes later, sighing. Charlotte was new in town, a reporter for the *Oracle*. She had a daughter a couple of years older than Vita who came into the clinic for her checkups. They'd recognized each other the way expatriates might in a foreign city, though they didn't know each other well. Charlotte had called to find out what she could about Sabine's death, and of course that led them to gossip. "Hannah didn't want the state police to think our townspeople are bad housekeepers."

Of course not. LaRee thought of the woods behind Hannah's father's house, the carcasses of old cars . . . and everything else . . . piled there. Georgie Bottles lived in an abandoned school bus back there, and there were maybe twenty toilets all lined up from the days when the town had to switch over to a one-gallon flush. Heaven knew what use they could possibly be, but Jeb Stone couldn't help holding on to things. "I can imagine what neatness might mean to Hannah," LaRee said.

"And the rescue squad tromped all through the snow, around the kitchen, everywhere. They can't find a whole footprint, or a tire track, and Hannah washed up the wineglasses."

"My God, anyone who's ever watched a cop show knows you don't wash the wineglasses!"

"I think it was second nature. Death is bad enough; she didn't want Sabine to be embarrassed, too. When in doubt, a Portagee cleans."

LaRee laughed. "And a washashore drinks. Do you know anything more about Vita? Did she see . . . whatever happened? Or . . ."

"It sounds like she was asleep upstairs, came down in the morning and found Sabine there. She tried to revive her—they found vitamin pills in her mouth that Vita must have put there. And a bag of little marshmallows she had tried to feed her. But Sabine would have died hours before—she was stabbed in the throat."

"Vita was there with her all day alone? Trying to bring her back to life? What . . . ?" What was she, or anyone, going to do, to save the child's heart and soul?

"That's what they think," Charlotte said. "I mean, they might be wrong. I'm so sorry."

"I can't believe it. I don't really believe it."

"Who would?" Charlotte asked. "I don't think Hannah or the guys on the rescue squad even thought there could have been a murder. They saw someone bleeding, and a baby . . . and a mess. They're questioning Franco, you know."

"Oh my God . . . can you imagine Franco Neves . . . ?"

"Of course not," Charlotte said. "But he has the motive, and the means. He was a longline swordfisherman years ago, apparently. You know what that is."

"Yes," she said. Miles of line, hundreds of hooks, and on a good day, a fish almost the size of a woman on each arm, to be hauled flailing into the boat and slit open with one stroke. She hoped Sabine had not put out her hand to protect herself. She did not want to think of her hands being cut.

Captions scrolled along the bottom of the television: "Oyster

Creek has for generations given safe harbor to all sorts of travelers, but a gruesome discovery has shocked this pristine New England village, and people who thought it couldn't happen in their home-town are thinking again." The camera panned the harbor with the roofs and steeples packed around it. "The tot found suckling at her dead mother's breast yesterday had apparently tried to care for the victim as her life ebbed away." And a close-up on the Facebook pic-ture again.

"I need to come home," Sabine had written to LaRee. She'd been in Italy for years. At first she was in love with a waiter from a café on Santo Spirito whose addiction to opium was in abeyance. Their af-fair, the beautiful union of two tortured souls, was consummated in the same room where Elizabeth Barrett Browning had once stayed. It made a good story, edgy—international, with a pinch of romantic poetry and a dash of pulp fiction. Sabine soon became distracted by another man, an itinerant fire-eater who added a Pre-Raphaelite aspect, making her the focal point of the triangle. Then it turned out that the fire-eater had been the opium addict's dealer (and lover) all along. "But there's no home to come to."

Of course LaRee had told her to come to Oyster Creek. And the minute Sabine stepped off the little plane in Provincetown, looking worn and rumpled, her fine hair blowing across her face, LaRee had regretted the invitation.

"You were right," Sabine had said, in a fragile, distant voice that reminded LaRee of her collegiate fixation on suicidal poets. "I be-lieve this light could cure anything."

Soon the opium addict and the fire-eater were forgotten; there was a new story under way. Franco made a wonderfully picturesque lover, leaning in the door of the harbormaster's shack with his slow smile, and behind him a dragger coming in from George's Bank with a load of cod. Falling for him was like falling in love with the whole town: the stinging wind off the water; the crabs popping in and out of their holes alongside the marsh; the layers of history back and back and back, through the mackerel fishery, the New York intellectuals and plein air painters, the whaling captains with their clipper ships. It was real—feet-planted-in-the-tide-bottom real. And nothing else was ever real anymore.

Now the television had their photos side by side, Franco in his peacoat and fisherman's cap, Sabine with a paintbrush in hand—the fisherman and the artist, the Portagee and the washashore. Cultures would clash; there was glamour, mystery, a romantic location. News directors were thanking the heavens.

LaRee had found herself kissing Franco once, years ago, in the side doorway of Doubloons Beach Bar after a long summer night of dancing. She was not yet married; his sons were still young. There was no lechery in him; he just fell in love all the time, and she could feel him slip into love with her, right there as he bent in toward her mouth. In his mind, he was the one submitting and she was the seducer.

She had laughed and sent him home to Danielle, but Sabine was hungrier, older, more desperate. She would take him because she needed him; she didn't care who suffered. Of course there was a catastrophe on the horizon, but . . . not a catastrophe like this.

The TV camera closed in on the harbormaster's shack. "Father of the victim's love child in custody," the caption read.

LaRee turned it off; she couldn't look. Two squirrels were chasing each other through the trees out back, leaping from branch to branch, tails twitching. The winter sky was bright, bright blue and clumps of snow had begun to drop from the branches. Thank God, something ordinary.

"Vita's asleep in my bed," she told Charlotte. "I mean—this is off the record; you won't tell anyone, will you? She thinks Sabine is going to wake up. And she's just . . . she's so new and open to the world, she doesn't have any protective layers." She realized she was begging. She couldn't face this alone.

"She's with you?" Charlotte asked.

"Where else would she be? She doesn't even know Franco's her father, and she doesn't have anyone else."

The pregnancy had jarred something loose in Sabine. Suddenly she'd wanted to pick blueberries on the back shore with LaRee, and while they were stooped there Sabine had poked fun at all her ex-boyfriends until finally she sat down in the bushes and laughed and laughed and said, "Who was I trying to be, anyway? Anyone but myself, I guess." And with one hand on her rounded stomach she had leaned back and looked up at the sun and said, so happily, "What a fool!"

She'd had a date with Franco that evening—carefully contrived. Usually they saw each other only when Danielle was at work at the pharmacy, but there was a meeting of the county harbormasters association in Hyannis, and he'd acted as if he were going up with the other guys. Instead, he was taking Sabine to Chatham for dinner. "No one has ever been this . . . just *nice* to me," Sabine said. "We're going for dinner and a walk on the beach and pretend we're tourists. We'll be another couple on the street. No one will recognize us out there."

She had looked so pretty, her face filled out by the pregnancy and flushed under the sun. And then, at midnight, the phone rang and she was sobbing, shattered, as if her whole life had tipped over a precipice. Franco had taken her to a restaurant with white tablecloths, roses in every vase, a sweeping view over the sound. He had taken her hand and praised her—starting with the delicacy of her feet and working upward, a plush carpet of praises, leading to a guillotine: He had loved Danielle since he was fifteen years old; he could no more take leave of her than he could cut off his right hand. He'd been raised a Catholic—he certainly understood that Sabine wanted the child, but she had told him she planned to return to Italy. Wasn't this the right time? At that he had taken something from his pocket—she'd bumped against it earlier and wondered if it was a jewelry box. It was a thousand dollars, in twenties, folded into a rubber band.

"He was trying to buy me off! With a thousand fucking dollars! Can you imagine?"

"Not to buy you off. To help you, I'm sure," LaRee had said, scrabbling for a consoling answer.

From that moment Sabine had despised Franco. The softness LaRee had seen in her that day was gone; she spent her time calculating, planning out new torments. She took any excuse to visit Danielle at the pharmacy. Sabine, buying her prenatal vitamins, solicited her advice, confided her story. "It's kicking—feel it!" she'd said, and Danielle had rested her hand on the stretched belly to feel her husband's child move there.

"That woman must be an imbecile if she can't guess who the father is," she'd said, the day she first took Vita in to show her off. LaRee had wondered if Danielle wasn't in fact a genius, turning Sabine's torture back on her. But there was no stopping Sabine. The fire-eater, the opium addict . . . she could name them the way some could recite the rosary—all the way back to her father the son of a bitch, and for every one of them she would exact a price from Franco.

"But he doesn't have any money," LaRee had said when she started asking for child support.

Sabine had squinted at her, confused. What did it matter how much money he had? The point was to ruin his life. "I suppose you knew all along . . ." Danielle had said to LaRee when she finally found out the truth, holding up a hand to stanch the apology, standing there behind the pharmacy counter in her white smock and her half-glasses. "What could you do? Franco got himself into this mess, the big dope." And then: "Still, it's more family. I always wanted a girl."

So Sabine had lost again, though the suit proceeded. With Vita she was as tender as a woman could be, serving her little bowls of strawberries with powdery sugar, dabbing the shampoo from her brow in the bath. Then the subject would turn to Franco and she'd bare her teeth and hiss. She suffered from her own anger, worse than anyone else.

"She wouldn't let it go," LaRee said to Charlotte. She was aware of the conversation as it passed, eavesdropping on herself—a few more moments of her own life gone. How she had cried yesterday over losing Rex; was there not a tear left for Sabine? "She just had to punish him somehow."

"You must know about Amalia Matos and Franco," Charlotte said.

"What?" Amalia Matos, Bobby's wife, was Franco's age—late forties somewhere—but her varnished hairdo made her seem a generation older. She had become more upright and censorious through the years until she was as rigid as a tuning fork, vibrating with moral superiority, offended by almost everything She was there, always there, behind the counter at Matos Fish Market, deft and efficient, setting down the fillet knife to rap sharply on the window when kids gathered on the sidewalk in front.

"Franco and Amalia . . . like, a love affair?" LaRee asked.

Amalia Matos in love? With Franco? Sabine would laugh into hiccups at this—LaRee had to call her. But her smartphone was not smart enough.

"Let's just say it has to do with their junior prom. Amalia is still feeling stood up."

"Oh God, I wish I didn't believe that," LaRee said. The things Drew said when he left—that he'd married her because he was too young to know what to do; that after all, she knew she wasn't his type, he liked the sexy type, he always had. Idiotic though they were, the words still stung. "And Amalia's there with her fishing knife, all day every day. Maybe she did it. Maybe she was trying to frame Franco."

"Or, Sabine questioned the freshness of the scallops?"

"That would move Amalia to homicide."

"She wouldn't need a knife, though. She'd accomplish it with a look."

"I know that look!" LaRee said, laughing. This, the fact that she and Charlotte had both suffered the disapproval of the same fishmonger, lifted the weight from her heart for a second. Which of course made her cry.

"You there?" Charlotte asked.

LaRee swallowed, managed to sound natural. "I just . . . can't believe it. Can't understand it."

"I know," Charlotte said kindly. "Me neither. If you think of anything, LaRee, please call me, will you? I . . . I'd honestly like to write the truth. Which isn't so easy."

"I will."

A drab little bird hopped through the bittersweet vines out back, plucking berries. LaRee and Drew had sited the house on the one level spot they had—behind it the hill sloped upward, blocking the morning sun, and the front dropped steeply to the west, wooded with low pines and knobby oaks whose leaves clung all winter. All covered with snow now, a sacred forest. The phone rang again.

"LaRee, it's Danielle, Danielle Neves." LaRee always hoped to get Danielle when she called in a prescription from the clinic; she would rush the amoxicillin if a child was miserable with an ear infection, while Mary, the other clerk, seemed to enjoy making things difficult, citing one rule or another, savoring her little ounce of power. But LaRee and Danielle had never talked about anything except prescriptions or weather before.

"Hi, Danielle. I guess you've heard?"

"Franco's at the police station," Danielle said. Her voice was low, matter-of-fact. She had lived her life much as she would if her family had stayed in Gelfa: finished high school, married, raised her children. When their house was repossessed, she had convinced Franco's boss at the Walrus and Carpenter to let them fix up the apartment over the bar. And she'd found all the good in the place; she'd made it a home. Danielle didn't have a calling, a life plan. She just did what was necessary every day.

"He didn't . . ."

"No, of course not," Danielle said. "But, LaRee . . . where's the baby?"

"Here, with me. Hannah brought her last night."

"What happened? Do you know? They say . . . they said Franco is under arrest for suspicion of murder." She sounded less frightened than amused—the cops all knew Franco; in fact, the harbormaster's office was just a branch of the police force. He was there among friends.

"Vita was alone with Sabine . . . with her body . . . for something like a whole day."

"Her body? Why? Who?"

"Believe me, I'm trying to imagine," LaRee said.

Danielle laughed, a low, dry sound. "Me, I suppose. I had the reason."

"I don't think anyone will think that."

Now Danielle gave a real hoot. "You must be a young soul," she said. "There are at least a hundred people in this town who would be just thrilled if I was tried for murder. I mean, where to begin? Sheila Lopes? She thinks Cabbage ought to be assistant harbormaster, just because he's a more *upstanding citizen* than Franco. Meaning that the guy's tail is so tight between his legs he wouldn't jaywalk across Sea Street at midnight in February for fear of getting a ticket. Or Elfa Soares, who won't ever forget that I was on the school board when her son didn't get hired to teach third grade. And that's not to mention all the people who'd throw me or anyone to the dogs just for a good story . . . a fishwife-with-fish-knife story."

"Guilty, guilty as charged," LaRee said. "But there'd be a lot of us on your side."

"Franco would miss me. And the Fitzsimmonses. They'd have to clean the cottage changeovers themselves. That's three."

"And me!" LaRee said. "Who'd put a rush on the amoxicillin prescriptions if you were in jail?"

They were laughing, but it would have been nice if this was a little further from the truth.

"I'll come over and pick up the baby," Danielle said.

LaRee sank down into the couch. She was cold and tired and frightened—not of some madman with a fishing knife, but of what was going to happen when Vita woke up.

"She's fast asleep, Danielle. Her hair is all matted with her mother's blood. I'm not going to . . ."

"A child needs her father," Danielle said, her voice rising.

"Yes, but she doesn't even know Franco is her father right now. . . . Listen, Danielle, come over here, why don't you. We can have a cup of tea, we can try to make some kind of sense . . ."

She regretted this instantly. She could not bear the weight of one more human need. Sabine had a will that made LaRee Vita's guardian. She had not expected to die, but she was damned if Franco—or worse yet, her mother the gorgon—was going to get anywhere near that child. Of course Franco might contest the will; blood relation must carry some weight. . . . But she did not want to explain any of this to anyone right now.

"Danielle, let's just do one thing at a time, okay? Get Franco back from the police station, get Vita a bath . . . just . . ."

"It's okay," Danielle said. "There's a news truck parked outside anyway. They're waiting for me and they can wait all damn week if they want." She laughed and LaRee did, too. Defiance they recognized, admired, and trusted, Portagee and washashore alike. "The cesspool's backed up; Vinny's supposed to be here with the pump. He was supposed to come yesterday."

"So, he'll be there within the week," LaRee said, absurdly grateful for this bit of connection, that they both knew Vinny Machado would get there when he got there, with the "honeypot," the pump truck. When the neighborhood was stinking, it meant Vinny was nearby, and Vinny was going to give you a look that reminded you it was your stink, not his, and that without him you'd be drowning in it.

"His father was my cousin," Danielle said, quietly reminding LaRee that she had no right to laugh at him. There was a soft thump, and LaRee heard the footsteps—the happy, deliberate footsteps of a child just awake and ready to begin another of the days children have. You might see a toad hop in the grass and then you might catch it, feel its cool, dry skin and its back legs pressing into your palm. You might learn to make an angel in the snow. Your mom might put rainbow sprinkles on the cupcake, or show you how to cut a heart out of construction paper, or . . .

Vita came bounding out of the bedroom wearing the old T-shirt LaRee had put her to bed in, her eyes sparkling, her hair still in one big snarl.

"When is Mama coming?" she asked, and jumped onto the couch beside LaRee.

Part Two

6

LEARNER'S PERMIT

"My boobs are bigger! Much bigger! They've grown just this week!" Vita cupped her breasts in her two hands with immense satisfaction.

"Most heartfelt congratulations," LaRee said. She didn't remember this all being quite such a big deal—but it was so far in the past, who knew? Vita had her mother's small stature; she was not likely to become voluptuous. She had Franco's wild dark hair, but her skin was as pale as Sabine's, and sometimes she had an intent, innocent expression that pierced LaRee's heart—as if she'd had a glimpse of Sabine before life hurt her and hardened her. If someone had protected Sabine, kept her safe from the rain of ordinary daily cruelty, she might have been someone entirely different, less inclined to toy with fate. She might be alive now.

LaRee stopped herself: might as well join the rest of the town and blame the murder on its victim. She had been tarred with the same brush as Sabine—a washashore, a loose woman. You did not find the local wives dancing at Doubloons on a summer night, wearing nothing but a little scrap of dress and an armful of gold bangles. And you did not find the local wives murdered in their own homes. LaRee had seen plenty of them at the clinic with black eyes, broken noses, yes, but these injuries were inflicted by their own husbands and boyfriends. From the time Sabine died, there was the quiet, pervasive assumption that she herself was to blame. What had she expected, seducing Franco when everyone *knew* he couldn't resist that kind of thing, and then carrying his child and raising her here, right in his wife's face, instead of moving away as any decent woman would have? People said they saw a red light in her bedroom, that she opened the door to the UPS man in nothing but her panties. . . . People said just about anything. When Vinny Machado was arrested for her murder, two years after it happened, the first thing anyone said was, "Wow, what'd she do to him?"

"Is that possible, though?" Vita asked, pulling the neck of her shirt out so she could peer into her bra. "I mean, a week ago they were just not the . . ."

"Basketballs? Watermelons? That they've become?"

"Exactly!"

Vita was giggling, happy—sitting in the driver's seat of the Subaru for the first time since she had passed her permit test, ready to take to the road. She adjusted the rearview mirror, smiled radiantly at her image there, adjusted it again. She had that same smug, delighted little look as the day she first learned to ride a tricycle, as if she had mastered life completely now. And her delight was LaRee's drug: One twinkle in that child's eye and all regrets, disappointments, and fears burst like soap bubbles in the sun.

"Oh, my girl! How did you get so grown-up?"

"I'm practically the last one to get my license," Vita said. They were in the driveway of Outer Cape High, on top of a hill that looked west over Mackerel Bay and east to the hard blue of the Atlantic Ocean. The kind of real estate development you could put on that property now would be worth millions. But back when the school was built it had been nothing but an old woodlot, of no use to anyone. Cars and trucks streamed past, driven by kids LaRee remembered dressed as snowflakes for their kindergarten concert, each carrying a rose in their eighth-grade graduation. How had life gone by this way? She reached across to wrap one of Vita's curls around her finger. Vita hated her hair and kept it yanked back into a ponytail so tightly that LaRee worried it would affect her circulation. LaRee thought it was the most beautiful hair she'd ever seen—like the tangible proof of Vita's resilience, curling every which way, with a will of its own, as they said. Vita wanted only to subdue it.

"Okay, can we go?" she asked.

"I'm ready when you are. Foot on the brake, take the emergency brake down . . . and . . . that's right, just a little press on the accelerator . . ."

The engine revved, loud but impotent, and Vita looked around to see who might have noticed.

"First you have to shift into drive," LaRee said evenly. Thirty hours of driving time and six months to do it—not so bad really. It was like everything about motherhood: You provided a calm, encouraging presence, and the kid just climbed up through the limbs toward the sun.

Vita shifted and the car lurched forward. They drove down the driveway and stopped at the road, or ten feet before it. Vita looked both ways.

"I can't see."

"You need to go up closer to the road."

"Mr. Webster said to stop *before* the Stop sign."

"Well, that's right, but not so far before the Stop sign."

"He's the driving teacher—I guess he knows better than you." Vita sat absolutely rigid, her hands at ten and two, her knuckles white.

"I'm sure he does, but I'm also pretty sure he means you should stop where you can see up and down the road you're turning into."

"All right, then." She drove halfway into the intersection, across one whole lane, and stopped. "Is that better?"

"Back up, back up!" Cars were coming both ways, half of them driven by sixteen-year-old boys with their nerves all bristling with testosterone.

"See?"

"Well, I didn't mean you should stop in the middle of the road, just closer to it."

"That's always the way, isn't it?" Vita said. "I'm always too close or too far. Nothing's good enough for you. I can do this, you know. Mr. Webster said I had very good defensive-driving skills."

"I'm sure he's right," LaRee managed to say. Vita would hear the strain in her voice and respond to it badly, but it was the best LaRee could do. What was more infuriating than sitting in the passenger's seat—the death seat—with a driver who, based on three minutes of experience, was certain she knew more than you did, although you knew very well that she could barely walk across a room without bumping into the furniture, was so damned stubborn she wouldn't wear a raincoat in a monsoon—and that every one of her failings was probably somehow your own fault? Fingernails digging into her palm, praying to sound relaxed and upbeat, LaRee continued. "So, here we are at the Stop sign. What next?"

Vita turned right, too widely, but she ended up in the right lane and they went nearly a mile with ease. Down the hill, through the light even, and LaRee had just gotten her heart rate down when they saw a bicyclist ahead: Georgie Bottles with a basket of clams over his handlebar.

"What is he doing way back here?" Vita asked.

"Living in the Fitzsimmons' cottage, I think," LaRee said. "I guess Jeb Stone's junkyard was spilling over onto National Seashore property and he had to get rid of those old cars. So Georgie's moved into the cottage and been there all winter, or that's what Charlotte said." Georgie's sister usually came out from New Bedford and got him cleaned up every few months, but her mother was dying and she hadn't been around.

"Do the Fitzsimmonses know?"

"I doubt it. But Danielle cleans for them, so when she opens the house for the summer I'm sure she'll get it fixed up—no one will be the wiser."

Georgie wobbled into the road, drinking from a beer in a paper bag.

"What do I do, LaRee? Oh my God, what do I do?"

"Well, you slow down and drive behind him until there's no one coming on the other side. Then you can cross a little bit into the other lane and pass."

"I'm going to hit someone—I know it!" She looked as if she was about to cover her eyes.

"No, you're not," LaRee said evenly. "Just go slower. . . ."

But the mufflerless Chevy behind them was tailgating as if it wanted to push them out of its way.

"Brandon," Vita said, checking the rearview mirror. "Oh my God, I *hate* him." Brandon pulled out and passed her, nearly running the driver in the opposite lane off the road.

"I can't do this, LaRee, I can't! Help!"

She was crawling along behind Georgie.

"Why don't I take over until we get to a quieter spot? Just slow down, let Georgie get ahead, and pull over."

Vita crossed the center line straight into the opposite lane, down which an oil truck was barreling.

"Oh my God, no! What are you thinking of! Stop right now!"

Vita slammed on the brake.

"No, I didn't mean to stop the car; I meant to stop driving in the wrong lane! What on earth? Pull over, pull over onto the shoulder!"

"Do what with my shoulder?"

LaRee grabbed the wheel and steered the car off onto the side, out of harm's way. "This is what 'pull over' means. Do you understand?"

"How would I know that? You said pull over! You didn't say which direction to pull over in!" Vita burst into tears, her head against the steering wheel so the horn blew suddenly, causing a new flood. "I can't do it. I can hear it in your voice that I can't do it and you know!"

"I'm sorry, honey. I'm just nervous. I'll try to do better." LaRee managed to laugh a little, to cover herself. Disaster had been averted after all, even if the lesson had not exactly been successful. How was it that Vita was still too afraid of the gas burner to make herself a bowl of soup? How was it that in spite of her wish for an immense bosom, she gave the appearance of an aspirant nun? The same delicate features had counted for beauty in her mother, but Vita resisted beauty, the way she resisted nearly everything. She was all bravado and no true confidence, holding herself stiff against any influence that might have shaped her. It was as if she had bound her natural instincts as tight as her hair, overthinking every movement she made so she lost track of how to do the simplest tasks. If LaRee had done differently, left her on her own more instead of rushing in to

fix everything all the time—or who knew what exactly, just anything different—things would have been otherwise. But she had
only done the best she could, and apparently that was going to have
life-threatening consequences.

She took a deep breath. She herself, in high school, had been
one of those girls who clung to a boyfriend as if she might otherwise drown. The boy had bangs down over his eyes and smelled of
hay and manure; he had to do barn chores before school. She had
been . . . well, no less lost than Vita was now.

"It was a mistake to start right here, right after school," she said,
watching Georgie pedal crookedly around the corner. Two girls
from school walked along on the other side of the road in flowered
skirts, glossy hair streaming. Perfectly normal high school kids,
talking about boys probably, or what they were going to wear to the
prom. Not that LaRee wished Vita would obsess over boys or
proms. It was just that, for all her love and effort, for all the trips
into Boston to see the specialist in children's grief, and the snow
scene made of cotton and glitter with figures skating on a mirror
under the Christmas tree every year, the fluffy kitten, Bumble, who
slept curled up behind Vita's bent knees, the dollhouse and the storybooks read over and over and the glow-in-the-dark stars in the
exact shape of Orion and the Big Dipper on her ceiling, Vita was
still suffering, still unsteady on her feet. And it meant LaRee had
failed.

"Mr. Webster didn't teach you what 'pull over' means?" she
asked. Surely someone else could have done that much, given her
just one of the thousand billion things a child needs to learn.

"I don't know—maybe he did. There's too much to remember
all at once, LaRee. I mean, you get out in the road and somehow
everyone just knows which lane to drive in? How is that supposed

to work? I can't do this. I just don't understand it. This is impossible. It's the kind of thing *your mother* has to teach you or you never get it right!"

Whatever went wrong, Vita was always going to assume that it was happening because Sabine was gone. And LaRee was always going to wonder if she was right. The last time she went to the dentist she'd had two cavities and he had said her molars were strangely soft. It was probably the lack of calcium. Vita had never liked milk, so Sabine had fed her hot chocolate with every meal. But since the night Sabine died, she had pushed the cup away, insisting that cocoa wasn't the same at LaRee's. Suppose Vita wasn't wired for driving? Sabine hadn't gotten a driver's license until she was forty, and never used her car if she could avoid it. And Franco was a sea captain, not a driver. There might be some loophole in Vita's mind that her parents would recognize and understand. Who knew what blood bond might have synchronized those three? She pulled Vita close with one arm, kissed the top of her head. They were not kin; there would be glitches between them. But all consolation went back to the great consolation, that first week, then the first year, of holding Vita tight against a grief so large it was beyond understanding. The connection there was different from that between a mother and daughter, but as strong as . . . well, she thought of the fishing line display at Gonsalves Bait Shop—strong as a spiderweb, some of them were, and they could go for miles.

"You'll get the hang of it; everyone does."

"I think I'm getting my period, that's all," Vita said, wiping her eyes. She had been gripping the wheel so hard that when she let it go, the color came back into her face and hands. "I'm fine, really. I'm sorry I'm yelling at you. You're such a good teacher. You're such a good mother."

"But not your own mother," LaRee said gently. It was important to keep the door open to the truth, for whatever good it might bring to Vita, who had, from the very beginning, a determination toward goodness as pronounced and sometimes as crippling as a clubfoot.

"You *are* my own mother," Vita insisted. "You always will be." There it was, that infernal attendance to LaRee's needs, just when LaRee was trying to minister to hers.

"Of course I am. I am!" LaRee said. "But . . . well, we don't have to set a place for Sabine at the table, as if she was Elijah. . . . We both know she's there."

"I don't even remember her, LaRee. It doesn't matter a damn."

"Ha-ha! It matters immensely. But you will learn to drive, and you will do it well. Mr. Webster already said so. It's even possible that I will learn not to panic when you're not sure what you're doing."

"*That* would be a miracle," Vita said.

"We can always hope! Ready to try again?"

"Mmm . . . maybe tomorrow. I've got cramps."

They switched seats. It was the beginning of May and the air was straight off the water, sharp and cold and smelling of seaweed. They'd stopped in front of the old Allerton farm—the land had long since been sold off for summer cottages but the farmhouse looked as it had two hundred years ago, daffodils ringing the old pump. "There, that's better," LaRee said, readjusting the mirror.

"Ibuprofen," Vita groaned.

"Check the glove compartment." She started the car, a big wagon she'd gotten when Vita was nine and they'd been part of a car pool. A hundred and thirty thousand miles and still going strong, though it could have been cleaner. "There's a half-full water bottle in the backseat, I think."

"Nice, LaRee. Very sanitary."

"Any port in a storm," LaRee said. She felt absolutely light-hearted now that she was back at the wheel. "We can stop at the SixMart instead, if you can stand to wait."

"I can't." Vita gulped the pills and sank against the window.

LaRee remembered the first time she'd bathed her, tipping her head back with the cloth over her eyes, pouring warm water to rinse the blood out of her curls, wishing she could rinse all of it away so easily. There was something about tending to a child—whatever piece of yourself was hurt and longing felt the comfort, too. She'd found an old pill bottle in the back of her medicine cabinet the other day—Valium, eight years out-of-date. She never felt anxious enough to need a pill anymore.

"We'll make a hot water bottle when you get home. Actually, that's probably why your chest got bigger all of a sudden. That tends to happen right before your period."

"It does?" Vita said. "No, it does not!" She sat straight up, wounded, appalled. "What kind of a thing is that to say? The best thing that's ever happened to me, the most important thing in the world, and you're saying it's just hormonal? You ... How can you?"

Now the tears she had carefully avoided began to pour. "What's wrong with me? What is it?" she asked. "Nobody likes me—they all want to hang around with one another and it's just like I'm always in their way. I think ... I don't know, but something's wrong." She put down the visor so she could examine herself in the mirror on the back, find the flaw.

"There is nothing wrong with you," LaRee said. Her own head was slamming; she'd thought she'd calmed Vita down. Having a teenage daughter was like having your own personal little tornado—always spinning, though you never knew where it might touch down. For one thing, they thought that television represented reality. This in itself was a catastrophe. Vita was sharp enough to know that people in general didn't live like the characters on *Gossip Girl*, but she couldn't help feeling that life was strangely unscripted, random, and lonely.

"You're a beautiful young girl," LaRee said. "A great student, and most of all, you're kind."

And kindness was no mean feat. There were days—more days than she liked to admit—when LaRee herself could barely manage it. Mary Attlekin had brought her twins to the clinic that morning, with measles. Measles! Mary was just twenty herself, and when LaRee asked for the twins' vaccination history, Mary had said that vaccinations were a scam, and she wasn't going to have her kids poisoned like Kyle Monder had been. Kyle Monder had fetal alcohol syndrome, which his mother, understandably, preferred to attribute to his vaccinations. Of course LaRee couldn't say that, or anything else, except to commiserate over the poor sick kids and settle them in examining rooms to wait for the doctor. A new doctor, Alice Nguyen, who was doing three years of rural medicine to reduce her student loans. She was no match for the parade of human frailties that ran through her office all day, and maybe least of all for Mary Attlekin, who had dropped out of high school when she got pregnant and lived pretty much according to her fears now. Alice lived by the cold light of current medical thinking, considering that it was a clinician's job to remind each hairy, flabby soul shivering on a steel bed in an open gown of the many and various failures that had led him down the sorry path to illness. LaRee had tried to explain to Alice that Mary Attlekin's allegiance to poverty and ignorance was a kind of loyalty to her family, who had always lived that way. Alice looked as if these were the cruelest words she'd ever heard. Well, maybe they were. LaRee was trying to respect Mary's plight. Alice respected her potential.

LaRee had lived here too long to remain optimistic. There was the time before Vita, then the time of trying to help her fit into the community, and finally the time of guiding her upward into a larger life than Oyster Creek could offer. If Vita were to thrive, to live with joy and energy and resilience, it would mean that LaRee was a success, a bigger success than Bill Gates or Oprah Winfrey, someone who had faced down her terrors and made the world safe for one person who would otherwise have been lost. "My little kangaroo baby," she used to call Vita, who would always zip herself into LaRee's sweatshirt, as if it wasn't enough to sit on her lap. Vita had been so delicate at heart that she'd seemed almost translucent, sticky, like a baby kangaroo, in need of a pocket. Twelve years later LaRee still felt as if the child's skin wasn't thick enough, that anything might harm her.

And now she had her learner's permit and she'd be driving away. They crossed the highway and drove through the familiar landscape, past rows of shuttered cottages along the deserted beach. This summer there would be laundry lines strung between them with bright towels and dripping bathing suits, and in every one a family with a dad grilling hamburgers and a mom calling the kids up off the beach for supper. Now the clouds were heavy and low and the bay a cold, opaque color that might as well be called Hypothermia Blue. The sign was up at Skipper's Fry Shack—it was opening at the end of the week; but the giant neon ice-cream cone at Ice Cream Tuesday was still wrapped in a heavy tarp against the weather. While the rest of Cape Cod had become wealthy and modern, Route 6 still looked like 1957. The mini-golf, the drive-in movie, the little cottages just the size you could dare to dream about, because that dream was small enough that it might come true.

"First rehearsal tomorrow!" LaRee said, falling back on the ancient maternal technique of distraction. High school hadn't changed much, apparently, since her time—its main purpose was to be sure someone was always left out, thus reassuring the others that they were not. Vita's uncertainty—her realization that there were many ways to see, many paths to try—left her utterly vulnerable at school, but at the theater she was loved for her openness and curiosity. In return she loved the theater—Mackerel Sky, their little summer theater with its one play a year—with an absolute passion. As soon as it started up in the spring Vita would be there every minute, rehearsing or working on the costumes or doing whatever was necessary.

Which meant she would not spend hours upon hours on the back shore, as she had been doing lately. LaRee told herself that, after all, Vita could have been addicted to video games or, Cape Cod being what it was, cocaine. In the winter when the sand was drifting against the snow fences and every parking lot held a shrink-wrapped boat, the kids would drive around the National Seashore sharing a blunt and a bottle of vodka, and call it friendship. And sometimes she thought she wouldn't have minded if Vita was one of those kids. It could not be healthy or right, for a girl of sixteen to spend so much time alone, especially not back on those high, windy bluffs that looked out on nothing but the heaving ocean as far as the eye could see.

Distraction worked. Excitement blazed up in Vita's eyes. "I feel like I can't wait another minute," she said. "Adam Capshaw is in it, too—did you know?"

"You may have mentioned that," LaRee said, teasing her.

"Oh, LaRee . . . he's just so . . . so perfect." Vita sighed. "Don't you want to hear more about him?"

And LaRee did, because when Vita was happy all the troubles on earth thinned and blew away, like fog on a breeze.

7

THE OUTER

"I think I'll take a walk while it's still light out," Vita said the minute they were home. She saw the flicker of concern on LaRee's face, and saw LaRee suppress it, but was infuriated anyway.

"You know, LaRee—if you could stop worrying for five whole minutes . . . or, maybe take it slower, stop worrying for just two or three minutes at a time."

"I thought you weren't feeling well."

"Sometimes a walk helps." She ran cross-country at school every fall; she was half addicted to the feeling of covering distance, each step pushing the last away.

"Fair enough," LaRee said. "I will try not to worry."

"Don't try. Just don't worry, okay? There's nothing to worry about, except your worrying!"

Then of course she was sorry, and she took LaRee's hand in both of hers. "LaRee, you're a good mother. A wonderful mother. You've been my mother for as long as I can remember, literally. I don't remember Sabine, not one thing about her. Nothing about that night, either. It's over and done; there's nothing there for you to fix. I'm no different from anyone else, a regular old girl from Mackerel Bay. You don't need to worry about me."

"I worry, therefore I am," LaRee said. "I think that's sort of a common thread among mothers. And I don't want you to forget Sabine . . . to lose her. But you're right—there is nothing to worry about. Go, have a good walk."

"I will," Vita chirped, and set off up the path behind the house, into the woods.

"Did you take a coat?" she heard LaRee call. "It's raw out there!"

"I took a coat!" Vita called back. To herself she said, *I took a goddamned coat.* It was raw, and breathing the cold air deep, she felt a calm come over her; her heart stopped the infuriating slam-slamslam that had totally to do with *people*, that sense they were always watching and she was always doing something wrong. This afternoon she had raced out of Western Civ so she could get to English class a minute early: Adam would be getting out of his class in that room and she'd have the chance to say hi. He had been the first one out, too—so he'd found her standing there waiting for him; she'd spit out her practiced greeting, "Hi, Adam! *The Tempest* tomorrow!" and died. He looked around to see who she was talking to in her "casual, natural" tone from a television show, and when he realized she was focused on him, he'd blushed and mumbled, "Oh, yeah, right," and looked down at the floor. Who did she think she was? A normal person with friends and a family? No, she was a circus curiosity, the girl with the dead mother. Adults snuck glances at her when they thought she wasn't looking; kids wanted to be sure she knew they were better than she was, that they were real Portagees, real citizens of this town. And Adam did not want her acting like she was his friend.

At the outer shore you could count on being alone, even in the middle of the summer. And on a cold spring day like this, with the shadblow trees blooming in the damp air and every other bud closed tight against the wind, she would not see a soul. Looking back through the trees, she saw the low roof of the house, the moss growing on the east side where the hillside blocked the sun. They needed to put a bleach solution on the shakes before the trees leafed out, and to prune the wisteria back. LaRee loved her bungalow and its half acre, but sometimes it seemed to Vita more like a burrow, a place to hide out from life.

Coming out onto the blacktop of Grace Pond Road, Vita heard a truck downshift on the highway at the bottom of the hill, and otherwise only the wind. If she'd lived in a different time, she might have come up here on some essential errand, maybe taking a cow to pasture or picking rose hips for a jam to prevent scurvy. She'd have looked out from the highest dune, scanning the horizon, hoping to see her father's ship returning.

Grace Pond Road ended at Outer Way, a flat, straight stretch of blacktop that ran along the high ridge of the cape, looking down to the barrier beaches on one side, and back through the furze—that's what Shakespeare would have called it: "Now would I give a thousand furlongs of sea for an acre of barren ground. Long heath, brown furze, anything."

The opening of *The Tempest*. That was the play they would begin to work on tomorrow, the perfect play for Oyster Creek, as Hugh, the director, had said. Were they not all stranded here, reliant on one another whether they could bear one another or not? Did they not live among heath and furze, short trees with branches like bony hands reaching from the grave, thorned and crusted in lichen, sprouting thick, brittle leaves and maybe sour little plums with huge pits? Beach plums, cranberries . . . hard, bitter fruits that grew tough enough, low enough to live where the wind never stopped blowing. LaRee would remind her there were apple trees, too, and even pear trees along the back roads—but she would remind LaRee that those trees were here only because a ship full of seedlings had wrecked off Cahoon Hollow years and years ago. This place was known for its grit, and its wreckage. *Rosa rugosa*—rugged rose. Jack pine and scrub oak, covered with windblown sand year on year so that only their tops protruded from the dune. And against the ground, the furze: blueberry, bearberry, cranberry, red-topped British soldier, and other plants that kept their heads down to survive.

The billboard for Doubloons loomed out of the hill, the only man-made thing in sight. OCEANFRONT DINING! RAW BAR! LIVE MUSIC! The letters had nearly been scoured away by blowing sand. A lone seagull hovered in close as if considering these options, but it was only looking for a bit of asphalt to smash a clam on, and it succeeded, flapping down, then pulling out the meat and soaring away. After Doubloons, the road curved southward, empty, and the ocean stretched east for a thousand miles.

Vita took the path through the bushes to the top of the bluff. The land stopped suddenly where the last storm had bitten it off, and there she stood, alone, high above the ocean, the waves slamming one on the next, surging up the beach. There were two shoals slightly offshore here, and between them a riptide would form when there was a storm nearby—last summer a young girl had been caught in it and carried out to sea. The family was visiting from Missouri; they didn't know anything about the ocean and the father had swum out thinking he would save his daughter, but both were pulled under and drowned. It had happened before, LaRee said, and they'd put up signs, but there were miles and miles of beach out here and no one could watch over all of it. Vita felt a strange satisfaction in looking down at that spot—knowing that savagery was part of nature, that it had torn up other families, too.

You weren't supposed to slide down the dune for fear of causing an avalanche, so she pulled herself up onto the porch of the Shillicoth house, a shuttered gray behemoth that had been a lifesaving station back in the days of clipper ships and shipwrecks. She always expected to feel a ghost catch her by the collar as she crossed the Shillicoths' deck, and she avoided the rotten board in the corner out of some superstition that she would be pulled through the hole.

A ghost—no such luck. The wind moaned constantly, but it was only wind, not a lost being returned for one last good-bye, offering a whisper of advice or admonition. Still Vita felt at home up here, in contact with something essential. Sere, stark, desolate . . . real. The closest thing she could come to remembering something of the long night when her mother's life bled away. No image was left, though—only the cold misery, the physical feeling.

She studied the horizon as carefully as she used to look for Sabine in a crowd when she was little. It was mortifying now, to remember how she used to "see" her mother, running through the woods out the side window, or passing the other end of the supermarket aisle. She would always call LaRee, who would miss the sighting by a second, then say something like, "Isn't it nice to know her spirit is still here with us?"

The right words, what she'd been taught by the grief man: Acknowledge the child's sense of things without denying the loss. LaRee was smart that way—she had known what Vita needed to believe in. But Vita was smart, too; she could hear LaRee humoring her, and she hated it. It had just been a part of her growing, that one day she stopped looking for her mother and found herself just looking, watching the horizon like a sailor. She stopped seeing Sabine, but she still saw plenty: the varying flight patterns of a swallow and a dove, the S-shaped track of a snake moving over a dune. She'd heard the whales were back already and she looked out for a spout now: a puff of mist that would blow up out of the water and hang just above the surface for an instant before the breeze swept it away. She saw only splashes, as the gannets drifted high, spotted fish, and plunged after them, straight down, fifty feet maybe, into the water. That was the kind of thing she noticed—the differences between splashes—and when she did notice, she felt the way she used to when she caught a glimpse of Sabine. It was like having a special power, one that she had learned from her mother.

An oil tanker was passing, way out in the gray distance where sea was indistinguishable from sky. She started down the steps to the beach. From there she could walk the wrack line, as the men from the lifesaving station had years ago. They lived here through the winter, watching from the belfry, walking the beach—four miles north, then four miles south, through every night of the winter—looking for ships that had foundered on the shoals, hoping to save the sailors. But the chances were slim. The same wind-driven waves that had pushed the ship toward land would batter it to splinters. Often enough the coast guardsmen couldn't get close enough to rescue a soul.

It was slack tide, a wide beach and . . . yes. The wreck—her wreck, as she considered it—was right there, its bones exposed like the ribs of a dead animal. The ship had been buried in the sand for years—centuries probably. Each rib was made of a single board, three inches thick and maybe thirty feet long, bent so it curved into the shape of a keel, secured by pegs. The big storm last week had uncovered it, but at this time of year no one walked here except Vita, and she did not mention it to anyone.

She wouldn't have paid attention to it, any more than any of the carcasses that washed up here—seagulls, sharks, once a gelatinous blob the size of an armchair in which she could find no eye, mouth, or fin. She wasn't one of those people who wrote poems about beach glass and counted a cast-off horseshoe crab shell as a sacred totem. But Hugh had said he wanted to build Caliban's hut out of driftwood, so she'd come out here one warm day in January and dragged home an old branch she found tangled in the seaweed along the wrack line. The next week she got a hurricane flag, square with a thick red border, still attached to the rope it had flown from. It must have come loose in the wind and blown out to sea, maybe at Chatham; the current flowed north from there.

It had become an obsession; the more wood she found, the happier Hugh would be, and the more she would belong at the theater. She'd get itchy if she hadn't been out to the beach for a while, worried that she had missed some essential flotsam the way some people worried they'd missed their chance to win the lottery.

The wreck had never been completely uncovered and it was already partly blanketed with sand again. But she had already broken pieces off— a backpack full of old, wormy-looking wood that had crumbled into pieces along its grain. The best piece was a massive joint that made her think of a giant's shoulder, crusted with salt, riddled with holes, stained black and rust from . . . well, she didn't know what. It would look just right as flotsam scavenged from an ancient shipwreck, because that was what it was. She couldn't wait to give it to Hugh.

There was a little hole, like a clam hole, in the sand, and though she hated clams she couldn't resist digging. She clawed through the sand, trying to come in six inches under the hole—and hit something hard, pulling it up in a cold handful of black sand. It was . . . a key, maybe? It was old, and it must belong to the ship somehow; and really, you weren't supposed to take as much as a single cranberry from the National Seashore. But it had been out here for centuries, buried in the sand with no one knowing—it might as well be on her dresser at home.

And it belonged to the ship, which, she had come to feel, belonged to her. Like every single thing that floated, it would have been named for someone's daughter. The *Teresa*, the *Sweet Shyanne*, the *Little Dorotea* . . . When Vita was little she used to watch them line up at the pier for the Blessing of the Fleet, every girl in her class riding with her family in a boat with her own name on it. She'd boil herself into a black fury over it back then. She wanted to be like the rest of them, with a father and a fishing boat to be sprinkled by the bishop of the Fall River diocese on the first day of summer. By now she understood that families, and boats, were fragile, subject to the wind and tide, likely to wreck on an unseen shoal. That was why art mattered. *The Tempest* would be whole and beautiful . . . full of truth. They would shape it together, she and Hugh and the others, and they would make it out of what they knew of life, what it had been like to live on an unmapped planet hundreds of years ago, and what it was like to live on an unmoored one now.

There, the day had been set right again. Her hands were freezing, but she had in her pocket another piece of whatever puzzle it was she was trying to put together for herself. She was ready to try driving again, to forgive LaRee. The Shillicoths had taken the last few feet of their beach steps in for the winter, so she had to grab the bottom of the handrail and pull herself up. Then up she went and across the porch again, and home by one of the fire roads that cut through the woods, on quick, light feet.

8

As Seen on TV

"It went over to my forgetting side," Vita had explained to the patient detectives who asked her again and again what she had seen that night, what she had overheard. She had believed, then, that by tilting her head she could shake things over into the dark and get rid of them. It worked like a lobster trap, though: easy to get things over to the forgetting side but almost impossible to pull them back. The psychiatrist LaRee used to take her to had asked if she wanted to keep her memories of her mother to herself, feeling as if she might lose Sabine if she talked about her.

"Sometimes it's hard to share when you don't have as much as you need for yourself," he'd said, his voice so careful she didn't trust it. She could never seem to think when she was in his office, even though she was allowed to go out into the waiting room as often as she needed to, to be sure LaRee was still there. Dr. Karp was a nice, nice man, and she had wanted to be nice back, but . . . she would end up singing, "*Sur le pont d'Avignon.*"

"That's a pretty song," he said. "Where did you learn it?"

"Can I go say hi to LaRee?"

He always said "of course" because he thought she'd feel safe enough to stop asking. But that was wrong. "I'm sorry," she'd said, starting to cry.

"Why?"

"Sorry I can't remember."

She knew what Sabine had looked like, from the picture on her bureau of a thin, anxious-looking woman with a round-eyed baby on her lap. It was the only picture she had of the two of them, and Vita had stared at it so hard for so long that it didn't seem to show real people any more than a valentine cutout did a real heart.

Her first clear memory was of seeing Sabine, though—seeing her out the window, soon after she went to live with LaRee. It was just a glimpse, but Vita had known it was her mother, moving among the trees on the hillside above the house.

"LaRee!" she'd said. "Mama's out there!"

"Oh, Vita . . ." LaRee had sounded so sad, had lifted her onto her lap and kissed her. "What do you mean? What did you see?"

"She went through the woods, right over there." Vita had pointed to the spot. She could see it exactly even now, the way the lower branch had broken and the vine looped down. The snow had been so sparkly, with tracks through it as if a single doe had crossed there. No footprints. Even now Vita could see the white snow and the black trees and her mother glancing over her shoulder as she slipped between them. It had not occurred to her to knock on the window, or to call for Sabine. Somehow she knew that wasn't how it worked. She'd cuddled deeper into LaRee's lap, sucking her thumb and looking out the window at the sunlight that fell across the space where her mother had been.

At first LaRee had been excited and happy when Vita said she'd seen Sabine, but later she would smile sadly; then she became perplexed and finally worried. It was LaRee who sat beside her all night when she was sick, telling her stories about the tiny girl who lived in a bird's nest and had adventures in the trees. LaRee was her guide to every beauty—the pearly seashells they gathered along the wrack line at low tide, the winter picnics on the iced pond, where they drank hot cider from a thermos at a table built of snow. When Vita had been frustrated to the point of fury, tearing up the pictures she'd colored because they didn't look exactly like what she saw, LaRee had pulled a book of impressionist paintings off the shelf for her. "Have you ever seen a starry night that looks like that? But starry nights feel like that sometimes." If someone was mean at school, Vita would put her hand over her heart and think of LaRee until she felt safe and steady again. She didn't want to hurt LaRee's feelings, so she had stopped telling LaRee when she saw Sabine. Which was sad, because nothing ever seemed quite real until she had told it to LaRee.

Of Franco she had all too many memories. On Tuesday nights LaRee would take her to the Walrus and Carpenter, where the bartender would bring her a Shirley Temple and, if it wasn't too crowded, sit down at the table with them. Sometimes he'd have a little gift for her—a tiny flowerpot with real flowers growing in it, or a Hello Kitty pencil. All week she looked forward to Tuesdays, until one midsummer day at the beach when she looked around to see fathers everywhere, chasing after volleyballs, building sand castles, even just sleeping in the sun. Where was hers?

LaRee decided the time had come. "He's right here, actually. Franco at the Walrus? He's your dad."

Vita had stamped her feet. This was wrong, a lie or a mistake like everything else, something she was supposed to believe even though she could see by the evidence that it wasn't true. A dad lived in the house with you, pushed you on the swing, lifted you sleeping out of the backseat of the car and carried you through the dark to tuck you safe in your bed. "He is not my dad. He's the bartender! How is he my dad?"

"Well, he and your mom were in love . . . before you were born . . . and . . ."

They made a date for him to come visit—it would be like Christmas, a time when people were filled with warmth and kindness just because of the day on the calendar. LaRee baked a blueberry pie with a lattice crust, Vita up on a stool helping. She would run into Franco's arms as if he were a soldier just home from the war, he'd swing her up and hold her tight in both arms, and at that moment he would begin to be her father and everything would feel solid and certain.

Except that he was not returning from war, he was emerging from a lie. He stood there with Danielle in the driveway, looking nervous and obsequious, guilty, while Vita clung to LaRee in the doorway.

"Come in, come in," LaRee said, and Danielle came toward them, smiling a big, candied, frightening smile, leading Franco by the hand.

"She's not my mother," Vita said, afraid LaRee meant to give her away.

"No, I'm not," Danielle had said, kneeling in front of her. "But Franco is your dad, and he's . . ."

"Go away!" Everyone knew that parents came in pairs.

And he had reached out to her suddenly, eyes full of a kind of love she'd never seen before. The nice man from the Walrus, with tears in his eyes, begging her to accept him. It was the first time she had understood that adults were not infallible, that they could be as uncertain as children, as fragile. The pie was on the counter, along with a little china pitcher of flowers from the garden; the room had the cool green feeling it got in the summer when the sun came through the leaves . . . and she was pierced by a cold fear. There was a trapdoor beneath, always, and at any minute it might give way and you'd be dropped into the dark and no one, not even a father, could save you.

"Why don't we just have some pie," LaRee said.

So they sat down at the table, Vita on LaRee's lap, Danielle talking and talking as if she was trying to drown out some dreadful sound in her mind. Franco fidgeted and tapped his foot.

"I only had boys before," he said finally. "It's . . . like . . . you throw a ball . . . or, there's fishing."

"Did you teach them to ride bikes?" LaRee asked.

"I guess you could call it that. They just got on and rode away."

"Well, Vita got a new bike for her birthday. Maybe in September, after Doubloons closes, you could take her up to the parking lot there?"

"No, *you* teach me," Vita said.

"Franco knows all the tricks," LaRee said.

"*You*," Vita said. What had she done, crying for a father? She certainly hadn't expected LaRee to produce one. She'd thought she would get to pick.

"We'll all go together," LaRee said. "Danielle, you'll come too?"

"I'd love to," Danielle said, watching Franco's face.

Even in memory this was faded like an old Polaroid. She had known it was momentous, though it felt, from every angle, wrong. He had been there all along, standing behind the bar at the Walrus, making her a special drink with a frilly toothpick. Why hadn't anyone told her before?

"You'd had enough," LaRee said. "We all wanted you to have a place you felt safe in. Your mom had asked me to take care of you if anything happened, and by the time everyone knew Franco hadn't . . . committed a crime . . . (Vita had already been aware of all the euphemisms people used for murder and death; it was quite satisfying to hear that little hesitation before someone said "passed away," to see people try to wriggle away from reality. She might be an awkward, orphaned girl, but unlike the rest of them she had already looked death in the eye.)

"By that time, you were cozy here with me. I couldn't send you to live with Franco. To have you lose your home twice, before you started second grade? Franco wouldn't let that happen to his daughter. And I'd have missed you too much! So we waited until the right time, and . . . this seemed like the right time."

Everyone would need to be patient, LaRee said, to keep trying, to be grateful and forgiving.

For ten years they had been patient. Vita spent every other Saturday with Franco, usually Franco and Danielle. Once they had flown to Seattle so she could meet her half brothers—one was an airline mechanic and the other worked in the accounting department at Boeing. Both had pretty wives and young children. The accountant was carefully polite, but the mechanic had hugged her warmly and said, "Welcome to the family! We wouldn't be real Creekers if we all had the same mom!"

Danielle had rolled her eyes and answered that she didn't think it was possible that she could be his mom, though she vividly remembered his birth. "Never so glad to see a pair of forceps in my life! I said, 'Get that thing out of me, now!' But you're still a big pain."

Vita had been glad for this story—it was something to tell LaRee. She spent all her time back then saving up stories, because they reminded her that LaRee would be there to listen. She was a real woman, not a mirage who would vanish while Vita was in the other room, or on the other coast.

"Are you cold, honey?" Danielle had draped her jacket over Vita's shoulders, but it wasn't that, it was the feeling that she ought to be standing guard at home, in case some harm might come. Oh, she was dizzy; she . . . "Danielle, can I call home? I need . . ."

"Of course, honey, of course."

And she had run into the bedroom to call home. All the time they were trying to draw her into their family, she was resisting. Always that feeling of how wrong it was, a puzzle with too many pieces, still missing its center. She'd opened Franco's Christmas presents—the stuffed panda as big as she was, the music box with a clipper ship inlaid in ivory—but even as she gave a carefully delighted cry, the wrongness would be sifting into the room like soot. The adults had reasons and explanations, but she only understood that he was her father and he'd been down the street pretending to be someone else for most of her life.

Of course, as she grew, she came to understand. No one would take a child whose mother had just been murdered and give her into the custody of the man suspected of that murder. She hadn't even known he was her father. By the time they arrested the real murderer, Vita was in kindergarten, settled with LaRee. Aside from the surreal moments when she was sure she'd just caught a glimpse of Sabine, she was happy. Even Franco had agreed it would be wrong to tear up her life a second time.

Franco had become famous in the meanwhile. The news truck that parked outside the Walrus and Carpenter the morning they found Sabine's body, waiting to interview him, had discovered a star. He had walked toward the camera, brimming with confidence and energy and . . . sweetness . . . as if he were walking toward a beautiful woman. It had been a bright January morning, the sun spilling across the bay, and he saw himself as a host to these visiting reporters. He had started to tell them about the town, the way it had been when he was young, how his mother would send him down to the pier to get a fish for dinner and anyone would have given him one. How they'd dive for quarters the tourists threw—he was always the quickest one, the one who could guess from a glimmer where to aim. He had a wealth of stories just waiting to be told and the world was full of people who'd been working in cubicles, whose dreams were something like his daily life. The camera loved him. *Nightline, Dateline, 48 Hours,* Anderson Cooper, *Nancy Grace*—they all wanted to hear what he had to say. Not because he was famous—because he was real.

Before the murder he'd been Franco Neves who lived over the bar because he'd let the *Rainha* slip through his grasp and couldn't afford his own place. Now he was Franco Neves as seen on TV. Now if the phone rang during dinner, Danielle would say, "It's the Larry King show," with just the same irritation as if it had been Hank Capshaw asking him to work an extra shift. And Franco would clear his throat, square his shoulders. Larry King had turned out to be a nice guy, and interested in Franco in a way no one in Oyster Creek ever had been.

Vita was too young to understand, though not too young to know that people looked twice when they saw her with Franco, that she was set apart somehow. She was too full of the storybooks LaRee read her: *Anne of Green Gables, The Wolves of Willoughby Chase.* School had frightened Vita; she didn't like to let LaRee out of her sight for a whole day. But the promise of a friendship such as the ones in these books exerted a great pull on her, though she might be quaking as she crossed the threshold into the kindergarten room every morning to face all those huge alphabet letters in their clashing colors, and the other kids, who might become *friends* (the word had a glow of secret joy for her, so that she couldn't speak it aloud) if only she could dare lift her eyes from the floor.

And it had happened. Dorotea Machado and she both liked to play with the family of stuffed rabbits, inventing little rabbit meals for them of carrots wrapped in a lettuce leaf, or peas and beans and chives, lining them up for storytime, laying them down under a blanket when the class had its afternoon rest. One day the teacher spoke of them as friends and they risked a quick glance at each other to see that yes, this was true. What glory! Plans were undertaken—LaRee said of course Dorotea could come over, any day, and the next morning Dorotea had come to school with a scrap of paper balled up in her fist. "Monday," it read. The little girls had hugged each other, held hands on the playground. Over the weekend, LaRee made a gingerbread house for them to decorate—there were peppermint pinwheels for the front path, Necco wafers for the roof, and spearmint leaves to make bushes beside the door.

On Monday, though, Dorotea had arrived at school in tears, shaking her head and refusing to go near Vita all day. And at the great moment when the two had been supposed to head home together, Amalia Matos had driven up to the school doorway to pick up her granddaughter Teresa, and speaking in Portuguese, told Dorotea to get in the car.

LaRee tapped on the window. "Amalia, is something wrong? Dorotea was going to come over to our house for the afternoon."

"Her mother wants me to take her," Amalia said, without turning her head.

"But—"

"Her mother *asked* me to pick her up," Amalia repeated, as if LaRee might not speak English. Then she spoke in Portuguese to Dorotea, who sat stiff in her seat, facing front as if her life depended on it, and they drove away.

Then the kindergarten teacher, just out of school herself, who had seen it all through the window, rushed out to lecture Vita on Accepting Cultural Differences, and LaRee had called her a little idiot when they were back in the car. "It's because I don't have a father," Vita said, and LaRee said, "Don't be silly. You do have a father." But she knew what Vita meant. She had called Fiona Tradescome, who was in second grade and thus considered by Vita to be a goddess, to come help with the gingerbread house. "Yeah, they hate us," Fiona piped absentmindedly, lining up gumdrops along the path. "Just hang around with someone else; it's not a big deal."

And it had not been a big deal. After that she and Dorotea avoided each other's glances and the family of stuffed rabbits lay neglected in the corner. By middle school they went to Outer Cape Regional with kids from all the different towns. Vita was in the red group, which everyone knew was the smart group, and Dorotea was in blue. And it turned out that nobody had a father. Teresa's dad was fishing out of New Bedford. Brandon's had been in town as a tourist and conceived a son with one of the waitresses at Doubloons—no one had ever seen him again. There were dads in rehab, dads in the Marines, dads in jail. It was like the red group and the blue group, a matter of etiquette: You didn't bring up the subject of fathers, didn't ask a lot of questions, didn't make a big deal about Father's Day.

9

How She Walked Away

Vita got out of the car down at Mackerel Bay Park, where they were rehearsing *The Tempest*, and started to skip across the wide lawn before she caught herself and settled into a measured, adult pace. LaRee watched from the car, half praying. It was all walking away now; there was nothing to do but watch from an ever-growing distance, with the faith that some light from the past would shine on every forward step. Vita took a quick look back at her, and waved a hand to shoo her off. Heaven forbid the people at the theater should associate her with some . . . mother. Which was as it should be. LaRee let up on the brake and started toward home.

It was the first plankton bloom and the fresh bright smell cleared LaRee's mind of every doubt. She drove up the road from the harbor, past the simple frame houses where fishermen and merchants had made their homes two hundred years ago, and turned down Front Street, thinking—*here I am, done with another day at the job I've had for twenty years, going home to the house I helped build, getting some dinner for my daughter*—my daughter! Who'd have imagined it? Some people hated the term *washashore*, but she had always liked it. It was true to the way she'd turned up here, driving a twenty-year-old Volvo with all her possessions stuffed in the back. Worked all summer at anything that paid, went on unemployment the minute the season ended, put down roots without even realizing. Heartbreaking and backbreaking things had happened, she'd been confused and stumbled blindly through, but somehow everything had led to something else, and the life she'd built of rags and shards had knitted itself up into something beautiful and whole.

She usually avoided Matos Fish Market. It was better to go a little out of her way than to feel the draft of cold disapproval that came with the bay scallops Amalia Matos handed across the counter. She still remembered her first encounter with Amalia, back when she'd just arrived. She had pointed to a piece of cod that looked particularly nice and Amalia had deliberately put a different one on the scale. When she said again that she wanted the first, Amalia had said with asperity, "*You* don't *get* to choose."

Back then only tourists went into the market. Anyone who lived here either caught their own fish or bought it down on the pier when a boat came in. Hannah Stone said you could get into Amalia's good graces by bringing her flowers and complimenting her grandchildren, but years of LaRee's obsequiousness had had no effect. Amalia bristled during every transaction, as if LaRee was asking for something much more important than a pound of fish.

Which, of course, she was. She was asking to be considered a fellow member of the community. It was crazy, she thought, cocking her head vaguely and studying the empty refrigerator case just to avert her eyes. Why should Amalia Matos have the power to accept or reject her when she had lived here for two decades and some, cleaned cottages in the summer on top of her schedule at the clinic, lived the same life as the rest? Arteries severed by oyster shells, feet crusted with barnacle infections, fingers and once a whole hand severed by a fishing line . . . not to mention a foot caught in a boat propeller . . . jellyfish stings, poisonous dogfish spines— she had dealt with all of them, every kind of marine misery. She'd administered measles/mumps/rubella vaccinations to two generations, seen boys grow into men and marry and begin again. When Lynnie Testa got leukemia at age seven, LaRee had managed the search for a bone marrow donor, though she'd known Lynnie had almost no chance of surviving. But she'd understood that the community itself would sicken if it didn't have some concrete way to help. It was that kind of thing: years of small efforts and kind words that made you belong to a place.

Or that was the way LaRee saw it. Amalia would disagree. Amalia considered that LaRee was dithering now, posing in front of the freezer case aware of her willowy height, the hair pulled back so simply with wisps escaping, her dreamy expression as she felt the top of her head for her glasses, checking the date on a bottle of clam juice, as if she had all the time in the world. Amalia was a small, muscular woman, about sixty. She had taken over the operation of Matos Fish Market the day she returned from her honeymoon. (Fort Lauderdale, where she had spent every day lying beside a pool while Bobby fished for marlin. At night they shopped for gold necklaces and danced in the hotel lounge.) Whatever fantasies she might have had about married life, or life on the mainland, had died in Florida, and from then on she followed her mother's example in all things, raising her daughter as she would if they'd still lived in Gelfa (of which she remembered only the sunlight reflecting mirrorbright off the sea, the whiteness of the houses, and a dog that lay in the middle of the street all day).

That was what belonging meant to Amalia. It meant surviving in this place where the sun never shone as bright as it did in Gelfa, and holding tight to the old ways. The washashores came over the bridge with the idea they could buy their way in here, that everyone would fall at their feet because they'd been lawyers or doctors in Boston or New York. And they called themselves locals! Let 'em shuck a hundred pounds of cherrystones on the stern of a dragger in a biting wind. They thought their children were natives! If their cat had kittens in the oven, would they have called them muffins?

She had been picking lobster meat in the back room when she heard the bell, had washed her hands and come out into the shop to find LaRee Farnham standing there saying "hmm," and cocking her head this way and that, as if she didn't care whether she kept Amalia waiting or not. Amalia's life did not allow for little luxuries, decisions between one treat and another. She had the market and the rental cottages on Try Point; when it came time to retire she would sell everything and go back to Gelfa, while the taxes she had paid all her life went to support people like LaRee, who lived only for pleasure and wouldn't have bothered to save.

LaRee could feel Amalia's impatience and it caused her to linger over the clam juice, partly from spite, partly because she didn't want to turn and face the cold. By now she hated Amalia. *Hate* was not too strong a word. She knew that look Amalia had had the day (ten years ago, yes) when she drove Dorotea away from school while Vita sobbed. It was the look of a woman who would step over you if you were bleeding in the street.

"Can I help you?" Amalia asked, in her thin, bitter voice.

"I'm just thinking," LaRee said airily over her shoulder, pulling her glasses off the top of her head and putting them back on her face, turning, and looking past Amalia to read the blackboard:

Scrod was $11.50 a pound. Salmon was cheaper, but she had spinach already and Vita loved spinach with scrod.

Amalia wanted to say that she had ten more lobsters to pick, four bushels of silt-covered littlenecks to scrub, cod to fillet, sea clams to chop for pie. LaRee had stayed in the examining room with her the last time she went to the clinic. Amalia did not allow her own husband to see her undressed, and for LaRee Farnham to see her, to sneer, probably, at the thick dark body so unlike her own . . . No. LaRee, like her friend Sabine, had come here from the mainland, bringing with them the values that had devastated this town. Everyone knew that when the lust roared out of a man, violence was sure to follow.

That was what Amalia's brother-in-law, who was chief of police, had said after Vinny Machado, in a rage at his wife, Maria, picked up the butcher knife and told her he had killed Sabine Gray and he could kill her, too. She called the police, regretted it an hour later and tried to recant, but it was too late. "I wouldn't have thought Vinny had it in him," the chief said, and then, "It's a shame on all of us."

There had always been something wrong with Vinny. The family moved to New Bedford when he was a little boy, but it didn't work out and in three years they were back—so Vinny was slow-witted *and* an outsider. Then his father went down on the *Suzie Belle*, and he and his mother became, essentially, wards of the town. Amalia had steered them through it, finding his mother a job behind the counter at Skipper's, keeping an eye on Vinny so she could work, lending them money to cover the mortgage. Vinny was around on the street, and Franco would let him sit at the bar and serve him a Coke, because Vinny liked to feel he was one of the guys. Then a stroke of luck changed everything. Vinny got Maria Carriero pregnant. Of course they must be married, though Maria was just sixteen. She was a big girl with a cleft lip clumsily repaired. She had dreamed of a wedding, of course, but to find herself in a white lace dress with rose petals scattered in her path? Straight out of a fairy tale.

Now Vinny was Maria's problem. He got work at the transfer station sorting plastics and cardboard until the septic pumping job came up. He almost never spoke except to champion the Red Sox, but he had that grin, as if he had a depraved secret and was sure you had one, too. He would no more have fallen into a relationship with Sabine Gray than he would have written a letter to his congressman or signed up for yoga. But somehow, for some reason, he had killed her.

"I guess . . ." LaRee was saying, turning back to the counter with its pans of slick fillets and tangles of squid, "just a pound of scrod. Please. It looks so fresh."

"Of course it's fresh," Amalia snapped. *Blood is thicker than water* was what she wanted to say. Vita should be living with her father, not with LaRee Farnham. It was easy to guess the real reason; they didn't think Franco was good enough. So he, and the Portuguese community, had lost this child, and LaRee had inherited her, and the fortune that came with her, rumored to be millions. Vita would have been in communion class, except LaRee didn't belong to Our Lady, or any other church. While the little girls in their stiff white dresses had filed silently up the steps for first communion, Vita had come skipping down the sidewalk, holding LaRee's hand and talking a mile a minute. Vita would see Rome and Paris one day, but she would probably never visit Gelfa.

Amalia didn't go straight to the scrod, instead inserting her knife behind the gill of a haddock that had been laid out on a board and filleting it in three quick strokes, as if to highlight its freshness. She touched her tongs to a scrod fillet and LaRee said, "No, that one, at the back. The thinner one." She said this as much to prove to herself that she wasn't intimidated as anything else.

Amalia gave her the one she wanted. She wasn't a tourist anymore but a more or less regular customer.

"Do you need a lemon?"

"No, thanks." The lobsters clicked against one another in the tank, brandishing their banded claws. LaRee slid the Visa card out of her wallet.

"We don't take charge cards for purchases under fifteen dollars," Amalia was so pleased to say, pointing to a sign taped to the cash register.

LaRee found a ten, and (going through her purse with great care, taking her time while Amalia stood reddening at the register) fished out two more dollars and thirteen cents for exact change.

"Have a pleasant day," Amalia said.

"The same to you." It was as good as a curse. *Oh, Amalia, may you have a pleasant life, free of tenderness, longing, triumph, revelation. But very, very pleasant.*

The scrod made LaRee happy, though. She had felt pretty much like a lioness since that frozen night thirteen years ago—off all day tearing the heads off wildebeests and such, pursuing the best morsels for her child. Vita at sixteen still ate as she had at six: pasta with butter, chicken in pristine slices without so much as a membrane showing, and scrod baked on spinach. She needed more protein, more iron, more calcium, more confidence, more courage, more sense of connection, more hope, more . . . Well, the scrod was a step.

For all the worries, LaRee was prouder of Vita than she probably ought to be. Vita was so full of thought and love and honor and kindness that when she appeared in a doorway it was the same as seeing the sun come up out of the bay. Yes, she was awkward, she dressed as if she was trying to hide, she didn't know what "pull over" meant. But she had a natural equilibrium; it had been with her even the night she arrived. She would do one thing and another, and if things went awry she would keep at it steadily until they went right again, until she reached whatever goal she had in mind. If LaRee had said to her, "I hate Amalia Matos," she would have laughed. "You hate Amalia Matos for an expression she had on her face ten years ago? You're crazy!" And then LaRee would have to laugh too and admit that Amalia might be irritating but she was hardly a gorgon. The nights they had slept out in the backyard when Vita was younger, tangled in their blankets in the tent, watching out the front flap for shooting stars and opossums lumbering by . . . showing Vita all the simple magic in life, LaRee had known it herself.

"LaRee's the practical one," Sabine used to say, meaning that she, Sabine, was the romantic, glamorous one. For some reason this had hurt LaRee then. Now it seemed like a lucky break. She wasn't lost without Drew anymore; she was settled in her own life. Her beauty was more or less gone, but honestly, she didn't need it. When she was young she'd looked in the mirror a hundred times a day, to reassure herself: Would someone love her? Maybe from this angle, or that? All those pangs—they were inconceivable now. Her vocation was the mothering of Vita Gray, her great challenge was to blaze the way for Vita. It was a thrilling profession, a life of great luxuries, such as baking a perfectly fresh fillet of cod on a cold spring evening, sending your daughter—your own daughter—out to pick the new chives. Still, this time was drawing to a close.

She hopped into the car in the fish market parking lot and backed it around . . . and heard, before she felt, the crunch as she hit something. Ugh. She'd been lost in her thoughts. This parking lot was always empty in the off-season, and she, like everyone else, was in the habit of driving like a cowboy all winter, parking on the sidewalk, stopping to roll down the window for a ten-minute chat with a friend in the opposite lane. And zipping around backward without checking the mirror—because it was midweek in May and no one else was supposed to be there. Just a second ago everything was fine. The clock would lose only one second if she could go back and put on the brake. No one would notice!

"What the—" A man's angry voice.

"Well, 'what the' yourself!" she said, turning to see the back of an old gray pickup, its tailgate fallen, bags of oysters jarred down the truck bed by the collision.

"Did you even look?"

"Matt, is that you?" It was. Matt Paradel, the one man she had made love to—to be honest, the one man she had even kissed—in the last ten years.

"LaRee." He said this as if he had known all his life that she was going to smash into the back of his truck.

"I'm sorry."

"No, no, I'm sorry," he said. "I was coming from the side. I just assumed . . ."

"Let me—"

"No!" he said, seeing her about to drive forward. "You're holding the tailgate up. The oysters . . ."

She got out. Well, here they were. She'd passed him on the highway, seen him at the gas pump at SixMart, said hello when she saw him in the beer tent at the Oyster Festival, but there had been no chance for conversation in years.

"I'm so sorry, Matt."

"No," he said. "I wasn't paying attention—I always back out

that way and I was in a hurry, I didn't check. . . . There's just too much on my mind." He raked his fingers through his hair. There was less of it than the last time she'd seen him, but he was still broad-shouldered and with his flannel shirt half untucked his presence seemed homey, welcoming. She wished she were wearing lipstick and her hand went straight to the loose skin of her neck. Still, his eyes, his whole face lit up, as if she was the best sight he'd seen in a while.

"So," he said, taking a deep breath, becoming earnest. "How are you?"

"Oh, fine, fine. . . . How are you?"

"No. I mean really. . . ."

"Oh, God, how could I ever answer? It's too complex; there are too many layers . . . and it's been too long since we talked to give a proper answer."

He smiled fondly. "You can say a lot without giving 'a proper answer.' You always could."

"What am I saying?"

He peered at her. "That we're not the same people we were, last time we . . . saw each other."

"Do you drive around thinking of deep conversations to have with women who back into your truck?"

"All I asked was how you are."

He had come into the clinic one evening when LaRee was on call, carrying his three-year-old son in his arms. The little boy's name was Oak; his fever was a hundred and three. He'd started to convulse in his sleep and Matt had wrapped him in a blanket and run down the street, crossed the highway with the boy in his arms, not stopping even to put on shoes. He kept explaining that his wife was away, as if that had caused the illness, and watched LaRee take the boy's vital signs as if he'd be able to read the diagnosis in her face.

Of course a spark struck. At the follow-up visit he'd admitted that his wife wasn't "away"; she had left him. Very slowly, they had moved toward each other. They had to be careful and discreet, for the kids' sake—or that was how they put it. Really, neither one could bear to be hurt by love again. Matt was a ranger for the National Seashore, and dove for lobsters, kept an oyster claim, and had built a sailboat from plans he'd found when his father died. "She barely leaves a wake," he said proudly. He took LaRee out on the bay one evening: It was like stepping through a looking glass to see the town from that perspective. All the lines and contours were unfamiliar, beautiful in a whole new way.

The things she'd allowed herself to imagine! A whole, happy family, Vita with a fatherly presence, and she ... well, it was embarrassing to remember the mirage of bliss she had seen ahead. One weekend—they'd had to plan carefully, with sleepovers for Oak and Vita—Matt had come for dinner, and to stay the night. He brought a bottle of champagne he'd found on the wrack line on the Outer Beach—Veuve Clicquot. He figured it had fallen off someone's yacht. "You never have to worry in Oyster Creek," he'd said. "Whatever you need, it just floats in." She was shaking when he kissed her, she who had gotten rid of her virginity to the first boy who dared, back in high school. Now that she was older, she knew what was at stake. And that knowing, the sense that they were discovering a new world together ... He'd slept, but she couldn't, for fear of losing one minute of that night.

At dawn she woke, pulled him down the path to the pond, and they swam while the morning mist hung in the air above them. A golden September day: September 10, 2001. When he left she went back down to sit at the end of the dock; as her feet touched the water she knew it was real, a real open love like an element she'd never moved in before.

The next evening, Matt's wife returned. She'd known it was a terrible mistake to leave, she said, but it wasn't until she saw the towers fall that she knew she had to ask forgiveness. She loved him, she always had; she had barely felt alive without her family. She would go to counseling, do whatever he asked.

And that had been that. Probably it was good to have ended things then, so it would always be perfect in memory, with no chance for the mess of ordinary life to dull its beauty. She would always have that image, of the dark water and the sun in the trees above, and a new life beginning right there. Better to be separated before the beautiful vision was disrupted. And now her heart was beating in a manner entirely out of proportion to the situation, which was after all a parking lot bump between two very well-used vehicles.

"I am good," she said. "I am. My life is very . . . whole. And you?"

"Doing well, doing well," he said, with a certain gravity, a respect for . . . call it the past. "Oak's in eighth grade—he's finally living up to his name."

"Wow—I still think of him as . . . an acorn! Does he like school?"

"He seems to think it's a football team that requires some irritating paperwork."

"And how's work?"

"Well, you know the National Seashore. The tide broke through the Outer Beach in the April storm. Not sure how we're going to deal with that; the maps will have to be redrawn. Rebuilding the path over the tide marsh. Same old, same old, really. How about you? How's Vita?"

"Matt," she said . . . and it all came back to her, the way he had let her talk on, brag on about Vita, the way his gaze had felt like sunlight. "She's just so . . . oh, I wish you could see her."

"I'm not surprised," he said. "And you? Do you . . . ? Are you . . . ?"

"Oh, good, good. Old . . . you know, but . . ." She started to put the bags of oysters back in the truck bed. She wanted to be the one to say good-bye first this time.

They pushed together to lift the tailgate and hook it shut again. He laughed. "This truck is so beat up, I don't really have much to lose."

"I feel that way about my whole being." She laughed. Honestly, she didn't like to have him see her. Her skin had lost its glow, her waist was gone, her slenderness had begun to look like severity.

"Yes," he said, rubbing his forehead where his hair used to be. "I know just what you mean. Well, nice to run into you, ha-ha."

"Nice to run into you!"

He opened the door to get back in the truck and stopped, turned back. "Tracey left again," he said. "I mean, it's fine, it's the right thing. She went back to Raleigh. Her sister has a stable there and she always loved horses, so . . . Oak wanted to stay with the football team, so I have him until summer."

"Oh, I . . . I'm sorry." Was that what she was supposed to say? Or to feel?

"Don't be. I just . . . I thought I should tell you. It doesn't mean . . ."

Years ago she'd have stepped on this sentence before he could snatch it back. What didn't it mean? What did it?

"No, of course," she said quickly. "Nice to see you." And she drove away. So there. It was maybe the first time in her life a man had left a door open and she hadn't felt obliged to walk through it. She and Matt might have—well, but they hadn't. And the time was past now; those feelings didn't move in her anymore. LaRee wasn't going to try to revive them just because his wife had finally carried out her intentions. It was a good feeling, as if her heart were weathertight.

Across the street from the market, Sea Street turned off Front Street and led down to the wharf. Franco's boat, the *Rainha*, was tied on the inland side, among the few other draggers that still worked from the pier. Every hull was painted: red and silver or brilliant blue . . . and just as brightly stained with rust. The *Rainha* was, or had been, a pale green rim above a deep purple hull—the most beautiful boat in town. From this distance it didn't look more dilapidated than the others, but LaRee knew it wasn't up to the voyage to the fishing grounds anymore, or any other voyage, except the yearly passage under the bishop's sprinkle of holy water at the Blessing of the Fleet.

A ray of sunlight escaped the passing clouds and blazed a silver path across the bay. Turning the corner by the old Wisteria Inn, she saw they'd set the rockers out on the porch. Another year—the pulse of the town quickening as young people arrived to look for summer jobs. Most would spend a few months and return to the city, where they would try and perhaps succeed at achieving something. But there would be some like LaRee, who would feel they belonged here and would have to stay. Amalia would say they were hiding from real life, and she might be right. If LaRee had stayed on the mainland, she'd have gone to work in a hospital, become a nurse-practitioner, a nurse-anesthetist . . . or . . . something much more important than she was here. She'd have married a doctor, would have kids in private school, and maybe have an air of self-assurance, a quiet command of things. Instead, here she was, LaRee Farnham, the "girl who works at the clinic," driving a car with two hundred thousand miles on it and yet another dent today, through a town whose era of greatness was a century gone.

Then she came over the hill and started down toward Mackerel Bay Park, where Vita and the others were standing in the glow cast by the late sun. A flock of ducks was skimming the surface of the water behind them and settled together at the edge of the ebbing tide. And there was Vita, silhouetted against the bay, talking to Adam Capshaw. So she'd be full of excitement and happiness. What else could possibly matter?

10

OFF BROADWAY

The theater, or what they had come to call the theater, was in the public park beside Mackerel Bay Beach, a wide lawn with picnic tables scattered across it, with the pier and the harbormaster's shack on one side, a locust grove on the other. The trees were too tall and slender, like art nouveau beauties waving their handkerchiefs in the breeze, and if you ran between them in the dusk, with Mackerel Bay all liquid silver behind you, you could feel you were in a dream.

Seeing them there, around the picnic table listening to Hugh's plans for *The Tempest* set, Vita felt happier than she'd been in forever. These were her people—the Mackerel Sky Theatre Company on Mackerel Bay. Hugh Shiverick, the director, had been a professor before he retired. Orson Desroches, the company's benefactor, was a short, round, whiskery man with a booming baritone who seemed to take as much pride in his weaknesses—for liquor, and theater, and red-cheeked young men—as in his strengths. Vita wanted to leap into their arms and lick their faces like a little lapdog, she was so glad to see them.

But she stood rooted to her spot, feeling they wouldn't remember her from the year before. She had the wood from the wreck in her backpack. Its weight was a joy compared to that of the usual textbooks. It had been a long, stupid day at school, though no different from any other. LaRee always asked about her day, but she would never really get it. High school, if it were a painting, would be a Hieronymous Bosch, where children worked feverishly to operate the immense bodies and egos they had suddenly grown, stumbling through a world of terrors, grasping at whatever support they could find. Would LaRee guess, for instance, that there was always, *always* one girl or another crying in the corner of the ladies' room? Today it had been Kayla, and Vita had made the mistake of asking what was wrong.

"*This*, that's what's wrong," she'd said, smacking the bulge below her waist hard with the flat of her hand, then wiping her eyes. She was pregnant, and proud of it, as she'd tell you defiantly, just as she'd been proud to lose her virginity, proud of beating up Teresa Matos when Teresa slept with her boyfriend, and proud that she didn't care when that boyfriend left her. So it should take something pretty dire to make her cry. "Ugh, you have no idea," she'd said, pushing past Vita to the mirror to redo her makeup, which was as thick as armor. Dorotea Machado came in then, set her backpack down with a grunt, and she and Kayla had glanced at Vita and then at each other, laughing.

"You just have no idea, do you?" Kayla asked her.

"No idea about what?"

They looked at her again, and at Kayla's belly. Where to begin with the things Vita didn't know? The whole world of things a girl named Vita Gray would have been sheltered from—who could name them all? It was clear, though, from her name and her way of crossing her legs, and the little book she carried with her (*The Tempest*; George Lyman Kittredge, ed., on loan from Orson Desroches— the physical proof that she would one day cross the bridge and escape Outer Cape High) that she had never been slapped, never been fucked. She didn't have the faintest notion what real life was.

And they were right in their way. They knew things she didn't know, that she never would know. Back in middle school Kayla had offered to teach Vita how to beat up a girl. And on that one day back in kindergarten Dorotea had taught her plenty, about the way people saw danger in others, even when the others were five years old. They rode the same bus, they were in the same math class, but the invisible fence laid in place back then was still live, and neither of them thought of crossing it. Dorotea had not been allowed to be friends with anyone except Teresa Matos, but now Teresa was on the soccer team, which traveled together like a school of fish while Dorotea dragged around as if hobbled, her thick curls gelled so heavily it looked like she'd dunked her head in oil. Her mother worked double shifts at Infinite Horizons nursing home, and Vita had come to feel protective of her. Which Dorotea saw as an insult. Vita Gray had no reason to feel sorry for her; she was supposed to feel sorry for Vita Gray.

"No idea about anything," Dorotea said. "And you've got toilet paper stuck to your shoe."

There had indeed been toilet paper stuck to Vita's shoe, and she pulled it off, and standing up she almost started to tell them what she knew that they didn't. But that would have been cruel, so she gave up and went back out into the cacophonous hall, counting the minutes until she would be here at Mackerel Sky. She was playing the very smallest part in *The Tempest*, but who cared? What did it matter? For the next three months she was a member of the company, and she would have a role, an essential role, to play. The show opened on June 21 and didn't close until August. And during that time they would all be safe in a bubble of art, thinking together about life, creating a communal vision and through that vision traveling back in time to live lives William Shakespeare had imagined....

Hugh smiled to see her, with the backpack full of wood and the driftwood branches under her arm. He liked her, for qualities nobody noticed at school. "Hello," she said, two notes like a songbird.

"Hello, my little one!" Hugh was a tall man, with a thin, sharp face and deep-set, piercing eyes. He had been retired and living in Oyster Creek for three years now, but he still smelled professorial: old books, chalk, stale pipe smoke. He kissed Vita's left cheek, then her right.

"You're ready for more Mackerel Sky, are you? A glutton for punishment."

"I can't wait," she said, though now that she was here she was tongue-tied. It seemed too much to hope that these men could really be glad to have her among them. They were too grown-up and accomplished. Hugh always said he'd founded Mackerel Sky Theatre in order to atone for the sins he had committed as the Charles Emerson Bray Chair in Shakespearean Studies. From that august position he had bloviated to generations of collegians, his all-knowing palaver overruling every youthful notion, every fresh idea. He was a revered authority, but as he grew older, small regrets had begun to haunt him. How deftly he had skewered the young students whose naive passions he'd found so irritating. He had shown them who was more knowledgeable—oh yes, he had. And one by one, they had drifted away, feeling a bit too small for Shakespeare and for Hugh Shiverick. Hugh had taught for twenty-eight years, but walking through the park in June a few years back, with the locust blossoms snowing down, he'd noticed a clump of violets in the grass, bent down to pick one, and it had come to him: These plays were meant to be staged, not studied. Why not do that, here in Oyster Creek, give the plays back the life he had been flogging out of them in the classroom all these years?

He had started with *A Midsummer Night's Dream*, gathering a company of the hopeful and the disappointed, some of them talented, some only loud. He was lucky to have Sam Rosenmayer, who had just graduated from the conservatory and was so very beautiful that Orson would have done anything to be near him. And Sam's boyfriend, Leo Ward, a dancer who'd come to Oyster Creek for a weekend, seen Sam spinning dough into pizza, and known right there that his life was going to change. Others might not have classical training, but they were real people with real faces. Orson's spider veins and hunched back would make him a perfect Caliban.

And here was little Vita Gray, whom he had cast as a fairy because she came to the audition and he didn't like to disappoint a child. He'd expected she would drop out after one or two rehearsals, but instead she'd been there every minute, proudly carrying Peaseblossom's gossamer train and taking on any other task that was asked of her, just grateful to be one of the group.

"Who is this young person?" Orson asked, lifting an imaginary lorgnette to his eyes. "Not our very own Vita Gray, a small child I used to know?"

"Yes, Orson, it's me."

"A most impressive transformation," he said. "Are we of age, suddenly? Ah yes, and blushing! A formidable addition to your womanly arsenal."

"Orson, you don't care about womanly arsenals!" Vita blushed deeper, hearing the flirtation in her own voice. It was the way girls talked to boys at school, and it made her think they were fools.

"Or, you might say that my appreciation of women is so great that I do not care to remove them from their pedestals and—what is the phrase?—rip their bodices."

Orson said "rip their bodices" with such precise Victorian gusto that he seemed to be committing satire on the whole of heterosexual life.

"Orson, Orson, I'm sixteen!"

"Exactly what I was afraid of, my dear. But it does become you."

Vita glanced over to Hugh, who came twinkling to the rescue. "Down, Orson. You are well cast as the rainbow goddess, Vita, no question. And you come bearing flotsam!"

"Look." The branches, worn to points like antlers, she laid on the table, but she had to struggle to get the wood out of her pack.

"Hmm . . . a stump," Hugh said, feigning interest. Of course. It wasn't right. The driftwood would look perfect as part of the hut, but this was just a piece of junk. And she'd worked so hard to break it off and lug it back up that endless stairway, over the Shillicoths' deck. . . .

"Don't know if we can find a use for that," Hugh said, "but these will be perfect. I'll make a structure of chicken wire and we can attach them."

"And this . . ." The hurricane flag was wadded in her pocket like a used handkerchief.

"Hah," he said, "the real thing! This must be twenty years old, if not forty. Can't have been in the water too long, though, or it would never be this whole. I can always count on you, Vita." He flapped the pale rag in the air. "Caliban's family crest, this would be," he said to himself, pulling it taut between his hands.

Vita had to look at the ground. Her smile gave away something far too important for anyone to see. If anyone at school saw, it would just confirm the general opinion. . . . They all moved like a school of fish, turning together, diving together, at some invisible signal. . . . They laughed at the same things, sneered at the same things . . . and then there was Vita, searching out rags on the beach in hopes of pleasing some old man.

At school, honestly, she was too frightened to pay attention. The teachers were just waiting to pounce; when she had said that Odysseus's bed was carved from a tree, the English teacher had asked, "What *kind* of a tree?" as if she were prosecuting a murder and Vita was the defendant. Vita wondered about the man who killed her mother—she tried to push him out of her mind but he would creep in through any opening and she'd find herself wondering who he had been, how he could have come to kill, what it would have felt like to be sentenced to life in a prison by people who hated you. LaRee had said he'd been passing through town, had broken into the house intending to rob them, but that couldn't be true. If it was, people would still lock their doors; they would still talk about it, warn their children. Look how afraid they were of strangers and kidnappings, and as far as Vita knew, such a thing had never happened on Cape Cod. And phrases dropped from LaRee's phone conversations, things like "Sabine always said no man would get the best of her." When Vita's mind wandered, this is where it went— back to something that she had no memory of. When she turned eighteen she was going to find the murderer, visit him in jail, make him tell her the truth.

And he would, because he was an outcast, like she was. At lunch, Brandon Skiles had told her he had a bottle of whiskey hidden in the National Seashore forest behind the school; he'd invited her to come drink with him at lunch. She was lame, he said, and everyone knew it, but if they saw her with him they'd think she was cool. Her first impulse was to go with him; then she felt so ashamed that she said, "Brandon, I'd rather spend the rest of my life alone than be friends with you," and ran as if for her life, down the hall toward her locker, nearly smashing into Shyanne Holtz, slut-goddess of the senior class, who had seemed to be posing for some imaginary camera in the middle of the hall.

Shyanne was walking toward her now, across the grass from the parking lot—walking with Adam no less. Vita edged closer to Hugh, wishing she could hide behind him. Adam had a beard lately, a soft-looking beard with two little peaks under his lips. He looked like a baby devil. His hair was curly, or at least springy, and she imagined the stubs of little horns growing on his head.

Just as Vita thought this, Shyanne reached over and tousled Adam's hair, as if the same thing had occurred to her. He pulled away but he was laughing at the same time. Shyanne saw Hugh's attention turn toward Vita and ground her hips against Adam to keep it. "You're such a beanpole, you inspire a pole dance," she said. He smiled, stupidly.

"Vita, do you know Shyanne?" Hugh asked. "She's playing Miranda."

Vita's blood turned to vinegar. Of course. Shyanne was the star of the school shows, too. People said she was a natural, and there she was, as always, striding out to the center of the stage with none of Vita's qualms, as if she'd been born with some protective coating, something that shielded her from the ordinary run of awkwardness and confusion so that she would always be loved and admired, and didn't have to work for anything. Meanwhile, Vita stumbled, mumbled, blundered, apologized, shrank back for fear of being noticed, shouted her lines for fear of being ignored. Except at Mackerel Sky, where she had been safe. Until now. Shyanne could not be part of this; she couldn't. Vita's instinct was to run at her with bared teeth, but she managed to keep still. Shyanne glanced toward her, saw she was no competition, and turned back to Adam.

It seemed to be exactly at that moment that the foghorn sounded and the breeze swung west, over the water. Why couldn't they have a real theater, instead of the plein air? In a theater you were all really together, enclosed in a building, like a family, safe and warm. Vita was wearing her red corduroy jacket from the church thrift shop; the wind cut right through it. She was afraid she was going to cry, and worse, she saw that Hugh realized she was hurt.

"Hi, Shyanne," Vita said. "We know each other from school," she explained to Hugh, but Shyanne was carefully ignoring her, afraid to become a loser by association.

"Vita's in her third year with us," Hugh said, trying to help. "She's one of the most faithful members of the company. In fact, she's spent the winter gathering properties . . ."

Oh dear God, he wasn't going to . . . He wasn't, was he?

He was. He pulled out the hurricane flag—a wretched rag—with a flourish and announced boomingly, "Caliban's standard!"

Shyanne looked as if she'd stepped in something. At least he left "the stump," as he'd called it, under the table—a bunch of old water-logged wood crusted with barnacles. Vita could imagine Shyanne retelling this story tomorrow, the girls at her table turning to laugh at Vita, who in her third year at Mackerel Sky had a part with seven lines, while Shyanne played Prospero's beloved, protected daughter, the star. She'd have a love scene with Adam, they'd kiss, he'd become her boyfriend, and fine, fine, that was fine. She could have

Adam, and her father's boat, the *Sweet Shyanne*, was tied up at the end of the wharf. But she couldn't have Mackerel Sky.

Of course Franco was right there, too, at work in the harbor-master's shack, which had been a mackerel shed about a million years ago, when there were still mackerel in Mackerel Bay. "Oughta call it Old Boot Bay," Manny Soares, the old harbormaster, would say. When Manny retired he said he was moving south, and he did ... to a folding chair about fifty feet down the pier, where he was available to give an opinion on anything from the price of cod to global warming. The back of the harbormaster's shack was a garage bay, open onto the boat ramp at the base of the wharf, so Manny could keep an eye on Hank Capshaw and Franco. He wasn't one to second-guess—he'd been around too long to think that one man's decision could have much of an effect on the world, or even on the harbor. But he didn't like to miss anything. Every morning Franco would arrive on his bike, unlock the doors, and take out the kayak to go out and collect water samples from the shellfishing areas. Manny would come in a bit later, get his chair out of the shack and set it up in his spot, which was protected from the west wind but open to the sun, and looked out over the entrance to the harbor. On a wet day he put up an umbrella. Fifty years ago, there would have been a constant commotion to watch, draggers loading and un-loading, men lined up hoping for work as day laborers, tankers coming in to shelter from a storm, yachts through whose windows you could see liveried waiters serving dinner at night.

Vita didn't turn her head toward the shack; she didn't want to have any awkward moments with Franco. They had done their best, both of them, but though they lived in the same tiny, isolated town, knew the same people, inhaled the same air whose smell they could both parse like a poem, they were from different worlds, and every gesture seemed to go awry. LaRee told Vita he was proud to bursting and talked about her all the time, but she felt as if Franco was afraid of her in some way, afraid she was going to turn into her mother.

"So, are we all here?" Hugh asked. "Wait—Sam and Leo? Vita, would you . . . ?"

Of course she would. She would consider it an honor. She ran in a giddy streak across the lawn to the little cottage, Sea Spray, where Sam and Leo lived. "You guys, you're late for rehearsal."

Sam came around from the back with the towels he'd been hanging on the line. "Oh, it is! Leo—come on, we're late."

"I'm moussing my hai-air!" Leo replied.

"Well, mousse it la-ter!" Sam sang. "Everyone knows you don't mess with Vita Gray!"

She stood there looking too shy to live, but in heaven nonetheless. Sam and Leo were a mesmerizing pair: in love and showing it off, and because they were actors they could do this with every slightest glance or move. Light flickered between them, and every time they touched, even to hand the script back and forth, Vita could feel it. And their cottage, another of the million little Monopoly houses for rent by the week on Cape Cod, was freshly painted, white with the shutters a seafoam green, and window boxes full of pink geraniums and cascading ivy. They were aware that they were blessing the others with their presence and Vita fell in behind them so as not to diminish the effect.

"There you are," Orson said dreamily.

"A full cast . . . or nearly," Hugh said.

The harbormaster's boat was on its way back from Barrel Point. Vita could almost feel its progress, because Franco would likely be on it and she always kept close track of him. It was an old Boston

Whaler, struggling through the choppy water. Every year they begged the town to replace it but the town wasn't a seagoing place anymore and the voters barely understood what the harbormaster did. A new Crown Victoria for the police chief was one thing . . .

"We can double characters to a certain extent," Hugh said. "But the boatswain . . ." He watched as the boat cut its engine, momentum propelling it silently to the dock. Franco came out of the shack, caught the boat's rope and looped it around the bollard.

"Mr. Sipes might be good," Vita said quickly. "He loves Shakespeare." Mr. Sipes was a large, mushroomy English teacher with a great enthusiasm for iambic pentameter. She didn't suppose he'd ever been on a boat, but it was bad enough having Shyanne here; she just couldn't have them all going mad over Franco's authenticity.

She could tell he was aware that they were watching him—his movements were sharper and charged with pride suddenly. After the murder, when the TV crews came to shine their lights into every corner and made Franco a celebrity for a while, he'd learned what was wanted and how to provide it. He might be a fisherman on an empty sea, but that gave him an enviable connection to earthly, watery reality. Too many people spent their days combing through columns of figures and went home to apartments that gazed out into canyons of other apartments. They vacationed at Disney World! They'd been longing for a murder, a really good murder like Sabine's, to pop life open at a seam, so they could see in, smell it, taste it, drink it down like a fresh, salty oyster.

Franco strode along the dock to lift the hatch on the upweller, check the oysters growing there. They were all proud of the upweller, which forced water over the oysters so they were able to suck twice as much nutrition every day, and grow twice as fast. Twice the crop meant twice the income—it meant the town might hope to live by sea farming one day. Franco was wearing a striped shirt and a red bandanna. His legs were slightly bowed. It was hopeless. . . .

"Sipes," Hugh said vaguely. "Does anyone know that guy over there?"

Everything stopped. No one spoke, but they all, except for Hugh apparently, knew the story. Vita could tell by the way they averted their eyes from her. It was the best a small town could offer in the way of privacy, like the way Vita always took care to say "your parents" to Dorotea Machado, as if she didn't know Dorotea's father was in jail. Adam, Shyanne, Orson, all had that look Vita recognized—they had heard about her, talked about her, and her mother, and Franco. They knew her story from the television and the newspapers, in a way that had nothing to do with her.

"He's the assistant harbormaster," she told Hugh, hoping to sound noncommittal. "He lives over the Walrus and Carpenter, up on Main Street."

Hugh, who had been preoccupied while filling the Charles Emerson Bray Chair, knew nothing of the murder. He did not watch *Dateline*, *Nightline*, or *48 Hours*, nor did he read the *New York Post* or even the *Daily News*. He glanced around, puzzled by the silence, but he was concerned with finding an actor and let his question go.

"No harm in asking," Orson said. "Why don't I just have a word . . . ?"

Sam glanced at Vita, over Shyanne's head. Of course he was curious. Everyone was. Vita wished to heaven that she could pull her head in like a turtle. There always seemed to be a little spotlight following her, a light that made her look all wrong.

They watched Orson go, his small figure enclosed in a heavy wool cape whose ends caught the wind that was scuffing whitecaps from glass green waves. Franco had come out of the back and was leaning in that doorway, looking toward them with those Neves eyes that could see fish fifty yards underwater. He welcomed Orson with a glad smile, the way he welcomed almost anyone. Of course. Orson drank at the Walrus and Carpenter; Franco knew him as well as if he were family. Or better. As she watched, Vita realized how well she did know her father. She'd been studying him all her life, with a fierce intensity. There he was, gracious, smiling—you'd think he was standing on the steps of the White House, not in the tilting doorway of the harbormaster's shack. Somehow the murder that had left her lost and confused had made him the town's unofficial mayor.

She turned away, with a stone of defiance in her chest, and found herself face-to-face with Adam.

"Hi," she said.

He looked as if one of the locust trees had piped up, and she realized she'd never dared speak to him before. Then he smiled.

"Hi."

"That's my father," she admitted.

"Yeah, I know." He spoke kindly and Vita remembered suddenly that his mother had fallen in love with a woman a few years back, and left her family, only to return full of regret a few months later. She took up fitness and was always in some sort of Lycra outfit now, pedaling by or running by or swimming by, so there was never an opportunity to chat and you really couldn't mention her without praising her. The waters of propriety had closed over the incident; it would be rude to bring it up now. So maybe Adam understood better than someone else might.

"There must be fifty other boatswain types in town. Why him?" Vita said.

Shyanne shot them a glance that would have silenced Vita any other time, but now, cheeks flaming, she kept talking. Franco was walking back toward them with Orson. She would not let him see how shy and awkward she was.

"Do you know what your costume will be?" she asked Adam. It was the only sentence she could grab hold of.

"No," he said. "Which I'm kind of glad about, since I'm sure it'll involve tights."

It was her turn to speak. Franco was coming closer, looking serious as he explained something to Orson.

"I like tights," Vita blurted. "I've always thought I'd have my first kiss with a man in tights."

An icicle went through her heart. What had she said? If she'd had a flirtatious, salacious lilt like Shyanne, it might have been okay, but she had actually confessed something, and she had said it in a naked, open voice, as if she and Adam had been friends forever, as if . . . oh, she couldn't think at all.

He blinked, and looked at her again, surprised.

"I mean," she began . . . but she couldn't think of a way to cover it. That was why she never said anything, because every time she opened her damned mouth, she'd speak one of those truths everyone else had secretly agreed not to mention.

Shyanne stepped behind Adam and her hands slipped around his chest, pulling him back against her. She was so exalted in the hierarchy at school that she had the absolute right to do this and whatever else she liked. But his face tensed and he squirmed away from her.

"Why, do you think?" he asked, and Vita realized she knew the answer.

"Because . . ." She was staring at the blazing green grass around her sneakers; her eyes were stuck there. "If it's in Shakespeare, then it has to be beautiful." She had exposed the tenderest piece of herself, that part that imagined love must come with great, brave, Shakespearean grandeur, a pas de deux between a man and a woman whose spirits would swirl together like tigers turning to butter. A little girl's foolish dream. She prepared to feel him rip it in two.

"I guess you haven't read *King Lear*," he said, not in the dickhead way most boys would have, but with a sweet, inquiring smile, as if he felt the same way she did, but with less optimism.

"We're looking for someone with a certain . . . maritime flair," Hugh was saying, and Vita saw the word *flair* catch Franco: His shoulders straightened; he began to glow.

"It's a small part—the boatswain—but an essential one. Shakespeare . . ."

"Shakespeare?" Franco said, with a crooked smile. His face was creased and weathered, an old fisherman's complexion, but his eyes were full of life and humor. He had not graduated from high school; the fish had been teeming back then and his first son was on the way. He might never have spoken the name Shakespeare before—it was a password to a realm where he didn't belong. But it pleased him that the current of his life had carried him here. Nervous, he undid the top button of his shirt; this always had an effect. He looked the part, and felt it. Fishing was his heritage, and if it had left him without financial resources, it had nevertheless given him the most surprising benefits. Suspected of murder, he'd become famous. Next? Shakespeare.

"Shakespeare has been ruined by the academics," Hugh rushed to explain. It was a confession he forced himself to make often. "He intended to entertain, and so do we."

"Danielle likes me home . . ." Franco said.

"Danielle will be proud!" Orson said. "Franco, who else could play the part of the boatswain? Antone Pavao? Manny Soares?"

He was appealing to the truest and most secret of Franco's vanities. Yes, he was a native, in the local definition of the word: His father had come from Gelfa, he'd been baptized at Our Lady and married there, had gone to work on his father's boat. His mother kept to her house, rarely venturing beyond the backyard. His father drove the length of the wharf—the Portuguese trail, they called it— every day, stopping to smoke and talk with his friends. Franco's openness, his curiosity, his energy, had carried him further. The strangers who lived in Oyster Creek, painters, editors, psychoanalysts, might have been giraffes, lizards, and owls to his parents: to be avoided, ignored or occasionally discussed with a smile and a shake of the head. But Franco was a man of the world.

"Manny and Antone, they're good guys," he said, automatically defensive. They both owned new houses back in Cranberry Corners, Ford F150 pickups, and big fast boats, though they'd long since given up fishing. But they'd never crossed the threshold into the other world, except maybe to install a new appliance.

"Fine fellows, absolutely," Orson agreed. Neither of these men would have answered Orson if he'd tried to strike up a conversation. In their younger days they'd have shoved him off the sidewalk and if he had grumbled, they would have beaten him bloody on principle. Shakespeareans they were not. "But they were never described as . . . 'dark and broad-shouldered,' was it?"

"'Like a sailor just returned from a three-years voyage.' That was the *New York Times*," Franco said. The reporter had seemed so prim and dour, he wouldn't have imagined she could think that way. But women were constantly surprising him, and there was always some moment in any conversation when he would feel himself slipping, falling under a woman's sway. And then, she would fall under his. Sabine had been an artist, an intellectual, and still he had made his impression. He took the group in—Orson he had known forever; two gay guys such as would never come into the Walrus or out on the clam flats; Adam Capshaw, Hank's son; Shyanne, who reminded him of her mother at that age—that same plush swaybacked blonde . . . and . . . He blinked. Dear God, it was Vita. Ten steps away, but he hadn't recognized her. Her hood was up, her hands shoved in her sweatshirt pockets. Yes, LaRee saw to it he was invited to everything, and he and Danielle went to her chorus recitals, and to see her get the English Department prize, but . . . she was a teenager, you couldn't expect too much. And he wasn't going to make a fool of himself at some parent-teacher meeting, when Vita would have written papers on books he'd never heard of, never mind read. If she'd been a boy, they could have tossed a ball around, studied Morse code—that would have counted as a bond. If she'd been Shyanne—she and Danielle would have gone shopping together and gotten manicures and those things, and they'd have loved him together, the way mothers and daughters did. But she wasn't Shyanne; she was Sabine's daughter somehow, not his.

If he were capable of saying no, his life would have been entirely different. "I work all summer, almost every night," he tried.

"We'll rehearse around your schedule," Hugh said. "We'll make it work."

"You'll enjoy it, Franco. You're a natural," Orson said. Couldn't one person, one time, say Vita was "a natural"? Never. She was the one who tried so hard they gave her a part because they felt sorry for her. Franco, looking around at his new friends, met his daughter's eyes. She instantly averted them.

"Excellent!" Hugh said. "This is our little troupe. Orson you know, of course, and this is Sam, and Leo (they came forward together, Leo's hand gently against Sam's back), Shyanne, Adam, Vita . . ."

She put out her hand; she was not going to let Hugh guess the truth. "Nice to meet you," she said loudly. It was practically true. Leo cocked an eyebrow and this felt like reassurance.

"Vita . . ." Too much rushed into his heart—regret, disappointment; a frustrated, battered kind of love. Danielle had managed in spite of his failures, his boys had taken the best of him and used it to push on, to get over the bridge and become Americans, instead of living in an extended immigrant twilight here as Portagees. He remembered the way Danielle had held Vita when she was a little girl, so tight. She had always wanted a girl, and now he had one, who couldn't be hers. He saw Sabine's face, warm and full of tender interest at first, and finally twisted and hateful, a shrew. All of the old muck was raked up every time he saw the child.

"You're an actress," he said, trying to sound intrigued, impressed, proud. "Gonna grow up to be a movie star."

"An actor," she said crisply, even haughtily. "On a stage. I hate the movies."

Of course he would assume she was looking for fame! What she wanted was understanding, to step into another skin and know how it might feel. His assumptions only showed his own limits; they didn't matter a damn. Looking past his shoulder, she saw a hawk circling, so low she could see the soft down ruffling under its wings. And the water stretching away for miles . . . All lives are vast, infinite. Her mother's was over, hers was just beginning. She felt the same as when she was standing on the high dune over the Outer Beach: Some things were so desolate they began to be beautiful.

11

Salvage

When LaRee arrived to pick her up, Vita made a little show of not noticing, continuing her conversation with Adam, nodding super-seriously at whatever he was saying. She didn't need LaRee the way she used to—did everyone see? The clouds were racing away to the east. Blue sky emerged, and a sun so low that the locust trees cast serpentine shadows. Halyards rang against their masts. Leo tapped Vita on the shoulder and pointed to LaRee's car. And here Vita came, hands plunged into the pockets of her jacket, her ponytail bobbing. She hopped in lightly, then crossed her arms and scrunched her face into a frown so tight LaRee nearly laughed.

"What's the matter?"

"*He's* there. Didn't you see?"

"You mean Franco?"

"He's in the show, LaRee. They put him in the show."

"He's in the show?" LaRee gave a little hoot. Franco's knack for popping up wherever there was a spotlight would never cease to amaze her. Vita was tensed into a fury and looked the way she used to before a temper tantrum when she was four. The trick was to get her to laugh.

"Is he portraying a suave country-club type?" LaRee asked. "Or a wise old man, dispensing parables from the mouth of a cave?"

"LaRee, it's Shakespeare," Vita said, refusing to crack a smile.

"Bottom, then? Puck? Does he do a funny little dance? Does he smoke a cigar?"

"He's the boatswain."

"Typecasting! Abhorrent."

They were driving up Back Street, past the little houses that had belonged to fishermen and shopkeepers a hundred years ago, though only the wealthy could afford them now. They were simple, solid houses built tight as ships' hulls, and from their upper windows you could see over the bay. Some of them had the old Indian shutters, attached inside the windows so they could be closed against intruders.

The town was built on a cluster of three hills around the harbor, and this, the northernmost, had once been crowned by the Calliope Hotel, a gabled, turreted Victorian fantasia with little balconies and pennants flying and a row of rocking chairs along the front porch—a last vestige of the town's time of elegance, when trains brought families from New York and Boston to the seaside, and plein air painters lined the pier with their easels. LaRee's first job in Oyster Creek had been waitressing at the Calliope, but it had already been fading by then, and the next winter it burned down.

The Calliope fire was one of those defining moments in the town's history, like the Gray murder, except that where people whispered about the murder, they spoke of the fire with nostalgia; they went over every moment again and again. How wonderful it had been to come together like that against a terrible threat! "Spontaneous combustion," people would say still, shaking their heads, and you'd know immediately that they were seeing that night, the town's skyline lit orange, great flaming wings overhead—that was what it had looked like, as the wind took shingles and curtains and anything it could, blowing them across the rooftops to start new fires wherever they landed. Every man in town belonged to the fire department, and the women had followed the wind east, using garden hoses to wet everything down until the departments from Wellfleet and Provincetown arrived. The best night ever—that was how it had felt. The night she and Drew fell in love. When he left he said all the drama of the fire had confused him, turned him from the path he'd meant to follow. And she had asked him how twelve years could constitute a detour—twelve years during which he'd refused to consider having children and . . . oh, it was water under the bridge. He'd done the best he could; they both had.

"LaRee, you know what it's going to be like," Vita said. "They're all going to gather around him and go on about what an interesting type he is and . . . it's just going to be famous murder all over again."

LaRee laughed, though it might have been more honest to cry. If the fire had resulted from neglect, old wiring plus a roof leak in a building the owners couldn't afford to renovate . . . well, the murder was that way, too. Except the materials weren't chemical but emotional, and the disaster hadn't brought people together but pushed them apart. The fire could be recalled with pride, but someone needed to bear the shame of the murder, to take the onus off the town.

"Funny. Ha-ha," Vita said, but she was laughing, too.

"Well, don't be witty if you don't want me to laugh." LaRee reached over and took her daughter's hand. All the years . . . Holding Vita tight through the first night, Sabine's funeral, the child understanding and not understanding that her mother was gone forever . . . helping her balance on the ice skates later that winter, seeing her stand up suddenly and say, "I can do it," and skate off across the ice with those little clicking steps that had never approached gliding but had gotten her where she meant to go . . . Finding ways to make life safe and steady, making sure there were beautiful surprises along with the discouraging ones—cookies when she came home from school, the miniature rose in a pot on the table, Bumble the cat curled up in a patch of afternoon sun. Holding the ice pack on the bruise, explaining that the mean girl had the problem, reinforcing the sugar cube model of the United States Capitol with popsicle sticks, making sure the gossip about Sabine never reached her, that the tabloids with their headlines were folded away out of sight . . . helping her see, when she didn't win the blue or the red or even the yellow ribbon, that she still had reason to be proud. And always, wanting to grab someone, anyone, by the lapels and say, "She has suffered enough. The world *owes* her happiness from now on."

These little actions had made LaRee Vita's mother, as much as the pain of labor ever would have. And in becoming Vita's mother, she had lost the LaRee who needed one drug for ordinary anxiety and one drug for extreme anxiety. She was still not as good at life as she wished, but to have mothered one child well meant she had made some contribution.

"Franco is probably excited to be part of something with you," she said.

"You know," Vita said, "I do try to understand. I try to be nice about him, I do!"

"You don't have to try to be nice about him," LaRee replied.

"Yes, I do! If he was really my father, he'd get it. He wouldn't horn in on Mackerel Sky any more than you'd try to join the girls' soccer team at school! You wouldn't, because you understand."

"Fathers don't understand. They bumble around trying to be helpful and get in the way. That's the whole point of them. If Franco lived with us, you'd see."

"I wish you were married." Vita leaned her head against the window, sulking, half earnest, half comic.

"Whoever I was married to would still be irritating. Humans just are."

"We never see Matt anymore," Vita said suddenly.

"Oh, we do—it's just that . . ." That LaRee didn't point him out anymore. It used to be that she'd see him go by in the park ranger's truck and say, "There goes Matt, off to work," and now that she thought about it she realized she must have sounded hollow and left behind, as if she were saying, "There goes Matt, off to the moon." Vita would have felt that; she knew the shades of LaRee's voice the way her father knew the bay.

"Funny you should mention Matt," she said. "I ran into him earlier."

"Did you ask him to marry you?"

"No, I just backed into his truck and left it at that."

"Really?"

"More or less."

"Was he okay? Are you?"

"We're both fine. Just feeling slightly stupider than usual. You know, even if I was married, Franco would still be your father."

Vita made a growling noise and sank deep into her seat. "My DNA is nothing like Franco's," she said.

What was there to say? Washashore and Portagee rubbed each other raw. When Vita was younger and spent a weekend a month over at Franco's, they always went to church. Not that Franco had ever had one sacred impulse, except maybe when he was out on the fishing grounds, but his parents had taken him to church every Sunday and he had taken his sons when they were little, and it seemed the right thing to do. Vita had learned to genuflect and say the Lord's Prayer, and from the kids in the parish hall afterward she had learned that in the afterlife she would burn in hell. Having eavesdropped assiduously on LaRee's conversations, she was able to reply that religion was more likely to breed hatred than love, and there was no hell or heaven either and . . . generally to get herself into deeper trouble. But even then she'd had that strength, to follow her own path. LaRee tried to imitate that strength sometimes.

She stopped at Route 6, waiting for the traffic to pass. Carpenters and plumbers and electricians streamed back from Provincetown at this hour, heading home from their day of renovating waterfront mansions. It was strange work, laying exotic wood floors for whoever had just bought a house, knowing that you might well be back the next year to rip all of it out for a new owner who preferred Carrera marble. But that was how most people lived here, now—at the whims, and on the leavings, of the rich.

The ambulance was coming up behind them, around the corner. LaRee pulled over, waving to the driver as he passed.

"He's heading toward the hospital," she said. If he'd been heading toward the clinic, she'd have had to go back. "And he came from town. I wonder who it is. . . ."

"I hope it's Shyanne Holtz," Vita said. "Broke her back sticking her boobs in Adam's face."

LaRee laughed. "It's not a happy thing, you know, to think a man's only going to like you for your boobs."

"Oh, God, you sound like such a mom," Vita said, but smiling. They watched the flashing lights disappear over the crest of the hill.

"Well, it won't be a riptide," Vita said, thinking of the girl and her father who had died the summer before. You must let it suck you away, no matter how frightening, and it would bring you back, land you safe on a new shore. If you fought it, you'd drown. Vita couldn't stop thinking about the man diving after his daughter, dying with her. She had outgrown her fixation on ghosts and visitations . . . but she could not, in her secret heart, escape the idea that Sabine was out there beating on an invisible wall, trying to get back to her. She was haunted, not by a ghost but by this idea.

They turned up their road, through the woods where dark red and pale yellow leaves were just letting down from their buds. With the last sunlight from the west it looked as if the air were full of butterflies. There was the stark white tree at the end of their driveway; they were home.

"I got scrod for supper," LaRee said, but there was no answer. At least they were home. Coming around the back of the car, she saw that she'd underestimated the damage. Matt's truck bed was higher than her bumper and her taillight was broken. She did not need to spend five hundred dollars on the damned car right now.

Bumble had been watching from the little shed roof over the front door, and she jumped down to the plant table and to the ground and came galloping, rolling in the sand at their feet.

"You're a good kitty, Bumble. You'll be happy about the scrod."

"I'm sorry, LaRee," Vita said, dropping her backpack the minute she got in the door, heading into her bedroom. LaRee leaned back against the counter and closed her eyes—the best escape she had. Sabine, like Shyanne Holtz, had had that glamour that came out of need. She prided herself on never buying makeup when it was so easy to palm, and she was the same with people, sneaking in close to absorb their mystique or wealth or whatever she envied. She had admired a rosebush LaRee grew from a cutting. One year LaRee got home from work and found Sabine standing there with a shopping bag full of pink roses. She had clipped off every bloom.

"You always said I was welcome to anything," she'd said. She'd seduced Franco in that same spirit; being a real fisherman, a real townie, he had more cachet than any other man in Oyster Creek. Sabine got a child out of him the way she'd slip a tube of lipstick up her sleeve. Except that it had been LaRee who'd wanted a child.

And LaRee had wished her ill, waited for the comeuppance that must be just around the corner. A wish that had come way too true.

"Anyway, I pretended I'd never met him," Vita said later, with a kind of airy bitterness. She'd showered and scrubbed her face with some substance meant to clear her skin, and she settled into her chair, pulling up her knees and resting her chin on them so she looked like a small marsupial with large eyes, something that would cling in a tree. She was so alive and alert and resilient—the woman Sabine might have been herself if her life had had a little more kindness in it somewhere. "I just said, 'Hello, I'm Vita Gray,' and shook his hand. Hugh didn't notice. I don't think anyone did, except Leo and Adam."

Vita had that look on her face that came just before she launched into a dreamy rhapsody about a boy.

LaRee poured herself a glass of wine. "But Adam figured it out right away, huh?" An open door.

"He's just so smart," Vita said. "And so sweet. He looks like a baby devil." She might have been talking about a kitten. "His hair isn't curly exactly, but it sticks up a little and . . . and you can imagine there might be just the stubs of little horns starting there."

"God help us," LaRee said under her breath.

"What?"

"Oh, nothing—I'm sorry, go ahead." In sixth grade Vita had

come home with a simple health class assignment: She was to choose one person, a buddy who would help her resist the lure of sexual love through her teenage years. LaRee, listening out of one ear as she drove Vita home that day, heard this and said, reflexively, "Well, don't look at me!"

"LaRee! What do you mean?" Vita had been horrified. The nice teacher at school had explained it so clearly. It had made perfect sense and now LaRee ... "It has to be you!" Vita had said. "Who else would it be?"

"Well!" LaRee said. "Well, it's just ..." She'd felt herself opening and closing her mouth like a fish. "Well, what I mean is ... it's not as easy as it sounds, to resist that kind of feeling. I mean, of course, I'll be your ... abstinence buddy. I mean, if it seems appropriate."

Vita's hair had been down to her waist back then, and she had undone her braids as she spoke, fluffing the bristly mass of it out with her fingers before she began to braid it again, her hands moving as fast and sure as a lacemaker's.

"I want to have children," she'd said, doubling the elastics. "So I guess I'll have to have sex. Unless ... Maybe I'll get Chinese girls."

"Now *that's* colonialism," LaRee had said, laughing. She hadn't guessed how fast the years would pass, how quickly Vita would grow and change. The night before she started high school Vita had parted the endless hair carefully into sections, made ten braids, and cut each one off at about four inches.

"Your generation has a thing about looks," she'd said. Then she took a shower and the next morning there was a beautiful mop of curls, Franco's curls, and she had burst into tears and pulled them back tight. "The stubs of little horns—how adorable," LaRee said now, keeping her face turned so Vita couldn't see her expression.

"You're laughing at me," Vita said to her back.

"Smiling, not laughing. When someone describes a man the way you just did, I smile. Because I've been in love myself," LaRee said.

In love and out the other side. From this distance it looked like one of those conditions that had to be borne because no vaccine had yet been found. She could remember sobbing when Drew left, as if she'd been ripped open. Such misery, and it was only a few years later that she was crazy for Bill Shipman, the surveyor, and would find any excuse to be near him. Nothing was left of that now except a vague embarrassment when she saw him in the supermarket. And Matt . . . well, she could still get her heart to beat a bit faster for him, if she really worked at it. And sometimes she wanted to work at it, to remember what it had felt like when love went through her defenses like a hatpin and everything was new.

Mostly she was grateful that those days had passed, that she was safe on the solid ground of her own life. Her thighs were just lumpy extra flesh now—why bother anyone else with them? Whatever had been revealed to her by love, she could learn from a long swim in the pond. Contentment meant another log on the woodstove, Bumble on her lap, *Law & Order* on TV. For a night out, one of Vita's choral concerts at school.

"And his beard is like a little devil beard!" Vita said happily.

"His beard?" He was a boy, where did he get a beard? Vita had said the word *Adam* as if it were a two syllable prayer. . . . What if he didn't answer?

"It's so soft-looking, it makes him look even sweeter. A lot of the guys have those beards that make them look mean."

"A lot of the guys . . . ?" LaRee turned to the sink so Vita couldn't see her face. Of course Kayla Anderson came in for her prenatal visits, other girls from Vita's class were on the pill, but Vita . . . she was still a child!

"The raccoon's been in the compost again," LaRee said, looking out the window. "It's all over the place. I swear, he gets mad when I put bread in there."

"Maybe he has rabies."

"We don't have rabies out here. They put meat out with vaccine in it, along the canal, so the rabies doesn't travel. I'm surprised you even know about rabies."

"It's in our English book."

"What's that?"

"*Their Eyes Were Watching God.*"

"I've never read it."

"You should," Vita said, in the tone adults were prone to take when lecturing teenagers. "It's really good."

"I will. I always like the books you suggest."

She propped the colander in the sink. She had perfected the maternal art of hovering, disguising it under one and another little chore so she was always somewhere in the background, able to put in a quiet word.

"You have good taste in people, too," she added.

"I do, don't I?" Vita said. "In fact we had a very nice conversation today, Adam and me."

She blushed, though, remembering—even her ears felt hot; had she spoken the word *kiss* in front of Adam Capshaw? And then that mush about Shakespeare and beauty, so of course he had teased her about *King Lear*—the senior English classes were reading it. Ugh, what was she thinking? Why not just wear a big sign that read I'M A FOOL? And Shyanne squirming all over him with her face in those pornographic expressions.

"I can't believe Shyanne's playing Miranda," she said.

"I'm sure it's just because she's older, honey. She looks more..."

"No joke. I'm surprised she doesn't wear neon arrows pointing to her cleavage," Vita said bitterly. "And you know what? She's all wrong for it. Miranda is supposed to be innocent!"

LaRee washed spinach. She wasn't going to get it. Shyanne's shy, "demure" Miranda was profane as far as Vita could see—a mockery of the grave, gentle character Vita would have played. Vita had studied and worked and prayed as if Shakespeare were her god! A wave of bitterness rose in her throat. She had seen Franco's gaze rest on Shyanne, and the earth went out from beneath her when she did. There was something missing from her, something Franco had taken, and it left her alone and awkward while Shyanne stalked around in two pairs of false eyelashes grabbing whatever she liked. And apparently Vita's own father admired her for it.

"Hillary didn't invite me to her birthday party," Vita said into the air. "Everyone who sits at the lunch table except me. It's not that I care—I wouldn't have had a good time. I just . . . You know, it would be nice if one time someone wanted *me* to be the star, or wanted me to be their friend, or their date, or . . . anything at all."

"It sounds like Adam wanted to talk to you," LaRee tried.

"Probably he did. Now he can tell his friends how Vita Gray said whatever I said. And, 'Isn't she weird? You know about the murder, right? They say she lived off her mom's dead flesh for days.'"

"Vita, honey . . ."

"That's the kind of thing they say! We were going around in English class telling scary stories and suddenly somebody looked at me, and then they all looked at me, and then there was a dead silence and we were dismissed early."

"Sometimes I think we should have moved away," LaRee said. "I wanted to keep you near your father, and didn't realize what it was going to be like at school."

"Oh my God!" Vita said. "Thank *God* we didn't move! What would my life be like without Mackerel Sky? I can't even imagine it. And it's not the . . . past. It's not Portagee/washashore—or not so much. It's that we're not like everyone else. We're not so different, but you don't have to be very different. Life is frightening enough. People want to be with people who are just the same as they are, who like the same food and laugh at the same jokes. We go to school and learn about diversity, and a rich cultural mix with everyone bringing different things to it, and black and white and Asian people all laughing together in every single picture. And meanwhile the kids from the Church of God's Word are thinking no one else is Christian enough, and the indie kids are thinking no one else is weird enough, and Shyanne and her crowd think they're too cool for school—everyone has their group, and the slightest thing marks who belongs and who doesn't. We're a bunch of white people who all live on the same sandbar and we can't really say anything much to one another except maybe that racism is bad and the Red Sox need to win the World Series! Without Mackerel Sky I would literally be dead. How long till the fish is ready?"

"Fifteen minutes?" LaRee said. "You're a smart girl, Vita."

"For all that's worth."

"If you could invent a shirt with neon arrows you could make your fortune and open your own Shakespeare company."

Vita laughed, grudgingly.

"It's kind of cool to be playing Iris the rainbow goddess, I think. You do have that shimmer." And Vita did, too, when she was just herself at home, running down the narrow path to the pond on a summer morning, diving again and again from the float. Oh, when she just let herself be for a minute, she was such an amazing girl!

Vita rolled her eyes. "Don't be ridiculous, LaRee."

"It's not ridiculous! It's hard to invent a compliment without inspiration. Vita, listen to me—I've been alive . . . forever. Just live, just keep going, mistakes and everything. Your instincts are good. You like Adam, just let him see that; he'll respond. Trust me, there's no research necessary. At your age, hormones do the rest of the work! Then, once it's under way, you just get to sit back and watch the disaster unfold."

There, she'd let the cynicism of middle-age creep in. Vita did not need to hear her assume that love would always precipitate disaster.

"Yes, Mother," Vita said, mocking, but LaRee could see a very slight satisfaction warm her face. She ate hungrily and went off to write a paper about *Their Eyes Were Watching God*, and in half an hour or so LaRee could hear her reading *The Tempest* out loud— Miranda's lines, of course:

"'I do not know one of my sex, no woman's face remember, save, from my glass, mine own. Nor have I seen more that I may call men than you. . . .'" She worked it over and over, loud and soft, quick and light like a dizzy, confiding girl, then hesitant, like herself.

LaRee poked the fire—to keep the damp from settling. The fog was blowing up from the bay through the woods, so thick she couldn't even see down to the pond. There was a vine growing in around the window frame; she ought to pull it out. But she was fond of it; it felt right to let it in. The window had been the only one left intact from the Calliope after it burned down, and the owners had been glad to let Drew and LaRee carry it away. It was six feet high and nearly as wide, leaded, with two rows of stained-glass panes at the top, so when you looked out through it you seemed to see a huge painting, different every hour as the light and weather changed. Drew had built their walls out of timbers from the old stagecoach barn out on the King's Highway. The wineglass LaRee sipped from had belonged to Ada Towne, and before her to the Stewart family whose initials were etched around the rim. Even the knobby geranium on the sill had been salvaged from the porch of a summer house after the tenants went home for the winter. LaRee had made a life out of what others had left behind.

"'. . . I would not wish any companion in the world but you,'" Vita was saying. "'Nor can imagination form a shape besides yourself.'"

The fire snapped; a drop fell on the roof, then another. LaRee heard Vita's voice gather confidence as she started the little speech again, and then the bedroom door flew open and there she was, standing as proud as a statue.

"I can do it," she said. "It's good. Do you want to hear?"

"Of course!" LaRee was glad she hadn't turned the light on yet, so Vita didn't see her eyes fill as she listened to the story of a girl who came to the age of love on a distant island, with only the little she had learned in her shipwrecked life.

12

A Lothario

"It would have been different if I was harbormaster," Franco said. "She'd be living with us now."

They were finishing breakfast—scrambled eggs and sausage, the same as his mother would make on a morning when his father was heading out on the *Rainha*, and coffee so strong it seemed oily.

"Yeah, like when the boys were teenagers all they wanted to do was to be with their parents," Danielle said with a little laugh.

"Boys are something else completely," he said.

"I wasn't exactly close to my father when I was Vita's age," she said. "But then, I was already married to you."

"She shook my hand and said she was pleased to meet me!" he said. "She was daring me to say I'm her father."

"And did you?"

"No. I . . . wasn't sure it was the right thing."

"So you were being a good father."

He smiled. "Still, if she lived here . . ."

"Slay Case Lothario Wants Tyke Now." That had been the headline in the *Herald* the day after Franco filed for custody. Then there was "DA: Neves Neither Exonerated Nor Charged," and the one with a picture of LaRee emerging from the library with Vita on her hip, a cold wind blowing her hair across her face, and an expression of grim determination. "Kid Comes with a Fortune," it read, as if that was all anyone cared about. The fortune was two hundred and fifty thousand dollars, all Sabine had had, and left to Vita in her will. She had named LaRee Vita's guardian. Who else was there? Sabine's father had evaporated, her mother was dead, and her sister operated a body-piercing salon on the West Coast. LaRee was the closest thing to family Sabine had.

"It would be different," Danielle said. "I admit."

"'Harbormaster Seeks Custody of Orphaned Daughter,'" he said. "If that had been the headline, the whole state would have been on my side." Those summer mornings when he was skateboarding down Breakwater Road to see Sabine, you could smell the asphalt in the sun and the bay sparkled like it was full of stars. That it could have come to this! He'd wanted no child, and now he couldn't help loving her more painfully than he had ever loved anyone before.

"They wanted sensational headlines. The DA wanted to keep from looking like an idiot, Franco, that's all. You know how this stuff works. And plenty of people are on your side. The people who read those headlines wanted a story to take them out of their own lives for a minute. None of them gave a damn about you or Vita or me. None of it had anything to do with us."

"She ought to be here." The ground went out from under his voice for a second; he felt foolish and small. Vita ought to be here, with him, with Danielle, whose all-forgiving love had already stretched itself to cover her husband's illegitimate child.

"If you were harbormaster," Danielle said, "it wouldn't seem like such a big-shot job. What does the guy do except chase people who are speeding in the no-wake zone and give out tickets for lobster scrubbing? To hear you talk, you'd think he was harbor emperor. You're the one who's famous."

But the fame was long over. Their misery had lost its savor and the cameras had swiveled toward the next catastrophe, and the next. Meanwhile his daughter was growing up with LaRee Farnham.

"And Vita's not here because you did the right thing," Danielle said, as if she had read his mind. "She'd gotten used to living with LaRee and you weren't going to break that up, not after she lost Sabine the way she did. You ought to be proud of it!"

"Except . . ." Except Vita had come to belong to that world more than his world, and that was a world that looked down on him. He remembered how Sabine would seem to be listening for a distant music when she first sipped a glass of wine—she said she was waiting to experience the taste with all parts of her tongue. And he was a Portagee brute, not much use unless you needed him to lift something heavy, or scrabble down into a crawl space to fix a pipe.

Vita might have read all of Shakespeare but she didn't have the history of this town knit into her as she ought. LaRee couldn't teach her what it had been like to return from three days' fishing with a load of cod that made you feel like a king. LaRee had never waited for word, when a boat was missing, as he had when his uncle and his cousins, Paolo and Dan, went down on the *Maria B.* The family had crowded into the kitchen, the men drinking whiskey, the women coffee, knowing the truth long before the call came. The *Maria* had been so old it couldn't stand up to the weather—his uncle had needed just a couple more solid catches before he could afford the repairs. That was when his father gave up, turned the *Rainha* over to Franco, and got a job at the lumberyard.

Young and arrogant, Franco had weighed the price of cod against the price of cocaine and made the obvious choice. One trip a week to New Bedford, and his family was respectable suddenly, living in the house at Cranberry Corners with an in-ground pool. Franco coached the Little League team, Danielle supervised lobster roll suppers at church. For five years all went smoothly. Then one night two men were waiting for him on the dock. Soldierly, machine guns at their sides, they boarded the boat and came back to Wellfleet with him, rolling cigarettes, speaking to each other in Spanish. They had a businesslike, almost friendly manner, but when he started to use the radio he felt the gun in the small of his back and put it down. He usually unloaded down at Try Point, where the houses were boarded up for the winter, but this time he went straight to the wharf, thinking someone might come to his aid, though in the middle of a March night this was a slim hope. He stepped off the boat and started to tie it up, but the one raised his gun again, so he dropped the rope, and watched as they backed up and headed into the dark at no-wake speed.

Three days later the Coast Guard found the *Rainha* drifting southward and towed her back to port. It was like seeing a corpse. She'd been stripped of every inch of brass, the mahogany ship's wheel, the copper pipes, even the stove from the galley. Bobby Matos offered to buy her for two hundred dollars, said he'd sell her for scrap.

"That boat was my father's pride and joy," Franco had said. "I'm not sinking it for an oyster reef."

Bobby had shrugged, a very slight, crisp motion. It didn't matter to him.

Danielle had said, "Of course, of course," when he said he would never let the boat go. She hadn't understood yet that Franco's income had just disappeared, that they were going to lose the house. The town had been kind; of course it had been. Chris Taves had been happy to have Franco take over bartending at the Walrus—men would buy a drink just to be near him. The town always found a way to take care of its own.

"I opened up the Fitzsimmons place yesterday," Danielle said.

"How were the mice?" The year before, Danielle had missed a mouse nest built inside the stove, and when Mrs. Fitzsimmons put on a kettle of water for tea, the nest caught fire and baby mice came streaming out of the back burner.

"Irritated. But . . . this year the problem is a little more difficult to solve."

"What? Coyotes?"

"Georgie. He's been living in there."

"Huh?"

"Well, the Seashore got after Jeb Stone—he had all those old cars in the woods and they were talking about environmental hazards and . . ."

"Oh, right—God, I didn't think about Georgie."

"He couldn't live in the bus anymore. So he went to live at the Fitzsimmonses."

"I guess I heard that."

"Now he's got to get out, and . . ."

"Poor guy," Franco said. "Where's his sister?"

"I don't know—the mom's sick, maybe there's a new man or . . . Anyway, I said I'd ask you if he could stay on the *Rainha*."

"What? On the *Rainha*? How—"

"It's better than an abandoned school bus."

"An abandoned school bus is back in the woods. The *Rainha's* tied up at the end of the pier!"

"He'll only come and go after dark. And it's only for a few days.

Fatima Machado said he could have her garage if he'd clean it out, so . . . maybe a week at the most."

"Eh, Georgie," he said, but he had pretty much lost any rights to say no to Danielle. "You know they want me to move that boat. I can't call any attention to her."

"I do know, and I'll tell him again. I . . . oh, I just feel bad for him, you know. And he's one of us, no matter . . ."

"I don't think Vita's ever been in the church, except the few times we used to take her," Franco said suddenly. "One of us" had jogged the image of the church full of townspeople, Christmas Eve when the boys were little.

"You, of course, never skip a mass." Danielle laughed. She stood against the light of the kitchen window, a haloed silhouette.

"It's different when you're young. You're there with everyone in town, and even though you're just reading out of the prayer book you're all admitting your faults together, swearing you'll do better. You're all on the same page. And singing the hymns, you feel like you're part of something. My parents didn't let me miss church until I was in high school."

Danielle had a deep laugh, the same laugh all women in town seemed to develop by forty, knowing and ironic, having given up hope that life would make any sense and begun to see it purely as entertainment. "Yes, and look how well you turned out," she said, filling his cup again and swiping at the resultant spill with the dishrag that was always in her hand.

"It's not natural. . . . My parents were both baptized there, I was; you were, the boys were. LaRee doesn't see the point," Franco said. When Danielle raised an eyebrow, he said, "You know what I mean, about locals. LaRee didn't go to school here, no, she grew up over the bridge. She doesn't know a thing about Vita's heritage—"

"And she wasn't a suspect in any murders," Danielle said, quite tenderly. "A horny old goat in a borrowed suit, trying to pass for an upstanding man."

Franco smiled, abashed but not quite ashamed. Danielle was so clever a wife that she could make "horny old goat" sound like praise. Franco might not have managed to be faithful to her, but he was utterly loyal. There were women, and then there was Danielle, and they didn't occupy the same realm in his mind. All the places they'd lived—the boat, the Cranberry Corners house, that dump in the hollow back of Old King's Highway—what did it matter? Danielle was his home.

"Paramour, lothario," he said, enjoying the words more than he should have. If he couldn't manage a respectable harbormaster's life, at least he could be glamorous in the headlines. "Lothario, indeed. I was like one of those insects the queen bee uses for insemination."

"You know the difference between men and insects, Franco?" Danielle asked. "Men have zippers."

He put an arm around her waist and pulled her into his lap. "You're putting thoughts in my head," he said, kissing her neck, right beneath her ear.

She laid her head against his. She had been the prettiest girl at Outer Cape High School thirty years ago, and she was a very pretty woman still. Her face had softened, but it had lost none of its kindness, its laughter. Her hair was dyed the same auburn she'd been born with. She still smelled like heaven. She still had that ache of love, toward him, toward everything—even his illegitimate child.

"She's your flesh and blood, your daughter," Danielle said, safe with his arms around her. "It doesn't matter if she's with us or not, she always will be. Church isn't going to make her a Portagee. Give her something that matters."

Franco's tattoo itched. It was guilt; he was always guilty. Maybe that was just a man's lot: Danielle seemed to have a sixth sense that told her what was right regardless of any rules, but he had never followed an instinct without finding himself in a hornet's nest. To raise the boys—he'd just done what she told him to. Now he needed her help with the daughter he'd conceived in betrayal. He pressed his temple; vertigo was threatening.

"I don't have anything to give her. If she could say, 'Well, my dad's the harbormaster....'"

"It has nothing to do with you or how fancy your job is," Danielle said into his ear. "Vita doesn't need anything from the harbormaster; she needs something from her father. Now, I've got to go tell Georgie it's okay before I go to work."

She kissed his cheek and went to the mirror with her lipstick. Franco, feeling foolish, headed down the back stairs, where his slicker and waders were hanging, and out into the green day. The Walrus wouldn't be open till noon and the parking lot was empty. The new leaves still hung damp and wrinkled from their buds. His bike was propped against the corner of the building and he swung his leg over and coasted down Commercial Street toward the harbor, his heart lightening again as he went. It was a perfect, sparkling morning; he could see right across the bay. The bike wheel ticked, the little waves slapped the seawall. A woman was walking toward him, wearing one of those wrap dresses that fell open with the tug of a string.

13

SEA VIEW AUTO REPAIR

"It needs the whole taillight assembly," Sal Bemba said. "A hundred fifty, more or less, and maybe two hours' labor, three if you need it right away. I'd have to go up to Hyannis and pick up the part. And the side piece here. It's fiberglass so it won't need to be painted if you don't mind the way it looks. I can always paint it later, once the season gets going."

LaRee cleaned rental cottages on summer Saturdays, like everyone, and would have more money come June. She could do four a day for fifty bucks apiece, and she put most of that money away—an extra two thousand dollars a year toward retirement. Not that she intended to retire, but saving money was a kind of vice for her; she was afraid of the future and every time she saved a little she felt safer.

"Thanks, Sal," she said. "That would be great. I feel so stupid. I was just backing out of a space without thinking."

"I've done it myself," he said. "Got too much on your mind is all. I can get the part by . . . Wednesday, I think. Can you leave it off Thursday morning? Just leave the key in the Camaro."

There was a purple Camaro on the lot with no front wheels but a paint job to die for, realistic lightning bolts racing along both sides to the back. Sal used the car mostly as a mailbox, though the hood also served as a bench from which to gaze over the bay. Sea View faced southwest on the hill that led down to the old sandpit. You could see across to Plymouth and all the way up to Provincetown from here. Some days the bay was so blue it hurt to look, though now there were dark clouds lowering and she could see rain falling to the south. But the real pleasure of Sea View Auto wasn't just the panorama—it was the sight of a man fixing things. The broken-down trucks and bashed vans at Sea View would be put back together with some combination of old and new parts, silicone, tape, and wire, sanded and painted so their owners could squeeze out another ten or twenty thousand miles. The school bus Georgie had lived in was behind the Camaro, and Sal had taken out a couple of the seats and propped them against the building in the sun. Even Sal's three-legged dog kept going, wagging his tail fervently whenever Sal came around the corner, watching the world eagerly.

A truck was bumping down the sand road toward them—the park ranger's truck. "Hello," Matt said, rolling the window down.

"What's up?" Sal asked.

Matt looked at LaRee and laughed. "Had a little fender bender in the fish market parking lot."

"I ran into him," LaRee admitted.

"Well, it was probably my fault."

"Let's see," Sal said, going around behind. "Taillight, eh?"

"And the tailgate is . . . unhinged, I think," Matt said. "LaRee, I thought you didn't have any damage."

"I didn't take a good look at it until I got home," she said. Sal had gone in to check on the price of a new taillight for Matt.

"Me neither," Matt said. "LaRee, I was thinking that maybe . . ."

"I don't think that would be such a good idea," she interrupted.

He smiled. "You don't think what would be a good idea?"

"What you're suggesting."

"What did I suggest?"

"You know perfectly well what you were going to suggest."

"So, you can still pretty much finish my sentences, but you don't think it would be a good idea to have dinner."

"No," she said. "I don't."

"You're probably right," he said, disappointing her. "It just seemed kind of . . . overly coincidental to bump into you twice in a row this way."

He was wearing his park ranger's uniform; the tucked-in shirt showed his paunch and hid his biceps. Thank God he'd left his hat in the truck. But then, she was over her old longings. For all she knew, she wouldn't recognize an attractive man anymore.

"If it didn't occur to you to be in touch before . . ."

"You mean, when Tracey left? I thought of it, but what would I do, call up and say, 'Okay, she's gone—let's pick up where we left off'? I . . . didn't know what to do," he admitted.

She felt all the old nerves and none of the old electricity; it was terrible. "If it was a good idea for us to . . . have dinner . . . you would have known what to do," she said, watching a dragger come around Barrel Point, glad to have something to fix her eyes on. "You'd have wanted to call me, wanted to see me and talk. It wouldn't have come up because I rammed into you in a random parking lot."

"I suppose you're right," he said, defeated, a little hurt, and maybe relieved.

She was pretty sure she was wrong, now that she'd said it, but she couldn't argue against herself without letting at least a few minutes lapse. She had closed off the memory of the night she'd spent with Matt, so she could get over it and live along without thinking about what she was missing. Now it felt like she'd sealed that door so tight there was no opening it again. They'd been close to each other, honest with each other. But almost ten years had passed— the things she'd have confided back then didn't even seem true anymore. Those ideas of a man as a deep, abiding intimate who would somehow protect her and be vulnerable to her at the same time... Well, it made a nice dream, it was something she hoped for Vita. But her own time was past.

"I mean, it was important to me back then, very important..." she said. If he had any idea!

"Me, too!" he said, defensive.

"But not so you'd make some way for us to talk, or be friends, or anything..."

"It would have seemed like I was... betraying her."

"I understand. That was important. It was probably the right thing to do. But it does mean you weren't concerned for me... or, if you were, you put me way down the priority list."

"Because..."

They heard Sal ending his phone call inside. "Because I felt guilty that you were so important to me," he whispered quickly.

"I can do it," Sal said, glad to be the bearer of good news. "No problem. Pick a day next week. Oh, LaRee, were you waiting for me?"

"No, just got talking to Matt. I'll bring the car in Thursday. Nice to see both of you."

I felt guilty that you were so important to me. It stuck in her mind, of course. Which was why it was better to avoid him. She knew too much now about the machinery of love. He had to have someone who was "too important to him," because his wife had walked out on him once and was all too likely to do it again. If LaRee kept away from him, he'd find someone new before he even noticed what was happening. There were plenty of women in town who'd be thrilled to have a man with a steady job and an even disposition. He was lucky they weren't chasing him down the street! One or another would marry him, and they would invent, together, a whole long list of reasons why they had to be each other's one and only. And he'd keep a little torch burning for her, LaRee—a torch with about the power of a nightlight. Just in case the new one left him, too.

She took the back way home, stopping at the beach parking lot for a minute to look out. The clouds had thinned to a veil, lit a soft pink by the low sun and reflected on the satin surface of the water. From the top of the dune she could see each wave fold gently on the last, and a pale, fragile moon rising. This yearning—what was it for if not love?

14

FAMOUS MURDER ALL OVER AGAIN

Vita bumped her locker shut with her hip; very satisfying, as if she were sealing her troubles up for good. She skirted behind Shyanne, around a little flock of freshmen who were keeping together for protection, and over Brandon's foot, which had been stuck out in hopes of tripping her or at least catching her attention. Adam was coming in from the courtyard, and he seemed to smile at her, or at least to make a little sign of recognition. But maybe that was meant for Shyanne, or someone else. Vita tried to glance at him in a way that would acknowledge the smile without basing any assumptions on it, but he had disappeared into the stairway by the time she had her face properly arranged. Her cheeks were blazing—she tried to cool them with her fingers. If she could have communicated by blushing instead of speaking, she would have been the most articulate person on earth. As it was . . . "Behold, the great blunderer," she said to herself, in Shakespearean. Then she tried Zora Neale Hurston: "And there she walked without seein' nobody, her eyes turned in on her own. . . ." Either one worked. Each was immersed in his own language and the music of it was as important as the words. The English test was going to want her to decipher symbols, though, so failure was pretty much assured.

Something bumped up against her, hard. Dorotea Machado's book bag.

"You never know where you're going, do you?" Dorotea said, disgusted.

"I'm sorry," Vita said. "I was just ..."

Dorotea dropped her head of gelled curls and pushed past Vita up the stairs. Even Dorotea, who had not a friend on earth, didn't want to be seen talking to Vita. Brandon Skiles and the tangle of "popular" kids were behind her, butting their heads into each other's shoulders, laughing like hyenas.

"Move, loser. You're in my way," Brandon told Vita.

He probably meant this as an endearment. There was no point in taking offense. Still, when Vita couldn't choke out a hello, how did he and the others manage to be so commanding? They acted like they owned the place and ... they did. Their parents had graduated from Outer Cape High, worked summers at Doubloons, surfing all morning, waiting tables in their cutoffs and halter tops into the night, pairing off into one marriage and then another until their kids might as well all be related. Grown up, they'd pile those kids into the boat every weekend and meet up at Barrel Point, the men with their fishing poles and beer, the women tanning and gabbing, calling out an occasional admonition to the kids. Brandon's dad owned Oyster Creek Marine; it put him in the center of everything.

Vita started up the stairs, but one after another Brandon's friends shoved past. They were a group; you didn't get between them. Brandon greeted each one with a casual insult—"Yo, bitch," and "Whattup, ma nigga?" Everyone admired him; everyone wanted to be his friend.

Vita swallowed. She was overthinking. She was too sensitive; people always said so. She stood at the sidelines trying to figure it all out while the others went ahead and did what they did. But ... she could hear LaRee telling her to "just live," shaking her head and laughing, that deep seen-it-all-and-thrown-up-my-hands laugh she had, as if she were talking about a story, instead of Vita's actual flesh-and-blood, actions-and-consequences life. Had it occurred to La-Ree that if Sabine had taken a little care with love, she might be alive right now? If they'd been a real family with a mother and a father and a little girl asleep upstairs, if she hadn't been drinking wine with some man from over the bridge, someone she barely knew ... She stood frozen there in the stairway, thinking about what might have been. Life was more than just a big comedy show rolling along for LaRee's entertainment.

"Everything happens for a reason," she could hear LaRee saying. "And that reason is that God has kind of a vicious wit."

Vita's heart dropped. She betrayed LaRee with every thought, LaRee who "just lived" to the extent that she had opened the door on that freezing night and taken Vita in without question, letting her own life veer into the unknown. No one else's heart had that kind of room in it, and no one else would have gone all this way beside her so staunchly, laughing when there was so much cause for tears. The other girls, the ones with real mothers, sulked and raged and couldn't wait to get away, while Vita would call LaRee at lunch just to hear her voice. It was pathetic, really, another of the qualities that made Vita the biggest loser in Loserville.

Everyone had gone up the stairs past her now; the ones who didn't like her because she was a loser, the ones who didn't like her because she was strange, and the ones who didn't like her because she wasn't a real townie.

She slipped into a seat in the back corner of geometry class. The teacher was late, and Brandon hitched his chair desk over beside Alyssa and Gina, whose smooth heads were bent together in gossip.

"Girl on girl," he said. "Can I get in here?"

"Suck my dick, Brandon," Gina said.

"Very ladylike," he told her.

"We'll never be as ladylike as you are," she said, miming a polite sip of tea with her little finger out. Vita giggled, and the two girls turned back with one movement. Where did Vita Gray get the idea that she was allowed to laugh at their jokes?

She looked away, but he'd caught her acting like his friend.

"Quit eavesdropping," Brandon said—sneered, really. If you were a friend of his, that meant you counted for something; if not, you weren't worth bothering with. So when his voice went hateful, the room got quiet. Everyone was afraid to get burned.

"Suck my dick," Vita managed, half audibly. It had worked for Gina, and she just wasn't going to let him win.

"Who'd wanna get that close to you?" he said.

Vita gave him the finger.

"Not that one, idiot, the middle one," Brandon said. She'd fumbled, putting up her fourth finger at first instead of her third. "Jesus, you don't even know how to flip someone off."

The whole room laughed, especially Dorotea, who wasn't used to being one of the ones laughing.

"I'm glad to see you're all in a good mood," the teacher said. "That should help you on the quiz. Pass the papers to the left—no calculators."

Brandon turned around to give Vita one last sneer. She looked him hard in the eye. She wasn't going to bend to his will. To think his meanness used to hurt her . . . well, it still did. But she had *The*

Tempest right here under her notebook; that was the important thing. They were deep into rehearsals now—this afternoon they would be blocking her scene, she'd be there with Adam, with Leo and Sam. They'd be synchronizing themselves, trying to step off into the same imaginary world together, listening, reacting to one another. At school it seemed like everyone had snapped their hearts and minds shut against their classmates, the way you'd lock a door against a thief.

The clock ticked; the rest of them were figuring the areas of obtuse triangles. It was too hot in the room. Vita's head swam. She took a deep breath, closed her eyes. *Ceres, most bounteous lady, thy rich leas* . . . Ten minutes later, she had written this speech carefully all around the edge of the quiz paper. She was going to fail; she told herself she didn't care.

At lunch she finished with Iris's lines and began to add Ceres' reply: *Hail, many-colored messenger* . . .

She was alone at the corner table, watching them all from a distance. It was funny how that worked—the others refused to see her, which gave her license to observe them boldly. Adam came in, hitching up his jeans with his wrists the way he did, looking awkward and self-conscious, scanning the room for a friend and catching her eye. She looked away but not quickly enough. If he hadn't guessed her feelings before, he would now, and . . . she was mortified. Shyanne came in, looking stoned and pouty, and said something that made Adam laugh.

Behind her, Mr. Delvecchio, the principal, was standing at the door, scanning the groups table by table. Mr. Delvecchio was a kind, quick-footed man, who could address a fractious student with such clear respect that the bad behavior, whatever it was, would simply evaporate. His eyes lit on Dorotea Machado now, and he gave a quick, reflexive nod and started toward her. He looked so grave and certain that he might as well have been carrying a scythe. When he touched Dorotea's shoulder, she flinched, then gathered her books and her purse and followed him, head down as always, hair hanging like a heavy curtain over her face.

"Delvecchio stood out on the path with her till someone came to pick her up," Brandon said, on the bus.

"Did she look sad? Or worried?" Vita asked.

He shrugged. "How would I know?"

"How wouldn't you know? Are you, like, blind?"

"They looked like a short bald guy standing there with a girl who's never, ever, going to get any," he said. "A girl like you."

Vita put her earphones back in and stared hard out the window. In a few months she'd have her driver's license and the bus would be just an awful memory.

LaRee was kneeling in the front garden, weeding behind the peonies, whose buds were just beginning to show. Vita came up the driveway past the white tree, singing tunelessly along with Lady Gaga. "Just dance, it'll be okay . . . just da-ance."

She flicked the earphones out of her ears and plopped down on the front step. "Hel-lo." Two notes, high and then low, as recognizable as a bird's call. "How are you?"

"I'm very good, thank you, and yourself?"

"I got the highest grade in the class on the Civil War essay— that's how I am," Vita said lightly. This was true. The geometry quiz was pushed out of her mind. She'd figure out what to do about it later. "He said, 'Shows original thinking.'"

"That's no surprise."

"What's for supper?"

"Spaghetti."

"Ooh!"

There was something bright at the back of the garden—yellow, maybe a plastic toy, or . . . LaRee reached through the peony stems and pushed some leaves away to get to it. It was a goldfinch, perfect in death, from his curled feet to the bright, wet eye, from which some ants from the peonies were drinking.

"Vita, look." LaRee picked the bird up and held him out for Vita to see; you could never look that closely at a live creature. "He must have hit the window. I mean, I don't know why I say 'he.' Oh, the color, of course. The females are drab."

"LaRee, did something happen to Dorotea's mother?"

"Not that I know of. She was at the clinic with old Mrs. Machado the other day. Why?"

"Mr. Delvecchio came and got Dorotea from the cafeteria."

"Maybe she got caught skipping school?" LaRee said. When a cloud dimmed the sun for a minute, Vita would always think someone's mother had died. "Maybe she won an award?" Though Dorotea Machado was not going to win any awards anytime soon. She went along as if she were at the end of a leash, being led like a slow, docile animal into a cramped, dark future.

"No. It was something really bad." Tears pricked in Vita's eyes, blurred her vision and closed her throat. "I could tell, LaRee. . . ." She cupped her hand under LaRee's to bring the poor bird a little closer. "It's so pretty," she said, the corner of her mouth trembling so LaRee bent in to kiss the top of her head.

"Should we make a little grave for him?"

"I'm not five anymore, LaRee! I'm not going to feel better because we make a little grave!" She balled her hands and struck out at the air, hitting LaRee's hand so the bird sailed into the brambles at the edge of the woods. "Stop treating me like a baby!"

"Ouch, ow!"

She had smacked her head into LaRee's mouth. "Ow! Jesus!" LaRee's lip was bleeding; Vita rubbed her scalp.

LaRee took the fists in her two hands. "I'm sorry. I . . . only wish you were five, so I could make it better." She had to keep talking to keep from slipping into tears herself. Keeping Vita steady and safe and always growing, she had steadied herself against life's discouraging forces. "Shh," she said, holding her tight, looking over her shoulder to see the white tree standing there, proud and graceful though it had been dead for years. It had been struck by lightning, and the bark had peeled away but it stood there at the edge of the driveway, the forest rising like a wall, fifty feet of sycamore and oak thatched with vines.

What to say? "We're all lost here, but adults have made a secret pact to pretend they know what they're doing so every child has to find out for himself."

The phone was ringing inside, thank God. Vita made a dash for it, but reading the caller ID, she thrust it out toward LaRee. "It's Franco. I'm not here."

"Hello," LaRee sang.

"LaRee, it's Danielle." That flat, husky voice, reporting a matter of fact. It was Danielle and that meant trouble.

"What's wrong?"

"I just heard."

"Heard what?"

"Vinny's dead. That's what people are saying."

"What? How?"

"Suicide."

"Why?" Ridiculous to ask; he expected to spend the rest of his life in prison—the real question was why he hadn't tried before.

"His mom died yesterday. I guess you know."

"I didn't."

She explained how he'd done it. "They'll blame Franco," Danielle said with a heavy sigh. "Everyone will. It's like, somehow, if Franco had kept his pants on, the sun would always be shinin' and the cod would be leapin' right up into the boat." She was keeping her voice low and LaRee pictured her looking out her front window between the curtains, down over Main Street. "Always gotta blame someone...."

"Some people will blame me," LaRee said, to cheer her up. "It's more fun to blame a woman. We take it to heart. Men barely even notice."

"Yeah," Danielle agreed. "Honestly, I'd always blame a woman first. Men just bumble around trying to do what's right; it's women who plot and plan. I know myself well enough to be suspicious of women." LaRee laughed, a grim hoot of recognition at the backward pageantry of life, the secret undertow beneath every advancing wave. You had to be past fifty to laugh this way, and hearing Danielle join in, LaRee realized that they had continued their awkward truce for so long that it had become a kind of friendship. Ha, whoever knew what was coming? Who could predict...?

But Vita was watching her, with the eyes of a young girl who believed in Good and Evil still.

"Vinny always wanted to be just like Franco," Danielle said, almost to herself. "'Specially after his father died. He was always hanging around the boys, trying to act like he was one of the family."

"What is it?" Vita was mouthing. "What happened?"

"Danielle, Vita ... I've got to ..." It only struck LaRee now, what had happened. The murder had opened up beneath them suddenly, like an old well that ought to have been sealed. The day they arrested Vinny, Vita had been six years old. LaRee had gone to pick her up at school and found her playing hopscotch with Dorotea. The teacher had looked over their heads to her ... with concern, probably, but LaRee had read it as a plea not to disturb the little balance they all managed every day. How would she ever have explained the truth? She said nothing, and heaven only knew what anyone said to Dorotea. There were more headlines: "Home Invasion, or the Date from Hell?" "Mismatched Pair Sipped Wine Before Murder." Vinny's court-appointed lawyer insisted that Vinny didn't have the intelligence to have acted on his own, implying that Sabine had been his accomplice as well as his victim. The town was seized by a silent spasm. The explanation they had clung to—that a bad man from across the bridge, the kind of man a sophisticated woman like Sabine would have been likely to know in her earlier, more suspicious life, had followed her here and killed her—didn't work. It was Vinny Machado—and they discovered that when he told his wife that he could kill her as easily as he had Sabine Gray.

LaRee remembered seeing Vinny's wife with a black eye and wondering if Vinny was responsible for it ... and doing nothing more. She was a nurse; she had taken a seminar on recognizing domestic violence as part of her continuing education. This had entitled her to a raise, but it hadn't pushed her to action. She hadn't wanted to suspect Vinny—it would be awkward and messy to prove the suspicion; it would be the same old thing, a washashore assuming the worst of a townie. His wife would defend him. The police, who would turn out to be, in some circuitous way, related to him, would harden against her. She had let it go.

Who would sit a six-year-old child down and try to explain it all? No one, and certainly not anyone who had just managed to guide that child through a black grief toward the light. And then... the waters had closed. By the time Vinny was convicted, the girls were in third grade. Vita could read every word she saw, up to and including *tyrannosaurus*. "Special Edition: Verdict in Gray Trial" would have given her no trouble. LaRee got her home, unplugged the phone and the television, and started baking. As long as they were up to their elbows in butter and sugar, they were safe.

There were two sections of each grade; she made sure that Vita and Dorotea were never in the same group again. Dorotea herself would never hear the truth. It would go into the vault with the rest of the town's secrets, become the kind of thing that was rude to bring up. By middle school the girls would have different friends; by high school they'd be in different galaxies. When did you say it, when the child turned ten, or twelve? "Dorotea's dad slashed your mother with a fishing knife and we'll never know why, but from what we can guess she'd been flirting with him and he was snorting oxycodone and . . ." If Vita hadn't been so bad at geometry, she'd never have been in Dorotea's math section and she would have forgotten who she was by now.

No, LaRee had not told Vita, and over the years she had nearly forgotten it herself.

"Of course," Danielle said. "I'll see you at the funeral, I guess."

"You were right," LaRee said to Vita, sitting her down on the couch, holding her two hands tight. "It was something bad. Dorotea's father died."

"But he's in jail."

LaRee swallowed. Of course, Vita knew this much. That was the way it was in Oyster Creek. Some dads were in jail. Maybe for cocaine, assault and battery with a dangerous weapon (shod foot). One had scratched his girlfriend's name on a bullet and put the gun to her head.

"Did he have a heart attack, or ... ?"

"He killed himself."

"Wo-o-ow. Just wow." Vita was afraid of mothers dying, not fathers. Her eyes widened and she looked absolutely thrilled, just like the people who drove up the tabloid sales after her mother's death. "How do you commit suicide in jail?" she asked.

"He hung himself with his bedsheet; that's what Danielle said."

LaRee was grateful to see Vita nod. She'd been afraid she'd have to tell her what hanging was. Like all parents, she was used to keeping secrets. Who filled the Christmas stocking? What happened at Abu Ghraib? Why isn't my father married to my mother? Why didn't I go to live with him?

"With a bedsheet?"

"You can twist it up like a rope," LaRee said by rote, watching as the disaster approached....

"But what would you hook it to?"

"I ... Maybe the top bunk? I don't know."

"Why?"

"His mom died the night before—that's why we saw the ambulance, I suppose. Maybe he was sad about that, or he didn't want to kill himself while she was alive? I guess everyone in prison wants to die. The prison system in this country ... I don't know. We don't give people any reason to hope, any tools to make their lives better, then they act out of despair and we slam them in prison. We'd rather build more prisons than more schools," LaRee went on, blindly, playing for time. Building this house, with all these windows, they'd been thinking of sunlight. But when clouds lowered, as they did now, they could dim the room so completely it felt like being underwater. Rain started pelting, big drops of cold spring rain. Vita's face was in shadow.

"And just leave his family, Dorotea and her mom?" she said. "Now he'll never see them again, when if he'd just waited a little longer, he could have been with them."

"Mmm, it's true," LaRee said. Though it wasn't. Vinny had been sentenced to life.

"When was he supposed to get out?"

"Not for a long time."

How had the damned prison failed to keep him alive? Of course Vita would have learned the truth eventually, but the story would have come slowly into focus. By the time the whole picture came together, she'd be out in the world, she'd know how complex even the most ordinary things were. LaRee would explain how fragile Sabine had been, so lonely that she would almost assume another identity to seduce a man, so lonely that someone like Vinny might have seemed like a kindred spirit in some way. By then Vita, grown into a confident, thoughtful woman, would smile sadly—would understand.

"For holding up the SixMart with a souvenir machete?"

"That wasn't Vinny! That was Ed Callows off his meds."

"Oh, I always thought that was Vinny. But then, what did Vinny do?"

It was like that; you didn't remember how children outgrew the safety measures, pulled the covers off the outlets, sprung the gate at the top of the stairs.

"What?"

"What was his crime? Drugs . . . or . . ."

LaRee's throat closed. She remembered Vinny trying to talk to the parrot Della kept in the coffee shop—"Polly wanna cracka?" The parrot had repeated "Polly wanna cracka," in a mocking tone, and Vinny had suddenly tried to wrench the cage door open, but his big fingers wouldn't fit between the wires. He'd hit the cage, knocking it to the ground. The parrot squawked and flapped: "Closing time, closing time!" over and over in self-defense. And Vinny stood there, humiliated as always, a man who could be hurt into fury by a talking parrot. If Sabine had seemed to promise him love, and then denied it ...

"He killed someone." What choice was there? Her mind raced for some escape—take Vita away for a week until it all blew over, or ... But no—she'd have her laptop, she'd look at Facebook, in two clicks she'd be reading the *Herald*, and then ...

Vita's gaze snapped into focus.

"Who did he kill?"

"Vita, you were too young. ... I couldn't tell you; it would have been wrong. ... It ..."

"Him?" Vita said. "Dorotea's father killed my mom?"

LaRee nodded. Oh, how she wanted a cigarette, though she'd given them up the day Vita's adoption was final. She'd made a pact with fate: As long as she didn't smoke, Vita would be strong and happy. It made it almost easy to quit.

"Yes," she said. "He did."

"But why?" And before LaRee could answer, Vita grew up. Her face changed, and her posture, and she wasn't LaRee's child anymore.

"He killed my mother," she said quietly. LaRee would rather she had yelled. "And ... no one told me—you just let ... you let me go to school without knowing. But they all know, don't they? I'm the only idiot who didn't know."

"Vita, you were six years old when Vinny was arrested. You ... you'd survived it, your little self was so strong ... you found ways to grow and live. Your mother lived in you. That she wasn't here ... it was terrible, but her love was still in you. And you missed her.... But ..."

LaRee couldn't find the words. They talked often of Sabine, how excited she had been when she was pregnant, how she had called LaRee with every little story—the first time Vita had kissed her mother good night; her first ice-cream cone, consumed in pensive silence over a long half hour. They didn't speak of Sabine's death any more than they spoke of the ground they walked on. It was just always there.

"But there were some things it was easier not to tell me," Vita said now, in a high, accusing voice. It seemed she had spent her life cross-legged under a table while the adults whispered about her mother's murder above. And maybe that was good: It kept them from prying at her, dripping their sentimental pity into her wounds. They chose their words carefully, which was funny, because it was the tone—the little insinuations, the savage curiosity or the singsong smarminess with which someone would refuse to be curious—that had bored through and made an impression on her heart.

"Whether I needed to know or not, you didn't tell me. You just kept me here like some kind of pet, when I was a human being who deserved to know the truth."

"Vita, don't be silly."

"What choice do I have? Ignorant *is* silly! Vinny hung himself, in prison. Because of my mom!"

"No, Vita, he hung himself because he couldn't live with himself after what he did to your mom."

"You know what she was—a *whore!*"

"Vita! What on earth? Where did this come from? Your mom was a beautiful, wonderful woman who loved you and . . . she loved your father, too. She didn't do anything to anyone. Vinny murdered her, because he was a violent man and he was on . . . meth, or God knows what."

"And why did she let a violent, drugged man into the house?"

"Oh, honey . . . look, we don't lock our doors here, even now. Why wouldn't she have let Vinny in? He'd pumped her septic tank the day before. She probably thought he was bringing the bill."

"No . . . because she was just like he was—depraved."

"Where did you get this idea, Vita? Who ever even considered such a thing?"

"Just every person who's ever looked at me, that's who. Everyone at school . . . they all *know* what happened—people were honest with *them*. That's why they hate me. That's why. . . . You've been lying to me, all these years?" She jumped to her feet as if she couldn't bear it sitting down.

"Vita, stop this right now and listen to me." LaRee had almost never had to speak sharply to Vita before. "I may have done wrong by keeping this from you. Maybe I did. I didn't know what to do; I *don't* always know. But we will try to understand it together, and we will manage, just like we've managed everything else."

Vita had stopped and taken a deep breath, just as LaRee had asked her to. LaRee reached to take her hands.

Vita spun away as if she were resisting the most pernicious temptation she had ever faced. "No!" she said. "No. No."

And she ran out the door, down the driveway, onto the street. It was so quiet, that spring quiet: no traffic on the highway yet. LaRee could hear every footfall. In cross-country season five miles a day was nothing. Who knew how far those long young legs would carry her? But maybe that was best; let her run it out of her system. The sense of her own strength would buoy her up, calm her.

The footsteps stopped, and a shriek echoed across the pond. It was as if a trapdoor had opened and dropped them back to that first night, when Vita had no words and there was nothing to do but howl in fear and fury.

PART THREE

15

SOMETHING IN COMMON

It was one thing to run away. But where did you run to? Vita didn't even ask herself at first. She flew down the long driveway, along the road toward the highway, breathing the wet spring air, the fresh scent blowing in off the bay. She felt as fast as a tiger, in love with the way her legs worked, the deliberate rhythm of her steps, down one hill and up the next without quickening or slowing. The pond lay still and black in its hollow. Coming to the top of Tavern Hill, she stopped, not to catch her breath but to notice she didn't need to— she could have run for days. The town with its three steeples on interlaced hills lay below her, the harbor with Barrel Point curving protectively around, then the long reach of the bay, and Plymouth a distant shadow on the other side. This little view, which she saw nearly every day of her life, touched a nerve in her now, as if it were an enchanted place that she could never return to. And where else could she go? The highway that came all the way from California ended ten miles north of here at a little roundabout in the middle of a salt marsh, as if to say, "Three thousand miles, and you're still in the middle of nowhere."

There *was* a bus. It came through at seven thirty in the morning and five in the evening, and you could change in Hyannis for Providence or Boston or New York. She had five dollars in her pocket, but her wallet was in her backpack, dropped by the front door at home. She could go to the harbormaster's office, she supposed, and ask Franco for money—except he was worse even than LaRee. He had kept the same secrets, told the same lies she had. She was not going to start relying on a traitor now. If only there were a rehearsal, where she could be safely following a script! Except there was only a tiny part for her in that script. Even they believed in Shyanne, not in her.

That was when she screamed, like an animal caught in a trap. LaRee would hear—she wanted LaRee to hear. Vita had grown up in the shadow of this murder, been shaped by it even as she became beautiful and strong. LaRee had protected her, fed and clothed and guided and comforted her, and Vita had picked up her speech patterns, her mannerisms, her way of singing to herself while she worked, her way of looking at the world around her ... everything. And now—it was all woven through with lies! If Vita wanted to escape the lies, and the murder, it would mean tearing herself away from everything that sustained her. She wanted LaRee to know how it felt.

LaRee stayed still in the doorway, biting her knuckle, long after the echo subsided. Where would Vita go? Maybe the library? It was in the old Presbyterian church and it still felt like a safe and sacred place. She'd collect herself in the quiet there and soon would come a text message: "Sry, so dumb. Come get me? Xoxo." And LaRee would reply, "Not dumb at all. See you soon. Xoxo." And they'd get pizza at the Walrus and bring it home, and LaRee would apologize and Vita would be understanding; then they'd sit down and probably figure out a way to help Dorotea and her mother—victims of the same man, after all. . . .

She heard a truck downshift, hurtling along the highway—probably the fish truck coming from Provincetown, the driver anxious to get back home to Fall River now. How long had she been standing there, pulling her sleeves over her hands, not wanting to move, to admit Vita had really gone? The sun found a thin place in the fog and struck sparkles against the dark surface of the pond. And there, the phone was ringing.

"Hi, honey."

"Ms. Farnham? Hi, this is Sue Salatin from the *Herald*."

Well, of course it was. She didn't know Sue Salatin, but she knew how the phone would ring whenever there was a new wrinkle in the case. Twelve years ago it had shrilled incessantly; then nine years ago when Vinny was tried, it had begun again. . . . By that time, Vita had reached the age of intuition and could have put everything together from overhearing three words and seeing a tension in LaRee's shoulders. "I'm sure you've heard that Vinny Machado has taken his own life."

"Yes, I have, thank you." This was where you said, "I have no comment," and hung up. But LaRee was just stupid enough to feel guilty for being short with a tabloid journalist.

"Does this change anything, from your point of view?"

"What would it change?" she asked. Why was she getting into this conversation?

"Do you feel he's escaped justice, evaded the penalty handed down by the court?"

LaRee laughed. "By hanging himself? No . . . I just . . . I'm just sorry, sorry about the whole thing."

"Why would you be sorry?"

"What else would I be? It's loss and heartbreak all around."

"So, you think he got what he deserved?" This girl had probably been in high school when Sabine died. She and her friends might have giggled over Franco's picture in *Cosmopolitan*. *Would you date this murder suspect?*

"What do people deserve?" LaRee asked her. "I mean, what would you say Vinny deserved?"

"Well, I don't know. I'm not close to the case."

"What do you deserve, do you think? When you sum up your life?"

"Excuse me?"

"I'm sorry for his family," LaRee said. "That's really all."

She put the receiver back very gently, so she wasn't so much hanging up on the woman as causing her to evaporate. Nurses must nurse; reporters must report. There was no reason for anger. Even the snoozy old *Oyster Creek Oracle* had roused itself to publish a special edition the day Vinny was sentenced, with two photos: one of Vinny looking back over his shoulder as he left the court and one of Vita, standing on the bench in front of the school as LaRee buttoned up her coat. The photographer, maddened by this chance at glory, had literally jumped out from behind a school bus to take the picture, scattering mothers and children like pigeons so as to catch LaRee's hands carefully buttoning as Vita stood straight and still, the image of a good little girl. He had caught a true moment, and LaRee still had a copy of the picture on her dresser.

LaRee still entertained herself by imagining her life in tabloid headlines: "Slay-Tot Speaks Out: Stepmom Lied."

It occurred to her suddenly that Sue Salatin might be calling from downtown. God knew who was waiting there to pounce on an unsuspecting child. LaRee had imagined Vita running past the Walrus and Carpenter, the pharmacy, and the *Fishermen's Memorial,* the bronze fisherman statue in the roundabout at the top of Sea Street, pulling open the heavy library door and dropping into an armchair to take comfort from the ticking of the grandfather clock. She'd imagined the town would keep Vita safe. But she'd forgotten that the thing that shattered when Sabine was killed had left a shard in every heart, and that old wounds would reopen now. God knew what anyone would say—the reporters were sharks; they'd fight one another for a bite of her. She dialed Vita's cell phone and heard a muffled "Hips Don't Lie" start playing across the room. Of course. Vita's phone was in her backpack, right there by the door.

"It's for your own good." That was what adults always said, how they rationalized every stupid thing they did. For Vita's own good, LaRee had scrambled the story, never mind that the story was all Vita had left of her mother. If Sabine really had been killed by a stranger—a bad man who had come over the bridge like rabies and was locked in prison now—everything would have been different. But no, Sabine had been murdered by a man she saw every day . . . who had slashed at her with a fishing knife and left her bleeding on the floor. A stranger wouldn't have guessed Vita was upstairs. A neighbor . . . Vinny Machado . . . He knew he was killing somebody's mother! That Vita would come down the stairs in her little footie pajamas in the morning, and find . . . No wonder everyone laughed at her. She was the only person in town who didn't know the real story of her own life! What a fool, what a stupid little fool.

She was not going to stay foolish; she was going to find out. What did she know, really, about her mother, except that she had slept with a married man and lived in Italy for a while, and been

LaRee's friend at college. Who could know, with LaRee guarding all the secrets, making up convenient fairy tales instead? What LaRee had hidden from her—these were the most important things in the world!

Coming down Sea Street, Vita saw what she thought was the Outer Cape Seafood truck parked at the harbormaster's shack, then realized it had a satellite dish on top. It was the mobile news from WHUB in Boston. The front door of the shack was wide open and the phone was ringing. She put her head in and found the office empty. In the back room the kayaks rested across the rafters and the rubber boots were lined up against the wall. The smell of brine and seaweed struck her broadside—it was the smell that had meant she was visiting Franco when she was little, a smell of hope and trepidation. Would he really be glad to see her? Would he be the father she imagined, or the awkward, distracted man who usually met her on these days? She started to cry. How had she even gotten here? She had run away from home and her feet had just carried her down the hill to the harbor, to her father . . . her dad. "My dad," people said, so simply, as if it weren't anything important at all. Had she ever in her life said "my dad"? No, and she'd sworn he didn't matter, and yet, here she was.

And there he was, leading the reporter and cameraman to the very end of the pier, where the *Rainha* was tied. She'd been rusting there for as long as Vita could remember, her net reel thick with seaweed, the cabin door rotting like a tooth. Why did Franco have to take the reporters all the way out to the end of the wharf? To be near his poor wreck of a boat? Or because it was the right backdrop for a boatswain? It caught the sense they were looking for, of some kind of real, concrete life, the kind of life all the people watching longed for. Franco in his peacoat, the restless water behind him, the boat with its rust and rot and seaweed . . . a whole man, with a life fully lived. Who wouldn't watch him with fascination?

The camera rolled; Vita watched from just inside the back door. Franco was speaking into the microphone, talking and talking. He was the foremost authority on the murder, called in yet again to explain it to the world, and he had the look, the stance of a man who was doing something Very Important. The wind switched and she could hear the reporter's voice: " . . . your daughter, Franco?"

"Oh, she's, she's fine," he said, but for once he had no answer; he was at a loss for words. Sabine had left him two things: a daughter, and a spotlight. And he sure did love that spotlight! She thought of running down the pier, grabbing the mike and pushing him away— one step back and he'd be in the water. Then she would say, "You want to know how his daughter is? This is how!"

As if she had the guts to do such a thing, but no, she was small as a mouse, quiet as a mouse, and like a mouse she edged along the wall out of sight. His bicycle was leaning there, and she took it, wheeling it around to the front of the shack while the others were distracted by the cameras, swinging a leg over and heading down Breakwater Road around the harbor. The marsh grass was a bright, cold green, and a man was mowing the lawn at the Winthrop Inn. All of life going on by quiet rote—how did it happen, how could that be? A man had killed a woman, left a motherless child, gone to prison, and finally had hung himself, in shame and despair . . . and there was another man coming out of the hardware store with a brand-new ladder, and a young couple crossing the little bridge over the marsh, holding hands. The most terrible thing was just another thread woven through ordinary life. That bridge led to a sandy path around the edge of an island, and then, except at the highest tide, to Sedge Point, where Adam lived. What would happen if she knocked on his door? She'd like to imagine he would take her in, understand it all, and they could run away together, hitchhiking across the country, sleeping in barns, doing odd jobs to earn their meals. She had read too many books. Adam's thoughtfulness made him awkward—if he saw her at the door he'd panic as he tried to think of the right thing to say, and say just the wrong thing, and she of course would say the wrong thing, too, and very soon she would say she had to leave, just because she wanted to save him from his embarrassment, and she'd see how grateful he was to see the last of her. So it was probably good luck that the bike wouldn't go on the sand path. The seat was too high for her, so she stood to pedal, and with each stroke the bike raced forward, carrying her past that turn, toward the day when she would leave here altogether and for good.

It occurred to her now that she wasn't alone. There was a whole community of the bereaved; almost everyone belonged. Most people had some hole in their lives, an abyss they spent every day toeing around, so their lives weren't so much aimed at getting anywhere, but just not sliding back into the dark. It was funny to think she'd been feeling left out, as if she had to be valedictorian or class president or the star of some show in order to belong—when she had been one of the group all the time. She might be failing geometry, but if there were a standardized test for living with grief, she would be in the ninety-ninth percentile.

And Dorotea Machado would need a tutor now. At the highway, Vita turned south toward Fox Hollow, and the Driftwood Cabins.

LaRee didn't like her riding her bike on the highway, though everyone did it. On the map, you could see how delicate the cape was, long and narrow and frayed into points and inlets like a rag, riddled with bogs and ponds and the streams that ran between them, with estuaries that forked so far inland they nearly reached the other shore. Out here, the strip of land was so thin there were only a few miles between the bay and the ocean, with the highway running straight down the middle, the only connection between one bumpy road and the next. And LaRee didn't understand that Vita had grown up, that she could fight her own battles, get where she wanted to go without help. There was a lot LaRee didn't understand. She hadn't been there when Sabine died. Vita didn't remember it, but only because it had become part of her, like another organ: her heart, her lungs, her liver, her mourning. Now that both Sabine and Vinny were dead, Vita was the only one left who *had* been there, though every single person in town had the story in his imagination, pinned to whichever truth he or she preferred.

Vita and Dorotea barely knew each other, though they took the same school bus every day. Dorotea was surrounded by her family, which was half the town by the time you counted the in-laws and cousins. She moved along, expressionless, following the Gelfa traditions, serving at the Our Lady altar, giving the censer a swing as Father Lomba laid out the cloth for communion. She worked at Skipper's takeout window, handing over a clam roll between two paper plates, pointing out the condiments, moving the orders down the line. She had been allowed to see only one movie in her life: *The Passion of the Christ*. Who would have guessed they had something in common?

A cold misery pierced Vita, a shard of the bleakness that would cause a man to take his own life. She pedaled as fast as she could, to get this stretch of highway over with. A car passed so close it nearly brushed her knee. Shyanne and her friend Steph were coming along on foot, both in burgundy dresses with white aprons: the waitstaff uniform at Pizza by the Sea. Vita rode out around them and they looked straight ahead as if they hadn't seen her.

She was riding so hard she felt as if the bicycle would take flight. Dorotea was the other person in town, maybe on earth, who had seen the underside of everything the same as she had. She swooped right, down Point Road, over the bridge and past what she and La-Ree called "the renovation house" because carpenters or landscapers or plumbers were always working on it, but never once had they seen anyone who appeared to live there. That was on the water side of the street, where the houses cost millions, which meant, oddly enough, that the people who owned them had many houses and didn't spend very much time in any of them. On the other side, backed up to the woods of the National Seashore, lived the people who could barely afford their one house—many in the Driftwood Cabins, a colony of tourist cottages turned to year-round rentals, and, on the two dirt roads that snaked around behind it, houses built on lots made of "fill" along the edges of the salt marsh.

It would be illegal to build here now, but Bobby Matos had sold this land as cheap building lots back when nobody thought about protecting the wetlands. Single-story houses with a few little windows on each side, a truck parked in back and maybe a shed for the oyster gear. It felt lonely here in spite of the beauty of the marsh. Or maybe because of it: the green flaring against the silver estuary, silent and full of mystery—it looked like you could paddle around a bend into another world. But instead you were in this world, where everyone was too tired and worried and frustrated with life to look out the window.

She found the Machado house by the wrought-iron sign affixed beside the door, with the name printed under a clipper ship. Their Christmas decorations were still up: a wreath gone brown and a tall plastic candle in a red base tipped over beside the front steps, as if a burst of good feeling in December had sagged back into discouragement. Vita leaned the bike against the side wall, just uphill from the basement window, through which a pump was draining spurts of brown water.

Her stomach turned; revulsion gave onto fear. She was about to get back on the bike and ride home except that a man came out of a house three doors down and shot a curious look at her, so she felt constrained to act normal, which meant somehow that she had to continue with an errand that seemed stupid and even dangerous now.

She rapped on the door, setting off a dog inside, but got no human response until finally a woman called, "Shut up, Viper, just shut up." The door opened a crack and Vita looked up into the dark, wary eyes of Maria Machado, Vinny's widow, Dorotea's mom.

"Hi," Vita said. "I . . . was out on my bike and I thought maybe Dorotea . . ." She didn't know how to finish the sentence but it didn't matter. Mrs. Machado's face relaxed and she pushed her hair back, wiping her hands on her T-shirt, to open the door. Viper was a big German shepherd with a long nose, wagging his tail in frantic welcome even as he continued to howl.

"Here," Mrs. Machado said, grabbing the dog's collar with both hands. Feet planted firmly, she threw all her weight back and managed to yank the dog inch by unwilling inch into the bathroom, and shut the door. There was a powerful stench; Vita tried to breathe through her mouth.

"Here, come in. I was just trying to get some chores done. . . ." She flapped a hand in the direction of a disorder such as Vita couldn't have imagined. There was a big television in the living room, and across from it a bare mattress with piles of clothing heaped on it. A refrigerator, a stove with a crusted pot on one burner, and a cupboard with cups hanging from hooks made a kind of kitchen along one side of the room. A half-full can of chicken soup sat on top of the dishes piled in the sink.

"I just can't seem to keep up with it," Mrs. Machado said. "I'm working double shifts and with . . . everything . . ."

Something moved in the corner—a spotted rabbit. It nosed along beside the mattress, stopping to relieve itself in the folds of a damp bath towel.

"Precious, now look!" Mrs. Machado said. "Dotty! Dotty? I have asked Dorotea to keep her in the cage," she said, "but you know how kids are, and I can't do everything around here. The vacuum's broken, that's the problem."

A door opened and Dorotea emerged.

"Oh, hey," she said, seeing Vita.

"It's your friend from school," Mrs. Machado said. Dorotea pulled in her chin—she had no friends at school and Vita knew that. Mrs. Machado was wearing clean lavender scrubs and white sneakers. When she left the house she would bring no trace of its disorder into the world. But the effort to appear whole would cost her so dearly that when she returned she would have to fall onto the mattress and stare at the soap operas just for the sake of a glimpse of ordinary life. To be able to say to her daughter, "It's your friend from school," was a luxury for her. If Vita could make her happy by acting the part, why not?

"Hi," Vita said. "I just thought . . . would you like to go get some ice cream?"

Dorotea looked at her as if she had gone mad.

"Ice cream?" Mrs. Machado said. "Ice cream! At the drive-in. Here, I've got . . ." She rummaged through the clothing on the bed until she found her purse, and scratched around in it until she found two dollar bills and a handful of change. "Ice cream. A nice day for two friends from school to go get some ice cream."

"Mom," Dorotea said, shrinking back into the doorway. "You wanted me to clean."

"Not when your friend from school is here," her mother said, pleading.

"It's so hot inside," Vita said. "Do you want to take a walk?"

"I don't open the windows," Mrs. Machado said. "The airs from the marsh, they're no good."

This alone made Vita dizzy. "I shouldn't have come," she admitted, leaning back against the wall, letting truth leak into her voice.

"Don't be rude to your friend," Mrs. Machado said now, poking the folded bills at Dorotea. "Go. Get ice cream." The dog began to bark again when she raised her voice. "'Go,' I said. I'm going to work."

"Will . . . will the rabbit be okay?" Vita asked, as they left the house. "The dog won't . . . do anything to it, will he?"

Dorotea rolled her eyes, shut the door and started down the steps. "Nobody likes you," she said. It was hard to tell if she meant this as an insult or an observation.

"I know," Vita said. "Well . . . Abby and Sarah like me."

"Nobody important, I mean."

"Who's important?"

Dorotea looked at Vita as if this question revealed a bottomless ignorance. "I don't have a bike. We have to walk."

"Oh, okay. I'll leave mine here."

"Well, yeah, where else would you leave it?"

They started down the road together.

"I heard about . . . you know . . ." Vita began.

"I don't know what you mean," Dorotea said.

"Well, I'm sorry," Vita said, though somehow it sounded more belligerent than sympathetic.

Dorotea said nothing. They scuffed along in the pine needles at the edge of the road.

"So, I sort of thought I should come over. Because, you know, we have something in common."

Again, nothing.

"And I don't have rehearsal today," Vita said. "I'm in *The Tempest*, you know, down at the park."

"Shyanne's the star, right?" There, Dorotea had hit where she was aiming. Her own life had been a series of blows and her usual choice was between escape and retaliation. Vita had left her no avenue of escape.

"I'm playing Iris, the goddess of the rainbow," Vita said.

"That's not a good part, is it?"

They rounded the bend at the back of the Driftwood Cabins and came out behind the Tradescome house, and the vista of the wide blue bay rose up to confront them.

"It's not," Vita said, in self-defense. "But my dad's in it, too, and it's nice to be doing something together."

That backed Dorotea into a corner. "Yeah," she said. "I only have my mom."

"That's why I came. Because . . . you could say we both have the same problem," Vita said. By now she barely remembered that she had meant to be kind.

"He didn't kill her," Dorotea hissed. "Get away from me."

"I'm your 'friend from school,' remember?" Vita said. Her tongue had been freed; it was frightening. "He was convicted of murder by a jury, and his appeal was refused."

"Doesn't mean he killed anyone," Dorotea said in a singsong.

"D . . . N . . . A! DNA, that's what! Did you fail biology, too? He killed someone! My mother!" Vita yelled this into Dorotea's shuttered face, causing something to flicker there before Dorotea looked up at the sky and broke into a chant.

"Did not, did not, did not! Loser, loser, loser! Everyone knows you're a big loser! Nobody likes you!"

The truth had felt so good, Vita couldn't stop. "And it's not your fault! You were just a baby, like me."

"La, la, la, la, I can't hear you!"

They headed up Point Road, behind the big fancy houses. Screaming began to feel inappropriate.

"I said," Vita said, lowering her voice, "that it's not your fault what your father did."

"You don't get to say what's my fault and what isn't, loser."

A truck rattled by—Dorotea's mother on her way to work.

"Friend from school?" Dorotea shouted after she passed. "It's Vita Gray, you retard!" But her mother's windows were up.

"Okay, forget it. I'll go back to your house and get my bike and go home," Vita said. "Your mom won't know we didn't go."

Dorotea kept walking. "What's your favorite ice cream?" she asked suddenly.

"Peppermint."

Dorotea glanced over. "I like chocolate," she said, as if this was proof that she was better than Vita. "I pray for you every night."

"What?"

"Because you're a heathen."

"What's a heathen?"

"See, you don't even know that. It's someone who doesn't have a religion, so they don't have any morals. So, I pray that you'll, you know, abstain until marriage and stuff."

"You pray that every night?"

"Well, sometimes I pray you'll find God, but I always pray for you."

"*You* pray for *me*?"

"Someone has to."

"Do you pray for Kayla?"

"Why would I pray for Kayla? It's not like she's getting an abortion or anything."

"It's not like she abstained until marriage, either. I mean, your father is . . . was . . . a murderer. Your house smells of shit. You look like a melted candle, the way you drag around. Why don't you pray for yourself?"

Vita covered her mouth with her hand—she couldn't believe she'd said such things. But she'd had to, to keep Dorotea from binding her up in these ideas.

"*My dad* would have lived with me if he could," Dorotea said quietly. It was the winning stroke, and with it she became graceful. "I still feel bad about it," she admitted, in the same dull, automatic voice.

"About what?" Vita guessed what—the day in kindergarten when they were supposed to play together after school. She wouldn't have thought Dorotea would remember.

"Yeah, the time they wouldn't let you come over," Dorotea said.

"Oh, yeah . . . I'd forgotten about that." In fact Vita could still see Dorotea running across the playground toward her, holding out the tiny note that read *Monday*, a scrap as small as a fortune cookie message.

"Don't worry about it," she said to Dorotea now. It was the last thing she wanted to talk about. "It happened like a century ago. It's not important."

"No, but they shouldn't have. . . ." Dorotea was trying to lift her head and speak out her own thoughts, and the honest attempt changed everything.

"It was so sad," Vita admitted. "I still remember. I guess I understand it better now, though."

"What do you mean?"

"Well, I thought your family was afraid of me because of . . . what happened, like you'd catch my disease or something. . . .Like revenge of the green slime—and you didn't want it getting all over you."

"Yeah, that was kind of it," Dorotea said, smugly, goading Vita.

"But really it was the other way around. His—your father's—awfulness had gotten all over me and he didn't want to see me because of it."

"That's not what it was. He didn't want me to play with you because you don't go to church. He was afraid you'd corrupt me."

"How do five-year-olds corrupt each other?"

"You know . . . like you'd convince me to do stuff that was wrong."

"Like what? Jumping in mud puddles?"

"Like you'd think it was right for a woman to have a married man's baby," Dorotea said, pious.

"Or I'd think it was right for murderers to go to jail."

"He didn't *kill* anyone!" Dorotea shrieked this, with her hands over her ears for fear of the reply. They were walking along the highway now and someone honked—probably Brandon or some other creep from school. Vita felt as if there were a brawl going on in her head—all the things she had thought and been told were punching and kicking each other and upending the tables.

"He killed himself," she said, in a high, triumphant voice. "So he has killed at least one person."

"You're not supposed to talk about that," Dorotea said.

"So, is that the kind of thing your father thought I'd corrupt you into doing? Talk about the people he killed? And at night, before you go to sleep, do you pray that I won't talk about it?" She felt herself taking the wrong path, but she couldn't stop. If she didn't confront all this . . . wrongness . . . right here, her whole life might be controlled by it, and the truth would be lost, and Sabine would be lost. Surely there was some way to be honest *and* kind? She couldn't find it.

"You'll end up in hell," Dorotea said.

"Is your father in hell?"

"You're a monster. Only a monster would say something like that. That's why nobody likes you. You're a monster and you never should have been born."

Then she whispered: "Daddy's in heaven, heaven, heaven," and sat down in the weeds at the side of the road with her forehead to her knees.

Vita sat beside her, pushing aside some little whiskey bottles, the right size for a doll. There were fiddleheads coming up out of the sand, like the ones in the stories LaRee used to tell her, about mice who lived in the woods. The mice would pull two of the scrolled fern tops together with a strand of grass to make the arch for their wedding chapel. An ache opened in the back of Vita's throat; she tried to swallow.

"My mother is dead, your father is dead," she said carefully, setting out plain facts one by one. "We need to try to stop the . . . the green slime, before it does any more damage."

She had no idea what this might mean, but keeping herself calm in the face of Dorotea's hysteria felt good, so she wanted to continue. It was a little like standing on a surfboard, trying to keep her balance as each new wave struck; with every lurch she was more aware of her own strength and stability.

"What are you talking about?" Dorotea said.

"Why would he kill her? Why would anyone kill anyone?"

"Everyone hated her."

"I didn't hate her."

"She did something to him, so he had to kill her. . . ."

"What could that be?"

"I don't know," Dorotea said, beginning to cry softly into her knees. "She was a slut," she said, weeping as she tried to explain. "She'd spread her legs for anyone." The cars were passing so close that Vita felt a dull awareness that they were in danger. "My dad wasn't a bad man," Dorotea continued. "Not until he met her. My mom made him mad sometimes, but he loved her."

The TV truck came over the rise way too fast , swerving when the driver saw them, nearly hitting Matt Paradel's pickup head-on. Vita took Dorotea by the shoulders and pulled her back away from the road, rolling over her, pulling her into the culvert .

"What is wrong with you?" Dorotea said, fighting her off. "Get offa me!"

"I'm trying to save your life, stupid."

"I don't want you to save my life, you queer." Dorotea stood up and brushed herself off. "Like you could save anyone's life—look at you! Who do you think you are? You and your stupid green slime. You don't know anything except that you think you're so much better than me, even though you're a bastard and your mother got herself killed from whoring." She started walking back toward Point Road. Over her shoulder she said, "Save your own goddamn life."

Vita watched her. She had no idea what to do next. What would LaRee have done? She always seemed to know. Even when LaRee was wrong, you could tell she was obeying some inner compass, working toward kindness. And that gave her courage—she would take over without even realizing what she was doing, because she trusted her impulses. When a fisherman came into the clinic with a hook embedded in his hand, having been damned if he was going to come all the way back into port at midmorning and lose one of the few fishing days he was allowed, LaRee was the one who could lance the wound, push the hook through and snip off the point, all the while lecturing the guy so sharply that he barely noticed the pain. She didn't go around *wanting* to save people's lives; she just did it because somebody had to.

"Wait!" Vita called, standing up, plucking at her pant legs, damp from the ground.

"What?" Dorotea kept walking.

"You're right."

She stopped. "What do you mean?"

Vita wasn't sure, except that she knew people would listen to you if you began your sentence with "You're right." "Everyone has to save their own life."

"Not me," Dorotea said. "My life is fine."

She turned off, into the woods. There was a spot where the ditch narrowed so you could step over it. The grass was worn away there—Dorotea and anyone else walking into town from the Drift-wood Cabins could save time by cutting through the woods, and enough of them brushed through the overgrowth every day that they had made a narrow path. Dorotea had taken Vita around by the road, either because Vita was too dainty to be exposed to the poison ivy and the catbriar looped like razor wire through the trees or because the path was a secret privilege not to be shared with her. It was a place for kids to drink and smoke dope, a way for people to get to the SixMart for beer and cigarettes and doughnuts and lottery tickets and the other small comforts they relied on back in the Cabins, and since it was a secret it had become a point of pride, of belonging. Dorotea was not going to share it with anyone, most certainly not with Vita Gray. She stood on the other side of the ditch—her side—and said, "It's you who ought to be ashamed."

16

KIDS

The mother fox had brought the cubs out from under the shed. That was how still LaRee had been, leaning in the doorframe, staring without seeing while the argument, and Vita's life, passed through her mind over and over. Twenty minutes, had it been, or an hour? The clouds were moving away and the sun angled in from the west, making a warm spot for the cubs to bat and pounce while their mother napped beside them.

It was only a few years since Vita had dreamed of taking a fox family in as pets. She still had her child's sense that she could become friends with any bright-eyed creature. . . . She and LaRee had fed chickadees from their palms so often that all they had to do was reach a hand up and birds would flit down to settle. To think of Vita running out to pick a parsley sprig for dinner, or starting off up the road to pick blueberries on a July afternoon . . . Their hill was a storybook of sunlit adventures, set like bricks in a wall against the past. She should have remembered the way walls come down. A slap of anger hit her over, of all things, the day ten years ago when Dorotea had been supposed to come over to make a gingerbread house. That insipid sheep of a kindergarten teacher telling Vita she must be respectful of those who excluded her. Then LaRee caught herself: murder, imprisonment, suicide . . . and she blamed the sentimentalist? The teacher had moved away; she was probably selling bumper stickers somewhere now.

Maybe LaRee should have taken that as a signal to move away, to start fresh. Vita had been so young she might have forgotten all of it, even forgotten Sabine. Once Vinny was arrested, LaRee had felt an obligation to stick here, to show them (whoever "they" were—Amalia and anyone else who'd ever looked at her cross-eyed) that this was her home, too. "They" seemed to blame her, as if it were Sabine's fault, and by extension LaRee's fault, that Vinny had committed murder and was going to jail.

She should have moved, sold the house and left the whole misbegotten thing behind. It wasn't like she was a shellfish farmer; nurses could always find work. Drew, in his guilt, had deeded the house to her for a dollar; she could have sold it, bought a condo in Boston, started a new life. She saw herself fumbling for keys on the front steps of a brownstone in a golden autumn light, with a little mitten-clad hand held tight in hers . . .

She's a nurse at Mercy Hospital, has a little girl. I don't think there's a man in the picture.

That was what the neighbors would say. No more. Nurses were like chipmunks: ubiquitous, unnoticed. Vita would have spent her weekends with Franco until the relationship attenuated and he became a distant memory, an ache on a rainy day. Sabine—she would have become a beautiful story, her life a creative adventure, a treasure for Vita to build on. The problem was not that LaRee hadn't told the truth to Vita; it was that she hadn't made up a big enough lie. LaRee herself might have met someone, a guy like Matt, only single, and when she felt safe enough she'd have confided it all, the murder and how she'd felt she had to leave. The story would weave the silk of family tighter between them; they'd have married.... She could see Vita playing with a dollhouse while she and this man made dinner. She'd have read about Vinny's death in the paper—the last chapter of an awful story. And then she'd have closed the newspaper and gone to pick up Vita—a Vita whose hair billowed into curls, who was a bit of a science geek, planning to go to college pre-med—at her school. And she wouldn't have mentioned it, not because she was keeping a secret but because it had slipped her mind.

But no, she hadn't had the courage to tear her own roots out of the soil here. She'd told herself things would settle down, go back to normal, as if that were even possible. She'd wanted to keep Vita near Franco, near the place she knew as home. Had she imagined the tide would wash over and smooth everything as clean and fresh as the morning beach?

Did you ever know for certain that any action was for the good? An hour ago, when Vita ran down the driveway, LaRee had been sure it was right to let her go. Vita was sixteen, she was learning to make her own choices, and LaRee had to learn not to rush in every time with her own answer to a problem. Vita had reason to be angry, and at her age there was no difference between being mad at the world and mad at your mom. She would escape, go downtown and maybe bump into Hugh or Adam or someone who'd cheer her up a bit. She'd come home, and she and LaRee would sit down and think things through. All of which would have made sense if Vita had been upset over a boy or a test score or any of the ordinary things. But leaving a girl whose life was made of grief to manage the next terrible consequence by herself? Was she out of her mind? She ran to the car, backed it around, and headed down the hill into town.

And into the fog. Everything was lavender, murky, unknown. The light turned red just as she reached it and she waited while the fish truck from Provincetown went by, then the mail truck, then the bus.

The bus. She followed it down Hallett Way, parked behind it when it stopped at the pharmacy, went in. Kyle Monder was there buying a ticket and a pack of cigarettes, his hood up as if to conceal his face. Behind the counter, Mary Attlekin rang him up and handed him his change and he went out the door, keeping his head low. Ashamed of . . . everything. Born because two wretched souls found a minute of warmth together, alive the way blind creatures are alive miles under the sea. Aware, in the vaguest way, that others lived in the light. Kyle got on the bus; the driver stood there for another minute, looking up and down the street, tossed his cigarette in the gutter, swung into his seat and pulled away.

"He's off to Boston, huh?" LaRee asked.

"Yeah, his dad lives up there," Mary said. "Boy, you couldn't get me up there."

"Not a Boston fan?"

"I don't like cities," Mary said. "I lived in Holyoke when I first had the twins. . . . Oh, no, you're not going to get me into a city. I do not like cities."

"Have you been to New York?"

"Nope. And got no plans."

"Mary, has Vita been in this afternoon?"

"Haven't seen her."

"If you do, would you ask her to call me?"

"I'm closing up in fifteen minutes."

"Well, just in case."

"She giving you trouble?"

"I'm a little worried about her, that's all."

Mary gave her a hard little glance. "Teenagers," she said with disdain, though as far as LaRee knew she was still a teenager herself. "Nothin' but trouble."

The lights were on in the library. The tall arched windows advertised warmth and comfort, thoughtful ease. It had been the Presbyterian church, built in 1857 when the town was a thriving port. It was said that you could walk across the bay to Plymouth on the backs of the whales then, and the sea captains built churches as solid and ornate as their homes, so God would see they were grateful. Mackerel Bay had been full of mackerel. By 1898, kerosene had replaced whale oil, steamships were replacing clipper ships, and mackerel were as scarce as Presbyterians. The church steeple was torn off in the Portland Gale and never rebuilt. A few steely fishermen from the Azores had found their way to town, and sent for their families, and built the Catholic church across the street. Presbyterians attended one another's funerals, their knobbed fingers folded in their laps, while weddings and christenings spilled from the doors of Our Lady, Star of the Sea. In 1995 a man who'd summered in Wellfleet and made millions in the first wave of the Internet boom bought the derelict church building and gave it to the town to use as a library.

LaRee unlatched the arched door into the entry. The place was silent except for Margaret Capshaw, who looked like a greyhound, running in place as she read the bulletin board. Was she addicted to exercise, and if so, why? Or was LaRee just jealous, not of the thinness but of the ability to change the course of one's life? Two curved staircases ascended on either side and she took the left one for the high window that looked out over Sedge Point, treading lightly on the stairs, aware of the muffling effect of the carpet, as if Vita were a fawn in the woods and she had to keep from startling her. The children's room was empty, but she heard a page turn above and continued up to the reading room on the third floor.

A girl was reading there, in one of the leather wing chairs with a view over the harbor—Fiona Tradescome. Her hair shone in the lamplight and she pushed it out of her face, looking up with a smile. She was two years older than Vita and light-years more poised.

"Hi, LaRee," she said brightly, and LaRee had to blink back tears suddenly. Why had this girl had a safe, solid life of the kind that left a person at ease in the world when Vita had so much to bear? Fiona played the violin and people would talk about it, how ironic that Henry Tradescome's daughter had that talent when Henry himself had lost the use of his right hand in the last polio epidemic.

"Hi, Fiona. How are you?"

"I'm good. Are you looking for something?"

"I'm looking for Vita."

"I've been up here for an hour, I guess, and I haven't seen her," Fiona said.

"Oh, well, she probably . . ." The pier lights started to come on, one by one, out the window. Where would Vita go, in the dark? "We probably just got our signals crossed," LaRee said. "If you see her, would you ask her to call me?"

"Sure," Fiona said. "I'm sure everything's fine, though."

"I am too, honey. Thank you." She started toward the stairs, then turned back, uncertain.

"Do you want me to . . . Is there anything else I can do to help?" Fiona asked.

Yes, I need your self-possession for Vita. You have two parents and that should be enough for anyone. That was what LaRee thought. "No, no," she said. "She's probably home already."

It was 6:42 and the wind was bringing the smell of seaweed up from the harbor. It was the new moon—the tide would be low, the men out working their oyster claims. The street was empty except for a cat rubbing itself against a broken picket on the old Snow house fence. All these years and it was still the lonely, dreamy street where LaRee had searched for a job that lost summer when she was twenty. Whatever you did in Oyster Creek, whether it was kissing a lover or knocking a stone out of your shoe, it had a little extra drama. The town acted like a stage set to remind you that every minute of your life was terribly, terribly important. That was reason enough to stick right here.

A shadow emerged from the back of Matos Fish, a small, solid figure with a tight coif and an officious stride. Amalia was finished for the day, going through her closing routine for maybe the ten-thousandth time in her life. She came around and tried the front door to be sure it was locked, peered in through the window, and, reassured, tucked her cash pouch under her arm and started toward the bank depository next door. Then she felt LaRee's presence and looked over her shoulder.

"Hello, LaRee," she said drily, as if she were used to finding La-Ree sniffing around in her garbage.

"Hello, Amalia. You're working late."

"Can't tell a load of lobsters to wait until morning," Amalia said. "Lobster divers have to make a living, too," she said, implying that LaRee didn't care whether lobster divers lived or died. Then she remembered that she had a sharper grudge. "And Maria asked me to look in on Dorotea."

LaRee could feel retorts forming, little needles to jab Amalia with.

"That's nice of you, Amalia," she said. "How is Dorotea?"

"She is just fine. She has plenty of family, and we're setting up a fund for her education."

"I'll make a contribution. This is so sad."

"It certainly is," Amalia said, pushing the bag into the depository slot with ironclad satisfaction. She was a certified victim and did not share one speck of the universal blame. She was carrying a book as well as the bank bag—*Their Eyes Were Watching God.*

"Teresa is reading it at school," she explained. Teresa was her granddaughter—one of the pack of girls who scooped at Ice Cream Tuesday in the summers and drank behind it in the off-season. She played soccer and fit in perfectly with her team, as she had with her Girl Scout troop years ago. Of course Amalia would cheer her on at soccer games, but, reading the books for English class? LaRee wouldn't have imagined it and it made her wonder what else she didn't know. Amalia straightened her back and her face, and clicked away on her heels, turning up School Street toward her mother's. The old woman's face peered like a ghost out the front window. Of course Amalia would go to her mother's. This was the kind of news that demanded company, a lightning flash that lit everything so bright for a second that it seemed to have revealed an alternate world. Sabine's murder had been another of these, and the night the Calliope Hotel burned down, and the loss of the *Suzie Belle.* Amalia's brother had been the captain of the *Suzie Belle,* and their mother had not left the house since the day it went down, though she would sometimes put up the window to speak to someone in the street.

LaRee also had a brother—his name was Robin. "He has the creative spirit," her mother would say, but it was more that Robin didn't dare take a step in any direction. He lived on disability now, after a back injury twenty years ago. Sometimes he'd get drunk and call up full of cheer, telling LaRee he was going to reinvent himself, that he'd been doing some watercolors and they were damn good, damn good. This was the genteel equivalent of going down on the *Suzie Belle*, LaRee supposed. Down the street she saw a breath of smoke dissipating under the lighted Walrus and Carpenter sign. Franco would be behind the bar—Vita might have gone to him. And even if she hadn't, LaRee needed to see someone else who had been part of this story all along.

The Walrus was full; there was a Red Sox game on television. Henry Tradescome, Fiona's father, was there, Westie Small beside him, and some guys LaRee recognized without really knowing them: Sal Bemba from Sea View Auto Repair, and Cabbage Lopes, whose real first name was long forgotten.

"People been saying they seen a ghost," Sal said. "A light in the wheelhouse of the *Rainha*, late at night." He laughed at the idea, looking down the row at the bar to see if anyone would take it up.

"If there was a ghost on the *Rainha*, it'd be your father, Franco."

"There's no ghost on the *Rainha*," Franco said. "If Vinny came back . . . I don't think he'd haunt a dragger. He never even went out on the wharf after his father passed away."

"I used to work with Vinny," Cabbage said. "His dad was in my class at school."

"I know," Franco said. "I was in your class at school, too."

"I wouldn't have guessed you'd remember that, Franco. Seeing I wasn't a girl."

Franco wiped the bar in front of Cabbage and set down another draft. LaRee couldn't help being glad to see him. Both of his jobs consisted mostly of shooting the breeze with other men—either on the dock or at the bar. He enforced the law with a fond regret. He was sorry about all of it—sorry that lobsters didn't just wash up with the tide as they once had, that there were so few that laws had been passed to protect them, that the laws made it harder yet for men to earn their living, sorry that they broke the law, and mostly sorry that he, who should have been at the helm of the dragger *Rainha do Mar*, cresting one wave after another with no boundaries, not so much as a stop sign to obey, should be left writing tickets for small infractions, enforcing the law on his friends. He was sorry to be so easily bewitched by women, so tender and confused toward Vita that he could hardly speak when he was around her; sorry about Sabine, and Vinny, of course; sorry he'd hurt Danielle; just sorry. He leaned on the bar with both arms, hanging his head for a moment, then looked up with a big, sheepish, glad-to-see-you smile.

"LaRee!" he said. "Tequila sunrise?"

"That was my drink—in 1985," she said. It felt like home here. She could trace the names carved in the bar, the sound of the men's voices over the television just the same as it had been always. The low, dark room was lit by a strand of Christmas lights and a few cheese graters with yellow bulbs, so the bottles over the bar looked full of amber light. And there was always the atmosphere of a wake—a sense of communal mourning, resignation, and good cheer. They didn't always have a person to mourn for, but there were plenty of departed hopes: Cabbage's wife had left him and taken the kids up to Maine; Henry was writing a book that never seemed to be finished. But they were here together—they'd survived to try again.

"See, I remember a lot," Franco said, turning his back to her to get down the gin for Henry Tradescome. "I remember when the leg came up in Bobby's net, too. I thought Vinny'd just shake until he crumbled."

"Vinny's father went down on the *Suzie Belle*?" LaRee asked.

Franco looked at her as if she'd asked whether George Washington had been president.

"At least they found part of 'im," Cabbage said. "It's a comfort, whether you think it would be or not. Otherwise you just keep wonderin'. . . ."

He trailed off and there was a moment of silent respect, observed instinctively by all.

"So," Franco said, then. "What can I get for you?"

"Franco . . . do you have a minute?" LaRee asked. The cook had come out to sit at the bar and watch the game, so she pulled Franco into the kitchen for privacy. "Have you heard from Vita?"

He laughed sadly, shook his head. "No, why?"

"Oh, she's upset . . . I mean, she's furious. When she found out about Vinny . . . she just . . . oh God, you can imagine."

Franco squinted, scratched his head. "She's upset about Vinny?"

"Of course."

"Did she even know him?"

"No, but you know his daughter's in her grade at school . . . so . . ."

"Dorotea," he said, nodding, absorbing. "But why would she be mad?" He looked through the window in the swinging door to see if anyone needed a drink, but unfortunately no one did.

"Franco . . ." LaRee watched him puzzling. "She's furious that we never told her . . ."

"Told her what?"

"That Vinny killed Sabine."

"We didn't?"

"Well, I didn't. And apparently you didn't. I should say she's not furious at you." That wouldn't have occurred to her.

"I never even thought . . . She was just a little girl. Why would anyone have told her?"

"I know. I said the bad man went to jail, that she was safe."

And Vita used to ask, too: Was the bad man still in jail? *Yes, he will be there forever.* And then, how could anyone be so bad that he would kill someone? *Because of drugs—he was crazy with needing drugs; he didn't know what he was doing. He must be very sad now, to think that he killed someone's mother.*

LaRee had to repeat the story over and over—a story she had completely invented. No one knew what had happened really, not even Vinny. He had sworn he was innocent, even after the DNA matched. He'd been drinking, and yes, maybe he'd had some cocaine. *The man was desperate to get money for drugs. He came to the door. Sabine was always so generous; of course she let him in. She offered him something to eat.* (There had been two wineglasses on the table, but Hannah had washed them. Hannah was used to cleaning up after people; she was not used to investigating murders. Still, it was hard to imagine Sabine having a glass of chardonnay with Vinny.) *But he asked her for money. She gave him all she had, but it wasn't very much. He needed more.* (In fact, her purse was still hanging on the kitchen chair with sixty dollars in the wallet.) *And he didn't know what he was doing* (he had slashed her with a fishing knife, a knife no one had been able to find) *and . . . he didn't know there was a little girl upstairs, a little girl who needed her mom.* And Vita, six years old, planning to adopt a fox cub one day, had worried for this poor man: Does his family visit him in jail? *I always think we should forgive one another as often as we possibly can, but sometimes . . .* "Would you forgive me, LaRee, if I killed someone?" *The only way you would kill anyone, Vita, would be in a horrible accident, and of course I would forgive you.* "What if it wasn't an accident?" *It would be an accident.* "But what if it wasn't?" *Vita, there are some things a grown-up just knows.* "Then why didn't my mom know the man might kill her?"

"It made sense to talk about it that way when she was little," LaRee said. "Oh, I wish . . ."

Franco's face furrowed—he was trying to understand too many things at once. Danielle had taken their boys through a steady progression of rules, responsibilities, and events that marked off the stages of their lives: christening, first steps, first communion, football, driver's license, graduation, wedding, fatherhood. LaRee was like some kind of snake charmer, guiding Vita upward by dint of perfect focus. It reminded him of his father, who understood fish so well that he would sense them and seem to see them even at twilight or in a fog so thick you couldn't see your hand in front of your face.

"I wish I'd thought it through better," LaRee was saying. "I'd have . . . Oh, I don't know what, but I'd have done it differently, that's all!"

Franco rubbed his temples, seeing Vita as she'd been the week before, a young woman pushing her shoulders forward and her head down, the hard look she had given him as she shook his hand. A surly teenager. Weren't they all?

"She's going through a phase," he tried.

"Franco, of course she's going through a phase. That's why she needs her parents!"

"I'm right here," he said. "She doesn't want me."

"No, Franco. It's not that. It's that she's not sure you want her. She . . . It's all been so strange and out of focus for her. . . . You were here and she didn't know you were her father, and her mom is gone, and everyone else is . . . Do you know that she's always wished there was a boat named after her?"

"Why?"

"Because every other girl in town has one! That's how men

name their boats, after their daughters. Yours comes from before she was born, but still. . . ."

"Wouldn't be much of a compliment to have an old bucket like the *Rainha* named for you," he said with a laugh.

"No, no . . . It's not the boat so much. It's . . ."

Franco thought of his kayak skimming along, away from land and all the troubles on land, his skateboard . . .

"Somebody stole my bike," he said suddenly.

LaRee hit the swinging door with the flat of her hand and walked out into the barroom. She must have been pretty desperate to look for help from Franco Neves. It was the fourth inning and from the din she guessed the Sox had just scored. Matt had come in while she was in the kitchen with Franco and had sat down on the other side of Henry Tradescome.

"Has anyone here seen Vita?" she asked. Cabbage poked his finger into his ear and scratched violently, as if her voice had irritated it. Westie said, "I haven't seen Vita since she was yea high. I'm not sure I'd recognize her."

Henry looked up. "What's the matter?"

"She's upset about Vinny . . . and everything. She went for a walk this afternoon and she hasn't come home."

"Did you check the library?" The lines on Henry's face were deep from years of thought and . . . pity, or rue, and this alleviated her dread. How far could Vita have gone, really? What cruelty could she really meet with, in Oyster Creek? Even Amalia was doing her best.

"Thanks, Henry, I did. Fiona's there, by the way."

"Hmmm . . . I think I'm supposed to pick her up,"

Matt touched her arm to catch her attention, holding her eye. He always had to remind her, they had this secret stream between them, like the aquifer Oyster Creek shared with Wellfleet. Oh, September 10, day of innocence, sunlight, plenty!

An ad came on and LaRee decided to try again. She tapped the side of a wineglass with a spoon. "Listen—if any one of you sees Vita, please ask her to call home, okay? I'm a little worried about her."

And they all looked up to the television, all at once. Were they idiots?

No. It was the news break, and there was Franco standing at the end of the pier with the derelict *Rainha* behind him, the rusted pulley there beside his head, and the heavy chain that hung down from it, and the rolled net with wisps of seaweed caught in it, and the gray surf sucking at the hull. He rubbed his chin like a seasoned commentator and said, "Vinny wasn't a bad guy, really," and a red banner flashed across the bottom of the screen: "Jailhouse Suicide: Slain Woman's Lover Speaks Out. WLLZ News at 11."

"Franco, has it never occurred to you to say, 'No comment'?"

His eyes opened wide. "He came all the way down from Boston, over the bridge," he said. "I couldn't send him back without saying something."

LaRee cast her eyes heavenward, and Franco realized he'd erred, without understanding how. "Vinny wasn't a bad kid. You have to remember what he went through...."

"I do," Cabbage said grimly. "I was the one who found 'im...."

Franco was shaking his head. "I don't know why it was," he said. "Somethin' about bein' tough enough, I guess, proving it."

"Found him where?" LaRee asked. "You mean, when they found his father's leg?"

"Nothin', nothin'," Cabbage said, but Franco had never learned how to say, "No comment."

"In the basement," he said. "They tied him up down there and . . ."

"And what?"

"We don' know what," Cabbage said firmly.

"You've gotta be tough when you're out on a dragger," Franco said. "Or you don't survive."

"He wasn't a townie," Cabbage said, "so they rode hard on him."

"He was born here, wasn't he? His mom grew up here too."

"But his father was fishing out of New Bedford and they lived there until Vinny was in third grade. So, to the kids, he wasn't one of us."

"So they were out to get him from the start," Franco said.

"They took his clothes," Cabbage said. "And he'd been sick all over himself. I had to wrap him in a plastic tarp, that was all there was down there."

"Did you call the police?" LaRee asked.

"It *was* the police," Franco said. "More or less—the chief's son had a mean streak. He's a security guard in Chelmsford, or he was the year Vinny went to prison. I don't know what he's up to now."

"He didn't hurt him, just scared him," Cabbage said. "There wasn't any blood.... Anyway, after that, and after Vinny's dad died, he wasn't the same. He liked driving the big truck, though. . . . He liked that pumper truck."

LaRee sat down on the stool beside Matt. "Whiskey, okay, Franco?"

So Vinny, who she knew from his stupid grin and the way he'd push his cap back to scratch his head, had been a small boy once, tied up and humiliated by the others. He'd been brought up to work on his father's boat, but the boat went down. Sabine had invited him in for a drink, been flirtatious with him because that's what she did with men, then pushed him away. "The same way a man treats a woman," she used to say. "Why not?" Her affairs began in either admiration or pity, but they always ended in revenge.

Matt watched her taking it all in, considering it. From the very little time they'd spent together, he really knew her and, she noticed, loved her. Meaning he was interested to know how she thought, to weave those thoughts in among his own.

"It's on the house," Franco said kindly, bringing her whiskey. Sabine would never have forgiven him for not falling in love with her, when she was young and beautiful and educated and worldly—so far, far above him. Seducing Vinny would remind him that he was just a dumb Portagee, that all the compliments she had paid him, about his knowledge of the sea and the town being worth more than any book learning, were only flattery.... Had he really believed her? Was he that much of a fool? The Sox were up again and Cabbage had left the conversation.

"They stripped him naked and tied him up and just left him there?" she asked Franco.

"Reminds me of my fraternity days," Henry said.

"You know how kids are," Franco said uncomfortably.

"I guess I don't."

He looked out the window over her shoulder. Finally he said, "We've all got ours back a thousand times over, for the things that happened...."

"Vita didn't do anything, Franco, except to be born."

She didn't expect an answer, and didn't get one. The whiskey he had given her was as smooth as silk, top shelf, a peace offering, like everything that went between them. Since she had never loved him, it was easy enough to forgive. He did the best he could, like everyone else.

"Listen, Vita's probably home already," he said, coming back up the bar to her. "Kids that age, they have to get in a little trouble. I mean, Danielle got pregnant when we were fifteen, and not by ac-

cident. Our parents tried to keep us apart and we knew if there was
a baby coming they'd make us get married instead. Kids don't know
what they're getting into."

"That's very consoling."

"Well, I don't mean Vita's gonna do that," he said. "But they all
have to do something. They have to tear themselves away or they'd
never go."

"I never thought of that."

Franco smiled. "Young Frankie, the first time he ever drank liquor, he was walking home and decided to dive off the pier. It was
low tide, he broke both his arms and one shoulder and he was lucky
it wasn't his neck. It's a stage they go through."

The Sox struck out. Cabbage turned back to them and said, "I
always thought you married Danielle because you were afraid of
Amalia."

"Nah," Franco said, "'Course not. Amalia was just so used to
bein' in charge, you know, 'cause of her dad. She wasn't a romantic
kind of girl."

"What would Amalia Matos have to do with you marrying
Danielle?" LaRee asked.

"Nothing. She had a crush on me. A schoolgirl crush, like
they say."

"She'd been saying she was goin' ta marry you from the time
she was ten years old," Cabbage put in. "She said her father promised her, and that he was in charge of the town."

Franco laughed. "And he was, too. Everyone was afraid of him."

"He thought he owned the town and everyone in it," Cabbage
said. "He couldn't believe it when you didn't ask Amalia to the
prom. It was supposed to be an honor that she liked you."

"You know, he was just used to different ways. They were the important family back in Gelfa, they had the biggest house, the newest boat.... He'd have picked his daughter's husband if they still lived there."

"I've got to go find Vita," LaRee said.

"Here, I'll come with you." Matt drained his beer and stood up.

"No. No, thank you but . . . I want to find her and talk to her by myself."

He sat back down, looking wounded.

"I'll call you," LaRee said. "I'm grateful for the help." If there was one thing she didn't need, it was some man listening earnestly and being honestly concerned; convincing her to rely on him just so he could pull the rug out from under her later on. "I'm sure it's some dumb teenaged thing just like Franco said, and I don't want to embarrass her."

"It's probably some kid took my bicycle," Franco said.

"Not Georgie? He forgets, these days."

A look crossed Franco's face: anger and resignation. "It was behind the harbormaster's shack. It's not like I left it out in the parking lot here."

The day after Drew left for good, LaRee had wheeled his bike down and leaned it up against the side of the Walrus and Carpenter. It was known that if you left a bicycle untethered there, some drunk would ride it home, and she just wanted to be rid of it. After two days it was gone, but she could remember the way she'd watched it, as if as long as it stayed there, there was a chance he'd come back home. No, but the handlebars had turned up as part of a sculpture a few years later, on display at a gallery on Back Street, and when the gallery became a restaurant the sculpture turned up as a coatrack beside the door. This she had noticed on her one date with Matt, who had hung her sweater up with chivalry, and without realizing he was hanging it on her ex-husband's handlebars. This town was made of stories like that, all woven together into a fabric so tight that every thread tugged a thousand others. Amalia was still smarting from a date she hadn't been asked on forty-five years ago; Vinny had pulled Sabine into a nightmare that began when he was in fourth grade. The kids here might not inherit a dollar or a half acre, but every fear, every disappointment, every anger had been passed down in perfect condition.

"Please, Franco, if you see her, ask her to call me," LaRee said. "I'm going to go . . . find her, somehow."

"She's a kid," Franco said to her back. "She's fine."

17

Flapdragon

Vita sat beside the highway for what seemed like a long time, digging her fingernails into her palm, thinking of the back shore, the sea heaving and crashing, that huge restless being that was her best comfort. She should have turned toward the water instead of the town, let the human world go to hell on its own. How had she imagined that she and Dorotea were going to make some kind of friendship when the poor girl's mind was like . . . Vita pictured a bubbling bowl of entrails with a scaly tail curving through, and that image was curious enough to shake her out of her trance. She stood, brushed the dead leaves and pine needles off her jeans, then couldn't help trying out Dorotea's posture, shoulders hunched, head pulled in as if she were bracing for a blow. Her low voice, stubborn and angry, was directed inward. There was no hope another human would hear when she said, "You're the one that oughta be ashamed."

By imitating Dorotea exactly, Vita had understood her a little better. So let Franco talk about her being an actor as if that meant she was stupid, that she dreamed of being a Disney princess. She wanted to become someone who understood people by slipping into their skins, moving as they did, speaking as they did, until she could very nearly feel with their guts. Franco didn't get that. LaRee did. But LaRee had lied, and lied, and lied, about Franco, and Vinny, and . . . who knew what else? Until her whole life was disordered, like a map torn and taped back together wrong.

She started toward town, toward home. It was a five-mile walk maybe, and the bicycle was back at Dorotea's. If she turned back they'd have let her use the phone at the SixMart. But she couldn't. It would be going farther from LaRee, and she felt that if she stretched that bond any farther it would break. Tim Cloutier drove by with his truck full of lobster traps—it was time for that; he'd be putting them on the boat tonight so he could get out first thing in the morning. Then some tourists with New York plates passed, and one with Montana plates towing a new sailboat. She'd heard some people from Montana had bought the old Narville place down on Tradescome Point; it was probably them. She started to cry. She knew everything about Oyster Creek and nothing about any other place. How would she ever get away? The tears streamed down her cheeks and, as she walked into the north wind, down her neck into her shirt. One trickled down her back like a spider. She had to go home; there was nowhere else for her. She was going to be here forever, stepping among the land mines planted years ago by her careless, thoughtless, asshole mother. Oh, they were all right. Sabine had deserved to die.

The brutal thought sobered her, the same as if she'd twisted a burning cigarette into the crook of her elbow. An adult needed to be ready for the violence of life. The books on the shelf over her bed at home . . . *Little House* here, *Little House* there—LaRee had read them all aloud to her, she had been so set on making a safe little nest. A safe, false little world.

The mail truck came over the rise and rattled past, full of all the letters and packages people were sending from Cape Cod, across the bridge into reality. Messages in bottles—*Save me, I'm stranded here.*

Behind the truck came Sam and Leo in their little old Chevy. She wiped her sleeve across her face—they couldn't see her like this, so upset she felt barely human. Maybe they wouldn't recognize her. But Sam waved—ugh, they would never like her now.

He stopped and came backing up along the shoulder of the road.

"Do you need a ride somewhere, honey?"

"No," she said. "No. No, I don't. I'm fine."

"That cannot possibly be true," Sam said. "No one who is standing on the roadside next to Route 6 has ever been *fine.* That person obviously needs a ride *somewhere.* Get in, and we will take you."

"I don't know where I'm going," she said. "Just . . . *away.*"

"Well, move the birdcage over, that's right. And we'll take you 'away.' Though you realize you're walking into town, not out of it."

"Oh," she said, and laughing, began to cry. They were so beautiful and they loved each other with such grace; there was a charge in the air around them wherever they went. Who would have thought they would even recognize her outside the theater, never mind stop for her! And here she was in the car with them, moving the birdcage and making room for herself amid the red tricorn hat and the long satin gown in which Leo had played Juliet to Sam's Romeo last spring. She couldn't wait to tell LaRee. Then she remembered that she was not going to speak to LaRee ever again.

"So, why are you going 'away'?" Leo asked. He and Sam exchanged a glance in the front seat—as if she were a stray kitten they'd found, a treasure. Vita felt she was in love with him, or really, with them, both of them together. She would just like to stand between them and feel it all and . . . Oh, sex as she imagined it was just magic, sacred magic. And people talked about it as if it were a disgusting joke. Who knew? She didn't want to. Sometimes there would come a break in rehearsal and Sam would lean up against Leo—he was a little shorter so he could rest his forehead against Leo's cheek—and say something Vita couldn't hear, but their smiles would sweeten and Sam's hand would rest at the small of Leo's back for a moment, and for ten seconds you felt something like the first warmth of spring.

"I've lived here all my life," she groaned. "I have to."

She was not going to tell them the truth, that her mother had seduced a poor stupid drug addict and he had killed her and now he had killed himself and somehow everyone in town, even she, blamed Sabine. It was a bloated, reeking shame. She put her hands over her face, to keep them from seeing it. "Isn't that bad enough? To have lived in one place your whole life, known the same old people all that time?"

"I don't know, I lived in Ann Arbor until I was eighteen," Sam said. "It was cozy."

"Well, Chattanooga was *not* cozy; it was clammy and the insects were enormous and I wanted to get out of there just as fast as I possibly could," Leo said. "Of course, I knew I'd have to dance my way out. And nobody'd ever heard of Billy Elliot back then, by the way. Chattanooga was a circle of hell . . . the ninth circle. Or maybe the eighth, but still . . . Every porch had a porch swing and on every porch swing was a daughter, waving and saying 'Le-o? Hi, Leo. Come on and have some sweet tea.' And you knew that just inside the door was a mother waiting, and a father with a shotgun. And I was just thinkin', Sam, I know you're out there, Sam, and . . .'"

His accent got stronger with every line—he couldn't help acting it, entertaining them. Oh, she loved him.

"We're here, love," Sam said suddenly. They had driven into the narrow shell driveway at Orson Desroches' house, a tiny, ornate structure at the top of Sea Street, all white shingles in diamond patterns, with a wide porch topped by a smaller porch topped by a dome that looked as if it were made of meringue. Vita had sold Orson Girl Scout cookies, magazine subscriptions for the cross-country team, and oranges for the music department, but she had never been invited inside.

"We didn't take Vita home," Leo said.

"She wasn't going home."

"Well, we didn't take her . . . away, either."

"This is away," she said eagerly, just as Orson stepped out his front door.

Sam squinted, Leo shrugged, and another car pulled into the driveway behind them. Hugh got out, wearing a tweed jacket, carrying a bottle of wine.

"Are you hungry?" Sam asked Vita.

"I . . . I don't want . . ." To intrude, to be in the way, any more than she had already been in this life. But Orson was standing at the top of the steps with one arm magisterially outstretched, and his gaze so perfectly affixed on Sam that it was clear that everyone else would be utterly invisible to him.

Or nearly. "We have a special guest, I see," he said, coming to the edge of the porch in his sock feet. "Hmmm . . . I may want to tidy up just an extra bit. Have you all seen the view from the side balcony? Why don't you take the circular staircase, right there, and I'll be out in just a minute or two."

All of the town was spread beneath them, the steeples silhouetted against the soft silver of the bay, a pale sunset reflecting pink in the lee of every wave. Adam's mom went running down Front Street with her light, measured steps, running in place for a minute as she spoke to Danielle, who was closing up the pharmacy.

Sam spread his arms and went up on pointe.

"Show-off," Leo said. "You're competing with a sunset; you're going to lose." But he struck a complementary pose. Vita pushed up onto the balls of her feet, too, to see what it might feel like to be Leo and Sam. A light came on in the old Moody house at the end of Sedge Point, a plain little place with a laundry line across the front and zinnias in the garden in summer. Then the streetlamps blinked on, one by one, all around the harbor, and some in among the pines on Sedge Point, maybe at Adam's house. And one in the *Rainha's* wheelhouse—no, of course not, it had just been a last glint from the sun. But it had made her happy for a second, as if it were a flicker from the candle her mother must be carrying through the afterlife.

"*Entrez, entrez,*" Orson called. "Martini, or cosmo?"

They came down onto the porch and into the house, which felt like a tiny white church, especially because of the staircase leading to the loft, the tall pointed windows, and the fact that the pictures on the wall were covered with bright silk scarves. Vita was still dressed in her jeans and sweatshirt from school and she felt as if the day's sweat and tears had made her filthy. They couldn't really be happy to have her here. Did LaRee even care that she was gone? Probably not. She had played her part well but after all, she was not really Vita's mother; they would never have that visceral bond. The principal had put his arm around Dorotea, she remembered suddenly—he was fatherly, concerned for her. He had never paid any such attention to Vita; in fact, he was always getting her name wrong, calling her Virginia and then apologizing and making it worse with some long explanation. She just didn't register; she was like a ghost herself. Too shy to make a sound, she shrank behind Sam and Leo.

Orson stood rapt in the kitchen doorway, stirring martinis in a chrome shaker.

"Can you hear it? There's a tone that comes when they're properly mixed. You could say that a perfect martini has its own chime. . . ."

"Perfect madness has a chime, too," Hugh said, twinkling. He looked like a blue heron, tall and angular with long spindly legs and a few long wisps of hair combed back over a bald spot. "Even now it is ever so faintly ringing."

"Madness is one of the luxuries of age," Orson replied. "You yourself may find some reserves as yet untapped, Shiverick."

Hugh laughed. Leo had lifted one of the scarves to peek at a painting and Sam gave his hand a playful slap. Orson came in carrying a tray of drinks.

"Hell is empty, and all the devils are here!" he toasted, and the men lifted their glasses.

"Come, come, Vita, join us!" Orson said.

"But it's . . ." She reached for a drink, a pink one.

"Is that a cosmo?" Sam asked suddenly.

Orson looked puzzled.

"Because *she* is sixteen years old."

Orson blinked very rapidly and removed a pair of glasses from his shirt pocket to make a further inspection. Once they were in place on his nose he said, "Oh! I see. And so, you don't want the cosmo?"

"Well, it's kind of . . . not . . . legal." She redid her hair quickly, pulling the ponytail tighter, and scrunched back into the couch, her sweatshirt sleeves down over her hands. "But, I . . ."

Leo glanced at her with sympathy. "She's not a cosmo kind of girl, Orson. Do you have . . . root beer?"

"Root beer?" Orson sounded as if he pictured witches brewing something in a forest.

"Orange juice?"

"Yes, I do have orange juice."

"Thank you," Vita managed to say, though only the "thank" was audible. Last night Bumble had slept behind her bent knees, edging her over until she nearly fell out of bed, and she had dragged herself up this morning feeling sick because she hadn't slept, and she was afraid of the geometry test, and . . . oh, to crawl back there! A cat that was too cuddly and fifteen equations in black ink on crisp paper with the answers to be revealed, clear and absolute, the next day? She should thank the gods for such problems! She pushed herself back into the arm of Orson's sofa, tucking her feet up underneath, an anxiousness beating its wings so furiously in her chest that she had to keep herself rigid to contain it. The black loneliness of life—*that* was the only truth. Sleeping curled up with Bumble, LaRee in the next room . . . It had never been real, just a moment's calm before the next abyss.

"How did you two ever find each other?" Orson asked Sam and Leo. Hugh was examining the bookshelves, his head crooked to the side so as to read the titles on the spines. She had become invisible, or very near it. And none of them knew about Vinny. Or if they did, they had thought it over for a minute or two and gone on to the next thing. They didn't blame her, or feel sorry for her, or anything. It just wasn't very important to them.

"Pizza," Leo said, with a sweet little smile. "I was working at Pizza by the Sea and Sam came in for a slice."

"What bliss."

"Actually it was kind of hot," Leo said. "Those wood-burning ovens."

"Those blue eyes . . ." Orson said.

"They're green!" Leo jumped up to look in the mirror.

"They're more reflective than most eyes," Sam said. "They change, like cats' eyes."

"Really?" Leo angled back and forth to try to find the effect in the mirror.

"Oh my God, you are shameless," Sam said. "Handsome is as handsome does. Didn't your mother ever say that?"

"She couldn't tear her eyes off me," Leo ruminated, causing Sam to cast his eyes skyward. "Well, she couldn't!" Leo said. "I think I've wrecked it all with this hair, though. It's too blond-tastic, don't you think?"

"It highlights your . . ." Orson began, and then decided words were not equal to the task. "Oh, really, I could just breathe you in. Both of you. Sam, I mean you no slight."

"Oh, gosh, of course not." Sam was not as easily self-admiring as Leo. . . . No one was except maybe Scarlett O'Hara. And Sam was really the handsome one, Vita thought. His mouth was very red, his hair curled, and he did not raise his voice to make his point but softened it, so it was so tender you had to listen to it, the way you had to watch a quiet snowfall. Then Leo smiled at him and Vita changed her mind and decided he was handsomer.

"Now, these morels come from Winsome Farm, up in Harwich," Orson said, putting pasta into bowls. "You can make a perfectly *silken* sauce if you start with the right broth. . . ."

"How wonderful, you serve morels," Hugh said. "I didn't know you had any."

"I don't have any of my own," Orson replied, delighted. "This is why we are so lucky to have an organic farm nearby." They went on happily, playing pickup sticks with the conversation, each line lifted delicately from the last. They asked nothing and Vita watched and listened like a child at her parents' feet.

"Ah, linguine, little tongues."

"Do you like mushrooms, Vita?" This was Leo, breaking through her invisible wall.

"Not really," she croaked.

"An im-morel pasta for Vita Gray!" Orson said. "Speaking of beauty..."

Vita shrank, if that was possible.

"No reason to blush, dear. Our Leo here would never blush."

"I do blush!" Leo said. "Don't I?"

"Come here, my punkin," Sam said. "Do you remember when you were sixteen?"

"Ugh. High school—don't remind me. My voice didn't change till I was a senior. Of course that was the first sign of my vocal range...."

Sam laughed. "What I remember is the art of the hanging wedgie. Not giving them, obviously, but surviving them with some shred of dignity."

"They had hanging wedgies back then?" Vita asked.

"It's hard to know which came first," Orson said. "Underwear or hanging wedgies..."

"It wasn't that long ago, you know," Sam said stiffly. "I'm only twenty-five."

"You?" Vita asked. He was as ageless as Apollo! She could not imagine there had ever been anyone who didn't bow down before him.

They sat around Orson's little wicker coffee table with their plates in their laps, but Orson stood now and drew himself up. He was not much more than five feet tall, even though he was wearing stilettos. Except for a few white whiskers here and there, he was bald, and plump in a way that worked, with the heels, to give him the step of a middle-aged woman, so that Vita expected to see apron ties around his waist as he walked away. He carried himself with fragile dignity, as if he had learned he must demand respect or be trod under every foot that passed. Vita tried to angle her head the way he did and found herself feeling embattled, but brave.

"I suppose you think I escaped this sort of thing because I was beneath notice," he said. "In fact, I stuttered." He stopped to let the majestic implications sink in. "Thus did I develop the fine diction for which I am celebrated town-wide."

Hugh laughed, as if nostalgic. "They hadn't invented school shootings back then, or I suppose I'd be in prison."

"*All* of you?" Vita asked. "But you're . . ."

"Even I'm surprised," Orson said. "I'd have imagined Leo at least would have been exempt from such earthly trials. And Sam, you would have experienced cruelty in the interest of art only."

Sam smiled, and Vita felt her blush rising again. She felt as attuned to him as if she were a mirror. What she knew of sex appalled her; she would never understand how people forced themselves to do it. But this physical telepathy came naturally, and with it a kind of hallucinatory bliss no drug could match. She imagined sleeping beside Leo, between him and Sam, so their feelings had to pass through her . . . and she'd better stop imagining anything because every thought she had seemed to telegraph itself across her face.

"You're the coolest people I know," she admitted.

"Of course we are," Leo said. "I used to call them the rhinos, those guys," he said. "Leathery, and plodding, but they had this big horn in the middle of their face that meant they didn't have much to be afraid of."

Orson nodded. "The lumpen teenage masses have little talent

save a strange, primitive ability to sense potential in others. And snuff it out."

"Really?" Vita asked.

"Take you, for instance. A young woman, full of thought and feeling, her very uncertainty proof of a fine-grained consciousness . . . not likely to meet with great success in high school. You're absolutely right to go about in disguise now."

"I'm not in disguise!"

They were making fun of her. Well, everyone did; what had she expected? She took another bite of the pasta. Hers had none of the mushroom sauce, only butter, but it was still somehow better than LaRee's pasta. She ate an olive out of the salad. Outside the pointed window the new birch leaves moved softly under the streetlight. The conversation had split; Orson and Hugh were talking about how to light the locust grove during the third act, while Sam and Leo practiced following each other's facial expressions for the sake of looking into each other's eyes. They were masters at the billion infinitesimal changes a mouth could register, and the range of intensities conveyed in a glance. Finally Sam laid his head on Leo's shoulder and Leo leaned down and kissed his mouth.

Watching them, Orson lost his ability to listen to Hugh, who found he had only Vita to talk to.

"And what do you intend to do with the rest of your life, young woman?" he asked.

"Me?" Ugh. She didn't want to answer. He would laugh at the aspirations of such an awkward girl. Shyanne was moving to Los Angeles after graduation, to get a start in the film business. Vita had heard Hugh saying every move Shyanne made was a sexual invitation; she seemed to come from a different, and much more valued, species than Vita did.

"I'm going to be an actor," she said, and it sounded like a threat. She knew she was going to get a lecture now about how this was the dream of a little girl, that she had better learn to wait tables and stand in endless lines at cattle calls . . . and all the reflexive condescension that adults couldn't seem to stop themselves from. She supposed it felt good to them, their own dreams having dribbled away. At least that gave them the right to a certain kind of superiority. Someday when she was playing an adult she would remember this. She ought to pay attention, to learn the world-weary intonation.

But Hugh was listening, gravely.

"Why?"

"I like acting." She still sounded surly and teenagerish, a sound she hated. "I like imagining myself as another person in another world."

A smile spread over his face and he leaned back in his chair. "That makes sense," he said.

"It's so cool when you're just thinking—how would this person stand, or how would she react to something . . . and you realize something about the character and then you understand something else and you're thinking about the whole history, the way Shakespeare might have been thinking. . . ." She trailed off into self-consciousness. "Sorry, I'm just . . . prattling."

He peered at her, listening with care. "I'm not sure you can prattle and use the word *prattle* at the same time," he said.

"What?"

"I came to Shakespeare as an English student. It was all reading, knowing . . . amassing an arsenal of interpretations, footnotes, allusions, so you would have more of them than the next man and win the contest. And of course there was always a contest, with whoever sat next to you in class or whose essay was published in the same anthology with yours."

She was puzzling through his words. "I mean," he said, "that I like your perspective."

This was a gift and she was unsure how to accept it. She couldn't think. "When do we build Caliban's hut?"

"It has to be soon," Hugh said. "Franco is taking me out to Barrel Point next week—apparently there's an eddy out there and a good bit of driftwood has collected on the shore. He's going to build a basic structure and we'll attach the wood. That . . . stump . . . you brought will go beside the opening. Then we'll string lights through the locust grove, and put them on several switches so the goddess Iris can turn them on after she enters, at the opening of the show."

Sam and Leo emerged from their dream, and Orson blinked and sniffed, coming back to reality.

"So you will be stepping out of your disguise," Orson said.

"No," she said.

"You'll wear a costume that reveals you. Shows your beauty."

"I don't care about beauty."

"You care about Shakespeare."

"That's different," she said stubbornly.

"It's funny," Sam said. "When I play a woman I always feel like a goddess. It's a feeling you just never have as a man. You're at the center of the universe and everyone is looking up at you, and you smile over them with love, and . . ."

"Pavlova?" Orson asked.

"No!" she said. "No! Just an actor, who goes to work in a different story every day. It's not that I want to have everyone looking at me. It's that I want to be invisible, inside somebody else!"

"I was merely asking whether you wanted some dessert."

"What?" she asked, mortified.

"Pavlova? Meringue and strawberries? And whipped cream?"

"Oh."

"You won't be sorry."

"Thanks, I'd love some," she said, too embarrassed to look up.

"I never thought of it that way. You really don't want everyone looking at you?" Leo said.

"Do I seem like a person who likes to be looked at?" she said, still staring at the floor.

"Do I seem like a person who likes to be looked at?" Leo asked.

"We weren't talking about *you*," Sam said. "Vita," he said, "you know you're a pretty girl, right?"

She made a miserable shrug. "I suppose."

"Come here. Sit down beside me." She did, and he hooked his finger through the elastic and pulled it from her hair, so the ponytail escaped into a big puff of curls.

"You see?" she said, grabbing it and doing it in two quick braids.

"And the glasses need to come off, too. Sam, is the makeup case in the car?"

"Backseat," Sam said.

"Anyone else? Pavlova?"

"The thing is, you want to be more than beautiful," Hugh continued, "to use your talent to show more depth in your characters . . . more truth."

"Yes! Yes, exactly!" Vita said. She looked up, without thinking, and they were all there, smiling, welcoming her into their odd brotherhood. All these kind faces, these bright, avid eyes watching her. Orson was holding the Pavlova, a big meringue peaked and swirled like a circus tent and covered with berries and cream.

"There, beauty!" Sam said. "It's right there in that smile!"

"You're a little like me," Leo said. He was back with the makeup, dusting a brush against a palette, paying her the greatest compliment he knew.

"How?" she asked. He was electric onstage. There always seemed to be a spotlight on him, wherever he went.

"Cheekbones, I guess," he said, stepping back.

"She is exactly like *me*," Sam said softly, intent on his project, looking straight into her eyes. "She is nothing like you at all."

"And Prosecco, of course." Orson handed tall, narrow glasses around.

"None for her," Sam said. "We are not going to totally corrupt this child."

"She's sixteen. She probably drinks more than we do!"

She shook her head.

"I daresay she can manage a few sips of Prosecco, for the sake of a toast," Orson said.

She took the glass. Tears were welling and her throat closed. She was an orphan, but they were taking her in. The Prosecco was bubbly and medicinal. She sipped dutifully, in order to belong. And then again.

"And that is quite enough for any sister of mine," Leo said. Which was good because she was drunk on her two sips, utterly giddy, the room spinning, and around it all of her life spinning, past and present and, well, future. What might happen? Who might she become? LaRee must be worried about her. She should call, or . . . Sam was doing her hair now, twisting it curl by curl around his finger, singing, "I put a little more mascara on," more or less to himself.

"There," he said, opening a compact so she could see herself in the mirror, transformed. "What do you think? Or, wait." He snapped the compact shut again. "For God's sake, this sweatshirt . . . And I'm not taking it over your head after I just did your makeup. You've got something on underneath? Okay, so . . . Orson, do you have scissors?"

He cut the sweatshirt up the front, and pulled it off as if she were a child, leaving her in her Outer Cape High T-shirt. "Try this," Orson said, offering her a little jacket-like thing, peach-colored silk with a soft ruffle all around and a bow to tie the neck. "It was my mother's," he explained. "I keep it for certain occasions."

"There." The mirror was proffered again; she hardly dared look.

"I . . ." There she was. She, Vita Gray. The curls weren't heavy, they bounced, and the awful frizz she got when she brushed it was gone. She had expected to come out looking like Shyanne, but she did not, not at all. Her face was brighter, her features sharper; she was more herself. "I . . ."

"Don't thank me, girl, I just couldn't help myself," Sam said. "Look, this took me two minutes!" he crowed to the others as if Vita had nothing to do with it at all. For this she would always love him.

"When I think of what it must have been, for you two to find each other . . . your first glance, your first recognition, first . . ." Orson continued about his worship, while Sam and Leo made small gestures of humility, and other small gestures: Leo kissing Sam's fingertips, for instance, showing off.

"When I was young, of course, such a . . . tenderness . . . was inconceivable. We felt a responsibility to be furtive, to move in an atmosphere of shame. We rather . . . *loved* it. We would never have looked in each other's eyes."

Leo and Sam looked directly, liquidly, into each other's eyes— a kindness to Orson.

"Let's play flapdragon!" Leo said. "You have some brandy, Orson?"

"Yes," he said, "I certainly do!"

Flapdragon, apparently, was a game from Shakespeare's time, in which participants vied to eat raisins from a flaming bowl of brandy, and Sam and Leo played with spirit while Orson said things like, "Singed my whiskers!" and "Vita, keep back!"

Hugh was at some great remove from it all. "When you think," he said, to Vita, or maybe to the bookshelf, "that most of us spend our lives learning 'discretion'—how to keep things quiet—until some no longer have words for the most important things in their lives. Shakespeare lived in the opposite direction, working to say things that no one had put into words before."

Everything blurred. Hugh's sentences swirled through Vita's mind like smoke rings. A hot raisin flew over her head. She ducked away from the couch to the front window, through which she could see the slow-blinking blue light of the harbormaster's boat as it came around the end of Barrel Point and crossed the harbor. It seemed like a sign, that someone was watching over them, keeping them safe.

"*Full fathom five thy father lies,*" Hugh repeated to himself, thoughtful.

"*Of his bones are coral made / Those are pearls that were his eyes / Nothing of him that doth fade / But doth suffer a sea-change / Into something rich and strange.*"

18

Rainha do Mar

Darkness. Leaving the Walrus, LaRee looked up Front Street, past the library, Our Lady, Star of the Sea, and the First Church of Christ with its belfry lit against the night. Each of these solid, spired buildings, built here to reassure the inhabitants of a town set at the end of a thin curl of land in the middle of the sea. The night the Calliope burned, those steeples stood against an orange sky, the flames billowing up the hill behind them. Fire trucks barreled in from the surrounding towns, their horns and sirens howling, bellowing as if they could scream the flames down.

And the next morning, the smell of wet ashes, the old hotel that everyone said looked like a wedding cake twisted and slumped in on itself. The carriage house had been the only thing left. Orson had restored it perfectly, painted it white and on summer nights would fly a long white pennant from the cupola. Light shone from his windows now but LaRee couldn't look that way without thinking of the wreckage, the way all the leaves had been scorched off the trees—this must be one cell of what Vita felt, looking ahead toward her life. The black lacquer sky, the white steeples could flash over into horror—it had happened before.

She headed down Sea Street, toward the locust grove and Mackerel Bay Park, and down the pier. The old fishermen would drive along it two and three times a day, gathering bits of news—the price someone had gotten for a tuna, an argument between neighbors moored side by side. It was quiet now except for a couple of men she didn't recognize carrying crates of sea clams up a gangway from their boat.

The pier turned right after the old fish-packing plant, but renovation money had run out before they could replace the pilings around the corner, and the *Rainha* continued rotting silently at her mooring there at the very end. Why Franco didn't do something with her . . . Well, maybe he couldn't bear to. LaRee ought to clean out her own closets, give away the pants that didn't fit anymore, the velvet shirt she'd bought that year when she imagined she'd be dating Matt through the fall. *Ha.* She'd seen herself laughing in it, holding a wineglass in the firelight like some model in a clothing catalog. It was embarrassing to remember all she'd dreamed, so embarrassing that she didn't care to look at the shirt for the three seconds it would take to stuff it in a thrift shop bag. Though, really, she had been lucky when Matt's wife returned. The idea of making room in her life for a man again, someone to worry about and care for, who would fail her and be failed by her . . . No.

It was right that Vita was the center of her orbit. If only she could find her. Where was she? Where would she go? Making a U-turn at the end of the wharf, LaRee thought she saw a light glimmer from the cabin of the *Rainha*. Would Franco keep a light on in there, a naked bulb such as they used to appease the ghosts in a theater? Heaven knew he had his ghosts, but . . . LaRee stopped the car, and when she did, the door of the *Rainha*'s wheelhouse opened a crack, then was pulled tight shut again from within.

LaRee rolled down the window. "Vita?" Was this where she had been, all those days when she said she was "out walking"? Smoking weed on the *Rainha* with her friends? It seemed like every other teenager had—even Fiona Tradescome, who looked as serene as a madonna, had fixed the GPS on her cell phone so her mother couldn't find her, or so Vita said.

Teenagers did not know what they were doing, not even Fiona, not even Vita. And when you were mad at your mother, you ran to your father, even if it seemed like the last resort. "Vita, are you there?"

No answer, but someone was aboard that boat. The tide was coming in around Barrel Point and the *Rainha* was rocking, just slightly, crosswise against the swell. LaRee got out of the car.

The fish plant blocked the view from the rest of the pier, the harbormaster's shack was locked up for the night, and the men with the sea clams would do their work, make their assumptions, and go back to New Bedford.

Most of the boats had gangways that rose and fell with the tide, but the *Rainha* was fastened with just a rope at the bow. The boat jostled the pier, bumping away and against, the water sloshing up suddenly over the rail. LaRee took a deep breath and climbed up and over, slipping on the deck so that she fell sideways against the trawl. So she was in—bruised, scraped, and wet along her side, but in. "Vita?"

Everything was gnarled and blistered with rust—the cables, the porthole, the trawl. The scallop chain seemed grown and swollen into itself. An orange life preserver ring hung on the outer wall of the cabin with part of the covering ripped away so she could see what looked like straw inside. Someone had nailed a board across the cabin door to keep it from splitting. She knocked. "Vita? Is someone in there?"

No answer. She pulled at the door, but it was hooked closed from inside.

"Shut up. Go 'way." A man's voice.

"I'm looking for Vita Gray!" she called.

The door opened a few inches and a huge dark face appeared, eyes popping. "Well, she ain't here, so go away!"

"Georgie! Does Franco know you're here?"

"Franco don't ever look sideways at this boat," Georgie said, lurching back as the boat shifted. He was drunk, and holding a bottle of beer. Something was cooking on a makeshift stove behind him—that was the light she'd seen, a can of Sterno flickering. "Go 'way now."

"Do you . . . Are you okay?"

"Go *away*," he hissed, looking up at her like a bullfrog, scrappy even though he was standing two steps below her. "Nobody bothers me here, and as long as they don't see you, they won't start."

"You haven't seen her?"

"Vita? I seen Vita this afternoon, ridin' her bicycle down the highway. . . . She might be in Brewster by now."

"Her bicycle? What bicycle? Her bicycle's at home."

But this made no sense to Georgie and he just shook his head and started back to his cooking. Then he looked back and saw her dripping sleeve.

"Go up on the bow," he said over his shoulder. "There's a step there, see. She's tied at the bow, so . . . you can get off without fallin' in." A skepticism crossed his face. "Probably," he added.

In the distance she saw a blue light slowly blinking—Hank

Capshaw coming back across the bay from Barrel Point in the harbormaster's boat. Any closer and he'd see her drive away, know someone was out here. She did not want to explain herself and she especially did not want to explain Georgie, so she went up on the bow, grateful for the wide soles of her nursing shoes, and stepped across onto the pier again. As she drove away down the pier, the sea clam guys looked up at her for the first time. One gave a perfunctory wave.

Turning back up Sea Street, she saw the blue light coming closer. He'd tie up and head home on foot across the bridge around the island to the little house on Shep's Alley that he and his wife had built. She'd be just back from a run or a yoga class, fixing a very healthy dinner for Adam and his little brother. At the moment La-Ree would have paid for a glimpse of their dinner table with the family around it: a divine mystery.

What could be going on at Barrel Point that would require Hank's presence, in the pitch-dark night like this? Someone poaching from an oyster claim? A whale stranding? They happened out there—the harbor was a bit like a weir in that creatures could find the way in but not out again. Then she felt everything stop. The other thing that happened at Barrel Point was suicide. First a man from the mainland who'd driven out here after his wife died shot himself on the beach, thinking the waves would carry him out to sea. He didn't know the currents—the cops had to clean up the site and three years later, the one who'd been first on the scene had become despondent and remembered that Barrel Point was the right kind of remote place. He'd taped a vacuum hose to his exhaust pipe and left a note saying no one should be sorry, that he'd died looking out over the bay. After that Barrel Point stuck in people's minds as the appropriate place for despair. Suicides, divorces, deaths, they were the broken threads that weakened the whole fabric. Then drugs got in and ...

Just as her blood turned cold, LaRee looked up to see something like an angel—Vita, a slender silhouette in Orson's arched window, against what she thought was candlelight. Her hair was loose, and she was standing ... confidently, with her arms stretched wide. Yes.

Yes. She was fine, she was just fine, and soon she would stride into the world with that halo of curls and that posture and ... a tear rolled down LaRee's cheek, then another. Then it was as if the world of sorrow Vita had interrupted when she arrived thirteen years ago yawned open again.

LaRee escaped that world by being Vita's mother, day by day by day, leading Vita out of her own loss and consequently, rescuing herself. Vita was safe at Orson's, doing exactly what a sixteen-year-old girl was supposed to—finding her way into life.

LaRee went home, to take a leaf from Amalia's book and read *Their Eyes Were Watching God*.

19

MORNING

Vita woke up on Orson's sofa, under a comforter as white and fluffy as last night's dessert. A slice of sunlight angled across her knees, with a Gothic point like the window it came through. It was all peace and order and light here. Of course. Orson had no relatives at all.

"Vita," he said, looking down from the top of the stairs. "Are you awake, dear?"

"Yes," she said, pulling the cover to her chin though she was still fully dressed underneath it. A burnt raisin rolled out from under her pillow, proof that last night had really happened.

"May I come down?"

"Of course! I ... What am I doing here?"

"You were sleeping so soundly, I couldn't bring myself to disturb you. I called your mother and she said just to let you stay. Do you drink coffee, dear?"

"Yes, thank you," she said, not wanting to sound childish, though she had never had coffee and the bitter smell repulsed her. "But she's not my mother."

Orson had tied a white scalloped apron over his clothes and brought her a mug of coffee and a linen napkin. His small, soft hands had dimples instead of knuckles, and seemed strangely bendable, as if he had cartilage instead of bones. But he propped up her pillows efficiently and threw the front door open to the world. There was the bay shining like a mirror, with the boats bobbing against the pier. A quiet morning, the summer people—college professors mostly, right now—here already, but the tourists, the day-trippers and barhoppers, yet to come. Her accusation rang in her ears as the childish insult it was, guaranteed to hurt LaRee only because she cared so much. She heard flip-flops and saw the top of a kayak go past down the lane. Orson lived in paradise, not a mile from Dorotea's hell.

"She's worried about you," Orson said simply.

"She lied to me. All this time I've been the only person in town who didn't know the truth about my own mother, Orson."

"What truth is that?"

"That Dorotea's father was in jail because he killed her. Everyone else knew that, except me."

He untied his apron, silent again. He was wearing a silk shirt and pin-striped pants. "Where are you going?"

"To Fatima Machado's funeral." He paused for an instant, gazing down with respect for the dead, Vita thought, until she realized he was contemplating the shoes in his closet.

"I didn't know you knew her," Vita said.

"I used to live next door to her, when I first came here. I'd buy her a tank of oil for Christmas, that kind of thing. She was already losing her memory when Vinny went to jail and she started to be suspicious when I went over to visit. Didn't like having a strange man in the house."

Vita pulled her knees up against her forehead. "My mother wrecked their lives," she said.

"What on earth can you mean?" Orson asked, sitting down across from her.

"That she was a . . ." She forced the word out. "A slut."

"I have never been clear about the meaning of that word," Orson said.

"Well, you're the only one who's not clear about it."

"Does it mean someone who deserves to be murdered?"

"No, of course not . . ."

The church bells down on Front Street started to ring, and Orson jumped up and went back to the closet for his suit jacket and opera cape.

"It means that she didn't have respect for love, that she didn't honor her own heart." Vita hardly knew what she was saying, but she had to get it out into the air.

He folded the cape over his arm and turned to look at her. She saw this was a new idea to him—that she, Vita Gray, who had failed geometry and been given the smallest part in the play, had just surprised the impossibly sophisticated Orson Desroches.

"I hadn't thought of it that way," he admitted. "I never really knew your mother—but what I saw of her was a pretty woman who loved her little girl. I'm sure she had her eccentricities. . . ." (He was slipping his feet into a pair of black pumps.) "We all do. But she did not ruin anyone's life. Vinny ended her life, and he might have ruined yours, but from here at least it doesn't look that way. It looks like you're a person who takes life in her hands and makes good of it."

"It does?" But even as she asked this she saw a glimmer—it was true that she had gone to talk to Dorotea, tried at least to come to terms—and not just to come to terms with an idea, but with another person. And what a mess that had made.

"You're on your way home from here, I presume?"

She flinched, every muscle. "No! I can't go home. I won't. It's not even really my home, Orson, and you know LaRee's not my mother." She said this with a child's high-pitched finality that made him smile for a second before kindness straightened his face.

"Vita—" he started.

"I've made up my mind. I'm Sabine Gray's daughter." As she said this, it occurred to her for some reason that she had beautiful hands, delicate with long, pale fingers. The kind of hands you didn't see much in Oyster Creek, where women were proud of their oyster-shucking abilities. She stretched her right hand in front of her, so Orson could see Sabine's ring on her finger, as if that would prove something.

"Quite an opal," Orson said. "Was that hers? An heirloom?"

"It was hers. I guess an heirloom." Who knew? Who knew anything?

He took her hand to see the light angle through the ring. "It's like looking into the bay—the peacock colors," he said. "And you're right. No matter what else happens, no matter who else you love, you will always be Sabine Gray's daughter. And Franco's daughter, too. And Oyster Creek will always be your home."

This left all the other questions, a great world of questions, to her.

"Just close the door behind you," he said. "No need to lock."

"Orson?"

"Yes."

"Why do you always wear high heels?"

"They give the illusion of a longer leg," he explained, and

headed down the steps, stopping to snap off a couple of lilies of the valley, smell them, and tuck them into his buttonhole. Then she heard his heels clicking as he went down the street. He probably didn't realize Vita was supposed to go to school.

She got up, folding the quilt and plumping the pillows so the room would stay perfectly orderly. She was alone entirely, in a little house such as she might live in herself one day, not as a frightened child trying to convince herself that her mother was only asleep but as an adult who, as Orson had said, had taken her life in her hands and made good of it. To think of it, a place of her own, built from salvage like LaRee's house or Caliban's hut, or white and perfect like Orson's . . . whatever she wanted to do.

Which, right now, was to sit on the porch, in the wicker chair, with her cup of coffee. The day was sunny and almost warm, though the fog lingered along Sedge Point as if it were caught in the pines there. At the bottom of the block four old women were coming along Front Street together, looking like pigeons in their dark clothes. Then Amalia Matos with her mother on her arm, and Franco and Danielle, with Danielle's parents behind them. She could still hear Hugh quoting Shakespeare—people spoke of a sea change as if it were some wonderful metamorphosis, a beginning. But Shakespeare said, "Suffer a sea change." He meant what happened to you after you died, when you were lost underwater and creatures were living in your bones and the people who had known you as a breathing, yearning soul were taking your memory and using it for whatever they wanted. Stealing it, making it into something of their own. It was worse than robbing a grave.

"Mom," she said, testing the sound, but it was too strange; she could not do it. "I'm sorry. . . ." This she could say aloud. Her mother, being her real mother, would know who it was meant for.

There at her feet was the newspaper, rolled up where it had landed when Cabbage, who delivered the papers in addition to his other jobs, had thrown it from his car window that morning. Vinny's mug shot was on the front page; she'd never seen it. He looked accursed, heavy eyelids half closed and a look of resignation on his face, as if he'd always expected to end up in prison. She couldn't help thinking that he'd been the bull, while Sabine was the toreador—sometimes there's an accident; the wrong one dies.

MACHADO FOUND DEAD IN CELL

"I'M SORRY," ADOPTIVE MOTHER ADMITS

Venceslau (Vinny) Machado, convicted ten years ago in the killing of Sabine Gray, a murder that shook the sleepy fishing village of Oyster Creek to its core and captured the national spotlight, is dead, apparently a victim of suicide, in his jail cell in Souza-Baranowski Correctional Facility. Machado was discovered Wednesday evening by a guard on his regular rounds.

"The guards check on inmates every half hour," a source said. "As a fisherman Machado had knowledge of ropes and knots and it appears he was able to hang himself from the top bunk while his cellmate made a visit to the infirmary."

"He was a good guy," said Franco Neves, harbormaster of Oyster Creek, who fathered the victim's daughter in an extramarital relationship and was a suspect in the murder for several years until Machado was apprehended.

"I'm just sorry for the family, sorry about all of it," said

LaRee Farnham, the child's adoptive mother, while refusing further comment. "There isn't anything else to say."

Machado's wife, reached at work at the Infinite Horizons Retirement Home, said, "Now they're sorry, sure."

It was strange. Vita had expected that the newspaper article would make her feel terrible, but it didn't. It was wrong in a million ways, from calling Franco the harbormaster to somehow making LaRee's sadness seem like guilt. But the wrongness was a comfort—the newspaper would get things wrong and tomorrow it would go out with the recycling and be forgotten. Life would go on and things would change.

The church bells had ceased. Vita heard the organ groaning as the funeral began. They were all in there: her father, Dorotea, Orson. His silver stilettos were beside the door and she slipped her feet into them and tottered toward the mirror. She had never been able to walk in heels—they made her feel as if she were balancing on the top of the Empire State Building. If Orson could do it, though—surely she could learn? She tottered across the room, but the shoes were four sizes too large. Last night the scarf-draped picture frames had seemed a natural part of the decoration—squares of bright color against the white walls, almost like stained-glass windows. One of the scarves had blown sideways when Orson shut the front door, and she reached to tuck it back over the frame, and saw that in fact it was covering a photograph, a black and white photograph of a man's penis, very close-up and artful, as if it were an orchid. Or a tarantula. She dropped the scarf and jumped back. What was the matter with adults? Orson, who had covered her so gently while she slept, who could say things that lit everything with a beautiful warm light, things about a theater full of people following a story together, or that acting was the art of speaking honestly . . . and he was collecting close-up pictures of penises the whole time? Was adulthood like a disease you grew into? Maybe that was what had happened yesterday, when she had gone to Dorotea's house thinking she'd find a kindred spirit and ended by screaming hateful things at her. A growth spurt.

She kicked Orson's shoes off, grabbed her high-tops, and ran out the front door, down the steps, into the street, which was steep enough that it propelled her toward Front Street and Our Lady, Star of the Sea.

LaRee was just rounding the corner in the Subaru and stopped dead when she saw her. Vita turned and started back up the street. But where to? And what was she running from? She ought to be over the bridge, lost in some huge city by now. Instead, she'd never crossed the town boundary of Oyster Creek. It was shameful, to be so tethered to your home and your mother. Looking back over her shoulder, she saw that the car had not moved. LaRee was still sitting there at the bottom of the street, not pursuing her, just waiting for her return. So. That was that. She was caught, discovered, trapped, saved.

20

ANOTHER ONE GONE

LaRee pulled her into the car, one hand under her arm, the other under her knee, as if she were saving her from drowning, or burning, or humiliating herself, or any of the fates from which mothers rescue their children.

"I'm sorry," she blurted, while she still had a grip on Vita, for fear she'd disappear again before she could get the words out, but Vita's head hit her so hard in the diaphragm that the apology became a footballer's grunt, and by the time she caught her breath she was laughing.

"Is that your job in life, to knock the wind out of me? You used to do the same thing when you were six years old and I picked you up at school!"

"Yes! That's why I was born," Vita said, and she started to cry. Traffic had backed up behind them. It was nearly Memorial Day and summer people were coming into town to pick up their beach permits and propane for their grills. Carpenters were finishing up their spring jobs before the season really hit. And as always when there was a funeral, all the parking spaces on both sides of the street were taken. One hand on

the wheel, one under Vita's arm to keep her in the car, LaRee maneu-
vered toward the curb with Vita's feet still out the door.

Vita got herself twisted around and sat up. "It's not your fault,"
she said, meaning to sound forgiving, though she only managed to
sound polite. Which implied distance, which cut LaRee to the
quick. Vita felt that—she always felt what LaRee felt—but there was
nothing she could do. "There was no answer, no good way around."

"I could have—" LaRee began, but thought better of it. Vita
couldn't grow up to assume all the blames and burdens in life; she
had to know that mothers fail, too. "Well, I don't know what I could
have done. But whatever it was, I didn't do it, and here we are. I
brought you something."

Cinnamon rolls from the Upper Crust Bakery—of course, it
was opening day, and it had been their tradition to go together,
since the time Vita was five years old and would skip beside LaRee,
holding her hand. The rolls were still warm. They smelled all
wrong, somehow—cloying, like a sweet, homemade lie.

"I'm not hungry. I mean, thank you. Why don't you have one,
LaRee?"

LaRee nearly snapped that she was not hungry either. "No, thanks,"
she said, as lightly as she could manage, looking straight ahead.

"This isn't the kind of thing that gets resolved with cinnamon
rolls," Vita said.

"I didn't expect them to resolve anything," LaRee said. Though
once they would have, because they were a tradition, a ritual that
was theirs together and belonged to no one else. LaRee looked away
so Vita wouldn't see her lip tremble.

"I mean, thank you. Really, thank you," Vita said, squeezing La-
Ree's hand. "I'll have some later. Or . . . we can come back tomorrow, LaRee, and have cinnamon rolls. Okay?"

She sounded the way LaRee had when Vita was disappointed about a dropped ice-cream cone, when she was little. It was terrible.

LaRee managed a laugh. "Thank you, my dear," she said. "The cinnamon rolls will be good all summer."

"I just want to get away from here!" Vita burst out.

"Who could blame you?" LaRee agreed.

"No. Not just from here, from you! To a place that feels like a real home, with a real family—"

She stopped. Was this what Vinny had felt when he stabbed Sabine, so angry that she would destroy whatever was nearest? She must remember it, in case she ever had to play a murderer. "LaRee! I'm sorry."

"There's no need to be," LaRee said. "No one ever wrote an etiquette guide for murder survivors."

When Vita didn't laugh at this, the world seemed to dissolve. LaRee wanted to cry, to say how she had been going on and on with no love or reassurance, just the daily grounding of motherhood, and the feeling that every tide was eroding that ground under her feet, that she had tried, done her best. . . . But the thing to do now was to give Vita the chance for anger. She could call Charlotte or . . . anyone, later, and weep.

Vita nodded. LaRee must have just had a shower; she could smell the almond oil soap. It seemed a very long time since she'd been home. "I can't go back to school," she said. "I can't ever go back there."

"Let's start by getting through today."

"No. I will not go back to that school, do you understand?" She pushed all the way to the other side of the seat, against the window.

"Of course, of course," LaRee said. "We'll . . . manage it."

"I need to know everything about the murder and about Sabine. Absolutely everything."

She scrunched over into the corner, wearing her slit sweatshirt like a cardigan, her hands pulled into the sleeves, arms crossed over her chest, nose red from crying. She looked like someone who wanted to know nothing.

"Truth, all of it." It was no less than Shakespeare would ask. "Not the polite, appropriate garbage. The real stuff."

"I will tell you. Every single thing, as much as I know. Not the polite, appropriate garbage and not the rude inappropriate garbage either. Just as much of the mixed-up, confusing truth as I can tell. If you just want to get out of here we can go away for a week . . . or more. Maybe a month . . ." LaRee suddenly envisioned a white-washed cottage on the coast of Ireland. "That would be fun, wouldn't it? Go someplace new and explore it so we're not just stewing in it the way we always are here."

"I have rehearsal," Vita said.

Across the street, the church doors opened and Fatima Macha-do's casket emerged, carried by Bobby Matos and Cabbage and some of the others, all looking deeply uncomfortable in their dark suits. Men in Oyster Creek started out cocky and ended up stoic. The oldest ones—Ilidio Codinha and Antone Guerra, whose son had died in a car crash the year before—stood erect, at attention, but staring off beyond the horizon as if grief and disappointment had turned them to stone. The women wore black shawls and heavy wool skirts, the same clothes they would put on for the Blessing of the Fleet next month. Amalia, standing with Maria Machado and Dorotea, glanced across the street and saw LaRee's car, and her face became tighter, tougher than ever.

"Oh God, of course," LaRee said. "Now we're spying on a funeral. Or clowning at a funeral? Or . . . just guilty as charged."

Amalia took Dorotea by her bare shoulders—she was wearing

her homecoming dress, strapless black satin with flesh brimming—and turned her away so she wouldn't see them. A gust blew a paper bag up the street and lifted the flaps on the men's jackets. A Mercedes convertible came through, driven by a man with silver hair and a look of sensual pride on his face. DC plates—maybe he was a senator. What would he see here? The last of an old world? Or a constituency so small and poor it wasn't worthy of notice? The hearse backed up and the men loaded the coffin in. Once the door shut, the pallbearers relaxed: They had discharged their obligation and could return to their lives. Only two or three cars followed the hearse to the cemetery.

"'Sorry for the family.' I'd think she would be," Amalia sniffed to her husband, who stood at attention and gave no sign of hearing.

Franco and Danielle were standing kitty-corner at the short edge of the grave; the remark was intended for them. If Franco had lived his life among his own people and according to their ways, LaRee Farnham wouldn't have been up on her high horse watching this last pathetic chapter from across the street, pitying them all in public. Franco paid no attention to the comment, focusing on the priest and keeping one arm tight around Danielle, who tucked her hair back, though the wind caught it instantly and blew it across her face again. Amalia's hair was so stiffly coifed it was impervious to wind. The years had sealed her over. If she'd stayed in Gelfa, she'd have been one of the women who sat watching the street from behind her shutters and warning her grandchildren: *"Estadia em casa." Stay in the house and you won't get in trouble.* You wouldn't get in trouble and you wouldn't have to change. Danielle had mixed in the world, been hurt and disillusioned, fought hard and forgiven hard. Everyone said how young she looked—a curious, interested face. The two women gazed down on Fatima Machado's coffin.

Fatima hadn't been able to trust much of anything in her life, except maybe cigarettes. She was supposed to be a fisherman's wife, not his widow. She was supposed to have a son who grew up strong and capable, took over his father's boat, had a family of his own. He was not supposed to be Vinny. But she'd managed, living on disability pay, staying in the house where she could dote on her son in peace. Well, the cigarettes had done their work, set her free.

The group looked larger because the grave had only three sides, the fourth being taken up by the earth that would shortly fill it, covered with a green velvet drape. The cemetery workers lowered the coffin and stepped back as the priest leaned over to murmur a blessing. The old part of the cemetery, where the sea captains rested with their wives and children, was at the crest of the hill, with cedars and apple trees growing between the headstones. Only the low, flat land was left now. Vinny's ashes would be interred with Fatima when the state sent them. His wife and daughter stood there stolid, Dorotea tugging alternately at the top and bottom of her dress, trying to cover herself. Franco took off his suit jacket and put it around her shoulders, and she started to cry.

Amalia stepped forward and dropped a white gladiola. Danielle had cut some of the pink roses that climbed over the picket fence outside the Walrus. Orson came from the back, detached his boutonniere, and let it fall. As they were turning to leave, and the cemetery workers were taking out their shovels, a dark, bowlegged figure came over the hill toward them, hurrying in spite of his awkward gait, carrying something.

It was Georgie Bottles with his beer in a brown bag, and as he came upon them he stopped short, embarrassed. Of course, he was taking the shortcut to the liquor store. Seeing them, he immediately struck a fighting pose.

"Don't fuck with me," he muttered.

Franco reached out and patted him on the back. "Good to see you, Georgie," he said, but Georgie pulled away.

"I'm not getting out of there," he said to Franco. "I got nowhere else." He threw the beer can into the grave and continued on.

"Georgie," Amalia began . . . but Danielle shook her head.

"He's off his meds," she said. "Prescriptions just piling up. I called his sister. Meanwhile . . ."

"Meds," Amalia said, looking around. Even a harsh, unyielding spirit seeks a kindred soul. She found none and stood a little straighter in the wind. "That's what it's come to."

Father Lomba peered into the grave.

"Leave it there, Father," Danielle said. "Fatima would appreciate it."

"What wrecked that family is there's no more fish," she said as soon as they were back in the car. "They weren't good for anything but fishin'."

"You could say the same thing about me," Franco said.

"No, you're good for propagation. You'll be gettin' more fan mail after last night. Funny, I never thought to send a mash note to a murder suspect. Just no imagination, I guess."

He laughed—more like a sigh. He couldn't think why she'd stuck by him, now the kids were grown and they'd lost the house and she knew about Vita and Sabine. She never once said, "I was the prettiest girl in the class, I could have married anybody I liked, I wouldn't have to live over the Walrus and Carpenter and hear the same jukebox songs coming up through the floor every single night." She didn't say, "You betrayed me," either. Not anymore. She laughed about it, did her best. She and Franco were kin. If they separated neither of them would stay whole. He put on the blinker.

"Where're we going?" she asked.

"The house?"

"Vinny's house?"

"We have to."

Danielle's shoulders sagged. "I didn't make a dish," she said.

"They won't care."

Danielle laughed. "They'll talk about it for the next forty years," she said. "I can hear it now: 'She couldn't even be bothered to bring a covered dish to the funeral.' God, poor little Vin. Remember how he used to love the broom? He always had that broom. He was sweepin', sweepin'. He felt so important with the broom in his hand."

"He shoulda been a janitor; he'd have had something to take pride in."

"He could never get in at the DPW. . . . He's not related to Bobby." In addition to owning the fish market, Bobby Matos was somehow the progenitor of the entire Department of Public Works. Everyone who worked there was a son, a nephew, an in-law. When it snowed, Matos Fish and all the family driveways were plowed before the roads. They had garbage pickup six days a week.

"He couldn't live on without his mother," Danielle said, resigned to the luncheon by now, staring out the window as they headed down Route 6 toward Tradescome Point. Ice Cream Tuesday was open, its red and white striped awnings unfurled, the UPS driver ordering a cone at the window. "Couldn't stand to live one day past her," Danielle continued. "Not one day."

Cars were streaming up the highway now, for the long weekend—New York plates, New Jersey, Ohio. Another summer and everything would happen again, just as it always had: Young people would arrive in search of work and love and adventure; the sound and smell of the surf would quicken their pulse, give them courage. Just because they were here they'd take new risks, try new loves, suffer a moment's taste of bliss that would linger in memory ever after, or conceive a child who would return to knock on the door in twenty years. A swimmer would be caught in the riptide and carried out to sea, and there'd be talk of closing off that beach, but it would be pointed out that locals knew how to deal with the tides and they'd decide to put up more signs. An old lady turning left off the highway would be rear-ended by a truck driver who was speeding around some poky tourists looking for the turn to Fox Hollow. There'd be an afternoon wedding under a tent beside the harbor with flower girls tottering along strewing rose petals, a baby born in a car stuck in traffic on the Fourth of July. These fates were just waiting here for the people who would step in and live them. In August, Skip McGee would moor his sailboat in the harbor and move in (so as to rent out his house—twelve thousand for the month). Every night he'd lean back in the stern at sunset and play his saxophone. And on land, people in the rental cottages would finish up their dinner dishes with a deep satisfaction, saturated with sun and seawater, ready to face another year.

"We'll never be rid of it," Danielle said now. "We're caught in that damned murder and it never goes away."

Franco shook his head. "We will," he said, in the tone of all-purpose reassurance a man learns from marriage. "We nearly were rid of it, before this."

He took her hand, that little hand with its sweet pink manicure, the same as when they were in high school. Then her hand had been perfect; now it was soft, with knotted veins showing and a constellation of age spots near the thumb, which only heightened his sense of her innocence, her fragility.

Her hand squeezed his. "I haven't planted my window boxes," she said.

"We'll stop on the way home and get some flowers."

She could hear in his voice the gratitude and tenderness that a marriage is supposed to hold.

"Vita's pretty," she offered. "Or she will be, once she learns to manage herself. She's got her mother's eyes. . . ."

He could feel her fishing around, trying to read his feelings for Sabine. "She does not," he said stoutly. "Sabine's eyes were shrewd and that was all. Don't say that about that poor girl."

"Well, she didn't get made from your rib, Franco."

"My genes just blotted hers right out," he said, rubbing his chin so she could hear his beard scratch. "Those tired old Yankee genes. Vita's a good Portagee girl, you'll see. LaRee told me she's sad she never had a boat named after her."

"Never thought of it," Danielle said, "but now I do, it doesn't surprise me. I suppose I took it for granted growing up, that my dad was captain of the *Little Danielle*. But it's good to be able to take things for granted. Remember the little dories you built for the boys?"

"I'd forgotten all about them," he said.

"You could make one for Vita."

"You're right," he said. "I could."

They turned in at the Driftwood Cabins and bumped over the dirt lanes between the cottages. The Machado house sat on a high, bare foundation—a storm tide would have the marsh flooding right up the driveway. There were four cars parked along the road—Maria's, Amalia's big white SUV, Cabbage's truck, and a brown Pontiac that looked twenty years old.

"It's a high school reunion," Franco said, sighing. What wasn't? Amalia, still hurt and resentful over a dance forty years ago . . . and he, even now, reverential toward Bobby, who had the most baskets, the quickest rebounds. . . . High school had set the course of their lives, and they hadn't known how to alter it; there was nothing that showed them another way.

"I wonder if Vinny killed himself because once his mother was dead there really wasn't any reason not to," Danielle said. "Maybe it wasn't that he couldn't live without her but that he stayed alive for her sake."

"I suppose," Franco said. Who knew? And why would anyone want to know? Vinny had lived and now he had died. Franco remembered that the Red Sox had won the night before; it would make for an easy conversation with Bobby.

There was his bicycle, leaning against the front staircase. "What the hell?"

"Georgie, maybe?"

"Nah," Franco said. "Georgie's on foot, remember?"

"We're stuck with him on the *Rainha*," Danielle said. "He can't go to Fatima's now."

The stench hit them when they opened the door. "Something died in the wall," Maria explained. "And just when company's coming. Come in."

". . . and they were just watching, from across the street," Amalia was saying indignantly. "Like she thought it was some kind of freak show." The room was neat; the rabbit was in the cage and the dog chained to the back steps, but you could feel disorder lurking. Linguica rolls and pastries were set out on the table but no one ate.

Franco and Danielle sat on the edge of the sofa, holding their coffee cups. "Some people thrive on the pain of others," Amalia said. "Sorry for the family, I don't wonder."

"Eh, Franco?" Bobby Matos said, holding up a bottle of aguardiente, and Franco held his cup out to receive it.

"I'm not good enough, Bobby?" Danielle said, reaching her cup out, too. Bobby chuckled and said you could never guess with the ladies, but Amalia shot him a poisoned glance. Aguardiente was for men—peasant men. Bobby drank it the same way he belched at the table, to assert his masculinity.

"How's your daughter, Franco?" Amalia asked.

"She's in the Shakespeare play, the one down at Mackerel Bay Park," he said.

"She's so *smart*," Danielle said, demonstrating her open-mindedness. It was tiring to go around demonstrating your open-mindedness all day when you'd just rather be home watching the soaps and reading mysteries.

"Seems pretty stupid to me," Dorotea said, sullen. "She was over here yesterday making a fool out of herself."

"She was?"

"Yeah, I don't know who she thinks she is, barging in like that right after my dad died."

"That was Vita?" her mother asked. "Your friend from school? I thought . . ." She looked over at Franco, puzzling. "I got her mixed up. . . ."

"Yeah, and you made me go walk with her."

"I didn't. . . ." Maria's voice broke, and she looked away, sucking her lip. Then: "You need to do something—look at you."

Maria had a plain, anxious face with small, dull eyes—like an opossum, Franco thought. She was sixteen when she was hustled into marriage, seventeen when Dorotea was born . . . twenty-three when Vinny went to prison. Amalia had kept an eye on her, helped her get the job at the nursing home. Franco's head ached; he rubbed his temples. It was a great relief to remember that he'd been on the news the night before, that they had sent the satellite truck all the way out to Oyster Creek to interview him, because he, Franco Neves, was, in this case, an authority.

"Randy Redwoods, he's a nice guy," he said.

"You mean, the news guy?" Bobby said.

Danielle closed her eyes and shook her head. "Yup, you got the big famous lothario, right here," she said, mostly to herself.

"Lothario," Franco mocked. But he lingered over the syllables. It was a better title than assistant harbormaster. Amalia raised an eyebrow to show she didn't find anything funny, which was a fact everyone already knew.

"Your college fund has five hundred dollars in it, as of this morning," she told Dorotea.

"I'm not goin' to college," Dorotea said quietly, stubbornly aggrieved.

"Thank you," her mother said emphatically. "For setting it up."

"Bobby'll talk to the VFW," Amalia said, her voice a bit thinner after Dorotea's rebuff. "We'll have a breakfast there, in August, and a supper later."

Tourists would go to a pancake breakfast, a lobster roll supper. They would pay a lot for anything that felt authentic, true to the place. And who wouldn't give something to a girl whose father had just died, who wanted to get an education?

"I don't even have my license," Dorotea protested.

"Well, when am I going to do driving hours with you?" Maria said. "The middle of the night's about the only time I'm not working."

"I'd take you driving, honey," Danielle said.

"Can't afford the permit anyway," Dorotea answered, pulling her head in.

"When I was your age I'd never yet crossed the Sagamore Bridge," Franco said.

"Well, I have," Dorotea said. "I been to Souza-Baranowski every visiting day for ten years, until she got too busy."

"Until I got a second shift at the Horizons," her mother said. "So you didn't have to drop out."

"There's more across the bridge than Souza-Baranowski," Amalia said. It wasn't that she believed this herself, really. It was that there was so little left on this side of the bridge that Dorotea—all of them—would have to leave.

"I don't want to go," Dorotea said, with a harsh tug at her slipping bodice.

"How did my bike get here?" Franco thought to ask.

Dorotea looked up. "That's Vita's," she said. "She left it here, but I guess it's finders keepers." She said this with bitter triumph, as if she had at least torn away one thing from Vita's huge pile of riches.

"You don't have a bicycle?"

"Where would I get a bicycle?"

"Franco could teach you to ride," Danielle said.

Franco turned to her with irritation and she gave the slightest shrug, and smile. "Be good for you," she said.

Cabbage was drinking his aguardiente straight from his coffee cup now.

"Lost two in one week. How many natives are left?" he asked.

"Lost two, lost ten, lost a whole world. Should have been standing room only in the church this morning," Amalia said, and she couldn't quite help glancing at Franco as she said it. "Can you imagine bringing someone in from Newburyport to be harbormaster? Because he understands 'pleasure boating'? Can you imagine?"

"Used to go down to the wharf before dinner and get a fish," Cabbage said. "Cod, or mackerel, or a sea clam for pie. Anyone would give me one, it was like askin' for a penny."

"Do you remember when the squid washed up in the bay?" Franco said. "That was back . . . oh, before high school. . . ."

"I remember," Amalia said. "You boys loved it."

"Yeah," Cabbage answered. "They were better'n water pistols, the way you could squirt the ink. Chased the girls all over until they slipped and there they were flailing around in the squid pile. . . . But *you* wouldn't let it go, Danielle."

"You put one down my shirt, I put one down your pants," Danielle said. "Came out even."

"Best day ever," Cabbage said.

"They were all good days. Everyone's father went out fishing on a dragger in the morning and was home for supper that night."

"We played all over town. There was always one mother or another watching us out the kitchen window."

"Couldn't imagine anythin' else."

The conversation guttered out, all of them staring past one another, remembering.

"Franco, you're sure you don't want to sell the *Rainha*?" Bobby said suddenly.

"For scrap?" Franco sounded injured, then smiled and shook his head at himself.

"Five hundred," Bobby said. "I'll sink her out past Barrel Point. I believe I'd have an oyster reef there within a couple of years."

Franco sighed. "Not . . . not now. Maybe next year. I had a guy wanted to buy her and fix 'er up. He'll be back in July, maybe then."

"Didn't say anything to me about it," Danielle said. "Did this guy actually see her?" Probably he'd been telling someone at the Walrus about the *Rainha*, the cypress wood in the cabin that wouldn't weather, the way she'd stayed stable and solid and rode out the highest waves. The longer he talked, the better that boat would have sounded, and the guy would have said, "I'd like to come see her sometime; I've been looking to buy something." And Franco would have filed that away, under HOPE, sneaking it into his unconscious without passing it by REALITY. He needed to; that she understood.

"Are you moving over to Fatima's now, Maria?" she asked. They couldn't sell the boat with Georgie on it.

Maria shook her head, slow and deliberate. "Can't," she said. "That house needs so much work, gotta sell it." Fatima's house tilted at the end of Whiddon Alley, up against the old cemetery, the lace curtains turning to rags in the windows, the paint long since worn away. It was easy to imagine the real estate ad: "In town, walk to beach! Good bones, antique features; ready for your inspiration." And a few hundred thousand of your dollars. But someone would renovate it, keeping true to history, turning the little yard into a patio with an arbor, adding a widow's walk if they could get around the zoning board. And there they'd be, every August, waking up to fill their lungs with salt air, start the ceviche and head for the beach, back in time for a martini and a shower before the guests arrived. Urbane laughter would float up the street, and they'd lean back listening for the saxophone, on the same street where Danielle's grandmother had called her kids in for dinner by beating a pot with a wooden spoon.

"Another one gone..." Amalia said.

"My shift starts in an hour," Danielle said, standing. "Maria, I'll call the first of next week and see what I can do, all right?"

Maria nodded, stood up to bid them good-bye. Seeing Danielle start out the door, she said suddenly, "They're sending his ashes tomorrow. In a hearse."

Danielle closed her eyes, nodded.

"You gotta... Someone's gotta..."

"I'll come over," Amalia said, stoic. She would bury them all, buy a one-way ticket to Lisbon, turn out the lights, and leave the town to the washashores. "Bobby can cover the shop. Do you mind if I use your . . ."

She started to open the door at the side of the room, but it pushed back. Maria had dragged all the clutter from the living room into the bedroom. To walk through you'd have to climb piles of laundry, a mattress folded over on itself, a television with an antenna improvised of tinfoil and wire, a Disney Cinderella costume that must have been Dorotea's years ago.

Amalia pulled the door shut, and for once she made no judgment, though bitterness shriveled her throat. To go down to the wharf after school and see them there, mending the nets, cleaning the decks, calling across to one another with the bay sparkling behind them . . . She had been dazzled to see her father at the wide wooden steering wheel. He'd been steering that boat since he was tall enough to see out the wheelhouse windows; he knew every shoal and channel and he could feel the weather by the movement of the waves underneath. You'd have been sure he had set the family on its way to glory. Instead, life had carried them here.

She squared her shoulders and bore it, the mess, the stink, the sorrow. "We need to open the store, Bobby," she said. When she got home she would read more of *Their Eyes Were Watching God*, though it seemed silly to her, some kind of hysteria. Like Sabine Gray, or LaRee, looking for love and "fulfillment," recognition . . . silly luxuries as far as she could see. After she got through the chapter, she'd clean the bathroom, getting between the tiles with a toothbrush as if there were some disease creeping in there that could be vanquished if you worked at it every single day.

21

THE TRUE TRUTH

"To think, I used to be happy here," Vita said, looking out the big window into the woods. "That was before I understood all that was out there in the world."

"Well, you've been away almost twenty hours!" LaRee said. "I'm surprised you recognize the place."

Oh, she was back, she was back, speaking the exact phrases a sixteen-year-old was meant to, after a great adventure during which she had come very close to crossing the border into the next town. LaRee wanted to pick her up and hug and kiss her and twirl her around, the way she would have without thinking ten years ago.

"You know what I mean, LaRee," Vita said, sulking and laughing at once, giving a little performance. She pressed her hands to the kitchen window for a second as if recalling the cell she'd escaped from.

"I do know what you mean," LaRee said. "There is so much out there in the world and you will get to see all of it, all of the beauty and mystery. It's all ahead."

"I've already seen the bad."

"Some of it."

"From now on, the truth, always . . ."

"I promise. I never meant to hide things from you, only to wait until you could understand better," she said.

Vita looked away, glanced back quickly as if she didn't trust this.

"It's not as easy as you might think, Vita," LaRee said. "Truth isn't a solid thing you can pass from one person to another. It's all rags and shards, like something you'd find washed up on the beach, and you pick it up and disentangle it from the weeds and look at it from every side and you begin to understand some piece of it. You kind of feel your way through."

"But there are *some* solid pieces," Vita said, resisting her.

"I'll try," LaRee said quickly. "I will try. I met your mom at a party, in the line for the ladies' room. We were freshmen, so we were in the same dorm even though I was a nursing major and she was in fine arts. She seemed very . . . aristocratic, or something . . . cool and discerning. She didn't care much about things that were terribly important to me. She never went home for holidays; she said her father 'spent his time whoring' and her mother was a pill popper and she'd rather eat pizza alone on Thanksgiving than feel the emptiness in that house."

"Okay," Vita said, guarded and waiting.

"But she took a lot of pills herself—speed. She was friends with all the chic people—they were too beautiful to sleep. They could talk about Paris, their favorite bistros and shops, and Soho, their favorite bistros and shops, and Aspen. . . . Well, you see what I mean. They thought they were better than I was, and . . . I thought they were better than I was, too."

"Maybe they *were* better than you," Vita said. Even now LaRee flinched inwardly.

"Maybe they were," she said. "It certainly seemed like they were. They'd talk about painters, how you didn't know Tintoretto until you'd been to the Uffizi. I didn't know what the Uffizi was. Once Sabine said the sky was 'Ang blue,' and I thought it was a paint color, like alizarin crimson or something, so I said, 'Closer to cobalt,' to try to sound like I knew something. And she said, 'Ang the painter.' As if she was so tired of having to explain things like that to me. She meant Ingres . . . a French painter who I'd never heard of, of course."

"You know so much . . ." Vita burst out in sympathy, then stiffened.

"Hardly," LaRee said. "Even now I'm expecting someone to correct my pronunciation. And I knew a lot less back then. I hadn't heard of anyone, or been anywhere, and there was Sabine. . . . Once, there was a visiting poet, and I went to hear him speak, and I was thinking how amazing it was to be at college and meet people like that who had Pulitzer prizes and talked about Yeats as if he was just their next-door neighbor. . . . And in the morning I went to Sabine's room to borrow her shampoo and there was the writer asleep next to her! And she . . ."

Vita was listening so intently, LaRee had to take a breath and think twice. Sabine had shrugged off her tryst with the great poet, said that she didn't see why women shouldn't be able to make conquests just like men, that once she'd gotten a famous sculptor to strip naked for her, and then when he was standing there fleshy and sagging, she told him she'd changed her mind and sent him away. That she was leaving out. "I was jealous of Sabine," she said. "Probably I shouldn't have been, but I was young and I would fall desperately in love with some boy or other. . . . But real men fell for your mom. She was beautiful and sophisticated and adventurous, and I was just another girl."

"LaRee," Vita said, her reserve breaking. "Nothing is better than being you."

"My lovely girl," LaRee said. "I do feel that now, but at the time, I was young and very uncertain."

Vita looked down. "Like me," she said.

"A little. Your mom named you after Vita Sackville-West, did you know that?"

"Who's that?"

"She was a writer, but she was famous for her love affairs really. Your mom wanted you to be free to live, not cramped by convention."

LaRee's given name was Laura, after a great-aunt who "was at the round table with Dorothy Parker," according to her mother, who had never, ever told a simple truth. LaRee figured Great-aunt Laura had been to the Algonquin once, perhaps during Dorothy Parker's life span, perhaps not. Her mother was always alluding to family members who were "very important during the Roosevelt years," but whatever glory there might have been once was utterly lost by the time LaRee was born. Her father was an optometrist, and they had lived in a small, plain house chosen because it had good parking and an office space attached. The poor man had stood by in wooden silence as his wife taunted him—he never got the bills sent out, never went after the debts owed, fell for any sob story, was still tangled in his mother's apron strings, had not the fire of true genius (as she, whose family was very important during the Roosevelt years, ought to know). . . . Then her car slid off the road into a telephone pole, in the first little snow of the year. The house went silent. Her brother, Robin, had been twelve and followed the prescribed path until he was in his mid-twenties and the back injury gave him reason to move back home. He continued to insult his father as if it were a way of keeping his mother alive. Their father barely seemed to notice, as if he was just glad for the company. When he wasn't in his office, he was reading the newspaper, sighing and shaking his head. "Well, people will always need eyeglasses," he'd say. "An optometrist never lacks."

Without noticing, she had followed in his footsteps. People would always need nurses, too. Laura had become Laurie in high school and it was easy enough to start emphasizing the second syllable when she got to college. It had seemed to sound French that way.

"But LaRee doesn't sound French at all," Sabine had said. France, up to and including Ingres and the Sorbonne, where she had studied one semester, was Sabine's territory. Sabine was named for her grandmother, whose portrait hung in the National Gallery. "Miss Sabine Newbold with her Canary." Her tuition was paid from the grandmother's trust, but she was one of six children from her father's four marriages. Her little inheritance from her mother was in trust for Vita's care now.

"Your mom was beautiful," LaRee said to Vita, with an effort of generosity. "And very delicate, and she'd grown up around art, so she was naturally artful."

"Which is why you're so disappointed in me."

"What on earth do you mean?"

"You know exactly what I mean," Vita said, tugging her hair back tight as an example. "You wish I wore little dresses and had perfect hair like the others. You'd like me to be more like . . . Shy-anne!"

"Shyanne? The girl with the neon brassiere? How could you think such a thing?"

"I see you looking at them, LaRee. And then you look at me like 'What's wrong with this picture?' You're like, 'Why don't you wear your hair out?' and 'You wear that sweater every day . . .' You think I'm ugly and you want to fix me."

"Oh, Vita . . ." Of course she would see it this way. If LaRee looked longingly at girls in pretty dresses it was because they seemed to have the happiness she wanted for Vita.

"I know you are beautiful, and I try to help bring that beauty out. You want all truth, the awful truth. But truth isn't necessarily awful."

"'Those are pearls that were his eyes,'" Vita quoted, to no one in particular. And to LaRee, harshly, "Some truth is awful. Maybe you hate me because you were jealous of Sabine."

"I suppose that could be." Let her think about it, see if she could feel it. "I think she was jealous of me, too," LaRee said.

"Why would anyone be jealous of you?" Vita asked, sitting down on the couch suddenly.

LaRee had to laugh. "Well, that does seem like a good question! I don't think it was anything I had but more that she was so at sea with herself, so afraid of being ordinary. And I *was* ordinary—a nurse who married a carpenter, opened a savings account, planted a vegetable garden. . . . But I didn't mind it. In fact I was more or less happy that way. When she first told me she was moving to Oyster Creek, I thought—'Of course, I always knew I'd end up taking care of her.'"

"So, you hated her."

"Oh God, yes I did. Sometimes, I hated her. After . . . after she died . . ." All that night while Vita slept, LaRee had realized in little waves how unkind she had been. She'd refused to be impressed, when it was so important to Sabine to impress people. The least she could have done would have been to say how brave her friend was, to pursue ... whatever she was pursuing ... so boldly. She could have said that it was wonderful to know a picture of your grandmother hung in the National Gallery, that it gave you ground to stand on, from which to reach higher. . . . Except, if she admitted such a thing, she'd have had to give in to Sabine and admit that she herself was less interesting, less worthy somehow. So she'd made sure to sound bored when Sabine told her about the painting, to raise an eyebrow just slightly at such bragging. Yes, the optometrist's daughter was very clear-sighted about the airs others gave themselves.

That was what she'd kept from Vita—her mother's genius. It was a last little act of revenge, and it was disguised as goodness: Of course she had kept the squalid story of the murder from the child, but she had hidden the rest, too.

"After she died I realized how fragile she'd been and how brave to keep living, going ahead, even when she must have felt completely lost. All the things I hated about her seemed so small they were hardly worth noticing, just ways of protecting herself from a frightening world. I called some of her old friends from the city and invited them to the funeral, and one man who she'd talked and talked about didn't even seem to remember her. But there were other things, and once she wasn't there, being more chic and worldly than I was all the time, I could see them."

She had never had Vita's attention so completely. But one dishonest syllable and the connection would break.

"Like what?"

"That she had loved the world enough to think how the sky might be the same color as a dress in a French painting."

"Enough to have an affair with a man who drove the septic truck."

"She was in love with your father, of all people. She was ... literally crazy in love with him."

"What do you mean, 'of all people'?"

"Well, he wasn't her usual type! She liked to have someone who would distinguish her, a professor, or an heir. But Franco? The assistant harbormaster of Oyster Creek, Massachusetts? He was sort of a comedown."

"LaRee!" But Vita was laughing, happily. Candor was building a tentative bridge between them.

"No one will ever be such a big deal in Rome as Franco is here. He understands the ocean, for God's sake! Sabine inherited a worndown fortune, Franco inherited a rusty dragger. And no fish in the bay. But he's rolled with the punches; he's managed a life in spite of all the changes in the world. To her, to marry Franco would have been better than marrying a prince!

"So, she'd go down to the Walrus and he was the bartender; it was his job to make her a drink. She had the idea that they were star-crossed lovers, that he stayed with Danielle because he was too guilty to leave. But ... Franco and Danielle have known each other all their lives. If he left her he'd be walking out of his own life. That didn't make sense to Sabine. She was younger and prettier and she'd had this glamorous life and she just couldn't believe Franco wouldn't drop everything to be with her. It was the last straw, and all the feeling that went into that love soured into retaliation. She'd accuse him of not caring about his own daughter, she forced him to tell Danielle about you, she sued him for child support."

"So, she was just what people say," Vita said, with bitter triumph. "Asking for it."

"Asking for what? Asking to be murdered? She was a little bit crazy, like a lot of people, but she was floundering toward love. She made mistakes, like everyone. If inviting Vinny in for a drink is 'asking for it,' what does that say about Vinny?"

"Before I was at Orson's yesterday . . . I went to see Dorotea."

"My God . . . way down in the Driftwood Cabins?"

"I took Franco's bike. . . ."

"Aha. Georgie Bottles said he saw you on a bicycle, but I couldn't figure it out."

"You asked Georgie Bottles about me? I wouldn't even think he knew who I was."

"I asked everyone I could find."

"Well, I'm not sorry. I ought to have something of Franco's. He's my father."

"I'm sure he would understand."

"Dorotea's house . . . It's a nightmare in there. I didn't know anyone lived like that, especially not in Oyster Creek."

"You know what the tourist brochures say: 'We've got it all in Oyster Creek.'"

Vita gave a crooked, grown-up smile, which dissolved into a plea. "What could Sabine have wanted with Vinny? What? He didn't just break in—she was drinking wine with him!"

"You want complete honesty, so I will tell you the truth: I don't know. I don't understand."

"I don't believe you! Was she buying drugs from him? Was it that?"

"No. Vinny was probably high, probably on meth. He hit his wife, so he was used to being violent. . . ."

"How do you know?"

"Because I treated her. Though when I did, she said he never hit her, and I never reported it. So you could say that I might be partly to blame."

"Good. That sounds true. I mean, it's the kind of thing that would be true."

"Yes, exactly. So he was a violent man, and Sabine probably provoked him. I don't know that either, but she did everything to infuriate Franco...."

"But what happened? Why? He went there for the sex. That's why everyone went there."

For the last two years or so, LaRee had had the sense that Vita wasn't so much growing up as coming into focus. The other girls drew a certain kind of clarity on their faces with makeup, but Vita of course refused that and she always looked much younger, more innocent, and in some ways more ignorant, than they. Lately, though, she had grown into her own face, and it struck LaRee now that she had been asserting her right to youth and innocence, giving herself time. Her expression had resolved, become thoughtful, questioning, clear-eyed. She was not looking for a mirror so much as for some understanding that might take her another step into life. LaRee had forgotten how little she knew, and what a phantasmagoria ignorance can be.

"If Vinny went to your house with the idea that your mother was a prostitute, that was because of his own stupidity, and maybe some kind of drugged idea—nothing real. We know what happened was terrible, but we don't know what it was."

"Amalia Matos knew my mother and I didn't!" Vita said. "I can't defend her.... I can't do anything!"

"What can it possibly matter to you what Amalia Matos thinks of your mother? Amalia never looked at her through any lens except the one she looks at everyone with, which makes Amalia big and everyone else very, very small."

"It matters, because ... because, LaRee, you're trying to spare me, to make the world all nice and neat and pretty for me. Amalia has no reason to lie."

She stood up—she seemed taller, and straighter, grown from her efforts to understand.

"Your mom would be so proud of you," LaRee said.

"I want to be proud of her."

"Well, you can be. She was as brave as a lion, going off to Rome to pursue her art, and she'd meet a new man and dive into his world and add a whole new piece to her life."

"So she dove into Vinny's world?"

"Well, no." She could hear Sabine now: *He's always staring at me. You have to wonder what it would be like to go to bed with a man like that, a man who's all instinct and no intellect—it's all movement and muscle with him. Vinny knows what it's like to be outcast; he gets things everyone else misses. Like me. I wonder what Franco would think if ...* All that swagger, from one small, sad woman who'd been disappointed in love.

"I was tired of her ego and her silliness and her never-ending vengeance against Franco," LaRee went on. "And I was caught up in my own life, my own misery ... and then she was gone and I was sitting in the church while they played 'Be Thou My Vision'— and I knew that if I'd just said something to her about it, that she was crazy to be flirting with someone like Vinny ... She loved you, Vita, and that love was changing her. She didn't give a damn if you ever slept through the night, as long as you knew she was right there for you. So you trusted her, and because of that you trusted people in general. That was her real legacy. You were three years old when you came to me, with all the faith and sweetness your mother had given you. If you hadn't dared trust me ... I don't know if you could have survived. But you did, and ...

here you are, and you can be proud of your mother for making that happen."

LaRee turned her head, wiped her eyes, got herself to laughing instead of crying.

"And that is the truth," she said. "The true truth, as you call it. Okay?"

Vita looked skeptical.

"The truth isn't always cruel, you know. Most of the time it's more just . . . sad."

Vita nodded. "Dorotea's house was sad," she said. "Really sad."

"Vinny's life was pretty brutal." She wasn't going to tell about the basement, no matter how truthful she meant to be.

"LaRee, *why* didn't you tell me before? Everyone else knew!"

"I don't think they knew very much. They knew little bits of gossip, plus whatever their parents told them, just like you did. And except for Dorotea and a few others—it didn't matter, because it wasn't their life. But . . . I am very sorry. I've always wanted to protect you from all of it, and instead I left you exposed."

Vita sat down again, took LaRee's hand.

"Here's a truth," LaRee said. "When your mom asked me if she could make me your guardian, in her will, I felt like it was a trap, a way of forcing me to stay close to her the way she tried to force Franco. But I said yes, and then I forgot all about it. Who could have imagined what would happen? And then, there you were, as if a stork had brought you! I had no idea what to do, none. But both of us alone in the world, and from then on—through everything, your first ice-cream cone, the first time we carved a pumpkin and we stood out in the dark to see it with the candle burning inside—you've been my daughter. How lucky is that?"

"You're crazy, LaRee," Vita said, snuggled in beside her, the way she used to when she was tiny. What it had been like, to hold her for the first time! A lifetime of sorrow had slid away—and simply disappeared, like a glacier falling into the sea.

Vita jumped up. "I'm going to the library. I have to read all the newspapers, everything everyone said. I'm going to understand it all."

"I have most of them here. In a trunk out in the shed."

"Really?" Vita turned wide eyes toward her. "You do?"

"I knew you'd want them someday. I thought, maybe in ten years or . . . Anyway, I couldn't throw them away."

So, here it was, the time of reckoning, with the dust and webs, the boxes full of salacious, idiotic old newspapers, and also of letters from Drew. She'd kept his love letters and then the letters from after he left, the ones that said he'd never loved her and she had "coerced" the love letters from him. These she had saved because she couldn't bear to think about them long enough to throw them away.

"I'm so sleepy, now, though," Vita said. And instead of rushing out the door, she slipped down with her head against the arm of the couch and her legs across LaRee's lap.

"No wonder."

"I guess I can look at that stuff tomorrow."

"Whenever you want to, honey. It's all there, all the headlines, even the picture of your father in *Cosmopolitan* magazine."

"What?" Vita said, opening her eyes.

"*Cosmopolitan* had this article on handsome murder suspects—it was kind of like—'Could you fall for this criminal?'"

Vita giggled. "We do have an interesting life, LaRee," she said.

"We do."

"Will you wake me up for rehearsal?"

"Of course, darlin'."

She went into the bedroom for the quilt and by the time she was back Vita was asleep. She had slept like that when she was tiny, cheeks flushed bright and the one little hand curled into a loose fist on the pillow, as if the engine of her ambition was still pressing forward in her dreams.

PART FOUR

22

WIDE-EYED

"Remember, they've been stranded here since Miranda was a baby," Hugh said. "She knows nothing of the world beyond this island; she is the epitome of innocence." He sounded a bit drier than usual. Shyanne, who had no problem acting lascivious or haughty, could not quite bring herself to the role of Miranda. She shot Hugh a seething glance and bit her lip in a porno parody of a schoolgirl.

"She's too damned naive to be able to act innocent," he growled to Orson. Vita heard it. Her hearing was as sharp as her sight was blurred, and her general sense of smallness in the face of the enormous adult world kept her still, and sometimes nearly invisible. "Mousy," Shyanne had called her to Adam. Yes, she'd heard that, too.

The bay was such a bright, hard blue it looked like you could shatter it with a hammer. The *Sweet Shyanne* was making a pass along Barrel Point, with Shyanne's father at the helm and her brothers on deck, shucking cherrystones as quick as they could go. The smell of fried clams came in on every south breeze, a smell you always noticed in June before it became an ordinary part of the summer air.

How did you ever change anything, when you were caught in the sway of home? Who could leave Oyster Creek, its sights and smells, the constant rhythm of the waves? Vita had lasted three days before she went back to school—she wanted to see what she'd gotten on her history paper, and she missed singing in chorus, hearing all the voices blending together like currents in a stream. School was what she did; it was part of her. And she wasn't going to let Brandon think that he'd frightened her away.

At first it seemed as if nothing had changed except her. She had traveled far and wide—to Dorotea's house, to Orson's house, and back to the time before she could remember, to all that had made her who she was today—whoever that might be. She saw everything and everyone through a different lens. But the same motes floated in the afternoon sunlight while Mr. Bergman wrote out the geometric formulas on the blackboard, and the boys still banded together, chanting "Octopus! Octopus!" all arms reaching high and low as she got up to leave the classroom. The cheerleaders pushed through, rubbing up against the boys while telling them this was the closest they were ever likely to get. Vita stood there, hands on hips, glaring. Then . . . well, one thing was different: Dorotea was illuminated, singled out and special by virtue of her father's death. No one teased her anymore. No one got near her. She still hung her head, but when she looked up you could see some kind of triumph on her face. She was the tragic one and as she came toward the octopus, it dissolved. Vita stepped through in her wake.

That was the other change, a change in herself. When Brandon belched in her face later, she said, "You disgust me," without giving a damn what anyone might think.

"That's what I meant to do," he said, all superior . . . but somehow this twisted back on him and the other guys held their laughter.

"So I guess *I* win," he said, waiting for affirmation. Nothing.

"What are you staring at?" he asked the others angrily. "*She's* the loser."

"Whatever makes you feel better, Brandon," she said. *Then* they laughed. He seemed to shrink away right there, changing from a terrifying threat to a boy with a foolish grin and pale, uncertain eyes.

Turning around, she came face-to-face with Adam. One corner of his mouth was crooked into a smile. She had an instinct to walk until she was right against him, and this instinct touched off a panic that kept her from moving at all. So that was still the same.

"Hi," she croaked.

"Do you want a ride to rehearsal?"

"I . . . I've got to go home first."

"We can stop at your house."

"It's out of the way. . . ." She always took the bus home, and ate something and told LaRee the whole story of the day, changed her clothes, and then LaRee drove her downtown. That was her routine; she hardly knew how to do different. And she liked Adam so much that the idea of being in a car alone with him for fifteen minutes frightened her out of her wits.

"Um, about three minutes out of the way." He shrugged. "But that's fine, I'll see you there. I just thought . . ."

"No . . . thank you . . . yes . . . I mean yes, thank you! If we can make a quick stop at my house, that would be great." She fell in beside him, walking stiffly toward the parking lot, hardly able to speak. The trees that had been like knobby old hands reaching up from the grave all winter were all leafed out now, immense and lush and moving with soft grace above.

"You turn on Grace Pond Road," she managed, "and left around the next corner, by the white tree. . . ."

Spring had turned to summer overnight. The fog cleared under a hot sun, the wisteria blossomed all at once, and the peony buds were suddenly as fat as golf balls, with tiny ants patrolling the honeyed edges of the petals. LaRee was kneeling among them and stood up when she heard the car. Why? A helpful person would have crouched in behind the daylilies and kept her head down. Vita tried to leap out of the car, imagining she could get into the house, grab the script, and get back in the car before LaRee could come over and make conversation, but her backpack strap caught on the stick shift and brought her up short.

"Hi," LaRee said, infuriatingly.

"Get down! I mean, thank you. Adam's giving me a ride to rehearsal, no worries, you can just keep working."

"Okay, have a good time," LaRee said, taking a step back as Vita seemed to be armed and dangerous. "Do you still want me to pick you up?"

"Yes. Please. You can keep planting. . . . Just keep planting."

"I'll keep planting," LaRee said, dropping back to her knees behind the new pea vines.

So, maybe a lot had changed. But none of it in the way she had expected. Adam drove her to rehearsal every day now, falling in beside her as she headed down the path after school. They had, by accident, become friends. If Orson hadn't signed Franco up as the boatswain, Vita would have been too shy to speak to Adam. So maybe that hadn't been the worst thing that had ever happened after all. She followed Adam's gaze across the water, watching a tall sail come around Barrel Point while Franco and the others roared through the end of the shipwreck scene, howling and accusing one another as their ship split beneath them, stranding them on Prospero's island.

"'Would thou mightst lie drowning . . . the washing of ten tides!'"

Franco's brow furrowed and he looked toward Hugh.

"A pirate's dead body was left through several tides, as if enough tides would scrub it clean enough for proper burial. It was sign of disrespect," Hugh said.

Franco repeated the line as a curse, and when Hugh suggested he try a lower, rasping voice, he sounded like Popeye the sailor man suddenly and everyone laughed.

Vita went through life unnoticed, blending into the background, while Franco emerged from the harbormaster's shack for five minutes and was anointed a star. And there he was, beaming, like the big old fool he was. But—

"She's my daughter," he said suddenly.

"What?" Hugh squinted in his direction.

"She's my daughter. Vita is," he said; and then, "Really, she is!"

Hugh turned to inspect her. She stood still and held her breath.

"I see it," he said. "Yes. But . . . ?"

"It's not important," Vita said, but Franco was undergoing a revelation.

"You don't know?" he asked. "You don't know who I am?"

"He doesn't believe in television," Orson explained. "He only reads the *New York Times.*"

"It's *not* important," Vita said between her teeth. She was clenching her toes to keep from clenching her fists. *The washing of ten tides . . .* it would have been . . . eight tides, at least, that Sabine had lain there bleeding, the long day and night and day that was lost to Vita's memory but indelible in her imagination. There. Indelible. The washing of ten tides or ten thousand would not erase what she had of Sabine. She did not have to clutch at it, to try to get back an exact memory. Sabine was more than her death—she was present, right there in the way Vita turned her face to the sun.

"It's a long story," she said to Hugh. "A long, long story." Orson would tell it as soon as she left. She glanced at Franco and dared to smile. Hugh's compliment had given him the courage to claim her as his daughter. She'd had it backward. All this time she'd been sure he was ashamed of her. In fact he'd assumed she'd be ashamed of him.

Sam and Shyanne entered, as Prospero and Miranda.

"No," Hugh said. "No, Shyanne. Miranda may indeed sulk; she's a teenaged girl and she's stuck on this damned island with her father. But she would not have expressed it with that slump. They were *wide-eyed*, all of them, in a way we can barely imagine, but we want to make it possible for the audience to feel something of it. When Shakespeare was writing *The Tempest*, the world was very much unexplored. The *Mayflower*, for instance, hadn't arrived on these shores."

Shyanne rolled her eyes. "Oh my God, she is *such* a loser," she said under her breath, but Hugh was entranced by his vision, waving a hand toward the water to remind them all that the *Mayflower* had indeed arrived just a few miles north of Mackerel Bay.

Vita tried to feel what it might have been like to live in 1580, looking out over an ocean that seemed infinite. Beyond the horizon mysterious societies flourished, and ships would go and come in spite of the serpents that lived in the sea, bringing gold and silk and spices.... Something washed through her, like a scent from that time.

"That Shakespeare should imagine Prospero might have magic powers—why not?" Hugh asked. "They were using dried toads as a medicine for plague; magic was only one step beyond."

Orson flashed a secretive grin—he had long imagined what mischief he might make if he had magical powers. Franco watched with open curiosity, reminded of the stories his father had told him of the Portuguese explorers. Sam had his arms around Leo's waist, his cheek against his shoulder—Vita edged a step closer to Adam.

"We live in a time of recycling, conservation," Hugh said. "They couldn't have conceived of it. They had boundless natural resources. *Knowledge*, however, was limited. Societies lived by imagination: dread and wonder. Prospero, Miranda, Ariel, these characters are very different from anyone who lives in our time. Do I make myself clear?"

"Yes!" Vita said, militant. Shyanne rolled her eyes.

"Okay, I get it," Shyanne said, tonguing her chewing gum to the back of her cheek and positioning herself opposite Adam, deferential toward Prospero and too shy to meet Ferdinand's eyes. She was getting closer to the real character. But Franco was watching Vita, with curiosity and maybe even admiration.

Vita stepped back away from the group—she didn't come onstage until Act Five anyway—and went to sit at the picnic table. Families would be having barbecues here soon; this was the perfect beach for them. Cape Cod formed a protective arm around the bay, and Barrel Point guarded the harbor from the surf. When the tide was out there was a vast expanse of flats where children could run and splash, dig new channels and collect hermit crabs. The Good Humor truck came around every hour in the summer. It was heaven on earth, this beach. And only Vita really understood that it could split with a stroke, fall away.

Ferdinand made his exit, and Adam sat down beside her. "I got into BC, off the wait list," he said. "My mom texted me—they just called."

"Congratulations!" She meant: "So, you're abandoning me, like everyone else."

They sat there, silent. Someone had chiseled a heart with initials into the tabletop, years ago when people still did things like that. Vita's gaze was caught there; she couldn't look away. "Why BC?" she asked finally.

"I hardly know," he admitted. "Gothic architecture, or something. When I was walking around on the tour, it felt kind of solid, you know. Like being in a church before you start asking yourself how there could possibly be a God."

She couldn't think of a thing to say, not a thing.

"God, what crap," he said. "I'm sorry."

"No, it's not! It's more real than the stuff people usually say."

"Oh God, that's bad."

"It's good!"

"I've always wondered . . . what it was like for you," he said. "I mean . . ."

"I know what you mean," she interrupted, because she didn't want him to put it wrong, and no matter what he said it would feel wrong; it always did. She was going to hear some judgment in it. It would be prurient, gooey with curiosity disguised as concern, or casual, as if brutality was nothing out of the ordinary. And so it would infuriate her, and she did not want to be infuriated right now, when she was feeling almost close to someone. "You mean my mom being murdered."

"Yes, that," he said, embarrassed. She was embarrassed, too. It was something you didn't mention, though it had changed the landscape they lived on just as if it were a tornado that had ripped through the town. "I don't know how you managed to live. I don't think I could have."

"I don't remember it," she explained. "So, it's okay. Your mom was gone . . . for a while . . . right?"

"Yeah. But she was just up in Provincetown, not . . ."

"Dead," she said, simply. The corner of her mouth tugged and trembled and insisted on sadness. That was what she got, for demanding the truth.

Adam's hand moved toward hers but didn't dare touch it. "You're the bravest person I know," he said.

23

QUEEN OF THE SEA

Franco had woken up the morning after Fatima's funeral with an image of clean, new wood in his mind. He could see the grain, smell the sawdust. It had been years since he'd built anything, and driving to the lumberyard he felt as carefree as when his boys were little and he would have one of them always beside him in the truck. His tools were in the basement, and Hank was happy to let him work in the garage bay at the back of the harbormaster's shack. He was building a dory named *Vita*, but as he worked, planing and sanding until every inch was smooth, sealing with epoxy and covering the hull with fiberglass so it was watertight, painting her a luminous pale green that would stand out against the water, with a deep purple rim that would be visible in the fog, he kept hearing his daughter's grave young voice saying, "I'm an actor," as if this were a sacred calling. The way she listened to Hugh, the way she worked with Leo to learn how the goddess Iris might move . . . her ambition and the way she carried it out. Imagine having a daughter like this! She had taken the best in him—his openness—and made an art of it. In some back corner of his mind he was thrilled she had taken his bicycle: It proved that she too felt their relation. By the time he came to paint the dory's name, he knew it ought to be the *Iris*. And here she was, a fine, compact craft, named for Vita and for her aspiration.

Danielle had redone her window boxes with some of the leftover paint from the dory. She was standing on the front deck watering them when she heard the explosion and saw the plume of black smoke puff up behind the town hall. The building blocked her view of the pier, but she could see the harbormaster's shack, and Hank Capshaw, who ran out the front door and around the side of the building toward the pier. For a moment there was absolute silence, except for the sound of . . . flames; that was what it was. They sounded like a heavy flag flapping in a gale. Danielle was always expecting an emergency. There had been so many when she was young—from her brother putting the shucking knife through the meat of his thumb and hitting the artery, forty years ago, and the sinking of the *Suzie Belle*, to the Calliope fire, when she'd had to use the garden hose to wet down the roof of the Walrus and all the other buildings around it. Sometimes there were sirens and commotion, sometimes, as with Sabine's death, icy silence. There was always a kind of relief in catastrophe, though—after all the waiting and worry, here it was, to be grappled with at last. She slipped her feet into sandals and set off down the street, untying her apron as she went.

It sounded like a cannon, Amalia would say later. One heavy boom and then a complete, expectant silence, as if the whole town were holding its breath. She could hear the *slap, slap* as someone ran down Sea Street in flip-flops. The screen door of the fish market looked away from the harbor, but she could see the tourists stopping in midamble, turning toward the sound. Then someone started yelling, "Fire, call the fire department!" and Matt Paradel's truck came careening around the corner. She dialed 911 because it was the appropriate thing to do, but of course they said the firemen were on the way. She locked the market up tight, walking right past an elderly couple with a Florida plate who had just pulled into the parking lot. The sirens began to howl. Amalia bustled down to the street entrance to take down the OPEN flag, leaning it across the front door to make her point again to the customers, and started off toward the pier. Danielle was ten steps ahead of her and she slowed her pace to avoid catching up.

At the clinic, LaRee heard it come over the scanner: Code 111, 10-44, 10-46—fire at the pier, request ambulance, request police.

"It's okay," Alice Nguyen said. "A boat . . . exploded? . . . at the end of the wharf, but it sank right away and . . . I guess it put itself out? The ambulance is coming up with . . . the former harbormaster, I guess? He fell over in his chair? They think he has a concussion?"

The question marks meant "What am I doing in this godforsaken place, treating the injuries of neglect and despair?" Who could answer? Alice's parents had been professors back in Vietnam. When they got to the United States, her father took a job as a gas station attendant in Lowell and saved enough to buy the place, and to send Alice to med school. So here she was in Oyster Creek, treating Manny Soares for a folding-chair injury.

"What boat was it?" LaRee asked, though she hardly had to. Of course it was the *Rainha*.

"I don't know," Alice said, tight-lipped. Her time here would soon be up; she'd go work in a city hospital, meet a suitable man, marry, work hard, save scrupulously, and invest intelligently. They would name their son after Alice's infant brother, who had died in the refugee camp, and their daughter for a goddess. When she was twenty they would have her portrait painted . . . like Miss Sabine Newbold with her Canary. . . .

LaRee would stay here in Oyster Creek. Her roots had gone too deep here and branched too finely; she had no choice. The ambulance had arrived and was backing around to the door.

"Hello, darlin'," Manny said as he was wheeled past LaRee on the gurney. He sounded glad to see her . . . as glad as if she were his daughter. He'd had a daughter, she remembered, but she had married and moved away.

"How do you feel, Manny?"

"Like a damned fool. I always said I'd die down on the pier, but I didn't expect to break my neck falling over in my chair."

"Well, seems like you've survived," she said. "Let's take a look at you, be sure nothing's broken. Then I'll call your wife to come get you."

"She's gonna be mad."

"Manny, was Georgie Bottles . . . Georgie . . . Wasn't he living on the *Rainha*?"

Manny shook his head, then nodded.

"Yeah," he admitted. "Yeah, he was. Supposed to be for a couple of nights while he looked for another place, somewhere to get in out of the cold, you know. But he got used to it. If it was low tide he'd go down the ladder at the end of the pier, and walk up under the wharf to the landing so nobody would see him. Even I only saw him a couple of times and I'm out there every day. Of course, my neck is stiff; I pretty much look the other way, toward Barrel Point, out to sea."

"What did he use for a bathroom?"

"Probably the library, or under the wharf. He's one of our own; we couldn't just leave him without shelter. He wasn't doing any harm."

"Where is he now?" LaRee asked. Manny lifted his head suddenly, as if he'd just realized Georgie might be in danger. He was such a part of their daily landscape they'd almost forgotten he was a living man.

"I don't see anything," someone said—a random tourist who had wandered over because of the commotion. There was nothing to see unless you looked over the edge where the *Rainha* had been tied. The explosion had knocked her on her side and she sank almost instantly, taking the piling she was tied to with her, so that end of the pier slumped into the water. The town's two police cruisers and three fire trucks were all there, and Matt, who was the first volunteer firefighter to arrive, was just closing the back door of the ambulance, which headed off, swaying, up the hill.

"Can't go any farther, ladies and gentlemen," Hank Capshaw said. "It just isn't safe." Amalia had found her husband and Bobby walked a step ahead of her down the pier, striding swiftly around Hank to show who was really the authority, while Amalia waited at the edge of the crowd, watching him. Fire hoses were coiled everywhere—useless, but they had to follow protocol. The tide had just turned, but the water was high enough to completely cover the *Rainha*.

"Not much to see," Hannah Stone said to Amalia. She was stretching yellow caution tape across from one bollard to another.

"It's a shame," Amalia said to her, sizzling with disapproval.

"Sad," Hannah agreed.

"Shameful. An accident waiting to happen. This kind of thing . . . Manny Soares wouldn't have allowed it. No one would have, before . . . this." "This" referred to Hank, who, though his sideburns were graying after years on the job, had still not learned to respect the natural order of things here. "When Manny was harbormaster, there was so much traffic in this harbor there was no room to tie up a derelict boat . . . never mind . . ."

Her voice grew louder on the phrase "derelict boat," and she shot a glance at Danielle, who was standing with Franco, staring at the spot where the *Rainha* had always been before. If Franco had married Amalia, there would have been no dereliction of any kind. Bobby stepped back over the caution tape. "Nothing to see," he said.

"Did anyone see Georgie?" Danielle asked. "Today, I mean?"

"Why?"

"He . . . might have been . . . sleeping on the boat. Probably not, but . . ."

There was a splash as, hearing this, Matt dove in and began swimming toward the wreck.

"No!" Hank said. "No! Jesus Christ, there could be another explosion! Or . . . anything. Jesus Christ!"

It seemed a very long time but finally Matt's head popped up out of the water like a seal's. He shook the water out of his hair, wiped his face across his arm, then swam a few quick strokes and pulled himself back up onto the pier.

"No one I can find," he said, shaking violently. "I didn't think about the cold," he managed to say. Hannah went around to the back of the cruiser and pulled out a silver emergency blanket. "Maybe you need to go to the clinic, too," she said.

"Can the Coast Guard come in?" Danielle asked. "To look for Georgie?"

"It'd be nice to confirm there's a body . . . I mean, a victim. First," Hank said. "When was the last inspection?" he asked Franco. Hank rubbed his temples, then Franco rubbed his, both of them looking at the ground. Hank shouldn't have let Franco leave the boat there all this time—it wouldn't have happened, wouldn't have been conceivable, in Newburyport. But you couldn't just arrive in a town and start ordering people off the pier their grandparents had built. Franco shouldn't have let Georgie stay on the boat, but Georgie . . . well, if you knew his life, you'd find you couldn't say no.

"Has Georgie Bottles been living on the *Rainha*?" Hank asked.

"Didn't know what else to do," Franco said, more or less to himself.

"No . . . no, I see," Hank said. "I'll call the Coast Guard, though really there's not much chance."

"Call the liquor store first," Danielle said.

"Good idea."

Danielle put an arm around Franco. This was one of those moments she would never be able to forget, and though the tide was brimming and there was not a cloud in the sky, it would be the fire hose snaking around her feet, the caution tape, and the crazy tilt of the pier that would stick in her mind—the disorder. "She'd come to the end of the line, you know that," she said.

The tide sucked at the pilings. They were going to have to take that arm of the pier down, and decide whether it was worth replacing. "I'll call the salvage guys out tomorrow," Franco said. "We don't have to tell the insurance company . . . anything else."

"Franco," Danielle said, "honey, we haven't paid insurance on that boat for years." She touched his cheek and he could see she was going to cry. Not for the boat—she'd never given a damn about the boat—but for his dream.

Dorotea Machado came down Sea Street, wheeling Franco's bicycle. The firemen were pulling the hoses in and one of the trucks was beeping loudly as it backed around to leave. The tourists who'd been watching stepped out of Dorotea's way; she walked toward Franco and Danielle as if she didn't see anyone else. That was the way it was here; maybe it was the only way to get by in a town as small and isolated as Oyster Creek. In cities you had neighborhoods; in the country you had acres of farmland in between the houses. Here you just had to avert your eyes and pretend the people who made you nervous didn't exist.

Amalia stepped forward. "Dorotea," she said sharply, the way she'd have spoken to her own daughter, but Dorotea didn't turn her head. She walked straight to Danielle and Franco. "I thought I could learn by myself," she said. "But . . . you said . . ."

"It's not hard," Franco said. "We can work on it this afternoon."

Dorotea smiled, widely. She was still young enough, Franco thought. There was still time to help her find a way forward. Over Dorotea's head Danielle held Franco's gaze. It was time to let the *Rainha* and the past go, for the sake of the future.

"You!" LaRee said, finding Matt standing in a puddle at the clinic's front desk, with the silver space blanket around his shoulders. "What on earth?"

"You said Georgie was living on the *Rainha*," he said. "I had to go in after him. It was only twenty feet of water."

"Come on," she said, taking him back into the examining room, grabbing a handful of towels on the way. "Get the clothes off, and we'll get you dry."

"I'm fine," he said. "Just cold."

"A fifty-year-old person has a fifty-fifty chance of surviving a fifty-yard swim in fifty-degree water," she said. It was straight from the textbook.

"Well, it's my lucky day, then. I didn't swim any distance at all, and here I am. I survived."

"Step out, here." She knelt and pulled the pant legs off, one foot at a time, eyes politely averted.

"There's nothing here you haven't seen before," he teased.

"Maybe there's nothing there I want to see again. Did you think of that?" But her voice was tender and fond; it felt so good to know that night was still back there in both their memories.

He wrapped a towel around his waist, holding it closed with one hand, and she put the other around his shoulders. He looked ridiculous—he had a tattoo of a leaping tiger on his chest that would have been a proud sight once, but was droopy and sway-backed now. LaRee was wearing scrubs with tropical fish on them and had her bun secured with a pencil. Her right hand had more age spots than her left; she tried not to use it.

"We used to be better-looking," she said, wishing she'd bothered with makeup that morning. Her own signs of age were just ugly, whereas his seemed marks of honor, showing all he had taken on and how well he had borne it.

"That's true," he said, as sincerely as if he were swearing on a Bible. "I remember every minute of that night, so I know it's true."

"Matt . . ." She could not stand to feel it all again.

"I understand. I just wanted you to know. It's funny how memory sorts things out for you."

All this time she'd thought herself pathetic, for letting that night feel so important. It seemed like anyone else would have shrugged and moved on. She rubbed Matt's shoulders through the towel, and would have hugged him just for the sake of consolation, except that he might misunderstand.

"That's nice of you to say," she said. "No sign of Georgie?"

"No. It happened so fast. I saw the flames from Front Street and by the time I got to the pier the boat had sunk. The tide goes out pretty fiercely right there—there's no telling how far it could have pulled him."

24

THE WASHING OF TEN TIDES

"There comes a time when whatever is unfinished must be left as it is," Hugh said. "And sometimes that's what makes the show. It makes an entry point for the imagination, a mystery that carries on through time. It might be that someone in tonight's audience will remember a moment in this play years from now, that it will cross his mind casually, and suddenly some small thing will come clear to him in a new way. And we will have done our job, or at least part of it."

Well, it sounded good, and there was nothing to do but say it. *The Tempest* was going to open in forty-eight hours. It was not what Hugh had imagined, but then, what ever was? They'd put up the tent the day before, and strung the lights through the locust grove, but it had not created the right effect and Sam and Leo had had to take them all down. So they had worked through the night, Vita and Orson replacing every third white bulb with a blue one and handing the strands up to Sam and Leo on ladders. Vita was asleep at the picnic table when they finished. "An enchanted forest?" Leo asked, shaking her awake.

She looked up into the brilliant predawn blue, the last stars still shining, the locust grove. . . . "Yes," she said. "An enchanted forest for sure. Oh, Leo, it's amazing! And Sam . . ."

"And you!" Sam said. "I think we've got it."

At this all four of them began to sing "The Rain in Spain." Vita felt Orson's cape slip off her shoulders and picked it up before the dew could soak into it. They'd been watching over her as she slept; of course they had.

"It's catching up with us," Orson said, looking east where a red glow was spreading ahead of the sun.

"Done with just minutes to spare!" Leo crowed. Sam leaned against him. "And now, to bed . . ." They'd headed back through the locust grove to their cottage while Orson gave Vita a lift home, where she had kissed LaRee, who was scrambling an egg for herself before work, and fallen back asleep until rehearsal started up again that afternoon. School was out. Summer had come. She had survived a C in geometry, and so many other failed equations. More than survived—she had absorbed them, reckoned with them, made a certain kind of peace. The old fears seemed almost like steadying influences now.

"The flaws, the errors become part of the whole and the new growth shapes itself to fit," Hugh said, thinking how far he must have come to even feel such a thing, never mind give voice to it. "Beauty is serendipitous, and fleeting."

He still spoke as if he were standing at a lectern in a marble-columned lecture hall, instead of before a public barbecue grill. And as they listened they looked past him, out over Mackerel Bay where not a single mackerel had been caught in years. But as far as Vita was concerned, it might as well have been the Vatican, and Hugh was speaking unshakable truths.

Behind him was Caliban's hut, with a bundle of sticks at the doorway and burlap sacks on a laundry line behind, and the ragged hurricane flag fluttering. They had thrown a rag over the joint of wood that Vita had salvaged from the wreck, with the idea that it would look like Caliban's dinner table.

And behind that, moored by a heavy chain to a rusted buoy ball, was the last of the *Rainha do Mar*. Orson had paid to haul her up, and there she lay on her burnt-out side, splintered and sooty, the window broken, the boom askew.

"Get some use out of her, anyway," Franco said. He—all of them—were in costume. Franco wore a striped jersey with a red bandanna knotted around his neck. Vita felt lighter than air in a silk slip, silver blue just like the water on a still day, with colored scarves floating out from her shoulders. There was joy in this—the costume laid out for Shyanne was a kind of burlap toga.

"Not exactly a galleon, but it's realistic," Sam said of the *Rainha*. "There won't be any doubt it's a shipwreck."

"Did you see what else we found?" Orson asked, coming around from behind Caliban's hut, carrying the *Rainha*'s cabin door.

"It was floating out there," he said. "I saw it from my widow's walk. It must have been torn off by the force of the explosion." He turned it over and set it on the picnic table so they could all see. The inside face of the door was covered with a mosaic made of shells, showing the town as it looked—or as it had looked years ago—from the pier: the pattern of roofs, the spires of the three churches, and the Calliope Hotel cupola.

"Georgie did this?" Franco asked.

"I imagine so," Orson said.

"He was always carving something with a jackknife," Franco said. "I mean, back when he was a little boy. I didn't know he'd kept it up."

"Georgie . . . the drunk?" Sam said. "He couldn't bicycle in a straight line."

Franco looked past him to keep from taking offense. When you'd gone to school with a guy, remembered him enlisting—enlisting!—in the army when everyone else was scheming to escape it, back in Vietnam . . . thinking he was going to show them all what a man he was . . . Yes, yes, he was Georgie the drunk, but he hadn't meant to be.

"Have they found his body?" Leo asked, tempering Sam's tone.

"No," Adam said, having just loped up from the beach in his ripped white sailor's uniform. "The Coast Guard charted the currents and they had divers out off Barrel Point for two days, but they never found him. The channel is so deep—they think he was maybe carried out to sea."

"It's the right death for him," Franco said.

"How's that?" Hugh asked. They had been so uncomfortable with each other at first, Hugh speaking heartily as if Franco's lack of a Shakespearean education might have made him deaf, Franco self-consciously adding big words wherever he could fit one. But they had something in common, some way of seeing as from a great distance, with tenderness, and fascination. "He was part of the place, same as if nothing had changed since whaling," Franco said. "He lived on what he caught. He'd row miles if he needed to, if he heard the stripers were running out off Provincetown. I almost never heard him say two words, but he was made of iron. He was . . . fated . . . to die at sea." Franco would never have spoken the word "fated" if it hadn't been for *The Tempest*.

"He hath the drowning mark upon him!" Vita said, thinking of the play. "But your complexion is perfect gallows."

They laughed without thinking, without noticing it was Vita—little Vita—who'd spoken. She was just one of them now.

"Who'd have guessed an 'iron man' could do such delicate work?" Hugh said.

Franco shook his head, laughed, then pushed his cap up on his forehead. "Not me," he said. "Never."

Georgie had used the shells that covered the beach at low tide: tiny iridescent mussels, scallops and periwinkles and translucent peach-colored circles, and he had carved mother-of-pearl out of oyster shells and pared it to different shapes, gluing it to the back of the wooden door.

"This must have taken hours and hours and hours," Hugh said. "You never really know, do you?"

"The whole cabin was lined with it," Franco said. "A view of the town from Sedge Point, forty years ago, back when it was . . ." He had started to say "ours."

"And all from his memory," Orson said. "Look, here are the fish shacks that were cleared out for the park. And the pilings left from Barrel Wharf before it washed away. It's all done so carefully. I wouldn't have guessed Georgie ever thought of anything except where his next meal was coming from and whether the liquor store was open."

"You never know," Hugh said, looking out across the bay. "Every single life is such a journey, every one."

"I feel bound to point out that Georgie didn't die a heroic death at sea," Orson said. "He died of using Everclear as a solvent while he was cooking over an open flame."

"In the cabin of the leaky old bucket called *Rainha do Mar*," Franco said.

"Is that what happened?" Sam asked.

"The evidence suggests . . ."

"He left a legacy," Hugh said, looking down at the mosaic.

"Does Georgie have relatives?" Orson asked.

"Sure," Franco said. "I mean, he's Danielle's cousin . . . or second cousin, on her grandma Bemba's side. Which means he must be related to Bobby Matos, too, and probably—"

"Anyone close?"

"The sister in Fall River. I haven't seen her since we were young. Josie, Josefine. I'm not sure what her name would be now. They've called her, I'm sure."

"It's not like we have a body."

"But we do have a show to produce," Hugh said. "So, let us proceed?"

"Enter Ariel, like a water nymph," Leo said with a delighted pirouette. "That may be my favorite stage direction in history."

"I have a . . . text message . . . from Shyanne," Hugh said. "She can't make the rehearsal, so . . . Vita, would you mind reading Miranda, just so we can get through this scene?"

Hugh didn't lift his eyes from the page as he said this; he wasn't thinking of the things Vita had confided at Orson's party. Dreams. Yes, well. He himself had dreamed of becoming a distinguished professor, his voice deep, his pronouncements wise, as round and perfect as smoke rings, rising to the highest point in the lecture hall as a hundred pens scratched a note, underlining it so as to recall the words of the great man. This dream, this bright image in the distance, had become more and more diffuse, vague, cloudy as he came toward it, as if he had pushed his way down the aisle to touch a movie screen only to have the image blur and dissolve around him. Dreams made him itch now; he had a play to produce and an audience of people who would come to be entertained, to let their minds wander for a couple of hours in the sea air, while these characters pranced (he must slip something of a rein over Sam's lovely shoulders, yes) through an old story, so much like their own—the story of an isolated, superstitious community, its inhabitants scheming against one another, relying on one another, on their own enchanted island.

Hugh needed to run through two more scenes before four thirty, when Orson had to catch the bus to Boston. He had a ticket to *Sweet Bird of Youth* that night at the Huntington, had his valise packed and ready. "Vita! Vita Gray! Do not sit there as if entranced, please. This is reality! Would you please stand in as Miranda?"

Vita had prayed for this so often she hadn't believed it at first. She knew Shyanne had a new boyfriend, and had told Adam she was sorry she'd gotten involved with Mackerel Sky, that she hadn't realized how "lame" the whole thing would be. But to just not show up ... well, it was nearly a miracle. Here it was, Vita's chance to show them all. She hopped to attention like a fireman poised to slide down a pole, redid her ponytail in two urgent motions, and skipped into her place, with the locust blossoms floating down through the air over her.

It *was* her place—she knew it. She knew the lines, had memorized them by accident as she watched the scenes over and over. She felt the sense of Miranda come into her as if she were drawing it out of the ground. Miranda would be like Marie Antoinette, a young girl so privileged by her relation with power that she had no idea her whims couldn't be chiseled straight into law. She banished Caliban as coldly as Vita herself would once have got rid of Franco. Seeing Orson go with the crooked arthritic gait he had developed for the part, she felt a pang—Miranda might have too, and how would she have shown it? And here was Ferdinand, the first young man Miranda had ever seen.

"*What is't? a spirit? Lord, how it looks about! Believe me, sir, It carries a brave form. But 'tis a spirit.*"

Her thoughts chased each other so fast she could barely get hold of them. Act the part, blush at the sight of Adam . . . because he's Ferdinand. If he were just Adam, of course, the thing would be to avoid blushing. But Adam would understand she was only blushing as Miranda, that the soft hush in her voice was only for Ferdinand. He wouldn't think she meant all that feeling for him . . . except that she did. Her mind raced on as she spoke and glanced and blushed, beseeching Prospero's kindness, keeping her diction clear, trying to use every ounce of her feeling for Adam to show Miranda's for Ferdinand, without, God forbid, causing Adam to *assume* . . .

As she spoke the lines, it struck her that Miranda was like her. She too had seen her mother killed, and lived on with some memory from "the dark backward and abysm of time" haunting her. She had lived at sea, waiting, hoping, trying, but it was like climbing back up the dune on the back shore—you couldn't. The ground kept slipping down beneath you.

She felt a sympathy for the character that she had never felt for herself. Of course she was solitary and awkward—the poor girl.

"*My affections are then most humble. I have no wish to see a goodlier man.*" Tears started as she spoke the line. She felt it as if it were her own. What it would be, to meet a kindred spirit after a life spent alone!

"And . . . you two stand there charmed, transfixed by each other. You can't move," Hugh said. "Ferdinand, Prospero's powers are pulling you away, but you reach back, a hand at her waist. You know you'll lose, but you have to show her how you feel before you're taken. . . ."

Licensed by Shakespeare, he reached toward her, too shy to give the movement any force, but his eyes were honest. She felt a trapdoor open and there she was, in a new world. The air smelled of honey from the locust blossoms; that fragrance would revive this feeling every June from now on. There were veins of rust and black through the tide flats and the brilliant silver of the still water as it ebbed, the carcass of the *Rainha*, and Sam and Leo and the others, moving through the landscape but no more than apparitions now....

"Good—that was good," Hugh said. "We'll go through it more completely when Shyanne's back, and a last dress rehearsal with full tech tomorrow, five p.m."

No! He had been supposed to see into her heart, find the radiance there, recognize her gift and tell her that from now on *she* would be playing Miranda! She was scalded. She looked around to see if they had noticed her shameful, ridiculous hope and seen it dashed, but they had forgotten her altogether.

"And one last announcement. Opening night will be held as a benefit for a local girl whose father just died. They're trying to get up a scholarship fund for her." He smiled at Franco. "A good cause and a good way to bring in an audience that's not familiar with Mackerel Sky yet. So it should be a full house."

"And a full moon," Orson said. "Fair weather for the next ten days at least."

"You coming?" Adam said, starting toward the car, looking away as if there was danger in looking at Vita. The closeness, his hand at her waist, had spun a web over them. She fell in behind him, and they drove in silence as if a word might break the feeling. They waited for a stream of BMWs and Mercedes to pass before they could cross the highway, but then they were back in their own territory. Grace Pond lay still and black in its hollow and the white tree marked the entrance to the driveway, two sandy tracks with a grassy middle and beach roses blooming along the side. And the

house—her home—looking as cozy as a hobbit hut with the clem-
atis vines flowering over the front door. LaRee wasn't back from
work yet; Bumble came trotting around from the corner, saw the
car, and rolled onto her back in the sand. When Vita reached to
undo her seat belt, Adam caught her hand and nature just pulled
them together, too suddenly, bumping against each other, her lip
bruised against his teeth.

"Wait." She put up her hands and took a breath. "Like this," she
said, kissing softly so it was like a question, and he seemed to understand, to give an answer with the next one. He was holding her
so tight, as if he was afraid she'd escape. Something gave way within
her and she was adrift in a new element, alive, awake as she had
never been. Had something beyond this mattered to her? Why?

25

A Visit to 1612

The kiss broke; they had to breathe. And there they were, two naturally awkward people who had followed some instinct down a blind alley and found themselves face-to-face. Adam's face was so beautiful—so amazed and unguarded—it drew her back to the kiss. Neither of them knew what else to do. LaRee would be home any second, though. She would drive in behind Adam's car and then would have to back out again so he could back out, and it would be unthinkably, unspeakably, tragically awkward.

"Let's . . . I have something I want to show you . . ." she said. "Let's drive up to the Outer Beach."

He blinked and she realized he was frightened. She was too. The sudden possibility of love made everything dangerous. It was right there in front of them; suppose they drove it away?

"It's just . . . a place where I like to walk to. It's where I got the wood for Caliban's hut."

"I'm supposed to go home. . . ."

"Oh. Okay. Okay, bye." She opened the door, hoping she could get into the house before she started crying.

"But—but! My mom's at yoga!"

Vita stopped, trying to think what this could mean.

"She won't care if I'm home," he explained. Vita hesitated. Having stood her ground with LaRee and survived, she had the courage to wait for him, to listen even though she might not like what she heard. "My affections are most humble . . ." he said. From the play.

"My affections are most humble, too," she said, making her voice as soft and confiding as Sam Rosenmayer's and putting her seat belt back on.

They started to park at Doubloons, but Shyanne's old Jeep convertible was in the lot. She had turned eighteen and would be waiting tables this summer, edging through the crowds in cutoffs and a clingy T-shirt, plucking up twenty-dollar bills. The same as her mom had years ago. Seeing the Jeep, Adam drove on.

"Park in the Shillicoth house—they never get here till the fourth," she said. "It's that big gray hulk up on the bluff."

"Yes, my lady."

They went up the steps and over the porch, which had been fixed and painted since Vita's last visit. It wasn't the stark, sere place she'd been haunting all winter; the sun was shining and the waves spilled up the beach one over another like lace. A man walking his dog had stopped to watch something—she saw a whale spout and then another, then a slick black tail.

"Kind sir," she said. "Look!"

"They're so happy out there. . . ." He took her hand—the whales seemed to have sanctioned this.

She led the way, running down the beach steps to the wreck. More sand had fallen away at the bottom, so it was a big jump—a celebration. They were fast and strong and able. Vita barely glanced at the shoals where the riptide had formed the summer before, leading Adam up the beach to the wreck.

"My wreck," she said. "They found it." It was cordoned off with stakes and caution tape and there were footprints all around it.

"Those bastards!" He leapt the caution tape and strode into the middle of the wreck, holding up an imaginary sword. "Whoreson, cur, this wrack belongs to my lady, and I shall strike thee thrice if thou com'st near!"

"Well, it does! I found it first!" But her feet wouldn't move; she was a good girl first and last. Her heart sank to think this—Miranda was the "more braver daughter" of the King of Naples. How could she hope to play such a role if she couldn't even cross the caution tape?

"I was out here with it months ago—I found it back in April after the big storm. I came out to . . ." Really, she'd come to visit the site of the riptide, where the father and daughter had died. Together. The way a family ought to. "I came out to see it every day."

"And it shall be yours until the sea covers it again . . . which will be soon, looks like." It was true. Silt had covered the front timbers already. A few more tides and the hull would be buried again—for years, or decades, or centuries.

"I want another piece before it goes," she said. To prove she'd been here, really seen this. Without some memento she might stop believing it had been real.

"Vita, you didn't—the wood in Caliban's hut didn't come from this wreck, did it?"

"Some of it," she said. "That big piece that's like a stump. And I've got stuff at home that I pried off the timbers—pieces of metal and stuff."

"You're not supposed to do that. This is like . . . a historic artifact." He knelt down and brushed the sand away where two beams were fixed together. "Look—there aren't nails, only pegs and notches—they put this whole ship together like a puzzle."

"It's just going to be covered up again, and eaten away by the water," Vita said. She had been alone with it, in her own stretch of wilderness, and now there was caution tape and footprints and she was breaking a law. . . .

"No," he said. "If I'd found this I'd have hauled the whole thing out if I could. It is massively cool." He started to examine all the joints, to sift the sand beside them—apparently the wreck was cooler than kissing.

"Look at this!" It was a long white shell, hollow at the center. She'd never seen one like it.

"It's a pipe stem, I think. My dad has some like it—he used to take me beachcombing when I was little. They had pipes made of clay."

The dog walker was gone; blue shadows fell across the dune face and over the wreck, though the water still sparkled way out and she saw another whale blowing, and gulls gathering around it.

"It's no different here from what it was then," she said. "There's nothing to say it's not 1612."

"I wonder what it was like back then?" he said. Somehow they both knew that in 1612 there would have been no barrier between them, no caution tape, no mistrust, not so much as a thin cotton shirt. He took her hand and she stepped over the tape into that century when they imagined love must have been easier to speak out. His eyes were gray, and amazed to be looking into hers. His beard seemed designed to show how soft his skin was. It scratched her when they kissed and made her want to kiss more.

"I love it here in 1612," she said.

"I'm so glad you brought me here."

26

MAGICAL CREATURES

O rson got back from Boston on the first bus. *Sweet Bird of Youth* had been a disappointment—all drained of sweat and longing so as to be crammed with clever cultural allusions instead—so he left at intermission, rented a room at the Mandarin Oriental and picked out a most excellent-seeming fellow on Manhunt.com. Heavy linen, beveled mirrors, velvet drapes, and a decidedly working-class bedmate . . . perfection. But the partner did not live up to expectations any better than the play had, and Orson dispatched him as quickly as possible, then sat at the window, allowing regret to lap over him like the incoming tide. By four a.m., he had fallen into a nostalgic daze, recalling the bus station encounters of his youth. To defile, to be defiled and exalted at once, in the service of some searing need . . . He packed his things and headed to the Trailways terminal.

It was spotless; even the bathrooms were made of some unassailable material so that nothing could be written on the walls. A skinny security guard sat at the door, playing a video game on his cell phone. This fellow's lust was likely directed toward some comic book heroine or one of those wet-eyed anime figures. Orson folded his cape under his head and napped until the first bus arrived. There were two other passengers, and in Hyannis they picked up two more, nurses' aides at Infinite Horizons, by the color of their scrubs. They'd be in Oyster Creek by eight a.m.

Summer was upon them. He could feel it as he stepped off the bus. The street was silent except for the dripping window boxes at the pharmacy. The warmth rising from the ground promised the fog would burn off, and the low tide smelled of clam chowder. He started up the hill toward home, but decided to walk over and check the theater first. Mackerel Sky's opening night was not generally much of an event, but now that they were doing it as a benefit he expected a crowd, and he wanted to be sure all was ready. Somehow even the disappointment of the trip began to inspire him. Nearly seventy years old, and he was still yearning, suffering— alive!

The lawn at Mackerel Bay Park was as luxurious as velvet now, green and cropped close the day before, with clumps of violets flowering, wet with dew. The cottages across the street had a fresh coat of white paint, yellow for the shutters. Sam and Leo's laundry was pinned up expertly but had been on the line overnight—they were too dewy themselves to understand dew, Orson thought, delighted with his own cleverness. What a foolish old goat he had been, looking for physical fulfillment when it was clear that his life's calling was to admire these boys, to dream back to his own youth and imagine himself in their place.

The screen door to the harbormaster's shack opened and shut—Hank opening up for work, putting out the BEACH PERMITS sign. The tent faced diagonally so the *Rainha* was the backdrop on the left side and the locust grove on the right. The chairs were set up for the audience, klieg lights on side posts; Caliban's hut had been moved in for the night and the tent sides were tied down to protect everything. A ghost light stood center stage, keeping watch over the scene. Orson poked his head in, then lifted the flap and took a seat at the back. Everything was settled, right. They'd incorporated Georgie's mosaic into the set—the shells made a softly reflective surface, a proper contrast to the knotty wood and thick old ropes Hugh had used for the rest.

He heard a small cry, as if doves were nesting in the corners— this had been troublesome the summer before.

"Hello?" he said, and pressing a hand against his throat, tried a dove call, a clucking coo. "I can't allow this, you know," he said fondly, walking toward the sound. "In theory, of course, it's quite lovely, but in practice . . ."

The voice, which was human, though high and soft like a dove, said, "Hello? Orson? Oh!"

This came from the hut. As he approached he saw something move inside.

"Is it morning?" the voice said sleepily.

He pushed aside some of the grasses woven into the chicken wire, and looked in. A girl was asleep there. Her dark curls fell against a shoulder white as a swan's wing.

"My goodness," he said.

"Orson! Mr. Desroches . . ." It was Adam Capshaw lifting his head but with one arm protectively holding the woman's head against his chest, his face sleepy, his eyes narrow as if still caught in a dream. "I'm sorry. We . . ."

The girl's shoulders tensed as if against a blow, and when Orson didn't speak, her hand emerged from the blanket to hold Adam's. On the third finger was Sabine Gray's opal ring.

"My dear young people," Orson said. "Do your parents know you're here?"

Vita had texted LaRee to say she'd be working through the night at the theater again, so LaRee had had the spring evening to herself, puttering in the garden, feeling a peculiar lightness as if she'd lost her center of gravity. Then it occurred to her that this wasn't a momentary thing, that Vita was sixteen, about to get her driver's license, about to go to college. She was at the edge of a new life; they both were. Matt popped into her mind at that moment, as if he'd been sitting there waiting for an opening. She resented it. There was a wide, empty canvas before her and she wasn't just going to scribble some man into the middle. That was a twenty-year-old's mistake. But she could imagine a motif, a ribbon running through.

She was drinking her coffee on the front step next morning when Adam and Vita drove up. As soon as they got out of the car, it was clear. They came forward together, caught somewhere between sheepishness and pride, their hands just touching.

"Hi," Vita said sleepily, and when Adam heard this he smiled as if she'd just confided a wonderful secret. His shirt was misbuttoned and Vita's hair was matted into a snarl, her cheeks blazing red and her eyes cast down.

"Good morning," LaRee said, looking up at them, shading her eyes from the sun.

Adam cleared his throat. "Good morning," he said, at least an octave too deep, so LaRee couldn't help laughing.

"You sound very Shakespearean." They edged closer to each other as if this might be some kind of verdict. Vita saw the buttoning error and began to undo and redo all Adam's shirt buttons with the happy air of a child dressing a doll.

"Big night tonight," LaRee said, seeing that this might go on for hours if she didn't speak. "Adam, you'd better go home and get some sleep. And Vita, do you remember when you were little, we had to use peanut butter to get the snarl out of your hair?"

"I remember when you used to make me blueberry pancakes," Vita said, resting her head on Adam's shoulder

"She loves blueberries," Adam said, as if this was the single most fascinating bit of information he had ever learned.

"For now, it's a day-old scone," LaRee said. "I have to go to work, and you look like a shower and a nap might be in order." Vita and Adam didn't seem to hear this. They were in their own world together, looking into each other's eyes.

"What I mean is . . . Adam, shoo, go away! You'll see each other tonight!" He did, looking over his shoulder as if she had cast him out of Eden.

Vita sat down beside her as soon as he was gone. The peonies were bowls of soft light. "You . . . used protection, right?" LaRee asked.

Vita jumped up. "HOW could you? How could you imagine that I would be so childish as . . . OH, OH, I cannot believe it! Do you really think that I am so stupid and immature that I would . . . *take a lover* . . . without having the proper protection? You have no faith in me. . . ."

This went on, but LaRee was laughing, and she could hear the ground eroding beneath Vita's outrage.

"I was just asking," she said finally. "I'm not mad at you. In fact I'm glad to see you cozy and giggly with Adam. I just thought it was important to double-check on the consequences."

Vita sat back down. "Really?"

"Of course. I mean, you're young. Maybe you're too young—I don't know. But he's clearly pretty fond of you. . . ."

"LaRee, he is so, so wonderful. . . . We can talk about anything at all, and he's not closed off to it—he's listening, he's interested to think about it. Nobody's like that, at least not anybody in high school."

"So he's worthy of you?" LaRee's eyes filled, her voice cracked; she hid it under a cough. Vita was grown; she was heading off into life.

"LaRee, last night was the nicest night of my life."

Vita would have gone on but was afraid to put it into words suddenly. Once she had stepped over the caution tape, they'd begun to trust that the feeling would stay with them, and they had climbed the dune and sat with the lighthouse looming above them to watch the moon come up. The changing light through the water, the beam from the giant lens flashing overhead, the line of his collarbone as she traced it . . . The world was entirely new. Once the sky was dark they went back to Mackerel Bay Park, where the thick lawn was soft underfoot and the set for *The Tempest*, closed in under the tent, felt like their own new home. Adam rolled up his jeans, waded into the bay, and said it was warm enough, but she didn't believe him until she felt it herself. They had both folded their clothes carefully and had averted their eyes until they were in the water. And that was when it was all natural and true and right. . . .

"You know how you can see the phosphorescence in the water at night? We went swimming, and when we came out our skin was lit up like we were magical creatures," Vita said.

"And you are, Vita. You both are." A weight was slipping away from her—the fear that Vita's heart would never be light, that she would never give in and let life surprise her . . . that she would never recover.

"How come we never have marshmallows around here? I mean, we grill all the time, we have fires at the beach, but we never have s'mores."

"I . . . What made you think of marshmallows?"

"We have them on the set—Prospero gives one to Caliban when he's good, and last night we got hungry and that was all there was. And I—I don't think I've ever had one before."

"Well . . . marshmallows. The night Hannah brought you here you said you always had marshmallows in your cocoa, but I didn't have any. And you got upset—but when I said we'd get some the next day, you realized that meant you weren't going home the next day. And I think that was when you realized your mother was really gone. So I just avoided the subject of marshmallows for the next . . . twelve or thirteen years."

Vita laughed, sadly, sitting back down on the step and resting her head on LaRee's shoulder.

"That poor girl," she said. "I feel so sorry for her. You'd hardly know she was me."

LaRee leaned her head against Vita's. "She's part of you," LaRee said. "I see that part all the time, and I'm always amazed by it. You've lived through fear and it's made you less afraid. You've been hurt and it's made you more sympathetic. I wish it always worked that way. . . ."

"I just laughed out of sadness, didn't I?" Vita said.

"I hadn't thought . . ."

"I did! Listen . . ." She tried it, and again. "It's so funny. I laughed where I could have cried."

"I suppose so."

"People do that. Characters do . . ."

"Vita Gray, you're making art out of this!"

"Don't you think my mother would approve?"

"She'd be so proud of you."

"I think she might," Vita said, looking down the driveway toward the white tree, its graceful, reaching form against the green profusion of the woods behind it. "Do you remember when I used to think I saw her all the time?"

"Of course. It broke my heart."

"Last night when Adam was asleep, the ghost light was on, on the stage, and it was shining on the stone of my ring, so I could make reflections with it. And I thought—well, she's right here, isn't she? I look like her. I am like her. She's right here."

"It's true," LaRee said. "We have to reckon with her, every day."

"*We*," Vita said emphatically.

"*We*. Always."

"LaRee?"

"Yes, my dear . . ."

"Do you promise not to die?"

That *was* the question.

"I will do my very best," LaRee said.

"Well, that's honest."

"You did insist on the truth."

"You know, I think I'll take a shower," Vita said, stretching. "I can't believe it's opening night!" She jumped up and went inside, but a minute later she popped back out, wrapped in a towel. "I've never been so happy in my life!" she bubbled. "LaRee, to think of all I didn't know yesterday . . ."

"Into the shower, my magical creature, into the shower! You may just have learned it, but I've only just managed to forget!"

Vita turned to leave, her arms crossed as if she were holding her memories tight around her. LaRee suddenly imagined wings budding beneath her sharp little shoulder blades, thickly feathered, muscular wings that would carry her a long, long way.

"Nothing else matters, nothing," Vita said. And then—"Except the show! Opening night! Oh my God!"

The plumbing went *clunk* as she turned the water on, and she began to sing, "There is sweet music here," the song she had been singing in chorus, at school. She could never seem to hit the high notes when she was practicing, but now they came one after another, clear and strong. And then, of all things, "*Sur le pont d'Avignon, l'on y danse . . .*" A song LaRee hadn't heard in years. Vita's voice was more mature, and she'd had three years of French, but hearing it, LaRee could see her again in her yellow sleep suit, dancing and singing with Sabine.

LaRee had left for work by the time Vita came out of the bathroom, her hair wrapped in a towel and LaRee's ratty old bathrobe cinched at her waist. LaRee had left a scone and butter and apricot jam on the little old café table she'd inherited from Sabine. The table had been rusted and wobbly when she got it but she'd stabilized the legs and painted it a soft blue that fit in with all the various greens in the garden. She'd set a place for Vita with a linen napkin and a yellow rose, and Vita sat down in her chair among the daylily blades. This perfect, beautiful life was what LaRee wanted for her—wanted the way Napoleon had wanted dominion over Europe. Vita could see her now, clipping the rose, poking it into the vase like a quill into an inkwell. This flower, like everything, was part of her grand plan to save Vita's heart, keep it fresh and open to life, when there was every reason for it to scar over and constrict and fail.

"You've done it, LaRee," she said aloud. "You have. So you can *stop* now." She'd expected to cry, but instead she was laughing. She was alive and whole and having a buttered scone in the garden. And wanting not the lovely resuscitation LaRee practiced on every single thing she touched, but real life, full of struggle and confusion and surprise.

27

His More Braver Daughter

"Is your father proud of you?" Hugh asked Vita. She was in her Iris costume, the silk scarves lifting and falling with the slightest breeze. The day was so calm that the one duck crossing the bay in front of them left a twenty-foot wake.

"He didn't say anything . . ." she said.

Hugh puzzled over this, one bristly eyebrow lowered, the other raised.

"You know, he's a man," she said, with a shrug. "He doesn't know how to say things like that."

"I used to be a man," Hugh said. "It wasn't much fun, but it seemed awfully important at the time. I clung to it for so long I forgot to have children. It's rather sad, really."

"Oh, Hugh! You have me."

She hugged him, without thinking, and felt his surprise and discomfort until his hands came to rest on her back and he said, "And you have me," stiff and formal. Life still made him uncomfortable when he didn't have a great author as intermediary.

Franco was standing beside the *Rainha*, or what was left of her, appearing to test the mooring, but really, Vita thought, paying his last respects. And Hugh must have seen the same thing because he said suddenly, "Do you know the Royal Shakespeare Company in Stratford uses a real skull as a prop? It was willed to them by a pianist who loved Shakespeare . . . something like having your ashes scattered at sea, I suppose."

"I'm going to leave my skull to Mackerel Sky!" Vita declared.

"Not for a long, long time, my dear," he said, setting his hand on the crown of braided ribbon that rested on her curls.

Beached, the *Rainha* dwarfed them all, their heads barely reaching the painted waterline. Adam and the others from the shipwreck scene had come across the lawn to join them.

"I never realized how big a dragger is," Vita said. It was all she could think of. She hadn't seen Adam since the morning and it seemed as if now that he was all dressed and combed, his warm, open self must have retreated back into its hiding place. But he caught her glance and held it—they had the best secret in the world together.

"Like they say about icebergs," Franco said. "Most of it's underwater."

"It's so sad, about the fire and everything," she said. It took a great effort to speak, for fear of saying the wrong thing, or acting the wrong way. He was her father, really. Biology drew a clear line between them. Everything else was murky, unknown . . . dangerous. But if you didn't grope through it . . . "I mean, it's your boat, your father's boat."

Franco sighed, smiled sideways at her, and she backed up against Adam, who touched the small of her back and made her smile.

"She'd had her day," Franco said. "But Georgie . . ."

Orson came up beside them. "Still no body?" he asked.

"No," Franco said. "The Coast Guard searched the channel, they had all the currents plotted, didn't find anything. And we thought, maybe when we lifted the wreck . . . but no."

"Who'd have guessed he'd leave something so beautiful behind?" Orson said. "Of all people . . ."

"Everything's like an iceberg," Vita said, nearly jumping at the sound of her own voice. For sixteen years she had been watching, listening, and suddenly she had things to say. "Or, everyone. So much underneath . . ."

Franco blinked, looked at her again. "I made you something," he said, surprising himself. As he was building the dory he had told himself that it was just a project, not really for Vita, that it would be easy enough to paint over the name and choose something else, auction it for Dorotea's scholarship fund maybe. . . . But now it struck him that there was plenty of time to make another. "Come with me."

It was moored behind the *Rainha*, a little boat whose sides belled out before rising to a point at bow and stern. It was the same green as the light angling through the low water, and the rim was the same purple as a patch of seaweed deep beneath. There were two plank seats and a pair of new oars, and if she could imagine navigating the serpentine channels of Oyster Creek in it, someone else would think of rowing out past Barrel Point when the bluefish were running.

"You made this for me?"

"I . . . thought you should have your own boat." She barely heard this, but in the years ahead it would grow louder in her memory, an honest declaration of love.

She took off her ballet slippers and lifted the long slip so she could wade in.

"Here," Franco said, tying the scarves loosely behind her to keep them dry. She stepped in—the water seemed colder than it had been the night before—and ran her hand along the rim, feeling the smooth new paint. *Iris* was painted in an old-fashioned script on the bow.

"She's named for you," Franco said. For a minute Vita didn't understand. Then she put her hand up to touch her makeshift crown and gave him such a glance that he knew it all, how lost she'd been, and how brave. It felt like he'd been prying, though, like this was something he shouldn't have seen, and he averted his eyes.

"She's light," he said, "so you don't want to take her out if it's choppy, but that means she'll be quick, too, if you just want to paddle along the bay or up Oyster Creek into Moon Pond, maybe."

"Thank you," she said, gravely. "I . . . thank you. I can't believe you named it Iris."

"Well, you're an actor. I thought it would be right to name it for a character you played." He smiled, rather shyly for a lothario. "It seems . . . right. I only had sons before, so . . . I didn't know."

"I took your bicycle," she blurted. "I'm so sorry. I left it at Dorotea's."

"I know," he said. "It's fine. . . . It's maybe a good thing. Dorotea wants to learn to ride, and I said I'd help her. It's good that she wants something."

Dorotea was just arriving, coming down the center aisle with her mother. She waved to Franco, with just her fingers, and he waved back.

"I'm thinking you can help me," he said to Vita. "With helping Dorotea. Maybe we can talk about it after the show?"

"Of course," Vita said. From her whole mad conversation with Dorotea she remembered one thing clearly: Dorotea's apology for their broken playdate in kindergarten. Ten years Dorotea had suffered, for her father's sins, and she still wanted to right that one small wrong. Vita did too. "I'd like to help."

The chairs were in rows with ribbons denoting a section for the Machado family. Mackerel Sky productions were usually pay-what-you-wish, but tonight tickets were twenty-five dollars apiece, with all proceeds going to benefit the Dorotea Machado fund. Amalia had the cash box tight in her hands, and a look of indignation ready for anyone who wanted change. This town was going to pay obeisance, finally, to the people who had built it, braved the seas and bent over the deep fryers in the clam shacks all summer, every day, just to keep themselves going another year.

LaRee's pancake-breakfast logic was apparently correct, because the parking lot was filling up, not just with the Volvos and BMWs of the summer people but with Chevy Impalas and Crown Victorias—the crowd from the Friday night fish fry at the Walrus and Carpenter was all here, too. And all of Bobby Matos's relatives: the whole DPW, in their gleaming pickup trucks.

"Imagine meeting you at a Shakespeare performance," Cabbage said to Sal Bemba. "High tea tomorrow, if you please?"

"Long as it's at the Walrus," Sal said.

And another pickup, anything but gleaming: Matt Paradel's truck. Who should get out of the passenger side but LaRee Farnham . . . or someone a lot like LaRee. At first Vita couldn't believe it was her. Not that she wasn't tall, with her hair twisted up quickly so that gray-blond wisps escaped all around; not that her glasses with their heavy black frames weren't propped up on her head, and she still walked as if she were weaving through a dream. But she seemed both more confident and more shy than usual. She was wearing her jeans, a gauzy black blouse that Vita had seen in the closet but never known her to wear, and a long gold scarf looped twice around her neck. And lipstick, a shade of red that on almost anyone else might have looked crazy. LaRee looked defiant against the sorrow and confusion of life, determined to follow whatever ray of light she could see, and in that way, beautiful. And she walked along beside Matt, talking and laughing lightly as if he were an old friend.

Adam came to stand with Vita behind the tent flap, watching the audience arrive. "Your mom . . . LaRee, I mean . . . looks pretty," he said. "Is that the park ranger she's here with? Is she . . . going out with him?"

"Not that I know of." But he must have asked her to come to the play with him, and clearly she'd said yes.

"So, here's your chance to kiss a man in tights," Adam said. Vita laughed and kissed him, and again.

"Oh, I love you," he said.

"I love you!" It was so easy, a pure statement of fact, as if Bumble the cat had been transfigured into a man. "I love you so!"

Shyanne was back, looking as tense as if she might bite someone. After some strained conversation with Hugh she had gotten into her costume and was stalking ferociously back and forth behind the tent, repeating her lines. "What do you think?" Orson asked Vita. He was hunched over and dragging his left foot, dressed in burlap with a kind of mask of brown felt oak leaves pulled over his face.

"Oh my God, I love it," Vita said. "It matches with your hut, too. Do you like the driftwood I brought?"

"I do," he said, straightening his posture a little so he looked a little less like a woodland gnome and more like the person they knew, their benefactor. "Where did you get that wood?"

THE HARBORMASTER'S DAUGHTER · 319

"Out on the back shore. It was part of an old wreck buried in the sand out there."

"A really old wreck, apparently."

"What do you mean?"

"Well, look at this. . . ." He had in his palm a black . . . shell? Or . . . ? It was smaller than a sand dollar, bigger than a quarter.

"What is it?"

"A coin, my dear. Here, take my reading glasses." These were suspended from a chain around his neck, hidden under his costume. "I feel strange without them," he admitted, bending forward so Vita could use them. She could make out the shape of a man astride a horse, and letters around the edge.

"I found it under my couch pillow," he said. "It must have been in your pocket, the night you slept there. It's silver, tarnished obviously. British I think . . . and 16-something."

"Dollars?"

"No, years. 1641? Maybe 1671? I can't make out the third digit."

"I'd been carrying it around in my backpack."

"I'm not sure," Orson said, "but I'm guessing this means you've found one of the oldest wrecks ever unearthed out there. And, in good old Cape Cod tradition, you plundered it." He twinkled, not just his eyes—he was a person who twinkled.

"Oh my God!"

"My dear, you've been needing to flout a few laws," Orson said. "It's nearly time, isn't it?"

It was, yes, time. Thanks to Dorotea they had a full house—and Vita recognized almost everyone in it. "Probably the first *Tempest* for most of the audience," Hugh said. "We've got to make it a great one."

They had a mirror set up in the corner with them, and Sam and Franco were jockeying for a last glimpse of themselves. Franco posed with shoulders back and a flinty, seaman's gaze. He had been so often photographed, filmed, interviewed, it had become a habit to strike an attitude, to guess which one would end up in print. Every summer there was a woman who wanted a photo with him— "I'm sort of a murder aficionado," one had said, without a flicker of embarrassment. "Do you watch Nancy Grace?" He hated Nancy Grace, who had not, apparently, realized that he was the authority on this murder, and had never even interviewed him but just huffed and puffed on about her own ideas.

Sam was trying another range of expressions—some that Franco wouldn't have dared, a liquid gentleness, a magnetic openness. A longing passed through Orson, a shudder of regret, but he let it dissolve, turning his gaze to Adam and Vita, who had each other and needed no mirror.

The players were to enter from the back, up the center aisle, each striking a pose at center stage before taking his or her place. Shyanne went first, in her burlap dress, with her hair curled into perfect ringlets. She was the star; Vita was a member of the ensemble. A minor member of the ensemble. Which meant—she really, absolutely, belonged. She stood at the back, waiting her turn, her heart full and, somehow, calm. This was one of those times when she would have seen Sabine, when she was little; she'd have been quite sure that her mother was right there in the audience, in one certain seat. She had had to save herself, and that was how she'd done it. Now she looked out over the water, past Barrel Point where the harbor opened to the sea, and her heart was pierced by the long, empty distance. Maybe this was not so different from seeing

Sabine—it was feeling her absence, standing face-to-face with the bleak understanding that was left behind.

"And . . . go," Sam whispered, behind her. She ran up the aisle in her ballet slippers, the scarves flying behind her, stopped for a moment on the stage, trying to obey Hugh's direction to "embody a perfect simplicity," and continued into the locust grove behind Caliban's hut, where she would be hiding during most of the play. By now she thought of it as her house, hers and Adam's.

"That was wonderful," Orson said, joining her.

"What was?"

"Your entrance."

"I've done it a million times."

"Never with that authority. You were always a little girl playing a flower fairy. Tonight, you were a goddess."

"Really?"

He nodded. She couldn't imagine what she had done differently, but she did feel different, as if there was a new weight in her, an anchor. Looking for answers, she had found harder questions; looking for comfort, she had found grief; looking for harmony, she had found a thousand squeaks and jangles. But her heart was full. Orson had seen that in the few seconds she was onstage? How?

She started to ask, but he put a finger to his lips—the play was about to begin. Vita crept behind the hut to look around it and see what was happening. Franco had entered, with Adam and the other shipwreck victims, then Shyanne holding Leo's—Prospero's—hand. Behind them came Hugh, who was going to give a curtain speech, thanking the audience, reminding them they were here for a good cause, and that there was a synopsis in their programs to which they might refer.

And behind him . . . heads turned. Who would come behind the director? The playwright? Well, why not, Vita thought, given the kinds of things she had discovered on the back shore?

But it was not William Shakespeare. It was Georgie Bottles, who had seen the procession heading toward the park and guessed that there would be food and drink available. So he had followed them and was continuing to follow them, right down the center aisle toward the stage. He had his beer in its paper bag and he looked around with huge eyes popping, a mad suspicion on his face, as if the entire town were somehow in collusion against him. Vita expected him to stride up to the stage and denounce them all. Then he saw the wreck of the *Rainha* and stopped still. "Orson," Vita said. "He's alive! It's Georgie!"

Orson peeped through the foliage arrayed over the hut. "This ought to surprise me," he said. A suppressed mirth spread through the crowd, everyone looking down so as not to catch another eye and laugh out loud. For once in their lives, they were all on the same side, feeling the same thing. LaRee's shoulders shook, while Danielle carefully studied her own hands.

Amalia coughed to clear any amusement, then whispered something to Bobby, who got up and guided Georgie into a seat. He was one of their own, after all. They sat bolt upright, Amalia looking something like the queen of England, Maria and Dorotea Machado beside her, Georgie disoriented, craning his neck to try to understand where he was and why, and Bobby with that *I'm a local and I have the right to kill you* glint in his eye.

Danielle sat with LaRee and Matt, in the seats Vita had saved, front row, far right, toward the locust grove. "It feels like church," she said, "the whole town here together."

"Father forgive us, for we have sinned," LaRee said, with half a smile. Hugh took the stage and began to speak in his wise professor's voice. "So much has changed since Shakespeare wrote *The Tempest*," he said. "Almost everything, except human nature. We suspect one another, based on the slightest of differences, even as we proclaim our intention to live together in peace...."

Was it LaRee's imagination, or did Amalia's neck muscles tense?

"Don't put them to sleep, Hugh," Orson whispered to himself, crouching behind Caliban's hut with Vita. "We can do that all by ourselves."

The wind was still; the low sun cast an iridescent sheen across the bay. Vita took a breath. It was almost time for the rainbow goddess to run through the locust grove, turning on all the lights in the trees.

ACKNOWLEDGMENTS

I'd like to thank my editor, Ellen Edwards, for her natural insight and humanity, and her patience. And my agent, Jennifer Carlson, for years of calm, kind guidance.

The Harbormaster's Daughter is a work of fiction. No character or event here is intended to represent any actual person or story. The town of Oyster Creek, all the surrounding area, its citizens, shops, and organizations, its history and even some of its geology, are invented, an imaginary hamlet not far from Wellfleet, Massachusetts.

Photo by Brad Fowler

Heidi Jon Schmidt is the author of *The Rose Thieves, Darling?, The Bride of Catastrophe,* and *The House on Oyster Creek.* Her stories and essays have been published in the *New York Times,* the *Atlantic, Grand Street, Yankee,* and featured on National Public Radio. She has won awards including the O'Henry, Ingram-Merrill, and James Michener awards. She teaches in the Workshops at the Fine Arts Work Center in Provincetown and lives on Cape Cod with her husband, Roger Skillings, and their daughter, Marisa Rose.

CONNECT ONLINE

www.heidijonschmidt.com
facebook.com/heidijonschmidt

The Harbormaster's Daughter

HEIDI JON SCHMIDT

This Conversation Guide is intended to enrich
the individual reading experience, as well as encourage us
to explore these topics together—because books,
and life, are meant for sharing.

A CONVERSATION WITH HEIDI JON SCHMIDT

Q. *This is your second novel set on Cape Cod. Why did you want to return there?*

A. So many of my favorite authors—Jane Austen, George Eliot, William Faulkner, Thomas Hardy, William Trevor—wrote, or write, out of a deep knowledge of one place and the people in it. I'm saturated with the beauty and trouble of this place. One of the characters in *The Harbormaster's Daughter* observes that every single life is a heroic journey, and you never see that as closely as you do among the neighbors in a small, isolated town.

Q. *This novel was originally sparked by a real-life murder. Can you explain?*

A. The Outer Cape is haunted by several murders, and they've all made me think, mostly about the way violence begets violence. Here both murderer and victim have been hurt, and toughened, by life—and each is willing to harm others because that's a standard they recognize. LaRee wants to help Vita break that cycle.

I have to reiterate that this book is absolutely fiction—it comes out of my own imagination and my own obsessions—it's searching for a truth that goes way beyond the facts of any one event.

Q. *The novel is in many ways a coming-of-age story. It's also a story about a mother and daughter. And a story about a father and daughter. How do you see it?*

A. All of the above, but maybe most of all a story of resilience. Every major character is keeping his or her balance despite serious loss. Vita is so young when her mother dies that she has no conscious memory to reckon with—just a cold dread that feels like truth to her. Yet there's an artistic flame burning in her that defies despair and keeps her moving forward, reckoning with life. Vita's own courage sets her course. That's a kind of inborn talent in itself—LaRee nurtures Vita so her natural gifts can bloom, which helps Franco come to understand and support his daughter, too. It all happens through community.

Q. *I'm struck by your deep understanding of the secondary characters, who are so vividly drawn—Sabine, Danielle, Orson, Dorotea, and Amalia, to name just some of the standouts. Your compassion for their frailties and your respect for their strengths shine through. Was it tempting to let each of their stories take over your main tale?*

A. Thank you—that's a high compliment. I'm so fond of these characters (yes, even Amalia). Each one makes a way through life with his own grit and grace. When disparate souls bump against each other, stories result. And, yes, I always want to follow all of those stories out.

Q. *I have to say, high school sounds just as daunting now as it was when I attended more years ago than I like to count. Where did you pick up your insider understanding of teenagers?*

A. My daughter just finished high school, and it has left me with a great respect for teenagers. They're learning to be independent and they make mistakes, just the way they did when they were learning to eat spaghetti, except that these mistakes are bigger and harder to clean up. Adults can hardly bear it—we're trying to forget we used to be that pimply and vulnerable. So sometimes we turn away just when we're needed the most. If I had to take up a new profession I'd become a guidance counselor. I could definitely spend every day helping kids work toward their ambitions.

Q. *Your description of Vita and Adam's romance beautifully captures the wonder and innocence of first love. I realized, to my surprise, that I haven't read an uncynical, nonjudgmental depiction of love between teenagers in a very long time. Why is that, do you suppose?*

A. I honestly think cynicism is the result of disappointment. But I don't believe there's a soul on earth who doesn't wish for an innocent, trusting love. Even the poet Charles Bukowski, who made a career out of tough-as-nails cynicism, has a poem (called

Bluebird) about the hopeful tenderness he hides for fear of being hurt! Vita suspects that her mother may have courted death out of cynicism, so her romance with Adam is doubly meaningful for her.

Q. *Why did you make a production of* The Tempest *such an important part of the novel? You seem to suggest that such amateur theatrical productions offer a vital opportunity for self-expression and discovery in a small town.*

A. My daughter was drawn to theater at a very early age—she hated that dollhouse we got her, because she couldn't fit inside it. She wanted to be the one dressed in costume, trying out other characters and other lives. So I started seeing a lot of theater locally and it struck me as a kind of sacred experience—everyone in the building living through something important together. And as a writer I love the idea that all the people in a town would come together to bring a playwright's vision to life.

Q. *Landscape is ever present in the novel—the sea, the light, the hills and marshes, the beautiful vistas, and the literal dumping grounds. Some characters are acutely knowledgeable of the natural world, others seek to exploit it or to find inspiration in it, and still others are indifferent. How has the Cape's landscape affected you?*

A. Like so many people, I'm obsessed with it. It's almost like another character—there's a sense of well-being that comes from the light on the water here that beats Prozac all to hell. People who've lived here for generations know firsthand that the sea is also a destructive force. The town of Oyster Creek is still suffering from the loss of the dragger *Suzie Belle*.

Q. *The novel makes clear that the decline of fishing is having a devastating impact on the local Portuguese community. Can you explain how catch limits affect people's ability to make a living, and how they are adapting? Over time, how do you see the loss of fishing altering the character of Cape Cod?*

A. Catch limits protect the future of the fishery—but meanwhile they're putting fishermen out of business. The limit to the number of fishing days allowed has been brutal. It means that once you've left the pier you have to get as big a catch as you can because you won't have many other chances. If someone gets hurt, or a storm blows up, your choice is between your livelihood and your safety.

The loss of the fish has long since devastated Cape Cod, much as the loss of small farms has had a brutal effect on areas all across the country. There's a pride that goes with working your own piece of land or sea that's unique and irreplaceable. But we live in an era of depletion and we're going to have to find a way through.

Q. *You know a lot about the history of Cape Cod. Is there any historical tidbit that stands out for you?*

A. So many! I suppose the one I come back to most often is the story of Billingsgate Island off Wellfleet: named for Billingsgate

Fish Market in London because the fish were once so plentiful there. A small community grew up on the island in the eighteen hundreds—thirty houses, a lighthouse and lightkeeper's cottage made of brick and granite. But the sea kept rising, forcing residents to move to the mainland (which meant floating their houses across the bay on rafts). Finally only the lighthouse was left standing; it was destroyed during a storm in 1915. It's a particularly concrete example of the power of nature over our lives, and a testament to human adaptability.

Q. Are you in a book club? Would you care to share something about your own reading preferences, or perhaps some recent discoveries?

A. I am in a book club. I was invited to discuss *The House on Oyster Creek* and never left! My reading preferences—honesty, awareness of the fragility and yearning of human life, how hard we try toward each other, how badly we fail. Short stories from Chekhov to Cheever to William Trevor and Alice Munro, because they catch all that happens in one ordinary moment. George Saunders and Sam Lipsyte, who make me laugh until I cry. All authors who "sing of human unsuccess, in a rapture of distress" (W. H. Auden).

Q. Are you planning more novels set on the Cape?

A. Oh yes, absolutely.

QUESTIONS FOR DISCUSSION

1. For many people, the true test of a novel lies in its ability to make them care deeply about the characters. Does *The Harbormaster's Daughter* pass the test for you?

2. Many of the characters in the novel are deeply flawed, yet the author seems generous and forgiving toward them. Do you share her attitude? Do you enjoy reading about characters who aren't necessarily easy to like?

3. LaRee has raised Vita with the goal of creating a safe, wondrous world for her, and protecting her from the full ramifications of her mother's murder. In some ways, that has kept Vita isolated from the community. What do you think of how LaRee has raised Vita? Would you have done it differently?

4. The media love Franco because he's "authentic." But is he? What does our attraction to people like him say about us?

5. Have you ever known a woman who shared some aspects of Sabine's character—her insecurity and the ways she tries to mask it, her benighted search for love, her devotion to her daughter?

6. As fishing declines, the Portuguese community suffers. Discuss how various characters adapt, or fail to adapt, to the subsequent losses—for example, bartender Franco, fatherless Dorotea, bitter Amalia. Do some of their choices add to their grief?

7. When Sabine is murdered, people assume an "outsider" did it. When they learn otherwise, they blame Sabine for somehow inciting her own killing. How do you explain this familiar pattern? Do the townspeople bear any responsibility for the murder?

8. LaRee is very accepting of Vita's first sexual experience at the age of sixteen. Why is that? What does her attitude say about what she wants for Vita? What do you think of the way she handles the situation?

9. Not everyone is lucky enough to experience a first love as sweet and wondrous as Vita's. Were you?

10. Vita is vitally aware of the natural world around her; she draws strength and healing from it. What role does the natural world play in your own life?

11. Oyster Creek is portrayed as a small town in which very different people, the Portuguese and the "washashores," are forced to interact through close proximity, their loves and resentments becoming entwined over the years and being perpetuated through rigid patterns of behavior. Have you ever lived in such a place? How does your experience compare with what happens in the novel?

12. Talk about that bicycle. What do you think is the author's intention?

13. Did you find the end of the novel satisfying? Why or why not?

Read on for an excerpt from

The House on Oyster Creek,

the first novel in

Heidi Jon Schmidt's series depicting life

in the fictional town of Oyster Creek,

on the tip of Cape Cod.

A LETTER FROM FATE

Charlotte had known when she married Henry that he would inherit Tradescome Point. It helped weave the little veil of romance over him: He was the only child of only children, from a long line of Maine Puritans whose names he knew only from the stones in the family plot. They'd been shipbuilders, ship captains, and his grandfather, having sailed around the tip of Cape Cod to avoid a gale, had found this crooked finger of land in Wellfleet and decided to retire there. Tradescome Point, called Mackerel Point back then, looked south over the serpentine estuary known as Oyster Creek, which opened into Mackerel Bay and then into Cape Cod Bay. The island at the bay's mouth had been named Billingsgate because fish seemed as plentiful there as in Billingsgate Fish Market in London. Lobsters washed up in heaps after a storm, and a man could rake in bushels of scallops at low tide, like leaves. And of course there were the famous oysters, reefs of them in the shallow water, and cod, and mackerel drying in sheaves on every one of the wharves that bristled out all along the shoreline—every fisherman was proud as a king.

By 1902, when Isaiah Tradescome arrived, almost every last mackerel had been caught. The big wharf at the end of the point had been swept off its pilings in the Portland Gale, and there was no reason to replace it—there were no mackerel left in Mackerel Bay, and the point, accessible only by water or by the narrow cartway alongside the creek, which lay under two feet of water at high tide, was of no use to anyone. Isaiah bought it, all eleven acres, for a hundred and eighty-seven dollars, built his house, and lived there the rest of his days.

Henry spoke of the place slightingly, as the last relic of a tradition he'd managed to escape. He was the last Tradescome except for his father, who lived in a nursing home outside Boston: a staring old man who crimped the edges of his blanket with nervous fingers all day and all night, waiting for death.

"Hold his hand," Charlotte prompted Henry the last time they visited him. It was four hours by train from Grand Central; they'd sit with his father and spend the night in a hotel, reassuring each other about what a good place they'd found, how clean and bright it was, how the nurses seemed genuinely concerned. Charlotte had put up pictures of Henry Senior, looking up from his desk at his insurance office, showing off a wire basket of littlenecks he'd dug out of the tide flats off the point. She wanted everyone to remember that he had once been a whole, living man.

"Or just rest your hand on his head, so he can tell you're here."

"He doesn't know me," Henry said with profound irritation. One of his hands had been weakened by polio years ago; the other was tensed along with his jaw at his wife's notions. She believed in the healing power of a touch, and other banalities.

"He'll feel it; he'll sense something, some deep memory. It'll comfort him even if he doesn't know it's you."

"Conventional wisdom," he said, seething. *Conventional* was his worst insult—he pronounced it with such contempt that Charlotte feared it as she would a red-hot poker. Emaciated, translucent, his father looked up at them with watery, frightened eyes.

"It can't hurt him," Charlotte insisted.

Henry gave in and took the crooked fingers in his. A little frown troubled his father's long, pale face and the old man pulled his hand away. One corner of Henry's mouth turned up—now did she get it? Tradescomes came from cold granite; they did not want comfort against life's blows.

"You're young, that's all," Henry said to Charlotte, with a chuckle. "Your view will darken; give it time."

Before she'd had Fiona, Charlotte had believed this, and most of the rest of what Henry told her. He was twenty years older than she was, an author, a staunch and learned man, and she'd been grateful to have him as a guide. Charlotte was made of empathy; she would accidentally glimpse the hopes and fears of the stranger behind her in a supermarket line. Her heart went out to people and she could never get it back. Henry's heart seemed to have hardened until it cracked; she'd been sure she could restore it, bring it back to life again. It hadn't occurred to her that Henry might not want that.

The phone call woke them all. The light on the Empire State Building was out; it must be after midnight. Charlotte took Fiona up from her crib and settled back in bed to nurse her.

"Thank God," Henry said. "Yes. No, there won't be a service. There's no one left to mourn him." He gave his characteristic bleak laugh and hung up, breathing a long sigh.

She reached her free hand out to him, and he allowed it to sit on his shoulder for a moment before picking it up and returning it to her.

"It's hardly bad news," he said.

"Still, it's sad." Fiona was drifting off again and Charlotte's nipple popped comically out of her mouth, though she kept trying to suck, making fish lips in her sleep. To think that Henry's father had been someone's baby; someone had gazed down at his face with this wondering love that amounted nearly to prayer. . . .

"An old, stale sadness," Henry said.

"So, sadness has, like, a shelf life?"

He did smile at that. "No," he said. "Which means it will still be there in the morning, so you might as well get some rest." He got up and went to the bathroom for the hot water bottle, pulling a T-shirt of Charlotte's out of the laundry to wrap it. The warmth and smell would trick Fiona back to sleep in the crib.

"Is this too hot?"

Charlotte pressed her wrist against it. "Just right," she said. Henry was nothing if not helpful. Getting the rice cereal to the perfect consistency, or the water bottle to the exact temperature, these duties he undertook in earnest. And he would hold Fiona whenever Charlotte needed a free hand, though always with a slightly rebellious look, as if just because there was a baby here in the crook of his arm didn't mean he had to feel anything for it. Certainly not.

He leaned down to make up the crib—his naked backside was poignant, two stick legs supporting his thick torso and the head of gray hair he raked with his good hand all day, racking his brain for exact phrases. His back hurt him, the doctor said he needed a new knee, and the bad hand hung strangely as always, an unclenchable fist, proof of the cruelty of life. He settled the water bottle in, smoothed the wrinkles out of the sheet, and Charlotte tiptoed behind him, leaning into the crib, careful to keep the baby tight against her until the last second. Fiona didn't wake up, just snuggled closer to the hot water bottle, and they stood over her, watching her sleep. It felt like they were a real, whole family, the kind where each brings his own spark so there's always a soft light burning, even in the darkest time.

"I'll read awhile," Henry said, going into the living room and turning on his lamp. It had been a bare bulb when Charlotte met him, shining harshly on the jammed bookshelves, the piles of books on the floor beside the armchair, the table where he pushed the books aside to make a bit of room for his dinner plate every night—usually scrambled eggs. He'd read until his eyes felt "like boiled owls," then go down the six flights of stairs and around the corner to McClellan's Tap. "He lives like an Athenian," one of his acolytes at the newspaper had explained. "His life is in the market-place. Home is just a place to sleep."

Charlotte had been another of those admirers, in awe of his devotion to work and thought, his stark austerity. She'd been so young, embarrassingly young, with no idea what mundane materials lives are made of. Wanting to distinguish herself, do something brave and important, she had gone to work for a pittance at the *East Village Mirror*, which Henry had started printing on a mimeograph when he first saw the danger looming in Vietnam. Now he was the visionary-in-residence, whose purity of journalistic heart made all the rules and tricks Charlotte had learned in grad school seem tainted. The *Mirror*'s tiny circulation did not trouble him—better to address a small group of serious readers than be a cog in some big, shining wheel. Did you see more deeply into the subject? Did you find the details that would etch the story absolutely into the reader's mind? Then you could hold your head high; never mind the byline, the prestige. His chin was always stubbly, his sweaters worn through at the elbows: He didn't waste a thought on such things. The trace of a Maine accent left in his speech added to the sense that he belonged to an earlier and much better time, and his left hand, flaccid at his side, gave a certain glamour, giving the easy explanation for his ferocity, his steely refusal to take part in the ordinary round of life. Everyone was curious—the men drank with him; the women slept with him. They made a myth of him and loved him for it. Only Charlotte, whose brand of hubris was emotional, had tried to get to know him.

And she'd succeeded; she'd made her way into his heart. And been so smug about it too, being favored by the great man. Henry was almost the age her father would be now. Her father had remarried soon after her mother's death (he was one of those men whose wife *was* his soul; he couldn't live long without one), and been absorbed into the new family, leaving Charlotte as a sort of fifth wheel. She'd call him on holidays, and they'd have a bit of conversation, but she wouldn't have thought to confide in him, and when he died one morning as he was setting off on his postal route, she'd felt only a dull, distant grief, an echo of something so old it had become ordinary. By then she had made this strange marriage and didn't know what to do.

She had only herself to blame. She and Henry had taken a trip to France together, in those early years. Provincial creature that she was, she was attracted to everything that glittered: Henry pulled her down alleyways into restaurants that seemed like caves, full of students smoking Gauloises. Paris had been Disneyfied beyond recognition, he said; only the beauty of the women was worthy of note anymore. Away from his desk, he was unmoored; nothing pleased him and he barely spoke, though his face would knot suddenly with fury and he'd address some bitter expostulation to the editor of the *International Herald Tribune*. Holed up in the garret hotel room with him, Charlotte had suffered a loneliness so bleak it seemed almost physical. On the train to Marseilles he went to the men's room and never came back; after an hour she went to look and found him in a different car, reading a history of the Dreyfus affair and looking fit to kill. She tiptoed back to her own seat, thinking she'd get off at some stop midway and go on alone. Except that Henry, having never owned a credit card, was carrying only a hundred dollars in traveler's checks. She couldn't abandon him, any more than she could have left a child alone. They alighted in Marseilles as married as ever. Charlotte saw a young couple striding past, deep in conversation, and Henry, watching her watch them, said with perfect tenderness: "Poor girl, that's what you ought to have had."

Now, with Fiona safely asleep, he tucked an old wool blanket (his father's) over himself and tried a few pairs of glasses from the side table before he found the right ones. The cat jumped into his lap. Bunbury was the ugliest cat Charlotte had ever seen—a square head, a mean face, and fur stiff as a bottlebrush—but he and Henry had some kind of understanding, and as Henry started to scratch behind the cat's ears, Charlotte saw grief overtake him. His shoulders went rigid, he clenched his fist, that was all. Charlotte tried to sleep—Fiona would need her again in a few hours—but it was impossible. She lay there trying to piece the dead man together, from the bits she knew. The man in those pictures, his linen suit and trim mustache, a certain energy and pride in his face . . . had he gotten some of what he hoped for, before he died? Face to the pillow so Henry couldn't hear, she cried for him. Somebody had to.

He had structured it all so smoothly, before he lost himself to dementia—probate went without a hitch. The nursing home had absorbed most of his savings, and after the taxes there was barely a dollar left. But Henry was the only heir, and they received by registered mail the key to a safe-deposit box that contained such jewelry as Charlotte could not have imagined—blue diamond teardrop earrings, a gift to Henry's grandmother on the occasion of his father's birth, and a cameo depicting a barefoot woman on horseback, thrusting a spear into the breast of a lion.

"Ship's captains," Henry said, barely glancing, as Charlotte held the brooch under the light. It was translucent pink, carved from a shell. "They brought things back...."

They were shut up in the anteroom off the safe-deposit vault. It was paneled in gleaming mahogany, and about the size of an elevator. "Dross..." Henry said under his breath, pushing aside a packet of old letters. Underneath, there was a set of brass knuckles, well used.

"Mutineers," he said with a gleam, trying them on his good hand. "You had to be ready for them. You have to be hard as a ball bearing, Grandfather used to say." He made a quick, tight jab in the air, with real hatred on his face, as if his enemy were right in front of him.

"Is this the deed?" Charlotte asked, to turn the subject. Clearly it was—a fold of thick, brittle paper, covered in tendriled script, tied with a stained satin ribbon. It looked like a letter from fate.

"'Know all men by these presents...'" she read out. "'In consideration of one hundred and eighty-seven dollars, I, Luther Travis, do hereby grant unto the said Isaiah Tradescome, his heirs and assigns forever, a parcel of upland and meadow in South Wellfleet, being about ten and three-quarter acres more or less, bounded northerly by the Oyster Creek cartway, seventy-three lengths of fence as the fence now stands, and southerly by the waters of Mackerel Bay, extending eastward to the bridge beside the boat meadow, and westward to Sedgewick's Gutter....'"

"Point Road was still the cartway when my grandfather bought the place," Henry said, rigid in the shoulders. "The road came later, after the automobile." He was the only person Charlotte had ever heard speak the word *automobile*, and he said it with some suspicion, as if it was still a newfangled idea as far as he was concerned. "Sedgewick's Gutter, I don't know."

"The Boat Meadow?"

"Oyster Creek is only full at high tide. It runs through the marshland—you can take a canoe through the channels but there's high grass on all sides, so it's as if you're paddling through a wheat field. I used to spend whole days in there. In some places the cord-grass is ten feet high. It's mysterious; you don't know what's around the next bend."

His voice was soft and distant, and he slid the brass knuckles off and took the deed out of her hand as if he might see himself there, a boy kneeling at the edge of the marsh, keeping still enough that the life of the place would continue, the hognose snake slithering off the bank and across the water, the fiddler crabs popping out of their holes.

"So, you do remember something from before you were twelve," Charlotte said. He'd always insisted that his first memories were the things he could see in the mirror over the iron lung, the year his parents took him out to Wellfleet to try to escape the polio outbreak. Nothing from before that mattered, anyway—it might as well have been someone else's two-handed life.

"I don't," he said, looking up from the deed. "A few flashes maybe—being out in the canoe, or all the women like black statues at my grandfather's funeral."

"And the game," Charlotte prompted. He'd lived for baseball back then, had begged until he was allowed to stay in Boston to pitch the first Little League game of the year. If they'd left when they wanted to, he might not have gotten sick; everything might have been different. "The one that was nearly a no-hitter."

"I do remember the game," he said. "I felt like I could fly."

This was a jeer at the naive boy he'd been. The one who emerged from the iron lung a month later had only scorn for such innocence. He'd kept hearing how lucky he was—how he should be grateful to God for sparing not only his life, but his right arm as well. That the left one hung there helpless was a very small thing when you thought of what might have happened. Of what happened every day. He'd had nothing to do but read while he was in the machine; he'd discovered all kinds of things. Things like Auschwitz.

"Lucky to be alive," he said now, treasuring the foolish phrase. "I'd believed in God up till then. . . . But there was the minister saying God had been watching over me. He sounded like a salesman. . . . I thought: 'This man must never have seen a newspaper.'"

Charlotte laughed. It was funny how people who had just been kicked in the teeth by life would go on profusely thanking God. It was not funny that Henry had lost hope when he was twelve and never seemed able to catch a glimpse of it again.

"A boat meadow," she said, hoping to change the subject before a rant could get started. "Fiona would love that, floating through a boat meadow."

Henry looked over the top of his glasses, amused. Fiona had just taken her first steps. He had no experience of children, no inkling how fast she would grow.

She went on reading the deed:

"'All of these boundaries, except the waterlines, are determined by the court to be shown on the plan, as listed in the Barnstable

County Registry of Deeds, book seven, page two seventeen. . . .' Well, we're landowners."

She spoke with the light drama Henry used to love, fifteen years back when she was the eager girl in the corner of the *Mirror's* tiny newsroom. She could bring the sparkle and mystery out of things; she'd seemed at first to be the cure for him, but she mostly irritated him now. She had no gravitas; had never fully accepted his authority, though he was vastly more experienced, better read than she was. When he refused to let her write the bigger pieces at the *Mirror* (nothing personal, it was just that she didn't come up to their editorial standards) she had, inconceivably, left the paper altogether to take a job at *Celeb* magazine, a fashion/gossip weekly Henry had never even looked at except once when he was waiting for a root canal.

"Landowners," he echoed, contemptuous, his dark gray eyes darkening further, his mouth pursed. He did not traffic in landownership, but in ideas. Well, she had wanted to please him, had tried for years, but having never been able to measure up, she'd turned it around and learned to enjoy flicking the red flag, watching him charge off in a rage. If you can't join 'em, beat 'em. She'd made real money at *Celeb* while he was holding the fort for serious journalism in his dark little office. She bought an orange patent-leather handbag, red stiletto heels with shark's teeth painted on the side, like hot rods for your feet. All very irritating, but calling him a landowner was the worst thing yet.

"By the waters of Mackerel Bay," she went on. "It's poetry! A 'boat meadow'? The idea of it . . ." Wellfleet was just a word to her, a word from that seminal text, the Oyster Bar menu—Wellfleet, Chincoteague, Blue Point, gusts from the seaside, where the lowing of foghorns, the fresh cold wind off the water, could make loneliness seem like a beautiful thing.

"We're rich! I can't believe it."

She knew this would drive him crazy. His glance was poison and he put a finger to his lips. Was that what she cared about, money? If they had to be rich, she could at least keep from mentioning it, and most certainly from trumpeting it while fanning herself with the deeds to their seaside properties, et cetera.

"It's only the truth, Henry." She laughed. "We . . . well, you . . . have inherited the place. What are you going to do with it?"

He sighed. He'd walked up the endless stairs to his rent-controlled apartment every day for thirty years, from the time he started the *Mirror* through the era of his little renown as a political reporter and critic, to today, when there would occasionally come a volume in the mail, a first edition of his collected essays, discovered at a garage sale, which some supplicant was begging him to autograph so as to fill out his (always *his*) collection of the representative works of the Vietnam era. These little packages made him shudder, reminding him of what he'd meant to become. And the shudder itself infuriated him—his ambitions had not borne out, so what? He could hardly call himself disappointed—he had expected little from life. At the *Mirror* he was the wise man, unfailingly thoughtful, open to all points of view. Charlotte was too young for him, lighthearted, light-minded, too. He'd had more serious, sophisticated women who would have made much better companions, but some idiot instinct had compelled him in this direction, caught him in this subliterary life. Fiona's crib stood where his desk used to be.

Back in the city, Charlotte looked down over Houston Street, where flocks of black-garbed young people were picking along through the icy puddles. It was the winter of 2003; she still couldn't help stopping at the corner of Sullivan to stare south, toward the empty sky where the Trade Center used to loom. The billboard across the way showed a woman whose stony face made a strange contrast to the breasts welling softly from her lace brassiere. If you bought the brassiere, maybe your face would get that hard and nothing would hurt you; maybe that was the point. Whatever, Fiona needed a wider view. She was a squiggle in a yellow sleep suit, who must sip up sweetness and strength until she blossomed into the whole, capacious creature Charlotte willed her to become. Yes, willed. Charlotte's own natural disquiet, that sense that any minute she'd put a foot wrong and fall off the edge of the earth, which she had prayed to transcend by becoming an adult, a journalist, a wife, had finally been stilled with her first look at Fiona's face (as she was lifted, bloody, from between Charlotte's thighs by the obstetrician). Of course. You walk toward the light, keeping the little hand tight in your own. That's all.

"So, what are we going to do with it . . . Tradescome Point?" she asked Henry.

"I am not going to *do* anything with it," he said, pressing his temples. "I have work to do. It's been closed up for years, and as long as it doesn't ask anything from me, I'll let it stay that way."

"It's land, Henry; they're not making it anymore. . . ."

"What would we 'do with it'?" he asked, his patience stretched to breaking.

"Float through the boat meadow, on the tide!"

If he'd laughed, or made any response, she'd have gone along. It was one of her gifts, the ability to go along. But instead he shuddered, a little spasm of disgust that touched the sorest spot in their marriage.

"We could live there . . ." she said lightly.

"I live *here*," he said, with icy finality.

Then he gave a small, spectral laugh: "I sounded just like him then—my father."